ASHES OF AMERICA

FERGUS MCNEILL

For Desaraye, and all my American family.
Truly Missouri's finest.

PROLOGUE

Draft of Charles Lindbergh's speech
America First rally, 1953, Des Moines, Iowa

I stood before you in 1941, to plead the case for American independence, and to warn against the madness of entering a European war.

This was never our fight. It was never our place to defend the interests of the British Empire, nor to calm the ancient prejudices of nations on the far side of the world.

Our leaders assured us that we could support our friends by providing them with the implements of war -- tools, machines, and raw materials -- but how much American blood has since been spilled on the battlefields of Europe?

This policy of intervention brought war to America, with the Japanese attack on Pearl Harbor, and for a time we were drawn into a larger conflict, fighting nations that we had no quarrel with. Yet, even through this time, America and Germany might still have been allies: two noble countries, united against the mindless hordes that threatened to sweep away our great civilizations. Because, for all that has been written about National Socialism, it is now clear that Communism was ever the real danger.

Germany knew this and, despite the British aggression which forced her into unwanted conflict, Germany never lost sight of the true enemy. After they negotiated a peaceful surrender to the western allies in 1945, it was German forces that turned to weather the storm of Soviet invasion, holding back the Russian army until American atomic bombs destroyed Moscow, and brought an end to the war.

But this was never our fight. And now, while France enjoys her freedom, and Britain rebuilds its vast empire, America is somehow still paying the price for a war it did not start.

Too many of our brave servicemen have fallen, sent overseas to fight other nations' battles, and too many of them are still there, risking their lives to restore order that other nations destroyed. It is time for us to bring them home. It is time to put America first.

Fall, 1953
Joplin, Missouri

1

Frank Rye exhaled – a long, contented sigh – then lifted himself and rolled over, falling back onto the pillow. Right now, as he stared up at the sunlit ceiling, everything was good, like that blissful first moment after waking…

Beside him, the rhythm of Beth's breathing gently slowed, fading back into the respectable quiet of the house.

'I wasn't expecting that,' she said, reaching out a slender hand to touch his arm. 'I thought you'd be hard at work this morning.'

Frank glanced over at her.

'I am,' he said.

Her brow wrinkled into a brief frown, then she blushed and gave him a half-hearted dig in the side.

'I *meant*, I didn't think you'd be here this morning.'

'I'm not here.' He tilted his head away from her to gaze up at the rosewood ceiling fan with its brass rotor. For some reason, he'd never liked that fan. 'I'm down in Newton County. Official police business.'

Beth propped herself up on one elbow. Her hand traced a slow line from his chest to his belly, and a faint smile played across her lips.

'Is *that* what I am?' she asked. 'Official police business?'

She lay there, studying his face, waiting for him to speak, but he wasn't ready for conversation. After a moment, her smile faded and she seemed to lose patience, twisting her body around to get out of bed.

'Must be nice, to get whatever you want,' she said.

Frank blinked, then sighed once more. *Satisfied yet unsatisfied...*

Rolling into a sitting position, he let his feet drop to the floor, pressing his toes onto the bare wooden boards. Absently, he leaned over to touch the ugly scar that ran like a smear of pink wax down his leg, but there was no feeling in it.

'You didn't do much to stop me,' he reminded her.

'No.' Beth hesitated, then gathered up the towel that she'd spread across the sheets, folding it ready to drop into the laundry. 'No, I suppose I didn't.'

He watched her, naked and pale, as she moved around the bed, quietly tidying up the room. Hers was a careful discretion... he liked that about her.

On a whim, he reached out as she went to move past him, grabbing her wrist and dragging her back. She pulled against him for a moment, then relented, wrapping her arms around his head, and hugging him close against her bare breast. He caught a whiff of perfumed soap, mingled with her own natural scent.

No words. He was glad of that. Closing his eyes, he allowed himself the last of the moment.

After a time, she released him, stepping back to gaze down into his face, then turning away and walking to the door. He watched her disappear into the hallway, heard the bathroom door close. With a yawn, he stood and began to gather up his clothes.

She was waiting at the foot of the stairs as he came down, a lit cigarette already in her hand. Beth looked good, wearing that prim yellow dress once more, her long brown hair tied back with a matching ribbon. He followed her through to the parlor, doing up the last of his shirt buttons as he went.

'It's almost lunchtime.' She spoke casually, but there was something in her voice. 'I could fix you a sandwich if you'd like...'

He dropped into one of the armchairs, keeping his eyes on her as he leaned forward to lace up his shoe.

'Thanks, but I'll get something later.'

She had taken the cigarette from her lips and blew out a stream of pale blue smoke. Reaching to his pocket, he started to take out his own pack, then checked himself and took one from the box on the coffee table instead.

While he was here, it was better that he smoked hers.

Beth turned the dial on the radio until it clicked, then moved to the liquor cabinet, her hand reaching out to lift a bottle.

'You want a drink?' she asked, turning towards him.

That tone of voice again. Frank glanced over, then shook his head.

'Wouldn't sit right with me, drinking another man's bourbon,' he replied.

Beth glared at him, then slammed the bottle down on its tray, rattling the glasses.

'You're a bastard, Frank Rye,' she said.

He held her gaze, then nodded slowly.

'True enough,' he said. 'And you know it better than most.'

She gave him a hurt look, then smoked in silence for a while, though her expression softened a little as the radio warmed up and Rudi Schuricke's voice crackled and swelled to fill the room.

One perfect day we'll be together,
One perfect day I'll hear you say,
That in my heart you'll stay forever,

And from my arms you'll never stray...

Neither of them spoke as the music played, but the song seemed to thaw the mood between them and, as it ended, Frank saw the familiar shy smile was returning to Beth's face. She smoothed down the front of her dress then moved over to stand by his chair.

'Won't you stay?' she asked. 'Just for a while?'

Frank looked up at her. It was tempting... but the longer he was away the more questions people would ask. He checked his watch then shook his head.

'I should probably go and call in,' he said, stubbing out his cigarette in the ash tray.

Beth nodded to herself. 'Busy day, right?'

'Won't know that until I call in.' Frank glanced up, caught the disappointment in her expression. 'How about you?'

Beth turned away and wandered back to the liquor cabinet.

'Oh... you know me.' She picked up a glass, then set it down again. 'Nothin' to do, and all day to get it done.'

Frank rose to his feet and walked over to stand behind her. Turning her gently, he lifted her chin so he could gaze down into her eyes, then kissed her softly on the forehead.

'Yeah. I know you,' he whispered.

He opened the back door, stepping out onto the porch and pulling on his hat. Pausing, he took a moment to check he hadn't left anything behind – wallet, keys, badge, gun – then took the two steps down and wandered quietly across the yard. It must have been quite a place when Beth's parents owned it, but now everything spoke of neglect. Two tattered lawn-chairs lay forgotten beside the barbecue, the grass was scorched yellow and the bleached wooden birdhouse leaned over on its tall pole. He resisted the temptation to straighten it – he had no business meddling with anything here.

The yard backed onto the railroad track and he stood silent for a moment, making sure there was nobody around, before calmly vaulting the fence. Brushing the dirt from his hands, he set off, walking between the shining steel rails.

It bothered him, the way Beth had wanted to give him lunch. Maybe it was nothing – just a courteous gesture – but gestures like that reminded him of caring, of attachment...

No place for that in what they had.

He liked Beth, liked the way she abandoned herself to him, but he knew he had to keep a little distance between them if he wanted to continue seeing her. And he did want that... he just knew that this was all it could ever be.

The track swept away in a gentle curve, cutting through a lonely line of dogwood trees, before it straightened out closer to the edge of town. Here, he stepped over the rail and down onto the bare ground, picking his way between the piles of ore and heading towards one of the old zinc mills that had stood empty since the war. Walking around the side of the abandoned building, he glanced up at the peeling posters, faded almost white in the sun, still reminding people that they should *Salvage scrap to blast the Jap*. He shook his head. It all seemed like a lifetime ago.

The patrol car was where he'd left it, tucked away out of sight in the shadows at the back of the main building. Getting in, he placed his hat on the seat and started the engine. Then, spitting up a plume of dust and grit behind him, he accelerated in a long arc around the empty lot and bumped the car out onto the road.

Main Street was quiet when he pulled in to the curb, just outside the theatre. Joplin had become a nothing-doing kind of town since the war finished. The mines had all but gone – even the streetcars had stopped running – and the whole place seemed to have forgotten why it was here... but that was fine by him. He liked the quiet, the isolation; it was why he'd come back.

Getting out of the car, he glanced up at the marquee. They were showing the new William Holden picture, *The Brave German*, but someone had scrawled the word *KRAUT* across the movie posters in red paint. He sighed to himself. Out here, opinions took time to change. After years of propaganda telling people that Germany was the enemy, it'd take years more to convince them that Germany was now a friend.

Crossing the street, he pushed the door of the diner and went inside. The waitress looked round as he walked in and set his hat down on the counter.

'Good afternoon, ma'am.'

'What can I get you, officer?' She was young, with curly brown hair that framed a sunny face, and large, innocent eyes.

Frank glanced up at the menu board.

'Well now... I reckon I'll have the scrambled eggs with bacon and toast,' he said.

'Coming right up,' she replied. 'Coffee?'

'Coffee. And could I use your telephone?'

'Sure.' She indicated along the counter. 'It's just there, in the back.'

He knew where the phone was, but she was obviously new here, so he looked where she was pointing, then smiled his thanks.

'I'm obliged, ma'am.'

Taking out a cigarette, he lit it, then walked along the counter and picked up the phone. He watched the waitress while he waited to be connected, catching her eye again as she set a cup down beside his hat, and nodding his thanks. A moment later, when the phone clicked, he heard Kirkland's voice and knew straight away that something was wrong.

'Where the hell have you been, Frank?'

'What do you mean?'

9

'I thought you were supposed to be down in Newton County this morning.'

Damn! Frank shut his eyes. How had Kirkland found out? The man had a real talent for sniffing out lies, hangovers, officers going AWOL...

He had to say something, but there might still be a chance he could talk his way out of this, *if* he was careful.

'I had an errand to run, and Pete wasn't busy so I had him go down instead.' He hesitated, wondering what Pete had said. 'Why? What's the problem?'

'What's the problem?' Kirkland's voice pitched up a notch. 'We've had the Newton County Sheriff on the phone. They found Pete's body. Some bastard killed him, Frank.'

2

Frank killed the engine and sat in silence, peering out through the windshield. He'd driven the twenty miles south with his foot to the floor but, now that he was here, he couldn't bring himself to get out of the car.

Why the hell hadn't he kept his dick in his pants and come down himself?

He stared along the side street, with its two-story brick buildings, noted the local patrol cars, nosed in at an angle to the sidewalk like they'd arrived in a hurry... but there was no point hurrying now. Pete wasn't going anywhere.

Why the hell would anyone want to kill Pete Barnes?

He shook his head and stared down at the napkin from the diner, where he'd scribbled the address they'd given him. It hadn't been hard to find the place – Neosho was a quiet town, draped neatly over the rolling green hills that ran down to the creek – but he hadn't sent Pete to *this* address; he'd sent him to collect some letters from a woman who worked at the Skordeno Upholstery factory, away on the other side of town. How the hell had the poor bastard wound up here?

And why were the Newton County boys so vague about what had happened?

Further along the street, just beyond the two patrol cars, Frank saw an officer emerge from a doorway and stop to light a cigarette.

One of the local deputies might be more forthcoming.

With a sigh, he got out of the car and slammed the door, then started towards the man. However bad the truth was, it couldn't be worse than the thoughts in his head.

The deputy had a restless way about him – early twenties, with a faint blond mustache that was probably meant to make him look older. His serious expression shifted to awkward sympathy as he recognized Frank's uniform, and he hurriedly tossed his cigarette as he stepped forward.

'Afternoon, sir.'

'Afternoon.' Frank noted his pallor, the slight tremble in the hands; maybe it was the kid's first corpse. 'I'm looking for Sheriff Carson?'

'Oh, he's inside.' The deputy jerked his thumb to indicate the building behind him. 'It's the second floor. If you just go on up, you'll... well, you'll see where.'

Frank looked past him, his eyes moving along the line of upstairs windows, then nodded to himself.

'Thank you.' He started towards the doorway, then paused. 'About Officer Barnes...'

'Sir?'

'Can you tell me... what happened to him?'

The deputy's face flickered from sympathy to discomfort.

'Did you know him, sir?'

Answering a question with a question; not a good sign.

Frank sighed. 'Yeah. I knew him.'

It was never easy, stepping into a room and seeing a body

sprawled out across the floor, but it was so much worse when the body belonged to someone you'd known. Frank stood in the doorway, forcing himself to look, to see the scene as a cop *should* see it.

Naked. Lying face-up, feet towards the door. Blood and bruising on the forearms, ribcage, head...

He took a step forward, leaning over to peer more closely at the misshapen skull, seeing the left side of the face all caved-in and wrong. It reminded him of that poor guy they'd found in the wreckage after the tornado hit Redings Mill last year. Except this time, he knew what the victim was *meant* to look like...

...knew almost everything about him.

Averting his eyes, Frank straightened up and took a breath. The room was small but clean, with bare floorboards and afternoon sunlight shafting in through the single window. Beside the steel-frame bed in the corner, a vase of yellow flowers stood on the tiny nightstand, undisturbed by whatever had happened here. There were photographs, cut from magazines and pinned to the wall – pictures of Paris and Rome and a few places Frank didn't recognize – a bed surrounded by dreams. The mattress dipped in the middle, like it had seen a lot of use, and the sheets were disturbed...

...but Pete wasn't the sort to go picking up women. Was he? There had to be more to it than that.

Staring at the discarded police uniform, lying crumpled on the floor, Frank felt a shadow of disappointment. It might have been better if his colleague really *had* been caught with his pants down. A happier way for someone to go, fooling around with some accommodating young woman. Perhaps that's why the other officers were so ready to believe it.

But this was Pete.

'I'm truly sorry, Frank.'

He turned around to see Sheriff Ray Carson standing in the

doorway, holding his hat in front of his broad belly – a gesture of respect that made him feel even worse.

'Yeah. Thanks, Ray.'

The big man came silently into the room, bringing a faint smell of whiskey with him. He had a solid reputation, despite some ugly rumors about his wayward son, and Frank had always found him easy to get along with. The two men stood side-by-side, gazing down at the corpse.

'I hate for you to see him like this, but I figured you'd want to understand the...' Carson paused, reaching up to stroke his thick mustache. '...the circumstances.'

Frank nodded. No doubt the old sheriff meant well, but Pete was still lying there, buck-naked and beaten in some girl's room.

'Maybe you could cover him up,' he said. 'Give him a little dignity?'

'Sure thing. Just as soon as we get the photographs.'

Frank sighed and turned away from the body, taking in the rest of the room.

'Is that the weapon?' he asked, pointing towards a baseball bat lying just below the window.

'Looks that way.' Carson trailed off, then glanced up at him, hesitant. 'Do you know if Barnes was down here because of work?'

'He was supposed to be working...' Frank paused, then frowned. '...but not here.'

'What do you mean?'

'I sent him to collect something from a woman over at the Skordeno Upholstery factory.' Frank looked up, his expression thoughtful. 'We should check whether he ever made it out there.'

'If you give me the woman's name, I'll send someone over.'

'It's Mary... something. I've got it in the car...' Frank trailed off, glancing around the room. 'Who'd you say this place belongs to?'

'Waitress. Name of Faye Griffith.' Carson said it with a hint of distaste, as though he'd already made his mind up about her.

'Been here just over a month, works at the grill over on Wood Street. And real pretty, according to the old guy downstairs.'

'Pretty, huh?'

Frank walked over to the bare-looking dressing table. There was a faint covering of spilt face powder, with several clean spots where items had been removed. Beside it, the heavy old closet stood open, with a waitress' uniform and a shabby-looking coat bunched up at the end of the rail.

She left in a hurry, and she didn't plan on coming back.

Carson was bending over, hands braced on his knees to steady himself. He gazed down at Pete like he was trying to read something in the remains, then straightened up with a grunt.

'You think maybe he'd been round here before?'

Frank eyed him warily.

'Is that your way of asking if Pete was screwing this waitress on the quiet?'

There was an edge to his voice now, yet Carson stood his ground.

'I'm sorry, Frank; you know I have to ask.'

They stared at each other for a moment, then Frank sighed and shook his head.

'Yeah, I know.' He waved away the apology and looked down at the body. 'Let's just say Pete was a decent guy, and I'd be surprised if he was doing anything like that.'

Very surprised.

They'd worked together for almost five years, got drunk together, talked together... Pete had trusted him completely. There was never anything to suggest that he was sleeping around, and Frank certainly knew what signs to look for.

The sheriff pulled a large hand across his flabby jaw.

'That your way of sayin' you don't know for sure?'

Frank gave him a dark look, then cracked a thin smile.

'Something like that.' He picked up a small bottle of perfume, smelled it, then put it carefully back in its place. 'So where's this Faye Griffith now?'

'We don't know. High-tailed it out of here after what happened, I guess.'

Frank's eyes flickered back to the heavy baseball bat, discarded on the floor.

An unusual weapon for a waitress to have lying around.

'She lived alone?' he asked.

'That's right. I already spoke to a friend of hers at the grill.'

'No husband? Boyfriend? You said she's pretty.'

'There's no indication of her being married,' Carson replied. 'Nobody remembers seeing her with a man, and everything in the closet is hers, so...'

'So she's single. Okay.' Frank glanced around the room. There were no photos of people. 'What about family? A brother, maybe? Or her father?'

Carson shook his head.

'Her folks came from Kansas City,' he explained. 'Haven't turned up any family round here yet.'

Frank nodded slowly, his finger tracing out an expanding spiral in the powder on the dressing table.

'Who found the body?' he asked.

Carson pointed at the floor. 'The old guy downstairs.'

'Okay.' Frank considered this. 'And how'd he happen to find it, all the way up in here? Something attracted his attention?'

Carson allowed himself a brief grin.

'I know what you're thinking,' he said. 'But the guy's seventy-five years old. He says he heard a woman screaming, some sort of commotion. Hobbled straight upstairs to see what was going on.'

'Was the door open or closed?'

Carson's grin vanished.

'I didn't ask,' he admitted.

'Did the old man pass anyone on the stairs?'

'No, I made sure of that. Didn't see a soul, except...' He

gestured awkwardly towards the corpse. '...except your friend here.'

Frank folded his arms, frowning.

'Is there a bathroom on this floor?' he asked.

'Just along the hall,' Carson told him. 'Why?'

Frank didn't answer. It seemed unlikely that Faye Griffith could have made it all the way to the end of the hall and down the stairs before the old guy started up. But maybe she'd hidden in the bathroom, then crept out while he was here in the room.

'Frank?'

'The old guy comes in here, sees the body... then he goes straight back down to call you?'

'That's right.' Carson nodded. 'Except the nearest phone is at the hardware store, just down on the corner.'

'So he had to leave the building?'

'Exactly.'

Frank looked around, remembering the half-empty closet. It would have taken a few minutes to sort through her clothes and possessions. She must have hidden in the bathroom, waited there until the old guy went downstairs before she came back to gather her things. Then she could slip away while he was down the street.

Pretty ballsy for a waitress.

'Nobody else in the building?' he asked. 'Nobody saw anyone leaving?'

Carson shook his head.

'It's always been a quiet neighborhood,' he said. 'Up until now.'

Frank walked over to the window and leaned on the sill, staring down into the street. It was almost empty, despite the two police cars.

He leaned forward, forehead against the glass, peering along the road.

'Where's Pete's car?' he asked, slowly.

Behind him, Carson paused.

'I don't know...' The sheriff cleared his throat. 'Maybe he parked it round the corner. If this was an illicit rendezvous, I mean.'

Frank shut his eyes.

'I wouldn't have thought of that,' he lied.

'No tellin' what a man will do when there's a woman involved,' Carson noted.

'Yeah.' Frank straightened up and turned his back on the window. 'Let's go downstairs, and I'll get you that name. I want to know if he made it out to the factory or not.'

'Sure.' Carson took a step towards the door, then hesitated. 'So, what do you want to do about...?'

He gestured towards the body.

'What do you mean?' Frank asked.

'Well, we have to conduct a proper investigation, track down the killer... but I don't see that we need to embarrass a fellow officer unduly. Maybe we can leave certain... details... out of the report?'

Frank looked at him, then gave a grateful nod.

'That's good of you, Ray.'

'We take care of our own, Frank.'

'I appreciate that.'

'Well... I saw his wedding ring.' Carson gave him an awkward smile and moved out into the hallway. 'I figured his wife didn't need to know how and where we found him.'

Frank stiffened as the thought he'd been avoiding finally pushed its way to the front of his mind.

'Ever met his wife?' the sheriff asked, holding the door open.

Frank glanced down at Pete's naked body, dead eyes staring up, like they must have stared up at the awful rosewood ceiling fan in his bedroom.

He swallowed. 'Yeah. I know her.'

3

He left the car in the shade of a gnarled old tree and stood for a moment, hitching up his pants and smoothing down the front of his uniform. It was a sweet August evening, with a warm breeze carrying the smell of cut grass from somewhere, but he felt cold inside as he made his way to the gate and walked slowly up the path. The old house looked down on him, tall and silent. It felt strange coming to the front. Wrong, somehow. But everything was wrong now.

Stepping up onto the porch, he knocked on the screen door, then stood back a little, waiting. After a moment, he heard her footsteps, and the door opened.

'Frank...' Beth looked surprised, but she gave him a broad smile, tilting her head to one side. 'What are you doing back again?'

Her hand went to touch her hair, then hesitated as she caught something in his manner. The smile faded from her face, eyes first.

'What's the matter?'

Frank took a step forward.

'May I come in?'

He could see *that* really worried her. How long had it been since he'd asked her permission for anything?

She stepped aside, beckoning him into the hallway.

'Frank...?'

He pushed the door closed behind him, suddenly feeling the vast emptiness of the house, yawning all around. Avoiding her eye, he turned and walked through to the parlor. Behind him, her footsteps clicked out a nervous rhythm on the wooden floor.

He took a breath, then turned to look back at her.

'Sit down, Beth.'

She stiffened, becoming even more upright for a moment.

'You're scaring me, Frank.'

He paused for a second, then walked over to the liquor cabinet. There were two glasses on the tray; picking up the bottle, he poured a long shot of bourbon into each one.

'Sit down and drink this,' he said, moving over to where she stood and handing her a glass.

'But what's the–'

'It's Pete,' he said.

She froze, staring up at him... then her eyes became distant and she looked past him, her face expressionless as she slowly slumped down onto the chair. He bowed his head in sympathy, wondering how to begin, but in the end it was Beth who spoke first.

'How did he find out?'

Frank stared at her, wrong-footed by her assumption. Normally, when a police officer showed up unexpectedly, ordinary people worried that someone was hurt, or worse. But she wasn't looking at him as a police officer, and she'd misunderstood because she was worried about their affair.

Slowly, deliberately, he shook his head.

There was a moment – the briefest moment – where he saw relief flicker in her eyes, before it was replaced by an awful dread as she realized what that meant.

'Did something... happen to him?' She'd guessed now, but she was building up to it, not ready to ask the real question.

Frank held her gaze, letting her see the answer in his face.

'Oh my Lord...' One slender hand fluttered to her mouth. 'He's dead, isn't he?'

Her shoulders slowly drooped, and her eyes became glassy and unfocused. For the first time, Frank glimpsed the child in her – the little girl she'd once been, before she grew into a woman – as all of her adult confidence fell away.

'I'm sorry, Beth.' He took a step closer to her. 'I wanted you to... to hear it from me...'

Her jaw suddenly stiffened and anger flared in her eyes, but only for a moment.

'Sorry, I didn't...' She shook her head, composing herself once more. 'Thanks for... you know... having the decency to tell me.'

Frank lowered his gaze.

Decency.

He turned away, knocking back his bourbon and setting the empty glass down silently on the table, before looking over at her again. Her head was bent forward now, staring past the drink held loosely in her hand. Long lashes hid her downcast eyes, and the yellow bow was conspicuously cheery against her dark hair.

Silently, he reached out to place a cautious hand on her shoulder. He half-expected her to flinch, but she remained eerily still. Then, very slowly, she raised her free hand to place it over his, clasping it tightly.

'What happened?' she asked.

He took a breath, not wanting to tell her, not wanting to make it worse.

'We don't really know yet.' Frank felt trapped; unable to withdraw from her question as her fingers gripped his. 'He'd been beaten... it looks like he was murdered.'

Beth's head lifted, a startled expression on her face.

'Murdered?' she gasped. '*Pete?*'

Frank nodded slowly.

'Newton County Sheriff found his body down in Neosho.' He wasn't going to tell her just *how* Pete was found. 'We're still trying to figure out what happened.'

Her expression darkened.

'Newton County...'

He could hear the unspoken accusation in her voice. Slowly, she raised her drink and drained the bourbon, watching him over the rim of the glass.

Frank sighed. He'd been dreading her anger and her screaming, but this cold calm was so much worse.

'Where *I* was supposed to go this morning, but I sent him instead.' He shook his head. 'It should've been me down there.'

Her large eyes glistened, not allowing him to look away.

'Yes,' she said, softly. 'It should.'

He stood there, frozen, but she finally lowered her gaze, resting her head against his arm and brushing her cheek on his sleeve to dry the tears.

'I'm so sorry, Beth.'

The words seemed loud against the hush of the parlor, empty words that hung between them, awkward and inadequate. He lapsed into silence for a while, not knowing what else to do except give her time to take it in.

Eventually, she spoke, her voice measured, even.

'I did love him. I know you might not think so, because of what I let you do to me... I know you probably think I'm a terrible wife, a terrible *person*...'

She broke off. Frank leaned forward, gently squeezing her shoulder.

'No, Beth. I don't–'

'...but I *did* love him.'

She sat up straight for a moment, shrugging off his hand, then slowly got to her feet. Wordlessly, she turned to him, her face inches from his, her eyes bright with tears. And then, she leaned forward to kiss him, just the lightest brush of her lips at first, then once again, deeper and more urgent.

Surprised, he kissed her back, feeling himself growing suddenly hard for her, as all the terrible emotions resolved into a powerful physical desire, no matter how wrong.

But Beth felt him pressing against her and broke away, blinking her long, wet lashes and giving him a sad shake of her head. He saw her expression, and understood... managed a brief nod of regret. This wasn't the sort of thing that *could* be resolved. Everything was different now; they weren't lovers any more.

'I'm so sorry,' he whispered.

She placed a small hand on his chest.

'I want you to find whoever did this,' she said, a note of steel in her voice.

'I will.' He looked down into her upturned face. 'I promise.'

She met his gaze for a moment longer, then her eyes filled with tears and she stepped closer, letting him gather her into his arms for a time. He held her while she sobbed quietly, feeling the warmth of her breath through his shirt, the press of her hands on his back.

When she finally drew apart from him, there was an unfamiliar weariness in her movements. She turned away, dabbing her eyes, distant now.

'You should go,' she murmured, leaning over to pick up the empty glasses from the table.

'But...'

'Just *go*, Frank.'

He stared at her, suddenly feeling hurt, despite himself.

'I'll have the whole damned family here, all wanting to help me,' she sighed, her shoulders slumping. 'I *can't* have you around. I can't keep up that kind of an act.'

He saw the despair in her face, and nodded foolishly. He'd lost her, but she'd lost everyone.

'If there's anything I can do...' he offered. More empty words.

She moved towards the door.

'You know what I want you to do.'

The sun was setting as he stepped outside, casting a red-golden glow over the front yard and the quiet street beyond. Beth stood like a statue on the porch as he walked down the path, but turned away when he looked back over his shoulder, going in and pulling the door shut behind her.

He didn't blame her. She was tougher than he'd ever guessed, but this was her whole life being turned upside down. And it was all on him.

Standing there, alone in the long shadow of the house, Frank bowed his head then strode away towards his car.

4

It was still warm, and the window of Kirkland's office was jammed open, bringing the sounds of late-night traffic on Main Street, and vague snatches of laughter from the malt shop on the corner. Frank stared at the line of framed police commendations on the wall, below a smaller frame that held an Army Soldier's Medal, proudly displayed on a bed of black velvet.

Kirkland didn't trust him.

The chief liked to think he knew everything about everyone, but those long gaps in Frank's military record had burned his curiosity and made him suspicious. He'd never liked Frank: late once too often, drunk once too often, insubordinate *way* too often...

And now there was this.

'So that's it?' Kirkland shifted, causing his chair to creak. For a big man, he was still in good shape, with a bull neck and a crew cut, though his scowling face bore a slight sheen of perspiration. 'That's all you've got to say?'

Frank kept his face carefully blank. It had been hard, explaining the day's events to the chief, and harder still to do it without mentioning his morning at Beth's, but she'd been through enough already.

'I'm truly sorry,' he said.

'Sorry ain't gonna cut it, Frank. A man's *dead*, don't you get that? A *fellow officer* is dead, and you sit there acting like it's no big deal?' He paused for breath, glaring across the desk, almost inviting a reaction. 'Damn it all, he should never have been down there in the first place, but to wind up naked in some girl's room...'

He shook his head, as if the whole thing was too offensive to discuss further.

Frank sat completely still, his eyes studying the objects on Kirkland's desk: cigar box, heavy glass ashtray, brass nameplate, a sturdy-looking pen. He sensed it wasn't time for him to speak just yet.

After a moment, Kirkland leaned forward a little.

'You talked to the Newton County boys,' he said. 'Did any of them know this waitress?'

'No,' Frank explained. 'She just arrived in town a few weeks ago.'

Kirkland slumped back in his chair, an oddly petulant action for a man of his bearing.

'So how the hell did Pete end up in her room,' he demanded, 'when you sent him to do *your* job at the Skordeno factory?'

Frank caught the accusing tone, but gritted his teeth, refusing to rise to it.

'Sheriff Carson thinks maybe there was something going on between them,' he replied. 'But he's just casting round for ideas. He doesn't *know* anything.'

Kirkland frowned.

'Well, if you find a naked man in a woman's bedroom, it sure seems like a possibility to me.' He trailed off for a moment, then looked hard at Frank. 'How about you?'

'Sir?'

'You knew Pete. You worked with him, got on with him...' Kirkland was watching him intently now. 'Any... trouble at home? Things okay with his wife?'

Behind his careful expression, Frank smoldered, wishing he could punch his superior in the face.

'I knew them both,' he said, then paused, aware of the line he was about to cross. Lying like this was serious, but the truth would nail him to the wall if it ever came out. He was already damned, no matter what he did now. 'They always seemed happy enough to me. I don't think they had any... problems.'

'So you don't think...?'

'I don't think Pete was fooling around with the waitress,' Frank finished for him. 'No, sir.'

Kirkland looked doubtful.

'Well,' he said, reaching across the desk to open the cigar box, 'that doesn't change the mess we're left with, now does it? When folks find out about it, they're still gonna think something sordid was going on.'

'Sheriff Carson seemed keen to spare any unnecessary embarrassment,' Frank noted. 'I think he'll be... discreet.'

Kirkland struck a match and proceeded to light a short cigar, watching him through the flame.

'Well, I guess that's something... for the widow, anyway.' He blew a cloud of thick grey smoke, snuffing out the match. 'Small comfort for Pete Barnes, though.'

Frank lowered his eyes.

What *had* Pete been doing? Why was he in that room? Pete certainly didn't have what it took to pick up women. Hell, he didn't even have what it took to hold on to his wife.

'So, you've talked all around it, but you still haven't told me.'

Frank looked up. Kirkland was staring at him, his expression suddenly calm, which was somehow more disconcerting than seeing the man angry.

'Told you what, sir?'

'Told me why Pete was down there. Instead of you.'

Frank felt himself tensing, but willed his shoulders to relax and stay loose.

'I asked him if he'd go,' he replied. 'He was okay about it.'

'Why didn't *you* go? Mary Cantell asked for you by name, didn't she?'

Frank stared at him.

'When I spoke to you on the phone this morning, you said you had an errand.' Kirkland took a long drag on his cigar. 'What was so important you couldn't do your damn job?'

Frank took a breath. *Just stay calm, keep it simple.*

'I wasn't feeling so good this morning,' he said. 'I just figured–'

'You were sick this morning?'

'Well, maybe a–'

'What kind of sick, Frank? *Hangover* kind?'

Frank's head snapped up, but the sharp denial died in his throat, and he remained silent. *Better that Kirkland believe that than to have him dig deeper and learn the truth.*

'Yeah, I thought so.' Kirkland reached over and set his cigar in the groove of the ashtray. 'As of right now, you're suspended, Frank. Without pay.'

'What?'

'Oh, you heard me just fine.' He jabbed an angry finger towards Frank. 'I want you out of here, till I figure out what to do with your sorry ass.'

'But–'

'Hell, you're lucky I don't wash you out right now... or lock you up.'

Frank rose to his feet, his chair scraping backwards over the wooden floor as he stood glaring down.

But Kirkland didn't flinch.

'I don't know what you were in the war,' he growled. 'But you sure didn't learn much about following orders... or having your friend's back.'

Frank's fists clenched by themselves, but he managed to fight down the dreadful urge to hit Kirkland.

'Anything else, sir?' he said through his teeth.

'Just get out, Frank.' Kirkland regarded him with disgust. 'Go home and have yourself another drink. It don't matter if you feel rough in the morning; you got no place you need to be for a while.'

Frank stood on the sidewalk outside police headquarters for some time, not sure what to do next. Gazing up into the gloom, his thoughts turned to Beth, to the kind of angry lovemaking that might numb two people's pain, if only for a little while. But he knew they couldn't comfort each other. Not now, not after this.

Frowning, he turned to look down the street. His patrol car was parked there and he still had the keys in his pocket. Glancing briefly back at the department building, he decided to take it. He was too tired to walk home, and anyway, *screw them*.

The steady growl of the engine relaxed him as he drove through the town, and there was something soothing about the succession of brightly-lit signs and storefronts slipping by in the darkness. It was almost midnight, and he hadn't eaten all day, but the drive-in on East 20th would still be open, and he was in no hurry to get home. He glanced in the mirror, then made a left turn.

When you've known what it is to be hungry, you always eat.

Bumping the car over the railroad crossing, he stared out at the road, wondering about Pete, about how much he'd known, or suspected. *Hopefully nothing; let the poor man rest in peace.*

He sighed. Ahead of him, the tall sign at Dezzie's Drive-In shone out against the night sky. Turning off into the parking lot, he pulled in under the bright lights and rolled his window down to order a steak burger and a soda.

Sitting there, waiting for his food, his thoughts drifted to the missing waitress, Faye Griffith. What was her involvement in all this, and where was she now? No doubt the Newton County boys would bring her in, sooner or later... but would she be wearing handcuffs or a body-bag when they did?

He looked up as the car-hop girl brought his order out and fixed the tray on the window for him.

'Can I get you anything else, mister?'

'No. Thanks.' Conscious that Kirkland had stopped his pay, he deliberately tipped her extra, then settled back in his seat and took a sip of his drink. As she walked away, his eyes swept the parking lot. A few yards to his left, a station wagon had pulled up – just another young couple at the end of their evening, some hair-creamed kid in a plaid shirt, driving his parents' car. The girl in the passenger seat was pretty, though, with wavy blonde hair and a pink polka-dot dress. As her boyfriend looked away to place their order, she glanced across at Frank. Seeing him watching her, she pursed her glossy red lips slightly, then gave him a faint smile.

Frank turned away and rubbed his eyes. He suddenly felt very tired.

He parked the patrol car at the side of the house, got out and stretched wearily. The air was cooler now, and he gazed up at the clear night sky for a moment, then yawned and went inside.

The floorboards creaked beneath his feet as he walked through to the kitchen and switched on the light, blinking at the sudden brightness. Setting his hat down on the counter, he took out his badge and looked at it for a moment, before placing it on the table. Then, he reached down and unholstered his .38, idly flipping the cylinder open and emptying out the six shells onto the table.

Kirkland wasn't messing around this time – the chief might cut you some slack when it suited him, but this was different and Frank knew it. He was on the outside now, and it would be a long road back.

Straightening up, he walked over to the cupboard by the sink, taking out a half bottle of bourbon and finding a clean glass. *Screw Kirkland.*

He took the last couple of cubes from the tray in the icebox, then poured himself a drink and switched the radio on. As the set warmed up, a newscaster's voice rose to speak in serious tones about the challenges facing US peacekeeping troops in the harsh climates of northern Russia, and the latest death tolls from Korea. Frank sighed.

What was the point of winning if the war didn't finish when you won?

Gathering up his badge, bullets and gun, he carried them over and dumped them into the kitchen drawer, slamming it firmly shut. Then he picked up his drink and wandered through to the den.

The room was sparsely furnished and none too tidy. Somehow he'd never quite got around to properly unpacking and there seemed little point now. He straightened the place out now and again, but only really made an effort when he brought women back... and that wasn't very often. Beth had been here just once – he could still see the uneasy expression on her face as she'd slipped her dress down – and they'd always met at hers after that.

Sitting down heavily on the couch, he tipped a couple of magazines onto the floor to reveal a half-full ashtray lying hidden on the coffee table. Leaning back, he lit a cigarette and sipped his bourbon, while the voice of the newscaster droned on in the kitchen.

A little after 1am, he got stiffly to his feet, switched everything off, and made his way through to the bedroom. Kicking off his shoes, he yawned, then undid the buckle on his holster, ready to drape it over the corner of the bed frame as he did every night. Seeing it empty now, he paused for a moment, thoughtful.

It should have been me.

Turning slowly, he went over to the heavy wooden closet. Opening both the doors wide, he squatted down, and hauled out the large army-green duffel bag he kept stowed there beneath his clothes – everything that really mattered, always ready to go – a nervous habit from his time in Europe that he'd never quite shaken off.

Unzipping the bag, he reached down the side of it and drew out a towel-wrapped bundle, which he unfolded to reveal his old .45 automatic. Checking the clip was full, he pulled back the slide to chamber a round, then walked over and placed the gun on the nightstand.

It should have been me.

𝕶𝖆𝖓𝖘𝖆𝖘 𝕮𝖎𝖙𝖞 𝕳𝖊𝖗𝖆𝖑𝖉

KANSAS CITY, MISSOURI   -   Tuesday, August 25, 1953

CITY CELEBRATES V-R DAY

EIGHT YEARS SINCE HISTORIC VICTORY OVER RUSSIA SIGNALLED END OF WAR

KANSAS CITY, Aug 25 - Veterans of two world wars were honored as thousands gathered at the city's Liberty Memorial to observe the eighth anniversary of V-R Day. Addressing the crowds, Mayor William Kemp praised the patriotism and great sacrifice of all who fought for freedom.

"Today, we remember the brave men and women who served their country during those dark times to bring the light of hope, through hard-won victory."

He also paid tribute to American servicemen who are still stationed overseas, particularly U.S. Peacekeepers in Siberia and Eastern Europe, many of whom are based out of Fort Riley, Kansas.

'A DAY REMEMBERED AROUND THE WORLD'

V-R Day marks the moment when the Russian Red Army formally announced their surrender, at noon on August 25th 1945, just days after the destruction of Moscow by the new 'atomic' bombs. Facing determined resistance from American and German troops, and with Stalin dead, the Russian surrender effectively brought World War II to an end.

(continued on page 3, column 4)

5

It had rained through the weekend, with dark skies that threatened storms, but now things were clearing up again, and this morning was uncomfortably bright. Frank swallowed the last of his cold coffee, then set the empty cup on the kitchen table. Reaching up to rub his eyes, his hand brushed across the unfamiliar roughness of his cheek.

Today was the day. And he'd have to clean himself up, sooner or later.

Pushing the chair back, he got stiffly to his feet and stretched, then padded slowly through to the bathroom. Bracing himself with his hands on the sides of the basin, he leaned forward until he was just inches from the mirror. A hollow man stared back at him. The eyes were the worst thing – dark and sunken – but his whole face looked ragged, like some boxcar hobo. A thick layer of untidy stubble covered his jaw, marking the days since Kirkland had kicked him out.

Sighing, he reached for his shaving brush and ran it under the faucet, then dipped it into the soap and started to work up a lather.

The past few days had become blurred, indistinct. He hadn't appreciated the subtlety of Kirkland's punishment at the time, but denying him the distraction of work had forced him to dwell on what he'd done, and the guilt had wrapped itself around him like a noose.

So he'd become what Kirkland believed he was; he'd gone to the liquor store, and he'd drank until things were bearable again.

Frank shut his eyes briefly, then straightened up to face his reflection, smoothing the lather along his jawline and working it in.

Sleeping through the empty days... restless nights spent prowling the house or driving aimlessly around town... how quickly he'd slipped back into that old darkness. It was like those first months after he'd come back from the war: suddenly robbed of purpose, an outsider in his home town, defined only by regret.

Lifting his chin, he turned his face to one side, and started to draw the razor over his skin.

He'd wanted to see Beth, of course. He'd driven by her place one night, and stared up at the light in her bedroom window, but what was the use? She'd be imprisoned by her family now, a tight little huddle of relatives making sure she didn't get a moment's peace.

He paused, wondering if maybe that was easier on her. *No time to think, no time to dwell on anything...*

He didn't know how she was; there'd been no word from her, no contact at all. He'd only found out about the funeral arrangements from Louie at the department, and part of him wished he hadn't. Still, it was a reason to get a hold of himself, smarten himself up.

He finished shaving and toweled off his face, then walked through to the bedroom. Opening the closet, he ran his hand across the hanging clothes, then hesitated.

Should he wear his police uniform?

He was suspended, and Kirkland would likely be there, along with half the department, no doubt. But what were they going to do? Make a scene at the graveside?

Nodding grimly to himself, Frank reached into the closet and lifted his uniform jacket off the rail.

He drove out of town, following the road north as it cut across open fields and skirted the edge of small woods, always climbing. Before long, he rounded a bend and lifted his foot off the gas; ahead of him, cars lined the side of the road and he slowed down, pulling in behind the last of them, then shutting off the engine. Getting out, he stood up and straightened his uniform before looking up the line. There had to be twenty vehicles here, but a police funeral *would* be well-attended.

Frank sighed. Pete was a nice enough guy, but until now he'd never thought of him as *mattering* very much. Staring grimly at the line of cars, he wondered how many of them would be here if it was *his* funeral.

Glancing at his watch, he started walking along the road. A few yards in front of him, a thin man in a blue suit was leaning against a smart-looking grey Chrysler, smoking a cigarette. He nodded respectfully as Frank passed, acknowledging the uniform.

The cemetery occupied a long stretch of open ground, bordered by trees. It fell away gently from the roadside, a grassy slope dotted with headstones and memorials, many of them recent-looking, additions from the war. The mourners were gathered in a broad arc – sombre faces and sombre clothes – around a neatly-dug pit. He walked slowly down, picking his way carefully between the grave plots, to stand on the edge of the group.

Before long, the black cars arrived, and a hush fell as people turned their heads. Staring back up the slope, Frank watched as the family members made their way down. He knew some of them – Pete's little brother, helping his mom over the uneven ground; Beth's uncle, dignified and sad...

And then he saw her, dressed in a plain black dress, with a black jacket and hat. Beth didn't look his way, walking stiffly to the grave, supported by her younger sister. The priest, an elderly man with a kindly face and tidy white hair, went over to say something to her, then turned towards the mourners.

'Join with me now in our hymn, *The Old Rugged Cross*.'

He bowed for a moment, then lifted his face and began to sing, the congregation adding their voices to his.

On a hill far away stood an old rugged cross,
The emblem of suff'ring and shame;
And I love that old cross where the Dearest and Best
For a world of lost sinners was slain.

Frank sang softly, his eyes on the road at the top of the slope, where the casket was now being carried slowly onto the path and down towards them. Four of the six pall-bearers wore police uniforms – Kirkland was there, his expression serious as he shouldered the weight of the dark wooden box, and set it gently beside the waiting grave.

The hymn finished, and the priest stepped forward, holding a black leather Bible in his hand.

'The Gospel of John tells us that death is not the end. In our loss, in our *suffering*, we can draw comfort in the sure and certain resurrection, bought at great price by our savior, Jesus Christ.' He paused, taking a moment to look around, studying the assembled faces. 'But I know that it's hard when someone is taken from us so young, so unexpectedly, as Pete Barnes was taken. At such times as this, we struggle with grief, and we wrestle with questions. We ask ourselves why?'

Why?

Frank's gaze flickered to Beth, but her head was bowed, her face mercifully hidden by the brim of her hat. Gritting his teeth, he raised his eyes to the distant trees, wishing he hadn't come.

The pallbearers eased the long straps through their hands, lowering the casket slowly into the ground, before standing to attention beside the grave. The priest spoke a final prayer, then turned away as the congregation relaxed and muted conversations began. Frank glanced briefly towards the road, wondering if he might be able to slip away, but all around him mourners were starting to drift slowly towards the family, ready to offer their condolences. It was his one chance to see Beth.

Waiting his turn, he caught glimpses of her through the crowd of dark suits. She looked beautiful but lost, her pale skin shining like porcelain against the black of her dress. As he drew nearer, he felt a sudden need to put his arm around her, to pull her close and kiss her once more, just as he had the last time he saw her... but she was flanked by dutiful relatives – her younger sister Kaitlyn, who lived in St Louis, and an aunt who'd moved to Oklahoma last summer – all back in town, all eager to help.

There'd be no chance to say anything to Beth. Nothing that mattered, anyway.

'Officer Rye...' Her little sister greeted him with a sad smile of recognition, one black-gloved hand outstretched. 'Thank you for coming.'

'Hello, Kaitlyn,' he said. She was pretty in her own way, shorter than Beth, but with that same, wavy brown hair. He searched her eyes for any hint that she knew about them, but there was nothing unusual in her gaze, just polite regret. He clasped her hand for a moment, then took a silent breath, and turned to face her sister.

'Beth?'

She raised her head and stared blankly at him, her expression unreadable.

'Frank.'

Instinctively, he began to reach out a hand to her, then stopped himself, unsure how fragile her composure might be.

'I'm so sorry, Beth. Pete was...' He faltered under the weight of the truth, realizing how his words might sound to her. 'He was a good man.'

Something in her demeanor changed, and her eyes seemed to sharpen, focusing on him. Here, surrounded by a crowd of solemn-faced mourners, he was the one person who understood what she was going through... and the one person who couldn't comfort her.

'If there's anything you need,' he said, softly. 'Anything I can do...'

Her stare seemed to harden, and he knew then what she was thinking.

I want you to find whoever did this.

She held his gaze for a moment longer, then finally lowered her eyes.

'Thank you, Frank. Thanks for coming.'

That was it. He stood there a moment longer, but she was done talking. Nodding awkwardly, he stepped back and turned away, his eyes resting briefly on the open grave. A terrible distance now stood between them. Everything they'd had, all burned up in that moment he'd told her Pete was gone.

Head bowed, he wandered across the grass, away from the little groups of black-clad people with their hushed conversations. He wanted to smoke, but not here, not on consecrated ground. Frowning, he started up the slope, picking his way carefully between the burial plots until he reached the road. Tapping a cigarette from the pack, he put it in his mouth, then flicked his lighter open. As he took the first, calming drag, a voice called out behind him.

'Frank?'

He turned to see Kirkland stepping up onto the asphalt, a terse expression on his face as he made his way over.

'Wasn't sure if you'd be here,' the big man said.

Frank lowered his eyes.

'I had to come,' he said, then added, 'for Pete.'

Kirkland considered this for a moment, then gave a grudging nod.

'You won't have heard, but there's a collection... for Pete's family.' He lifted a hand and rubbed the back of his neck. 'You knew 'em, so I guess you'll want to contribute.'

'Of course,' Frank agreed quickly. 'Thanks for letting me know.'

Kirkland seemed satisfied.

'Speak to Johnson about it,' he said, gesturing back over his shoulder. 'He's here somewhere.'

'I will.'

Kirkland made as if to leave, but Frank stopped him.

'Sir, I was just wondering...' He hesitated. '...about the suspension?'

Kirkland stiffened, and his eyes grew dark.

'Do I still need to spell it out for you, how much *trouble* you're in?' He leaned in close, his voice a low growl. 'Take a look around you, Frank. I just put Pete Barnes *in the ground*. This sure as hell ain't the time to rile me.'

Abruptly, he pushed past Frank and stalked away. A short

distance down the road, the man in the blue suit watched him stride past.

Frank waited until he saw Kirkland's patrol car drive away, then shut his eyes. It had been a mistake to come. Sighing, he turned around and made his way back into the cemetery to find Johnson.

6

Lenny's Rib Shack was a dingy little joint on the corner of 5th and Virginia Avenue, but it was on his way and it had a bar. The place *did* do great ribs, but right now Frank wasn't feeling hungry. He just needed somewhere quiet, somewhere that wasn't home.

The interior was dimly lit, filled with smoky cooking smells and the thin twang of country music from a tired old radio set on the counter.

'Hey, Frank.' Lenny looked up from his newspaper. He was a tall man in his forties, with thinning black hair, slicked back from his high forehead, and watchful dark eyes. 'Can I fix you something? We got ribs on.'

'Sorry.' Frank shook his head. 'I think I left my appetite at home.'

'Get you a drink?'

'Sure.' He stopped, then frowned. 'Say, can I use your telephone first?'

Lenny nodded and reached for his newspaper again.

'Go right ahead,' he said.

Frank wandered over to the back of the room, where an old

phone hung on the wall between the restroom door and the gleaming cigarette machine. Fumbling in his pants pocket, he drew out his notebook and flipped through the pages until he found the number he wanted. Dialing, he bowed his head and waited until the call was answered.

'Yeah, this is Frank Rye, from Joplin Police Department. May I speak with Sheriff Carson?'

He turned to look at the cigarette machine, wondering if he had the right coins for a pack of Camels, but then there was a click and he recognized Carson's rough voice on the other end of the line.

'Hello, Frank. How's it going?'

Frank sighed. 'Well, we just had Pete's funeral this afternoon, so...'

'Hey, I'm sorry Frank. It's tough saying goodbye to someone you worked with.'

'Thanks. Anyway, now that's done I guess I just want to keep busy, you know?'

'Yeah, I can understand that,' Carson said, more gently. 'So what can I do for you?'

Frank leaned back against the cigarette machine and rubbed his eyes. 'Well, I got to thinking about the patrol car, the one that Pete was driving. Did it ever show up?'

'Sure it did,' Carson replied. 'We found it parked in an alley-way, just a block away from the murder scene. Matter of fact, one of your boys came down and took it back up to Joplin. Didn't you know?'

Frank hesitated.

'No, I've been away for the past few days,' he lied. 'So I guess Pete must have driven there himself...'

'Looks that way. Haven't found anyone who remembers seeing him, though.'

Frowning, Frank considered this.

'What about the woman over at the Skordeno factory, the one he was going to visit? Did you speak to her yet?'

'Oh yeah, Mary Cantell?' Carson paused. 'We spoke to the Skordeno people, but here's the thing; they never heard of no Mary Cantell.'

Frank stood bolt upright.

'What do you mean? I was–' He shut his eyes, correcting himself. '*Pete* was supposed to go and collect some letters from her.'

'Maybe so, but there's nobody of that name working there,' Carson said. 'And nobody knew anything about a police officer stopping by either.'

This didn't make any sense. Frank shook his head, trying to fit it all together.

'So Pete *didn't* go over there?'

'He may have done, but nobody remembers seeing him.' Carson paused, then asked, 'Anything you wanna tell me about these letters? I'm kinda curious why you sent someone all the way down here, rather than just having us pick 'em up for you.'

There was a hint of suspicion in his voice.

'I don't know' Frank cast his mind back. Just a few days ago, but already it seemed like months. 'Somebody called the department, said they had some letters regarding old Howard Cooke...'

'The mill owner who killed himself last year?'

'That's right. Apparently they were "sensitive" but that's all I heard.'

Carson was quiet for a moment.

'Anything... *unusual* about that case?' he asked.

'No,' Frank said. 'There was some interest from the newspapers at the time, rumors that he owed money to some bad folk up in Kansas City, but that was just talk. It was a straight-up suicide: no mystery, no scandal.'

'Well... okay then.' Carson seemed at a loss. 'I guess that's it for now.'

44

'Guess so.' Frank stared across the room, his eyes coming to rest on a poster of a pin-up girl behind the bar. 'Oh... Ray?'

'Yeah?'

'Any news on that missing waitress? Faye...?'

'No sign of Miss Griffith,' Carson replied. 'She hasn't been back to work and her friend hasn't seen her.' His voice took on a slightly impatient tone. 'Now listen, Frank, you know I'm always happy to help a fellow officer, but I feel like I'm repeating myself here. I already told *all* of this to your folk in Joplin. Don't you boys talk to each other up there?'

Frank leaned his forehead against the wall. Newton County clearly didn't know he was suspended, and it was probably best to keep things that way.

'Yeah, of course,' he said, trying to sound as though the news about Faye had simply slipped his mind. 'I'm sorry... there's just been a lot happening, you know?'

Carson's voice softened.

'Aw hell, I understand. You just wanna do right by your friend, and I'd be the same in your position.' He took a deep breath, clearly audible down the phone. 'Look, I know it ain't easy to sit by and let someone else work a case like this, but we'll keep your department informed, don't you worry about that.'

Frank nodded to himself. *A kindly reassurance from a fellow officer... and a polite warning to back off and let them do their job.*

'Well, I appreciate all you're doing, Ray,' he said. There was no sense pushing any more, not right now. 'Thanks for bringing me up to date.'

'Any time, Frank.'

Hanging up the phone, he stood there for a moment, frowning.

How could there be no Mary Cantell?

Turning around, he walked slowly back to the bar and eased himself onto a seat, lost in thought. *Somebody* at the department had taken the call. If he could find out who, he could ask them about it... but now probably wasn't the best time to go digging around, not with Kirkland on the warpath.

'So?'

He looked up to find Lenny waiting expectantly.

'Can I get you something, or are you "on duty"?'

Frank looked at him, puzzled, then remembered he was still wearing his uniform from the funeral.

'Oh, right.' He turned to run his eyes along the bottles behind the bar. 'Bourbon.'

Lenny put down his paper and stood up.

'Bourbon it is.'

Frank leaned on the counter, resting his chin in his hands as Lenny poured his drink and pushed it towards him.

'Thanks,' he said, staring at the glass. 'And maybe I'll take a side of those ribs after all.'

'Thought you might.' Lenny gave him a broad grin, then turned and went through to the kitchen. 'Back in a minute.'

Watching him go, Frank's gaze drifted across the wall behind the bar, noting the array of different bottles, the heavy old register, the pin-up girl picture...

Faye Griffith.

He'd never believed she was the killer. When he'd been down in Neosho, seen the way Pete had been busted up, he'd felt sure there was a third person involved – the *real* killer – and that the missing waitress would probably turn up, dead, soon enough. But as the days went by he got a little less sure. Maybe she *was* dead, buried somewhere her body would never be found, but whoever killed Pete didn't bother to hide him, so why hide a waitress? No, the more he thought about it, the more likely it seemed that she was involved in the murder, an accomplice.

A woman who shouldn't have been trusted.

He frowned to himself, then knocked back his bourbon and set the empty glass on the bar.

.　.　.

Darkness was drawing in when he finally arrived home. He stopped the car at the side of the house, got out unsteadily, and stood for a moment. Across the street, he could see the Hendersons sitting in their illuminated front room, reading magazines. It was just another day to them; *every* day was just another day to them.

Perhaps ignorance really could be bliss.

Shaking his head, he walked slowly to the front door, pulling out his keys... then remembered his hat, still lying on the passenger seat. He started back when he heard the rev of an engine and looked up. There, just a little way back along the street, a car was pulling around in a sharp U-turn. Frank stopped in mid-stride.

It was a grey Chrysler.

He watched it complete the turn and drive away, disappearing back up the street the way it had come. It was the same car he'd seen at the funeral; he was sure of it.

Unlocking the front door, he pushed his way into the house. Kicking the door shut behind him, he strode quickly through to the bedroom and snatched up his .45 from the nightstand, feeling the reassuring weight in his hand.

There are no such things as coincidences, that was what his commanding officer, Major Swift, had told him when he was stationed in Switzerland. *There are only warnings.*

He took a deep breath, trying to shake off the warm fuzziness of the bourbon so he could think clearly.

The *same car*, parked outside the cemetery, and now here in his street. Someone had followed him home.

He shut his eyes for a moment, trying to recall the thin man he'd noticed earlier, leaning up against that Chrysler, smoking so calmly. Six feet tall, with an angular jaw and sunken eye sockets. Rough-looking, despite that smart hat and the expensive blue suit.

Frank opened his eyes.

47

Who wears a blue suit to a funeral? The guy sure as hell wasn't there to mourn.

He went through to the kitchen and put the gun down on the counter while he filled a glass under the faucet. Gulping down the water, he stared out the window across the back yard, lifting his eyes towards the last glow of sun behind the horizon. It would be completely dark soon.

It should have been me...

Frank stiffened. Maybe Pete was never the target... maybe *he* was, *still* was.

Suddenly, he became painfully aware that he was standing in front of the window, a big fat silhouette against the light of the kitchen. Picking up his gun, he stepped quickly to one side, reaching for the back door and rattling the handle to check it was locked. Then he turned and strode through the house, locking the front door and bolting it.

No coincidences... only warnings.

Stepping back, he turned around, his brow lined in thought. These were the only two ways into the house, unless you counted the windows, but they were too high above the ground to be easy. The important thing now was just to be smart, to be *ready*.

In the end, he propped a broom against the front door and a chair against the back, balancing them so they'd tumble onto the wooden floor if they were moved. Retreating into the bedroom, he left the door slightly open so he could hear if anything happened elsewhere in the house, but balanced a teak-handled clothes brush on the top edge, ready to fall. Nobody was sneaking in without him knowing about it.

Satisfied, he walked round to the far side of the room and yanked the drapes shut, then turned his attention to the bed.

Better to be safe.

Grasping some blankets, and one of the pillows, he hauled them off the mattress and down onto the floor below the window. Then, crouching low, he sat back against the wall and began unlacing his shoes. Seeing the room from this unfamiliar view-point took him back to his time in Europe; he'd slept on the floor quite often during those first days in France...

Settling down, he placed the .45 where he could reach it, then lowered his head onto the pillow. Staring under the bed frame, he watched the narrow gap in the door until his eyelids drooped and he fell asleep.

7

Frank woke with a start, blinking, confused at finding himself on the floor. His eyes focused on something dark and metallic – his .45, lying there, just a few inches from his face – and then he remembered.

He reached out quickly, fingers wrapping themselves about the gun, then held his breath as he listened... but there was no sound. Glancing under the bed, he could see the door was still slightly open, exactly as he'd left it. Relaxing just a little, he exhaled and let his head sink back onto the pillow.

Daylight came shafting down through the gap in the drapes, raising tiny dust motes from the wooden floor boards. He lay there for a moment, staring at them, then pushed himself wearily up onto his elbows, wincing at the stiffness in his muscles. He checked his watch; it was ten after eight. Rubbing his eyes, he gripped the .45 and got carefully to his feet. Moving quietly around the bed, he approached the door, remembering just in time to remove the clothes brush he'd balanced on top of it. Stepping cautiously into the hallway, he could see the broom resting against the front door; in the kitchen, the back door was still blocked by the chair. He lowered his right hand, letting the gun drop to his side. Everything was all right. For now.

He dressed quickly, choosing a white shirt and a dark grey suit; it was warm, but it made him look more like a plainclothes detective, and the jacket helped to conceal his gun. He left his badge on the nightstand, then changed his mind and snatched it up, jamming it into his pocket and hoping he wouldn't need to show it. Lifting his hat, he went to the front door and moved the broom aside.

There was no doubt in his mind now: Pete's murder had been a mistake, because *he* was the real target. But why? What the hell had *he* ever done? Was it an angry ex-con? That didn't seem likely. A jealous husband would be nearer the mark; ironically, Pete Barnes was the one person with a genuine motive for wanting him dead.

Taking a breath, he opened the front door. The street looked quiet enough. Stepping outside, he locked the house, then walked to his car.

He needed something more, something to help him make sense of all that had happened. Who *was* the thin man? He had to get a line on him, maybe see about tracking down that car.

But he couldn't go to the department.

Frank gripped the steering wheel in frustration. If Kirkland heard he was nosing around, he'd be busted out for good. No, he'd have to come up with another way, find some other loose ends to pull on...

The waitress.

If Faye Griffith wasn't dead, then maybe she'd left town. And maybe if he found her, he'd find her friend the thin man too.

Frowning, he came to the stop sign at the end of his street and sat there for a moment, looking up at it.

It was a long shot, but he knew he couldn't go to the police.

Not yet, anyway. And it sure beat sitting around, waiting for that grey Chrysler to come creeping up behind him.

Checking his rear-view mirror, Frank gunned the engine and accelerated out onto the main road.

There were two railroad depots in Neosho and he went to both of them. The first was out at the north end of town, a narrow little box of a building with tall windows, surrounded by trees. Inside, a delicate old man in a smart-looking uniform smiled at him politely from the ticket office window.

'What day would this have been?'

'Sometime in the last week,' Frank replied. 'She might have been traveling with a man – a thin guy in a blue suit.'

'Ah, well then...' The old man shook his head. 'I don't think I've seen her, and if she's pretty like you say, well, I'm sure I'd remember.'

Frank thanked him and went back to his car.

He drove down to the other depot, a much larger building, closer to the centre of town. Here, the middle-aged ticket agent was friendly enough to begin with, but grew wary when asked about Faye.

'Maybe you wanna tell me why you're looking for this woman,' he said, his expression darkening.

'It's a police matter,' Frank growled, pulling out his badge with some reluctance and showing it as briefly as he could. 'So I'd really appreciate any help you can give me.'

At this, the agent appeared to relax.

'Hey, no problem.' He shrugged. 'You're not the first guy to come in asking about her, that's all.'

Frank stared at him, then understood. *Of course; the Newton County boys would be making enquiries too.* He hurriedly pushed the badge back into his jacket pocket.

'We're... working with the Sheriff's Department,' he

explained. It was deliberately vague, and he hoped it would calm any suspicions the man might have. 'So *have* you seen anyone fitting the description?'

'Sorry, not recently,' the agent said. 'But hey, I was thinking; maybe she took the bus. Have you tried asking down at the square? Just head straight down Washington for four blocks, you can't miss it.'

The Jefferson Lines ticket agent was a serious man in his thirties with round eyeglasses and immaculate slicked-back hair. A large poster on the wall behind him showed a sleek new bus on a scenic mountain road.

'In the last week?' he said, frowning in concentration. 'No, I'm sorry. I know most of the people who come in here – by sight, at least – so I'm sure I'd remember if I'd seen the woman you're talking about.'

'Thanks anyway,' Frank said. 'Appreciate your time.'

He turned and went outside, pausing on the sidewalk to light a cigarette and gaze out across the broad square, with its two-story brick buildings and tidy storefronts. Ahead of him was a modern-looking courthouse finished in gleaming white stone and surrounded by mown grass and young trees. It all had that homely feel of a traditional small town...

...but someone had planned to kill him here.

He took a deep breath, frustrated by his lack of progress. He needed to defend himself, to strike back, but against who?

Scowling, he tossed the cigarette butt down, and ground it out with his shoe. He was about to head back to his car, when a street sign caught his eye.

Wood Street.

He frowned. Faye had been a waitress at a grill on Wood Street, hadn't she? He glanced down at his watch, then started along the sidewalk. Maybe he'd go and grab a bite to eat before he drove back to Joplin.

Barney's All-Day Grill was a modest little place a block south of the main square. Slowing, as though to glance at the menu in the window, Frank peered through the glass. There were a few customers but plenty of empty seats, and he could see a blond waitress standing at the counter. Pushing the door open, he went inside.

When the waitress came to his table, he glanced up at her with a smile. She was in her twenties, with a sky-blue uniform and a round, cheerful face.

'Hi. What can I get you?' she said, setting some water down in front of him, then pulling out her pad and pencil. Her name tag read *Wendy*.

'I think I'll have the cheesesteak,' he replied, looking up at her. 'And could you do me a favor?'

'Sure, what d'you need?' she asked.

'Could you pass me that paper?' he said, pointing past her towards an empty table in the corner. 'If nobody wants it.'

She glanced around, then reached over and handed him the newspaper.

'There you go.' She smiled. 'And your cheesesteak will be right out.'

He watched her moving away between the tables, everything familiar. Saw her greeting a regular customer coming in; she'd been working here for some time. This *must* be Faye's friend, the one Carson told him about.

Good.

He unfolded the newspaper, noting the headline: *N.Y. GOVERNOR INVESTIGATED OVER SECRET WARTIME MOB DEAL.* Hunching over the table, he started to read.

. . .

He pushed his plate away and sat back in his chair, feeling full. When the waitress returned, he greeted her with a satisfied smile.

'How was everything?' she asked.

'It was good,' he assured her. 'Real good.'

'Glad you liked it,' she said. 'Can I get you anything else?'

'No, but you can tell me about Faye Griffith.' He was still smiling, but his voice was suddenly quiet and serious. 'I need to find her.'

'Sorry, mister. Can't help you.' She shrugged, but he could already see it in her eyes. She knew something.

'Maybe I didn't make myself clear...' He took out his badge and put it on the table. 'You know what this means, right?'

'Okay. So you're a cop.' She gave him a sarcastic look and reached out to take his plate. 'I already told the sheriff, I don't kno–'

He took her wrist, holding it gently but firmly, the polite smile still fixed on his face as he stared deep into her eyes.

'It *means* I'm the law.'

He was pushing his luck here, but what was the alternative? Leave it all to Sheriff Carson? Wait for the thin man to get him in his sleep?

Frank lowered his voice further, leaning in a little so she could hear him.

'Wendy... do you have *any* idea what's gonna happen to you if you hold out on me and someone else dies?' he asked.

Hearing him use her name seemed to spook her, and her eyes widened.

'You're already in *way* over your head,' he told her softly. 'Now, where's Faye?'

'I...' She stared at him in desperation. 'I don't know where she is now.'

'What *do* you know?' he pressed her.

Wendy's shoulders dropped and she looked at the floor.

'Faye told me she needed a favor. That she needed to get out of town for a while.'

'No kidding.' Frank rolled his eyes.

'Hey, I didn't know!' Wendy hissed at him. 'About the guy who got killed, I mean. Not until after.'

Frank noted her indignation, then nodded slowly.

'So she needed to get out of town...' he prompted.

'Yeah, so I asked Jimmy – he's my boyfriend, and he's got a car – and he took her.'

'Took her where?'

'Racine. It's about ten miles west on–'

'I know where it is.' Frank frowned for a moment, thinking. 'Was anyone waiting for her? Did she meet someone there?'

'Jimmy just dropped her off at the gas station, then came back. That was what she wanted.'

'When was this?'

'It was...' Wendy looked at him uncomfortably. '...the same day everything happened.'

Frank sighed.

'Did she have a bag with her?' he asked.

'Yes, a bag and a suitcase. How did you know?'

'The same way I'll know if you mention this conversation to anyone,' he told her, his voice dropping to a whisper. '*Anyone*. Do you understand?'

She nodded quickly, then said, 'Yes.'

'Good.' Frank gave her a pleasant smile and released her wrist. Placing an extra dollar on the table, he picked up his badge and got to his feet. 'You've been very helpful, *Wendy*. I'll remember that.'

Folding the newspaper, he handed it back to her, then walked past her to the door.

8

The road was a long straight ribbon of asphalt, gently rising and falling as it ran through open country. Frank drove west, his eyes occasionally flicking to the rear-view mirror, but there was nobody behind him. After a while, the railroad crept in on the left, gleaming tracks visible between the patches of brush, running alongside in the middle of nowhere.

Why did Faye ask to come out here?

Eventually, the road swept through a pair of long bends and onto a low bridge that carried it over a twisting creek. Beyond the bridge was a crossroads, with a few small houses screened by trees. On his right, he could see the gas station. Frank slowed down and stopped at the intersection for a minute, gazing out through the windshield. Racine really *wasn't* a big place.

He pulled the car round to the right, crawling past the gas station and general store, and moving on up the hill. Ahead of him was a tiny post office with a tall flagpole, the stars and stripes hanging bright against the blue sky. Pulling in on a patch of dirt at the side of the road, he stopped the engine and got out. Stretching his shoulders to relieve the stiffness from his night on the floor, he paused, struck by how quiet the place was. There was no sound at all, except the faint rustle of the trees.

Why had she chosen Racine? There was nothing special round here, just a few scattered houses. He looked across the road, peering at their windows. Had she met someone here? Was she *still* here somewhere?

Frowning, he turned and walked over to the post office. It was a small, timber building, little more than a cabin. Someone had taken the trouble to plant flowers around the front of the place, but they were withered now, and autumn leaves littered the wooden porch. There was a handwritten note, pinned to the door - *Back in 20 Minutes.*

He moved across to peer through one of the windows, but there didn't seem to be anyone inside; the place was still and empty. Shaking his head, he started back towards the car.

Against the heavy quiet of the village, his footsteps seemed unnaturally loud... but he could hear something else now - the approaching rumble of a motor - and he looked back towards the crossroads. A bus was coming up the hill, slowing as it drew level with the gas station and pulling over. As it finally came to a stop, he heard the door swing open over the idle of the engine. A young man with an army crew cut got out, swung his bag up onto his shoulder, and set off down the road towards the intersection. *Another kid, back from Russia.*

Frank watched as the door shut and the bus pulled away, dust and dry leaves rising from the asphalt as it approached. He smelled the warm diesel fumes as it drove past him, noting the name *Jefferson Lines* written along the side.

This must be the first stop after Neosho. Was *that* why Faye had come here?

There was an old truck parked at the gas station, rust blooming across its faded paintwork, but nobody seemed to be around. He made his way past the pumps to the general store where several black tires were stacked up beside a newspaper stand. Pressed up against the glass, the front page headline read *GOVERNOR'S SECRET DEAL WITH MOBSTER LUCIANO.*

Frank pushed the door open and heard the ding of a little bell above his head. Inside, the air was cool, and the place smelled of pipe smoke and coffee. Racks of canned goods and provisions divided the floor into wide aisles. A counter ran along the far wall, and two men were standing there, looking at him with mild interest.

'Good afternoon to you.' Sitting beside the register, with a rack of cigarette cartons behind him, the storekeeper was a broad man in his fifties. He wore an open-collared shirt and a brown apron.

Leaning up against the counter, his friend looked older – a thin man with short silver hair and spectacles. He was wearing a US Postal Service short-sleeve shirt.

'Afternoon,' Frank said, walking over to them. 'I was hoping maybe you could help me out.'

'Do my best,' the storekeeper replied, standing up. 'What is it you need?'

'I'm looking for someone, and I thought she might have come by here.' Frank pulled out his badge so they could both see it, then slipped it back into his pocket. 'A woman in her twenties. Brown hair, pretty, maybe carrying a suitcase?'

The storekeeper was already nodding.

'Yeah, that would have been...' He paused. 'Let me see, now... 'bout a week ago?'

'You spoke to her?'

'Passed the time of day, that's all.'

'Is she in any trouble?' the Postal Service man interjected, obviously eager for gossip.

Frank ignored him.

'Did she buy anything?' he asked.

'Bought herself a soda,' the storekeeper explained. 'And a bus ticket.'

Frank leaned forward.

'You remember where that ticket was for?'

The storekeeper smiled and hooked his thumbs into his apron.

'I sure do,' he said. 'Kansas City, one-way.'

Frank took a deep breath and allowed himself a bleak little smile of satisfaction.

'Tell me,' he said. 'Is there a telephone round here that I could use?'

The payphone was over in the far corner of the store, partly hidden by a stack of soap boxes. Holding the receiver, Frank stared at the two men by the counter until they reluctantly looked away and resumed their own hushed conversation.

Carson's voice crackled in the earpiece.

'Good afternoon, Frank.'

'Hello Ray.' Frank turned his back on the others and leaned in close to the phone. 'I'm just following up on a couple of things here. Thought you might be able to fill in some gaps for me.'

'Is that so?' Carson's tone was agreeable, but non-committal.

'Yeah, it's about that waitress, Faye Griffith. You said she had family, back in Kansas City.'

'Just her brother, Stanley. What about him?'

Frank reached into his pocket, pulling out his notebook.

'I need an address for him.'

The line went quiet for a moment. Then Carson began to laugh.

'You really weren't gonna tell me, were you?'

Fumbling with his pen, Frank stopped and frowned.

'Tell you what?' he asked.

'You know damn well what.' The friendly tone was gone now. 'Think I wasn't gonna find out you'd been suspended?'

Damn! Frank bowed his head against the wall.

'Look, it's just–'

'No, *you* look!' Carson's raised voice crackled angrily in the earpiece. 'I've been the soul of courtesy with you, but you won't play straight with me? Well, you're out on your own now, and you better pray I don't tell Kirkland how one of his officers keeps calling up, poking their nose in.'

Gritting his teeth, Frank took a deep breath, straightening up to his full height. Kirkland was the least of his worries right now; someone was trying to kill him.

'Do we understand each other?' Carson was still talking, still unaware of what was really going on. Frank kicked the wall hard, rattling the shelves that surrounded the payphone, then screwed his eyes shut as he compressed all his frustration into an angry whisper.

'I *need* that address.'

There was an indignant snort at the other end of the line.

'Seems you didn't hear me–'

But now it was Frank's turn to raise his voice.

'Shut your *fat mouth*,' he snarled, stunning the sheriff into silence. 'I need that address and you're going to give it to me. And *you* better pray that *I* don't tell Kirkland what I heard about your son and that poor girl from Tipton Ford.'

He hadn't wanted things to go like this, but now he had no choice.

There was a long pause before Carson spoke again.

'You're a bastard, Frank,' he said quietly.

'I've been told that before,' Frank snapped. 'Now get me the damn address!'

'Just... just hang on.'

There was a thud as the receiver was set down, and he heard muffled sounds for a moment, until the sheriff returned.

'All right... it's 210 East 40th Street, apartment 16. You got that?'

'Apartment 16.' With the phone tucked into the crook of his

neck, Frank pressed his notepad against the wall and scribbled down the address. 'Yeah, I got it.'

'Then get *this*, too.' A growl crept into Carson's voice. 'If I hear any stories are going round, stories about me or my boy... well, then you'd better start sleeping with your eyes wide open, son.'

There was a sharp click as he slammed the phone down, and the line went dead.

Frank stood for a moment, then slowly exhaled, breathing out his anger.

Carson wasn't a bad guy – everyone knew that – but the dumb bastard shouldn't have got in his way. Not now, not over something like this.

He replaced the receiver, then turned to find the storekeeper and the postal worker staring at him.

'Have a good day,' he muttered as he walked, unsmiling, to the door.

Outside, the warmth of the sun touched his skin, and he stood for a time, squinting over at the road where the bus had stopped. Somewhere in the far distance, a train horn blew its mournful note.

Frank paused for a moment, wondering if the sheriff might really make good on his threat, then scowled and started walking back towards his car.

Screw Carson. Screw them all.

Late that afternoon, he walked out from the Union Depot building, stepping across the bright rails and up onto the platform. Setting down his heavy green duffel bag, he casually glanced left and right, but nobody was looking at him, and there was no sign of the thin man.

For now, at least.

He sighed, reaching back to rub the stiffness that remained in his shoulder, then looked up as the people around him began to stir. Sunlight glinted on the red and yellow locomotive that had emerged from under the nearby viaduct, and he watched as the long train rumbled slowly into the station, bathing him in a swirling crescendo of warm air and noise.

'Joplin, this is Joplin,' one of the porters, a negro with a rich clear voice, was shouting along the platform. 'Southern Belle, calling at Pittsburg and Kansas City.'

Hefting his bag, Frank moved forward with the other passengers, stepping up to climb aboard. Once inside, he stowed his bag then took a seat by a window in the chair car.

Why had Pete gone with Faye, followed her back to that room? *Why did he trust her?*

But Frank knew why. *We believe what we want to believe. We believe* who *we want to believe.*

There was a brief jolt, and the train began to move. Frowning, he turned to stare out through the glass as Joplin gradually slipped away.

Faye was a few days ahead of him, but *he* was ahead of the cops, and he knew what he was doing. When he found her, he was going to make her talk.

And he was going to make her pay.

Spring, 1944
Bern, Switzerland

𝕶𝖆𝖓𝖘𝖆𝖘 𝕮𝖎𝖙𝖞 𝕳𝖊𝖗𝖆𝖑𝖉

KANSAS CITY, MISSOURI - TUESDAY, June 6, 1944

ALLIED INVASION BEGINS

U.S. TROOPS LAND IN FRANCE; PORT OF LE HAVRE BOMBARDED; NORMANDY PENINSULA OCCUPIED

LONDON, Jun 6 – Berlin radio has reported that "British-American landing operations against the western coast of Europe now stretch over the entire region between Cherbourg and Le Havre."

The broadcast described a vast amphibious assault along a broad front between the mouth of the Seine and the Vire estuary.

'GREAT CRUSADE' DEMANDS 'FULL VICTORY'

General Eisenhower, who has called the invasion "a great crusade", told American, British and Canadian troops that "we will accept nothing except full victory."

Official announcement of the operation came at 7:32AM Greenwich Mean Time (3:32AM Eastern War Time) stating that "Allied naval forces supported by strong air forces began landing Allied armies this morning on the northern coast of France."

(continued on page 2, column 1)

9

The conductor made his way along the aisle, two lines of silver buttons gleaming on his black tunic, a tall peaked cap swaying with the movement of the train. As he drew level, Frank glanced up at him and raised a hand.

'Wann kommen wir in Bern an?' he asked. *How long until we arrive in Bern?*

The conductor paused and checked his watch.

'In etwa 15 Minuten,' he replied.

'Danke.'

'Bitte sehr.'

Frank turned away from him and went back to staring out of the window.

It had been a grueling journey, traveling hundreds of miles south to Spain just so he could re-enter France on diplomatic papers and take the train up through unoccupied territory to the border crossing at Geneva. There had been a moment, as the soldiers pulled him out of the line at the frontier checkpoint, when he'd feared it had all been in vain. But he'd kept his nerve, talked his way through, and his efforts had finally been rewarded; he'd made it to Switzerland.

The country he now looked out on was lush – rolling and green, with glimpses of blue lakes and silver rivers – a gentler landscape than the rocky Alpine passes he'd imagined. Here and there, the green was dotted with clusters of buildings – little white houses, with steeply pitched roofs and brightly painted shutters around small windows. Every now and then, he'd catch sight of mountains, hazy and blue in the far distance, their peaks capped with snow.

Leaning his forehead against the cool glass, he stared down at the blurring ground, the shining steel rails, then slowly closed his eyes. He still wasn't sure why they'd sent him here. It had all started at the transit camp in Normandy, with the questions about his mother...

'Your mother's a German... Ilse Dreschner, born in Hamburg; is that right?'

Standing in the C.O.'s office, he'd held himself a little straighter, avoiding eye contact with the new man behind the desk.

'Yes sir,' he replied. 'But my father's an American. Like me.'

Who the hell was this guy? He hadn't been around the unit before. He wore the rank of major, but lacked that usual military manner which had become so annoyingly familiar since enlisting.

'And you speak German fluently?'

Frank stared at the wall behind the desk.

'Ich weiß, wie man nach einem Bier fragt,' he said, then added, 'sir.'

The major glanced up from his dossier, then leaned back in his chair. He appeared to be in his thirties, slim and thoughtful, with combed black hair and a neat mustache. When he finally smiled, it was as though he'd learned how to do so from a book.

'At ease, Corporal Rye,' he said. 'Speaking other languages isn't necessarily a *bad* thing. In fact, there are times when it's really quite useful.'

That was how it started, but there had been many other interviews: sudden requests to go and meet people who were never introduced by name, and to answer odd questions. And then, after a few weeks, it had all stopped as suddenly as it began. There was never any explanation, so he assumed that whatever it was, they'd decided they didn't need him or want him any more.

But then, ten days ago, his old C.O. had taken him to one side and told him to pack up and report to regional HQ. Word had come through from on-high; he was being transferred.

...but why Bern? He opened his eyes again, looking through the trees and across the green landscape. Switzerland remained a neutral country, so he wore civilian clothes instead of uniform, and the papers in his jacket pocket listed him as a translation clerk, not a soldier. They wouldn't have hooked him out of his unit and gone to all this trouble just to get another translator, he was sure of that. But they'd been careful to avoid telling him the real reason.

The train was slowing now, the steady rhythm of wheels on rails disrupted as the tracks divided and spread out beneath a canopy of power lines. On the left, the ground had risen up into a towering wall, topped with grass and trees. All around, beautiful old stone buildings looked down, crowded together like a fairy-tale town. People began to move, gathering up their bags as the station slid into view, and the train squealed slowly to a halt.

When he stepped down onto the long curving platform, he paused for a moment, letting the other passengers flow around him, a babble of German and French conversations above the unfamiliar hum of the electric train. Then, gripping his suitcase tightly, he made his way along beneath the low canopies, past the posters advertising strange brands of chocolate and ladies' soap, towards the exit.

It felt strange stepping out from the station building into the open air, as if Bern hadn't been quite *real* until this moment, but here it was, exactly as they'd described it in the briefings. In front of him was the Bahnhofplatz, an impressive open square surrounded by large buildings, with vaulted arches supporting elegant stone façades. Streetcars stood in line, waiting to follow the overhead power cables that looped around the square and out across the city, and everywhere there were buses and automobiles, and busy people hurrying back and forth. It felt different to anywhere he'd known back home – not necessarily bigger, but somehow more *condensed*. And far, *far* older.

He glanced up at the clock by the front of the station, then peered across the square, reading the signs on the buildings until he found the one he was looking for: the Schweizerhof, a grand old six-story hotel, with a row of automobiles parked out front. Swinging his suitcase, he waited for a streetcar to go clanking by, then started walking across the slippery-smooth cobbles.

Inside, the hotel was even more impressive than its exterior had suggested. Passing through a revolving glass door, he found himself in a muted world of polished wooden floors and tall ceilings with glittering chandeliers. All the bustle of the square was left outside – in here, everything and everyone was quiet and composed. Remembering his instructions, he made his way through to the lounge bar, where he ordered a coffee, set his case beside a comfortable chair, and sat down feeling conspicuous.

There were several people seated around the room, and he watched as the waiter drifted from one table to the next, wondering which of them might be here to meet him. The smartly-dressed couple in the corner were too engrossed in each other, and the elderly man snoring softly in an armchair seemed unlikely, but the middle-aged man with the newspaper... he might be the one. Frank sipped his coffee, watching without being obvious about it, when he became aware of a tapping sound, getting steadily louder. Looking round, he saw a young man in a tweed jacket hobbling towards him. With tousled blond hair, and one leg very obviously lame, he was leaning heavily on a walking stick that tapped noisily on the floor.

'Mr Rye?' he called, hurrying over as fast as he was able, and extending his free left hand. 'So glad to meet you.'

Frank stood up, noting the man's British accent as he reached out to shake awkwardly with his own left.

'Good to meet you too, Mister...?'

'Sorry.' The young man laughed. 'It's actually Ranulph Cavanagh, but that's a bit of a mouthful, so everyone just calls me Rafe, which I much prefer.'

'Good to meet you Rafe. I'm Frank.'

'Oh, I know.' Rafe smiled. He sat down with some difficulty, relief apparent on his face when he finally sank into his chair and let the walking stick drop to the floor.

'That's better,' he sighed, relaxing. 'Now, we've got you a room, over on Bantigerstrasse. I'll take you across and get you settled in, but I think we might just have a drink first, seeing as we're both here.'

He grinned and raised a hand to summon the waiter over.

'Scotch?' he asked. 'It's not too bad in here, and anything's better than the ghastly schnapps.'

'Sure. Why not?' Frank shrugged.

'Zwei Whiskys, bitte,' Rafe told the waiter, who nodded and moved away. 'So, did you have a good trip?'

'It was okay, I guess.'

'First time in Europe?'

'Well, we spent some time in Germany when I was a kid.' He saw Rafe's interest and added, 'My mom's family are from there. It's my first time in Switzerland, though.'

The waiter returned with a tray, carefully setting two glasses on the low table, before bowing and turning away.

Rafe thanked him, then reached over to take his whiskey.

'Switzerland's not so very different to parts of Germany.' He stared at his drink, then frowned. 'Apart from all the wretched Nazis, of course.'

Frank gave a grim nod, then raised his own glass.

'To the Swiss,' he said.

'To the Swiss.' Rafe smiled.

They sat in silence for a moment. Frank took a sip of his whiskey, then set the glass down.

'So tell me,' he began, eager to understand more about his new posting but not wanting to display ignorance, 'what is it that you do here?'

'Apart from meet people from the station?' Rafe glanced down at his bad leg and his smile seemed to dim a little. 'I do what I can to make myself useful but... well, cripples aren't really best suited to active service.'

'Sorry,' Frank said, sitting back into his chair. 'Were you injured in the Africa campaign? Or was it France?'

'What?' Rafe seemed puzzled for a moment, then shook his head. 'Oh, no. This was just a silly motorcycle accident in England.'

'Oh, I just figured...'

'It all happened before the war, I'm afraid. So I'm the *wrong sort* of cripple.' He managed a rueful smile, then lowered his voice. 'But I do occasionally tell people I caught a bit of shrapnel in Libya, fighting Rommel. Everyone loves a wounded soldier.'

'Especially the girls.' Frank winked, raising his glass.

Rafe gave a slight shrug.

'Well, there's plenty of chaps worse off than me,' he said, brightening. 'I say, did you know that your President Roosevelt is a cripple?'

'You're kidding me.' Frank stared at him, thinking back to the newsreels he'd seen. 'I know he might be a bit lame but...'

'I'm quite serious,' Rafe went on. 'Think about it; when did you last see him actually walking? The old man says he can't even stand up anymore, not without special steel leg braces.'

He didn't sound as if he was joking. Frank took another sip of whiskey, then looked over at him thoughtfully.

'The old man?' he said.

Rafe appeared to hesitate.

'Mr Dulles,' he explained, after a moment. 'You'll meet him before long, I'm sure. He's met your president several times. Met Adolf Hitler, too, though he doesn't talk about that so much.'

'And this Dulles guy,' Frank pressed him, 'is he the boss?'

'I'm sure he can explain things much better than I can.' Rafe managed a polite little smile. 'But let's not worry about work now; plenty of time for that tomorrow. For now, the important thing is that you're here.'

He finished his whiskey and set his glass down on the table.

'Drink up, and I'll take you over to Bantigerstrasse. You can freshen up and unpack. Later we'll pop out and find something to eat, maybe meet some of the others.'

Leaning over, he stretched down and fumbled for his walking stick, teasing it with his fingertips until it was in reach.

Frank watched him, wishing he'd thought to help, then knocked back the last of his whiskey. He waited until Rafe was getting to his feet, then rose slowly, ready to support the other man if necessary.

'Is this Bantigerstrasse place very far?' he asked.

'Not too far,' Rafe replied, steadying himself with his walking stick. He glanced at Frank, then nodded gravely. 'I know... it seems a bit rich having someone like me doing *legwork*, but there is a war on, you know.'

His face broke into a broad grin and both men laughed.

'Welcome to Bern, Frank.'

10

Sitting on the edge of the bed, Frank rubbed his eyes then squinted at his watch. 6:45am. He stood up carefully; his tiny attic room had a low ceiling but as he turned towards the window and peered out beneath the overhang of the roof he was rewarded with a glorious view across the surrounding houses to the sunlit treetops that marked the woods at the end of the street and the forested hills beyond. Suddenly, the war seemed very far away. He gazed out for a moment longer, then turned to the small wooden chair where his clothes lay folded and began to get dressed.

Rationing was in force, so breakfast was basic: a slab of coarse brown bread with some kind of pale cheese. The elderly landlady sat in the corner of the downstairs parlor and gave the impression that she would watch him eat, so he excused himself politely and took his food with him.

Stepping out into the morning sunlight, he turned his face to the sky and drew a deep breath. There was a crisp freshness to everything, as though the air had come to him from some icy Alpine pass. Smiling, he took a bite of the bread and set off down the road. Lined with large stone houses, Bantigerstrasse was a small street in a quiet part of town. Here and there he saw little gardens, but many of the lawns and flowerbeds had been dug up and were now being used as vegetable plots. At the end of the road he cut between two houses, trying to remember the route that Rafe had showed him yesterday. A narrow dirt path meandered down through steeply sloping woods, where he caught tantalizing glimpses of the old town across the river, and descended through another neighborhood until he reached Dufourstrasse. Number 24 was at the far end, a three-story townhouse finished in stone.

There were steps leading up to the front door, which was open. Inside, he found himself in a silent hallway with white walls and a tiled floor. Straightening his jacket, he made his way up to the second floor where a single, closed door was set into the wall. He knocked and waited.

A woman in her twenties opened it. She was pretty, in an understated way, with brown hair pinned back from her face and prominent cheekbones.

'Yes?' She regarded him with mild interest.

'Hi. I'm Frank Rye.' He paused, then added, 'I believe I'm expected?'

A faint smile touched the woman's face.

'Of course,' she said, stepping back and opening the door wider. 'Do please come in.'

As she spoke, he noticed that she had a British accent.

'Thanks,' he said, and followed her inside.

She led him into a large open room, with tall windows and several desks arranged in the middle of the polished wooden floor. Rafe was sitting at one of them, but he looked up and smiled as they entered.

'Good morning, Frank.' He set down the paper he'd been studying and got to his feet, leaning heavily on his stick. 'Did you sleep well?'

'Just great, thanks.' Frank glanced around at the other empty desks. 'I'm not early, am I? You said eight...'

'No, no, it's fine,' Rafe assured him, then turned towards the woman who was standing beside them. 'This is Molly Pearson. Molly, this is Frank Rye.'

Frank hurriedly extended his hand to her, feeling a little awkward for not asking her name at the door.

'Pleasure to meet you, Miss Pearson,' he said.

She looked at him, a mischievous glint in her bright eyes, then took his hand and nodded demurely. 'And you, Mr Rye.'

Rafe beamed at them both.

'Good show,' he said. 'Now, there's lots to do, but Major Swift asked me to send you in when you got here. Shall I take you through now?'

Frank looked at him and shrugged.

'Sure, I guess.' He turned to Molly. 'See you later.'

Rafe took him into a narrow corridor where he knocked on a polished wooden door. A voice from within called, 'Enter'. Opening the door, Rafe ushered Frank inside.

This was a much smaller room, with a large single desk sitting in the middle of the dark patterned rug that covered most of the floor. Standing by the window was a broad-shouldered man in a shirt and tie, clean-shaven with tidy black hair and a strong jaw.

'Major Swift,' Rafe said. 'This is Frank Rye.'

'Ah, yes.' The man turned away from the window and stepped forward, a smile creasing his face as he extended his hand. 'Come on in, Frank.'

He had a faint East Coast accent: New York, or Boston maybe; it was hard to place. Unsure whether to salute or not, Frank reached across the desk and shook hands with him, feeling the man's powerful grip.

'Good morning, sir.'

Swift seemed to sense his uncertainty.

'At ease, soldier. Just think of me as James Swift rather than Major; we're very informal here.' He turned to Rafe. 'Thanks. That'll be all for now.'

Rafe flashed Frank a quick grin of encouragement, then turned and left the room.

As the door clicked shut, Swift indicated a chair.

'Make yourself comfortable, Frank.'

'Thank you, sir.'

They sat down, Swift settling back into his chair and steepling his fingers as he studied Frank.

'So,' he mused, after a long moment of uncomfortable silence, 'I imagine you're wondering why you're here.'

Frank affected a slight shrug.

'They didn't tell me much about this, so... yeah, I'm curious.'

Swift nodded thoughtfully, frowning as he considered what he was going to say.

'We're at war, Frank,' he began. 'It might not look that way in a pretty little town like this, but the war is raging here, just as it is everyplace else. The only difference is that *here* the war is raging quietly. Very quietly.'

He paused, reaching to retrieve a pipe and a box of matches from his desk. Frank watched as he lit up and tossed the spent match into a china ashtray.

'So we listen,' Swift continued. 'And we listen hard. In other places, battles are won and lost by artillery, or air power, or armor. *Our* battles are won and lost with information. Defensively, we need to know everything we can about the enemy, and we have to determine what's true and what's not. Offensively, we work to baffle him, feed him false information, so we can control what he *thinks*.'

Shifting in his seat, the broad man leaned forward. 'The point is this: Bern's an important listening post. In most places, the opposing sides can't come within a hundred yards of each other, but here we all move around the city together, Americans, Germans, British, Italians, French, all pretending to be civil, for the benefit of our Swiss hosts. And that... *proximity* allows people to talk. You can't imagine some of the information that passes through here. Which is why it's so important that we listen.'

Frank nodded. Now he began to understand why he'd been asked all those questions about his German language skills.

Swift took a long draw on his pipe, then blew out a plume of pale smoke.

'Officially, you're here as a translator, informally attached to the US legation. In reality, you'll be working for the Office of Strategic Services.' He stopped, fixing Frank with a stern look. 'And you're not to mention that name, to *anyone*. It's still quite a new department, so we're getting some support from our British friends in the SOE who've had more experience running this kind of thing – you've met Molly, I assume?'

'Yes, sir. Just this morning.'

'Well, don't let the fact that she's a woman fool you – she's one of the most capable agents I ever met. Sharp as a tack and tough as nails.'

Frank raised an eyebrow.

'I'll remember that, sir.'

'You do that. Now keep in mind, some of these people are Brits, not Americans. You can trust them, up to a point...' He trailed off, as though wondering how to word something. 'Just think of them as friends – good friends, actually – but *I'm* your family, okay?'

'Okay.'

Swift took another draw on his pipe.

'Good,' he said. 'So, anything you want to ask me?'

Looking through the window, Frank imagined he could just make out the hazy mountain peaks beyond the crowd of rooftops.

'Well, yes,' he said, turning his gaze on Swift again. 'I was just wondering: why me?'

'That's a fair question.' Swift leaned back in his chair and thought for a moment, as if deciding how best to answer. 'Let's just say that we wanted some extra manpower for the Bern station and, for various reasons, it seemed... *prudent* to recruit outside of our usual channels. Of the available options, you were the most suitable candidate.'

For a moment, it looked as though he might say more, but then his posture changed and he glanced up at Frank with a calm smile.

'Anything else?' he asked.

'Er... do I get a gun?'

'A *gun*?' Swift stared at him for a moment, then his face broke into a grin. 'Who are you planning to shoot?'

'I don't know, I just...' Frank shook his head.

Swift's grin faded.

'This is neutral territory,' he said seriously. 'Remember that, Frank. Because the Swiss police really *don't* like anyone who threatens the status quo.'

11

The morning passed, and Frank began settling into his place on the Dufourstrasse team. A smart young American woman had arrived while he was in with Swift. Jean Ellesworth had blonde hair and a welcoming smile; she came from Tulsa, but Frank's opinion of her sank when she dumped a stack of folders onto his desk and told him that he was expected to read them all. Molly and Rafe were in and out, scooting along the corridor to Swift's room with different papers, but one door in the far wall remained shut.

'What's in there?' Frank asked as Rafe hobbled back to his desk.

'Oh, that's Dulles' office.'

Frank cast his mind back to their conversation the day before.

'You mean *the old man*?'

'That's right.' Rafe grinned at him sheepishly. 'He's not here today, but I daresay you'll bump into him soon enough.'

Frank turned back to regard the stack of folders on his desk, then glanced at his watch.

'It must be lunchtime,' he noted. 'Is there anywhere to get a drink around here?'

Rafe looked at him and smiled.

'There's a decent little place around the corner,' he said. 'Give me a moment and I'll show you.'

They sat at one of the small tables outside the café. Frank raised his glass of beer.

'Here's mud in your eye.'

'Cheers,' Rafe replied.

The beer was surprisingly good, and Frank nodded his approval as he set the glass down with a contented sigh.

'So,' he began, eager to learn more about the people he was working for, 'Swift seems like an interesting guy.'

'Yes, he's a decent enough chap.'

Rafe spoke calmly, but his eyes flashed a quiet warning, and he inclined his head towards a grey-haired couple at a nearby table. Frank frowned and fell silent, annoyed at himself as he realized his error.

'I can't recall what part of America he said he was from,' Rafe continued. 'But you're from Missouri, is that right?'

'That's right.'

'I'm rather ashamed to say I don't know where that actually is. Is it one of the states in the middle?'

'Nearer the middle than the edges.'

He could tell that Rafe was carrying the conversation, steering them smoothly away from sensitive subjects, and he felt a sudden gratitude towards his new friend.

'Got a sweetheart waiting for you back there?'

'A *sweetheart*?' Something about the earnest way Rafe had asked made Frank chuckle, despite himself. He smiled, then slowly shook his head.

'There was a girl I had my eye on, but she won't be waiting for me... mostly because I never had the nerve to ask her out.' He raised his glass again. 'Maybe that's something I need to work on when I get back home.'

It was Rafe's turn to laugh.

'We'll concoct some heroic war stories for you to tell her.' He gave Frank a knowing wink. 'Trust me, I'm awfully good at making things up.'

Midway through the afternoon, Jean brought a set of German transcripts and set them down on his desk.

'Hey, slow down,' Frank protested. 'I haven't finished going through the other folders yet.'

'Those were just reading material,' Jean told him, with a shake of her head. '*These* are for translation. Type them up, single-sided, and make sure you number all the pages.'

'Thanks,' he said, without enthusiasm.

The typewriter, when he finally sat down in front of it, was infuriating. Sitting up straight with his hands curled like talons reminded him of childhood piano lessons, and his efforts now were equally disappointing. Resorting to just his index fingers, he labored through the first page, then glanced up to find Molly watching him with an expression that might have been sympathy or amusement. After that, the stuttering rhythm of keystrokes seemed embarrassingly loud, announcing his slow progress to everyone. He was glad when Rafe had mercy on him and suggested that he 'give it a rest and come at it fresh in the morning'.

They arranged to meet later for a drink, and Frank yanked the cover over his typewriter with relief.

As he made his way out into the stairwell, he heard the door behind him opening and looked back to see Swift coming out. The broad man hurried to catch up with him.

'So, how was your first day?' he asked as they started down the stairs.

'Fine, thank you.' Frank smiled, hoping that typing wouldn't be a big part of his job.

'I take it you've met everyone? Settled in?'

'Yes, sir. I think so, though...' He lowered his voice, conscious of the way the sound echoed around the stairwell. '...I'm still not entirely clear on my... *other* duties. Besides the translation work, I mean.'

Swift smiled and clapped a powerful hand on his shoulder.

'We listen, we follow orders, and we keep our mouths shut,' he explained. 'It's not a regular war here, so we never know what to expect. We simply know that it'll be necessary, and that we'll do what needs to be done. Okay?'

'Yes, sir.'

'Good man.'

They reached the ground floor and walked across the tiled floor to the front door. Swift paused on the steps.

'Frank?' He reached into his jacket pocket and drew out a small brown envelope, neatly folded in half. 'As it happens, there *is* something you could do for me. Nothing too tough, just a routine errand to start you out.'

'Of course.' Frank nodded eagerly, pleased at the thought of being useful after his afternoon in front of the typewriter. 'Whatever you need.'

Swift regarded him carefully, then spoke in a hushed voice.

'I want you to take this to Brunngasse, number 25, over in the old town.'

'Brunngasse 25,' Frank repeated. 'I'll find it.'

'You know where Casinoplatz is?'

'Yes.'

'Just walk north from there, and you'll see that big Zytglogge clock tower on your left. The street becomes Brunngasse after a couple of blocks.'

'Got it.'

Swift hesitated, the envelope still in his hand.

'The place you want has a green door, and there's a big stone plant pot right by the front step. If there's a matchstick propped up in that plant pot, then you pause to tie your shoelace, and push this envelope all the way behind the pot. If you *don't* see the matchstick you hold onto the envelope and just keep on walking.' He held out the envelope, his face stern. 'We'll speak tomorrow... and not a word to anyone else about this. Not Rafe, not anyone, is that clear?'

Frank took the envelope and slipped it into his pocket, his eyes never leaving Swift.

'Perfectly clear,' he said.

Swift smiled, and the serious manner evaporated.

'Excellent,' he said, his voice returning to normal. 'Well then, have a good evening.'

The sun was getting low. Frank made his way along Thunstrasse and followed the main thoroughfare as it swept up and right onto the exposed heights of the Kirchenfeld bridge. A cold wind teased at his jacket and ruffled his hair as he walked out towards the middle of the span, but he still slowed for a moment, gazing down at the river far below and listening to the steady rush of water as it spilled white over the weir. Ahead of him, the old town was set out along the crest of the hill like a sprawling fortress, with mighty stone buildings standing proud as battlements against the evening sky. His hand strayed to his pocket, brushing the corner of the envelope, until the clanking of a passing streetcar jarred him back to his senses, and he hurried on, following it over the bridge.

Brunngasse was a narrow, cobbled street of tall old buildings, which curved steeply away to the right in front of him. He moved over to walk on the left, so he could see as far ahead as possible, noting the street numbers as he went. *68... 66... 64...* The place would be on his right. Many of the buildings were fronted by the same vaulted arches he'd seen near the station, with covered arcades running underneath - useful in the snows of winter, he guessed, particularly as the road seemed to slope steadily downhill. He slowed his pace and tried to walk casually, not wanting to draw attention to himself, but there was nobody around. Before long, the street straightened out and, counting ahead, he saw a building with a green door and a large stone plant pot outside it. Slowing a little more, his eyes scanned the pot, searching for the match. It was difficult to see, still too far away but, as he came a little closer...

Yes, there it was! A single match with a red top, sticking up out of the dirt.

He glanced back over his shoulder, then immediately scolded himself for doing something so shifty. *Calm down, Frank. It's a routine drop; just do what you've been told.*

Approaching number 25, he reached into his pocket and calmly withdrew the folded envelope, holding it flat inside his palm. Then, he calmly scuffed his shoe on the cobbles and glanced down.

Don't think about the envelope, just concentrate on your shoe, and imagine the lace really is loose.

He halted, level with the plant pot, frowning as he dropped to one knee. Miming the action of tying his lace, he tightened the knot, then put a hand on the large plant pot for balance. Bracing himself, he rose to his feet, as his fingers eased the envelope down and behind the pot. He took a moment, brushing imaginary dust from the knee of his pants, while glancing across to make sure the envelope was completely out of sight. Then, he straightened up and walked on, carefully measuring his pace to keep it the same as before, fighting down the elation he felt at completing his first assignment.

Yes!

It was such an *ordinary* action, but he felt a thrill of excitement in his chest. He'd stepped into a secret world, a world that most people didn't know existed, though it was right there in plain sight. And he'd done his job well.

Brunngasse curved on like a deep ravine, slanting down through the towering stone buildings of the old town. The evening was drawing in now, and the first subdued lights were appearing in the windows as he raised his face to look at the dusky sky. Rafe had suggested they meet at a place near the river and Frank was working out the most direct way of getting there when something on the edge of his vision made him glance round.

There, on the left... standing in the shadows behind one of the arcade pillars, somebody smoking... dark suit and a fedora. The man was looking his way and stepped out into the street behind him as he passed, tossing the half-finished cigarette onto the cobbles.

'A word with you, please?' He had a gruff voice, heavily accented.

Frank stopped and turned around, immediately on his guard.

'What do you want?' he asked. The fact that he'd been addressed in English worried him.

The man took a single step towards him, then halted. He was in his forties, six feet tall, with a solemn expression and dark eyes.

'Over that way, please.' Nodding slightly, he indicated a narrow alley on the other side of the road.

Frank stiffened, but didn't move.

'What's wrong with talking right here?' he asked.

The stranger's face became bleak, and Frank saw him slipping a hand into his jacket pocket. Did he have a gun?

'Over there,' the man repeated.

Frank glanced up and down the street but there was nobody in sight. Reluctantly, he began moving towards the alley. The man stepped back a little, not allowing him to get too close, then followed him into the shadowy space between the tall buildings. There were several small windows and a closed door in the left-hand wall, but no way out and no cover.

'So? What's this about?' Frank demanded.

The stranger looked him up and down with apparent distaste.

'You're new in Bern, aren't you?' he said. 'What's your name?'

Something in the man's tone needled Frank, and he drew himself up a little.

'I reckon you got the wrong guy, *pal*,' he said, scowling. 'Why don't you tell me who *you're* looking for? Maybe I'll help you find him.'

He thought this might anger the stranger, goad him into something, but the only response was a weary shake of the head.

'I ask the questions. You answer them.'

'Yeah?' Frank took a step towards him. 'And why would I want to do that?'

The man rolled his eyes and pulled a pistol from his jacket pocket, leveling it at Frank.

'Now, we try again,' he sighed. 'Who are you?'

'Okay, okay...' Frank moved back a little, half-raising his hands. 'I'm an American, all right?'

An unpleasant smile crossed the stranger's face.

'Oh, I was aware of *that*, Mr Rye.'

The hairs rose on the back of Frank's neck, and he took another step back. How did this guy know his name?

'Now,' the man said, gesturing with the gun. 'I was wondering: what are you doing here in the old town?'

Frank stared at him.

'I... I was just walking home...' he stammered.

The stranger shook his head, sadly.

'But your room is on Bantigerstrasse. You're going the wrong way.'

Frank blinked stupidly, not knowing what to say.

'Unless you came here to meet someone?' the man suggested, raising an eyebrow. 'Isn't that so?'

Regaining a sliver of composure, Frank tried to affect a puzzled look.

'I don't know what you're talking about. I just–'

'The envelope,' the man interrupted him. 'I'm talking about the envelope you brought with you.'

Frank swallowed. He was out of his depth and he knew it, but he could sense the frustration rising inside him and allowed it into his voice to cover the fear.

'*What* envelope? Who the hell are you?'

The stranger sighed and took another step closer, the gun pointed steadily at Frank's stomach.

'You're trying my patience,' he said.

Frank shook his head.

'Look, this has to be a mistake. I'm an American–'

'Americans die all the time, Mr Rye. The Swiss police will be unhappy, of course... but the Swiss police are always unhappy about something.' Any trace of a smile was gone from the stranger's face now. He raised the gun and thumbed the hammer back. 'Tell me who you delivered the letter to. Right now.'

Frank glared at him. There was no point in saying anything. He knew, as soon as he answered, the man would probably shoot him anyway. His best chance was to tough it out and pray for an opportunity.

'*What* letter?' he demanded, trying to keep his voice from wavering.

The stranger pointed the gun directly at his face.

'Last chance,' he growled.

Frank drew a deep breath, tensing himself to stop from shaking. He continued to glare at the man, his anger rising.

Screw this guy.

Twisting suddenly to his right, he swung his elbow hard against one of the windows. The glass shattered and fell inward, and a small bowl was knocked from its place on the sill, crashing down onto the floor inside. Against the deep stillness of the street, the noise seemed impossibly loud.

Frank turned back towards his attacker, who stood gaping at him in surprise.

Above them, a light came on in one of the upper windows, and an angry voice called out in German.

The gunman glanced up, then scowled at Frank.

'Clever,' he hissed.

And then he was backing away, turning on his heel and disappearing around the corner. Frank stood rooted for a moment, as a wave of nausea surged through him, his heart pounding in his ears.

Fuck!

Gasping, he checked his elbow to make sure no glass had pierced the jacket sleeve, then noticed that his fingernails had gouged deep marks into his palms, yet somehow there was no pain. Taut and trembling, he paced back and forth for a moment, then kicked out at a trashcan and threw his head back with a yell of guttural rage. The can banged off a wall and went clattering over the cobblestones, filling the alley with a metallic ringing. Beside him, a light came on in the room with the broken window, and a voice called out 'Polizei! Polizei!'

Frank took a step backwards. He had to get out of here. Now!

Gulping down a quick breath, he forced himself to walk calmly out onto the road. There was no sign of the gunman. Lights were going on in surrounding buildings now, different voices calling out in concern. Turning right, Frank hurried away down the slope and disappeared into the shadows of the narrow streets.

12

'What the bloody hell happened to you last night?' Rafe was standing over by the window, glaring at him as he walked into the office.

Caught off guard by the question, Frank hesitated. *Last night... but how could they know?*

'What do you mean?' he asked, moving slowly over to his desk.

'What do I *mean*?' Rafe's eyes narrowed. 'I mean that I sat in that wretched cafe for *two hours* until I had the good sense to give up on you.'

Frank relaxed a little. He hadn't trusted himself to speak to anyone after his encounter and had gone straight back to his room. But he couldn't tell Rafe that.

'Damn, I'm so sorry.' He slipped off his jacket, trying to think of an excuse. 'I started feeling really sick, not long after I left here, and...'

He trailed off and shrugged, hoping that would be enough. But Rafe wasn't satisfied.

'You couldn't get me a message?' he demanded.

Frank hung his jacket over the back of his chair and sighed.

'I went back to the room, just for a half-hour rest, that's all. Then next thing I knew, it was morning.' He bowed his head, feeling bad about letting his new friend down, and worse about lying to him. 'I'm really sorry.'

Rafe turned away, shaking his head as he limped across to his desk.

'*Two hours* of pitying looks from people who thought I'd been stood up.' Gathering a stack of folders, he tucked them under his arm. 'Thanks a lot, chum.'

Scowling, he limped away down the corridor and went into Swift's room.

Frank stood there watching him until the door shut, then sat down heavily at his desk and rested his head in his hands. The last thing he wanted to do was upset Rafe, but Swift had been very specific. There was no way to mention the gunman without it leading to questions about what he'd been doing over on Brunngasse.

'He was worried about you.'

Startled, Frank looked up to find Molly, watching him from her desk.

'Sorry, I didn't know you were–' He stopped and frowned at her. 'What?'

Molly got to her feet. She walked over to the large bureau in the corner, opened it, and took out several sheets of carbon paper.

'I know he *sounds* annoyed,' she murmured, returning to her desk. 'But he was really quite worried about you.'

Frank looked away.

'I'm fine,' he growled. 'There's no reason to worry.'

Molly wound the sheets of carbon paper into her typewriter.

'People *do* disappear in Bern,' she said with a slight shrug. 'But I'm sure you know best.'

Peering down at something on her desk, she began typing.

Frank closed his eyes for a moment, annoyed at himself. They didn't understand, they didn't know what had happened, but he couldn't say anything. Not yet, anyway.

He opened his desk drawer and lifted out the bundle of transcripts from the day before, staring at them but unable to concentrate on the words.

'Molly?' he said, eventually. 'Is Swift in his room?'

'He's out with Dulles. Might be back later.' She paused from her typing and glanced over at him. 'Why?'

'No reason,' he shrugged, returning his attention to the transcripts.

It was going to be a long day.

Midway through the afternoon, Frank was busy scribbling down a translation on a piece of scrap paper. The pace of his typing was far too slow, and it required all his concentration to find the right keys; using a pen freed his mind to focus on the meaning of the German document before him. He could type the damn thing up later, preferably when there was nobody else around.

Behind him, he heard a door banging, then the sound of approaching footsteps and the tap of a walking stick. Rafe hurried into the room, clearly excited about something, and limped across to Molly's desk where he handed her a folded slip of paper. Glancing over at them, Frank saw Molly's eyebrows rising as she opened it and read the note. She looked up at Rafe, who nodded silently, then her face took on a grim smile. Frank lowered his eyes, not wanting them to see him watching. He heard something being whispered, but couldn't make it out, then there was a pause.

'I expect Swift will be in later,' Molly called over to him. 'But he may well be busy this evening, so just... speak to him when you can.'

Frank looked up, as though he hadn't been listening.

'Thanks,' he told her, then caught Rafe's eye and added, 'I really am sorry about yesterday.'

Rafe managed an awkward nod, then his face broke into a grin. Whatever was on that slip of paper had lifted his mood.

'All sins forgiven,' he said, pointing his stick at Frank and making the sign of cross.

It was after six when Swift finally appeared. He strode in, raising his hand in greeting, but there was a troubled expression on his face.

'Molly?' he said, inclining his head towards his room, then stalked away down the corridor without waiting.

Molly gave Rafe a meaningful look, then got to her feet and followed Swift.

Frank watched her go, then slumped back into his chair. Resigned to waiting, he glanced down at the last page of his translation notes, then turned to face the typewriter once more. Thankfully, Jean hadn't been in today so he'd had a chance to get through his workload without her adding to it.

Across the room from him, Rafe leaned back and put his hands behind his head.

'You're typing faster,' he noted.

'Doesn't feel like it.' Frank frowned, jabbing at the keys with his index fingers.

'No, I can hear it,' Rafe said. 'You're definitely getting quicker.'

'Don't tell Jean that.'

Frank heard Molly's footsteps and turned to see her coming back along the corridor.

'He's free now,' she told him as she passed.

Frank gathered his papers together and tucked them away in

the drawer. He got to his feet, trying to act casually, but made his way along to the other room quickly.

Swift glanced up from his desk, a piece of paper in his hand.

'Oh, hello, Frank.' He returned his attention to the paper, folding it into three, then looked up again, expectant. 'Yes?'

'Have you got a minute?' Frank asked.

Impatience flickered briefly on Swift's face, but he set the paper down.

'There's something... *important* happening right now, so it'll have to *be* just a minute but...' He indicated the chair in front of him. 'Come in.'

Frank stepped into the room and shut the door.

'It's about last night,' he said, moving around the chair to sit down.

Swift gave him a momentary blank look, then nodded in sudden recognition.

'Of course. Brunngasse 25. You delivered the envelope?'

'I delivered the envelope, but...'

Swift caught the tone in his voice and leaned forward.

'What?'

'Some guy approached me while I was there.'

'Did he see you drop the envelope?' Swift asked.

Frank shook his head.

'No, but that's the thing – he *knew* about the envelope, knew my name, where I'm staying. Bastard pulled a gun on me!'

Worry showed in Swift's eyes.

'What did you tell him?' he demanded.

'Tell him?' Frank glared for a moment, then shook his head in disgust. 'I didn't *tell* him a damn thing.'

Swift gave him a long, searching look, then settled back in his chair with a thoughtful expression on his face.

'All right,' he said finally. 'It was probably just the Swiss police. They can be kind of clumsy, trying to maintain their precious neutrality.'

Frank stared at him in disbelief.

Swift caught the look.

'You think it was the Nazis?'

'Yes,' Frank snapped, irritation breaking into his voice. Wasn't it obvious?

He drew a breath, ready to explain why it couldn't *possibly* be the damn Swiss... then hesitated. Something about the way Swift was acting bothered him, didn't feel right.

'Maybe...' He trailed off.

'Maybe what?' Swift pressed him.

Frank leaned back in his chair.

'Was this a test, sir?' he asked, quietly.

'A test?' Swift said, puzzled.

'Yes.' Frank spoke with more certainty now. 'Was it a test?'

Swift scowled at him for a moment, then a faint smile touched the corners of his mouth.

'A test in three parts,' he said, picking up the folded paper and reaching for an envelope.

Frank shook his head, not sure whether to feel pleased with himself or angry at Swift.

'Three parts,' he mused. 'Did I admit anything to the man, that's one. Did I follow orders and tell no-one but you, that's two...'

Swift slid the paper into the envelope and sealed it, then set it down on the desk and waited.

'I give up,' Frank shrugged. 'What was number three?'

'You worked out that it was a test,' Swift explained. 'And that's almost as important as the other two parts. We can't have stupid people working for us now, can we?'

He got slowly to his feet and came around the desk, reaching over to open the door.

'I'm sorry, but there really *is* something important happening just now,' he said.

'Yes, of course. Sorry.' Frank stood up and turned to leave, but Swift placed a hand on his shoulder.

'Be in the Casinoplatz tomorrow morning at nine,' he said. 'There's someone I think you should meet.'

13

Frank made his way along the broad, cobbled streets, climbing towards the top of the old town. Above him, grey clouds hurried across a morning sky that had been blue when he left his lodgings – the uncertainty of mountain weather. On either side of him, the beautiful stone arcades were bustling with people on their way to work, talking and laughing as though there wasn't a war raging all around their borders. He caught snatches of conversation – some in French, but most in German – and wondered how many of these people *were* German. Here, in the northern part of Switzerland, there must be quite a number, but he couldn't tell who. They looked the same as everyone else, just ordinary people.

He realized he had slowed down, and was standing beside a large stone fountain set in the centre of the road. On the opposite side of it, a pretty young woman with red hair and a dark green coat was gazing at him through the tinkling water. She gave a shy smile as their eyes met, then looked away. He watched her as she hurried away down the street, then turned and carried on walking up the hill, feeling his cheeks blush slightly. The old town wasn't all bad.

It was still a little before nine when he emerged onto Casino-platz – he'd set out in good time, not wanting to be late – and he took a moment to watch a streetcar rumble along the rails that cut diagonally through the long square. The surrounding stone buildings were grand and had a robust quality about them, as though they'd been designed to shrug off the worst winter snows, but at its southern end the square opened onto the high bridge, with its steady stream of people riding bicycles or walking to their morning work.

Frank scanned the passing faces as he walked across the cobbles – people smiling, serious, yawning wearily – all of them unfamiliar, until he approached the café at the street-corner. There was Swift, sat at a small table on the sidewalk, reading a newspaper. He had his back to the wall, commanding a good view of the square, but raised his hand in greeting while Frank was still some distance away, as though he'd somehow sensed his approach.

'Guten Morgen.' Swift greeted him as though he'd unexpect-edly spotted an old acquaintance in the crowd, and his accent was very natural. 'Wie geht es Ihnen?'

'Sehr gut, danke.' Frank caught himself before he responded in English and did his best to follow the chance meeting cue. 'Schön, Sie zu sehen.'

Swift flashed him an approving smile, then carefully folded up his newspaper and took the time to finish his coffee. Standing there watching him, Frank noticed that there was a second cup on the table, but said nothing.

'Well then,' Swift whispered, as he rose to his feet. 'Shall we go? It isn't very far.'

Herrengasse was a quiet street that led away from the opposite edge of the square, running along the side of the imposing casino block before sloping down into another curving street of old buildings and long arcades. Just behind the casino, Swift slowed his pace and indicated a large house on the right.

'Number 23,' he said, walking over to the front entrance. Frank followed him, noting a small plaque beside the arched wooden door with the words *Allen W. Dulles, Special Assistant to the American Minister*.

Swift rang the bell, then turned to face him.

'Be honest, be brief, and be *useful*,' he whispered. 'Oh, and if you hear him speaking German, don't correct him; he thinks he's fluent.'

They waited for a moment until the door swung gently open.

'Morning,' Swift said with easy familiarity, but Frank stiffened. Standing in the doorway was the man who had pulled a gun on him in Brunngasse two nights ago.

'Good morning, sir.' The man nodded politely to Swift, then gazed at Frank with calm formality. 'Good to see you again, Mr Rye. Please come in.'

Swift looked across at him and grinned.

'I believe you've already met Herr Groth,' he said, gesturing towards the man in the doorway. 'Come on, we don't want to keep Mr Dulles waiting.'

Inside, the entrance hall was light and elegant. A polished wooden floor ran all the way to the rear of the building, and a flight of marble stairs with ornate iron bannisters ascended to the upper levels.

'Second door on the left,' Groth said, pointing down the corridor.

Frank hesitated and looked at Swift.

'Aren't you coming in?' he asked.

'We have some things to discuss here,' Swift explained. 'But I'll see you later.'

'All right.' With a last wary look at Groth, Frank turned and made his way along the hallway. Stopping in front of the door, he knocked smartly and waited.

The door was eventually opened by a tall man in a tweed sports jacket. He was powerfully built with a small mustache and keen blue eyes behind rimless spectacles.

'Ah, Mr Rye!' he said, stepping forward and shaking hands enthusiastically. 'I'm Allen Dulles.'

'Glad to meet you, sir,' Frank replied.

'Forgive the imposition of bringing you over here,' Dulles said, beckoning him inside. 'I'd hoped we might speak at the office, but things have been unusually busy of late.'

'We live in busy times, sir.'

'We most assuredly do.' Dulles led Frank through to a wood-paneled study at the back of the building. Tall red drapes framed a window that looked out over some bushes to a stunning view of the river.

'Come in and take a seat,' he said, gesturing vaguely at the two comfortable chairs angled towards the large fireplace. 'May I offer you something to drink? Whiskey?'

Sitting down, Frank hesitated, unsure whether it was too early to accept a drink. He decided to pass.

'Nothing for me, thank you, sir.'

Dulles smiled. He walked over and lowered himself into the chair on the other side of the fireplace.

'I think we can dispense with that "sir" business,' he said. 'While we're here, at least.'

'All right.' Frank nodded.

'Capital.' Dulles grinned. 'So, tell me: how do you like our little Swiss outpost? What are your impressions of Bern?'

'It's quite a place,' Frank said, his eyes drawn briefly to the window. 'I think I'm going to like it here.'

'I find it most agreeable,' Dulles observed. 'Though we're afflicted by all manner of shortages, and that reminds me... do you play tennis?'

'Tennis?' Frank stared at him, wrong-footed by the question.

'Tennis.' Dulles eyed him eagerly. 'How's your game?'

'I'm... not sure,' Frank replied, shaking his head. 'I mean, I played a couple of times back in college but...'

Dulles sat back with a grave expression.

'Most unfortunate,' he sighed.

Frank shifted uncomfortably in his chair, feeling that the interview wasn't going well. The other man seemed to notice, and he laughed suddenly, his blue eyes glittering and his face becoming genial once more.

'Put it out of your mind, son. I just wanted to be sure I wasn't missing the opportunity of a worthy opponent, but that's not why you're here.'

Frank sat up a little straighter.

'Perhaps you can tell me why I *am* here?' he asked. 'I mean, Bern *is* beautiful but...'

Dulles laughed again.

'Admirably put, and I like a man who isn't afraid to ask questions.' He got to his feet and walked over to the desk, where he picked up a short briar pipe. 'As well as asking questions, I'm told that you're also a man who won't betray confidences.'

Frank met his gaze.

'I believe in loyalty.'

Dulles regarded him thoughtfully, then struck a match.

'That's good, or we shouldn't be speaking now.' He broke off to raise the match, holding it to the bowl of the pipe until it was lit. 'But I want to impress upon you the importance – the *national* importance – of what we do. Even if someone is loyal, they can still be careless, and that may be every bit as deadly as betrayal. Why, some men let state secrets slip and they don't even know they've done it. That's no use.' He snuffed out the match. 'Loyalty is nothing without care.'

Frank nodded.

'I understand,' he said.

Dulles walked back over to his chair, but remained standing.

'I hope so,' he said, jabbing his pipe at Frank and raising an eyebrow. 'You've arrived at a time of unexpected significance, so we'll have to dispense with many of the usual niceties.'

'Of course.' Frank glanced up, eager to demonstrate that he was attentive to what was going on. 'I got the impression that something was happening.'

'Really?' Dulles fixed him with a piercing stare. 'Explain?'

'I don't know any specifics, but...' Frank frowned. '...there just seemed to be a change at the office. A sort of quiet excitement?'

Dulles regarded him thoughtfully for a moment.

'Well, it does you some credit that you're noticing things.' He gave a brief smile, then his face became serious again. 'Better not to volunteer information, though. It's *trusting*, and trusting people is a dangerous habit to get into. Watch and listen always, speak only when you need to.'

Frank gave him a rueful smile and remained silent.

Dulles blew out a cloud of smoke and chuckled.

'That's the ticket,' he said, sitting down again. 'Now, while Bern may well be picturesque, it's also a city with some rather tiresome bureaucracy. How much do you know about the Swiss police?'

'I read the briefings but...' Frank shook his head. 'Not that much.'

'Well, the situation's straightforward enough,' Dulles said. 'Switzerland's a neutral territory, which makes it ideal for running certain types of intelligence and covert action. But the Swiss take their neutrality seriously, and they aren't stupid enough to trust anyone. So they monitor us to make sure there's nothing... *inappropriate* going on.'

'The police are watching us?'

'They're watching *everyone*.' Dulles smiled. 'Phones are tapped, people are followed. It's downright inconvenient, particularly when there are sensitive matters to be discussed and meetings to be arranged.'

Frank nodded, thinking back to his early-morning walk

through the old town, the different faces in the crowd. It wasn't just the Germans he had to be careful of; it was the Swiss as well.

'And that's where you come in.' Dulles pointed at him with the stem of his pipe. 'There are times when we're dealing with matters that are simply too important to let the Swiss anywhere near them.' He gave Frank a grim little smile. 'Tomorrow evening, you're going to help us keep them occupied, while something... *significant* occurs.'

14

Frank paced back and forth along the narrow, paved area at the back of the building, staring out across the rooftops to the twinkling lights on the other side of the river. He'd watched the night sky darken, seen the last glow of red fade below the horizon, and felt the temperature steadily dropping. Glancing over at the back door, he hugged himself to keep warm. *It must be nearly time.*

Unlike yesterday, he hadn't been invited into the house. Groth had greeted him when he'd arrived almost two hours ago and sent him round to the back, where he'd been given an overcoat and a hat to wear. At first, he'd waved the offer away, saying it wasn't that cold and he wouldn't need them. But then he'd understood: the coat and hat weren't for *his* benefit, and they *weren't* optional. He slipped his hands into the unfamiliar pockets, glad of them now, and turned back to stare into the night. The bridge was a little way along the valley and he could just make it out in the faint moonlight, towering high above the river that slithered round the base of the old town. The weir was almost directly below him here; in the darkness, he couldn't see it, but he could hear the constant rushing of the water as it cascaded down. The sound was oddly soothing, but he couldn't shake the sense of unease that had been growing in his stomach all evening.

This was very different to the nervous excitement he'd experienced when his unit first landed in France. There had been danger then, certainly, and every artillery shell and air attack had been frightening, but he'd been one man in a whole division back then, and there was a kind of safety in numbers. Here, there was no rumble of explosions, no approaching whine of diving airplanes, just a vast stillness that left him exposed and alone.

Shrinking back into the shadows at the corner of the building, he reached into his jacket and took out a cigarette. He knew to look away as he struck the match, knew to avoid staring at the flame so he could preserve his night vision, and he'd need that tonight. Taking a long draw, he blew out a slow stream of smoke and shut his eyes. It *had* to be time now, surely.

Beside him, he heard the soft click of a lock and a shaft of yellow light slid across the paving slabs. Groth stepped outside, glanced over at him, then quietly pushed the back door closed. He was wearing a coat and hat too.

Frank took a quick drag on his cigarette, then stubbed it out against the wall.

'Is it time?' he whispered.

Groth frowned and shook his head.

'Not yet,' he said, in a low voice. 'We wait for the ten o'clock blackout.'

'Right. Of course.' Frank jammed his hands back into his pockets, then turned to give Groth a sidelong glance. 'We look like twins.' He grinned, noting the similarity of their coats and hats.

'No.' Groth gave him a long, serious look. 'We do not.'

They lapsed into an uncomfortable silence. Frank began to pace again, treading slowly and softly, wishing they could just get started.

Suddenly, the expectant stillness was broken by a booming

chime from the cathedral, and the ring of answering bells from other clocktowers in the distance. Gazing out over the river, Frank saw the last few streetlights winking out until the whole city was shrouded in deep darkness.

Any minute now.

Groth glanced back towards the door, then gave a curt nod. Beckoning Frank to follow, he crept around the corner to the walled courtyard at the side of the house.

'All right,' he whispered. 'Remember: calm, steady pace. I'll wait for three minutes before I go.'

'Wish me luck,' Frank replied. He took a deep breath, turned up the collar on his coat, and pulled the brim of his hat down. Then, gripping the cold iron handle, he opened the tall wooden gate and stepped through, pulling it closed behind him.

He was on his own.

In front of him, Herrengasse was a corridor of shadows: the dim shapes of buildings described by moonlight, and the occasional faint glow of yellow bleeding out around the blackout blinds. He opened his eyes wide, unblinking as he stared across the empty street, but it was impossible to see if anyone was lurking in the gloom of the arcade opposite.

Three minutes...

Conscious of the time, his lips began moving in a silent count: *one Mississippi, two Mississippi, three... four... five.* Once he had the rhythm, he shoved his hands into his pockets, lowered his head, and started up the street.

He made his way along between the tall buildings, staying close to the wall where the darkness seemed deepest, walking in time with his count.

Forty-one... forty-two... forty-three... forty-four...

Fighting down the urge to look behind him, he listened hard, but his footsteps seemed to be the only sound in the heavy stillness. Unless...

He kept up his steady pace for a few yards, then took a

sudden shorter stride, placing his foot softly so it made no noise... and somewhere behind him, he heard the faint scuff of a shoe on the cobblestones.

Someone was following him.

Heart pounding, he walked on, not speeding up, giving no indication that he'd heard anything.

Sixty-four... sixty-five... sixty-six...

Approaching the end of the street, he peered ahead towards the dark expanse of Casinoplatz, his eyes searching for movement. Here, moonlight bathed the silent buildings and glimmered on the tram rails, but the place appeared deserted.

Seventy-seven... seventy-eight... seventy-nine...

Hugging the wall, he turned the corner and his pulse quickened. This was his chance – he could make a run for it right now, open up a gap between him and whoever was following him, get enough distance to lose him in the shadowy streets...

But that wasn't why he was out here. He had a job to do, and he was determined to see it through.

He made his way along the front of the casino, gazing up at the towering stone columns and the stars above. He imagined he could hear soft footsteps as his pursuer turned the corner a short way behind him, but he refused to look round.

Ninety-eight... ninety-nine... a hundred...

He passed beneath the trees that lined the casino overlook, gently rustling in the breeze, then stepped out onto the long open span of the bridge beneath the vast night sky.

There were no hiding places now, nowhere to go but forward. He could hear the rushing of the river again, but the valley below was lost in shadow. Approaching the middle of the bridge, a gust of wind caught him, whipping at his coat, and forcing him to hold onto his hat for a moment. He realized that he'd lost track of his count, but it didn't matter any more; he'd made it this far.

He'd drawn the police away from Herrengasse.

Slowing, he fumbled in his coat pocket and drew out a small

flashlight, holding it across his body. Then, glancing back towards the sharp silhouettes of the old town buildings, he flashed it in time with his walk – *on-off, on-off, on-off* – shining it out into the empty darkness.

Behind him, he heard the footsteps quickening and drawing nearer. Pushing the flashlight back into his pocket, he stopped and turned around. A lone figure was striding towards him, and Frank tensed himself in readiness.

What if Groth had made a mistake? What if this wasn't the Swiss police, what if it was the damn Nazis? The idea of a fight up here, with a hundred-foot drop beneath him...

The figure drew nearer, a tall man with a long coat that flapped in the breeze. He came closer, peering at Frank's face as he approached, then frowned and reached into his jacket for something. Did he have a gun?

'Was ist denn hier los?' Frank protested. He backed away, then blinked as a flashlight shone into his face, blinding him.

'Oh nein,' the man hissed, lowering the light and swearing as he realized he'd been duped. 'Scheiße!'

He seemed to hesitate for a moment, then turned around and hurried back across the bridge, quickly breaking into a run.

Frank rubbed his eyes, listening to the receding footsteps until they were lost in the sigh of the wind and the steady rush of the water below. His palms were clammy and his heart was pounding, but he took a deep breath and drew his overcoat about him. Turning to look along the jagged skyline, he saw the cathedral spire and, further along, the angular silhouette of the casino. Between them, in the darkness where the rear of Herrengasse 23 looked out across the river valley, an answering light flashed three times.

Frank stood for a moment, wondering who Dulles had been meeting there tonight, who the Swiss police had been so eager to intercept.

A secret courier from across the border? Maybe someone from the German resistance?

Whoever it was, that signal meant they'd slipped safely away into the night. With a grim smile, Frank hunched his shoulders against the wind and walked on into the gloom.

Fall, 1953
Kansas City, Missouri

Kansas City Herald

KANSAS CITY, MISSOURI   -   Wednesday, August 26, 1953

DID MOB BOSS BUY PARDON WITH SECRET WARTIME AID?

NEW ENQUIRY INTO 'LUCKY' LUCIANO CASE

NEW YORK, Aug 26 - A confidential report, which suggests that convicted gangster Charles Luciano may have had his prison sentence commuted in return for aiding the U.S. war effort, is raising difficult questions for New York Governor Thomas Dewey.

Governor Dewey, a former Republican presidential candidate, was the District Attorney who successfully prosecuted Luciano and secured a 30-year sentence for the Mafia kingpin. However, the mobster was released after just 10 years and deported to Italy. Rumours that he used his influence to ban labor strikes, and provided covert support to the U.S. military, led to speculation that he had effectively bought his way out of prison.

WHITE HOUSE 'WANTS INDEPENDENT ENQUIRY'

The allegations come at a difficult time for newly-elected President Eisenhower, who is under pressure to deliver on his campaign promise of bringing more U.S. troops home. Amid calls for greater openness about wartime government policies, this new development is an unwelcome distraction to an administration that is already under pressure.

(continued on page 2, column 3)

15

Evening was drawing in and the sun was lost as Frank leaned over to the window, cupping his hand against the glass to peer out. The rhythm of the rails had slowed and dark shapes drifted by as the train clanked over a set of switches, but all he could see was his own reflection, grim and tired, staring back out of the gloom. Around him, passengers were stirring, eagerly gathering their bags and belongings even before the lights of the platform slid into view. Frank shut his eyes and sighed. He was in no hurry. Nobody was waiting for him... or if they were, they didn't know it yet.

Outside, he heard the steady clanking of the bell, and a rich voice from the end of the chair car called out 'Kansas City, this is Kansas City. End of the line.'

The train squealed and jolted to a final halt, and people began crowding past, moving along the gangway. Slowly, Frank opened his eyes. It was the end of the line for someone.

He was the last person off the train. Stepping down to the platform, he tipped the negro porter a few coins, then set his bag down as he lit a cigarette.

'Carry that for you, sir?' the porter asked.

Frank exhaled and shook his head.

'It's okay,' he said. 'I got it.'

He hesitated, then held the carton out, offering it. The porter glanced back along the platform, then smiled and took a cigarette, tucking it away into his tunic pocket.

'Much obliged,' he said, inclining his head slightly.

Frank nodded, slipping the carton back into his jacket.

Obliged.

'Ever make a promise you weren't sure you could keep?' he asked.

The porter's face became thoughtful.

'More'n I care to remember,' he admitted. 'But I always meant 'em when I said it.'

Frank smiled at him ruefully.

'Me too,' he said, reaching down for his bag. 'You have yourself a good night now.'

'You too, sir.'

At the top of the stairs, the main hall of Union Station opened up like a cathedral. People hurried this way and that across the marble floors, a shifting congregation whose voices rose in a constant murmur that echoed around the vast space overhead. Frank glanced up at the mighty clock suspended from an archway high above. It was a little after eight, too late to start poking around asking questions tonight. For now, he just needed a place to stay. Turning towards the exit, he made his way across the familiar old hall.

How long since he was last up here? It must have been Adam O'Halloran's wedding, and that was over a year ago. Things were a lot simpler back then... before he got his eye on Beth Barnes and screwed everything up.

Outside, he hailed a yellow cab and slid into the back seat, keeping his bag beside him.

The driver was a pair of quick eyes watching him in the rear-view mirror.

'Where to, mister?'

'I want a hotel in town,' Frank said. 'Nothing fancy, but not a dive, okay?'

Without pay, he'd run out of money soon enough, so he had to be careful.

The cabbie's eyes flicked down as he started the meter, the back of his head nodding easily.

'Sure,' he said. 'I know some nice clean places.'

The taxi crept forward, sweeping around from the front of the station and pulling up at an intersection on the main road, then turning onto a broad bridge that crested the railroad tracks. Ahead, through the windshield, a succession of illuminated billboards advertised Braun electric shavers and Löwenbräu beer, while the towering buildings of the city lit up the darkening sky.

'So...' The cabbie's eyes were in the mirror again. 'Where are you in from?'

'Westville, Oklahoma,' Frank said, lying automatically as he glanced out at the store fronts slipping by. It wasn't likely that anyone would come asking, but there was no sense leaving a trail; that was a bad habit to get into.

'And what brings you to Kansas City?'

'I'm here to look someone up,' Frank said, staring out through the glass. 'A friend of a friend.'

Another lie. Faye Griffith hadn't been much of a friend to Pete Barnes. But then again, neither had he.

'Gonna be in town for long?' the cabbie asked.

Frank turned and stared at the eyes in the mirror until they blinked and looked away.

'What, are you writing a book?' he growled. Suddenly, the questions felt annoying, intrusive.

'Hey, just makin' conversation to pass the time,' the cabbie said, shrugging.

'Yeah, well, I don't know how long I'll be here,' he muttered.

It all depended on how long it took to hunt the woman down.

· · ·

He settled for the Bradbury, an anonymous-looking hotel on West 12th Street. It was the kind of place that people chose when they weren't trying to impress anyone. Gripping his bag, Frank paid the taxi, then stood on the sidewalk for a long moment, staring up at the fire escape that zig-zagged down the side of the building, his thoughts half a world away.

Then, with a sigh, he walked up the front steps. A printed sign stuck to the inside of the glass door read *Deutsche Gäste willkommen*. Germans welcome.

Inside, the hotel had the faded appearance of somewhere that had once been grand. Carpets were worn thin, elegant chairs showed sagging upholstery, even the desk manager was an elderly man, with light from the smoke-stained chandelier shining off his bald head. Glancing up at Frank through thick spectacles, he looked oddly pale against the wall of dark wooden pigeonholes where dusty keys lay in their shadowed recesses.

'Got any I.D?' he asked.

'Worried I'm a Russian?' Frank said with a sarcastic smile.

He signed in with a false name – *Mr Cavanagh* – and, while the manager turned his back to find the room key, he skimmed through the register, quickly noting the names of the other guests.

Patterson, Neumann, Grant, Ogilvy, Linden... yes, Edward Linden...

He could see himself as a Mr Linden. It was an old trick that Rafe had taught him, borrowing the identity of someone staying at the same place. Once again, his thoughts strayed back to his time in Switzerland.

'Room four-one-three,' said the elderly man, setting a key with a large brass fob down on the scratched desktop. 'Enjoy your stay.'

· · ·

The corridor was dimly lit and musty. Frank unlocked the door and swung it open, peering at the dark shapes inside. Stepping over the threshold, he started to reach for the light switch, then changed his mind and withdrew his hand, gently nudging the door shut behind him. Illuminated by the amber glow of the hotel sign outside the window, he set the key down on the dresser and dropped his bag on the floor. Making his way around the end of the bed, he went over to the window, gripped the frame and slid it open, letting in the sounds of the city and a swirl of cool night air. He bent forward, closing his eyes, feeling the breeze on his face.

Faye Griffith.

She was out there, somewhere, he could sense it.

And when he found her, she was going to lead him to her friend, the thin man, whether she liked it or not.

16

He slept late, but it didn't matter. There was no schedule to keep, no clock to watch. He was working on his own time now. Getting dressed, he straightened his jacket to cover the holster, then picked up his hat and made for the door. At the foot of the stairs, he glanced over to the desk, nodding at the young man who was now on duty, then strolled across the lobby and out onto the steps. He didn't want to eat at the hotel, but he'd woken up hungry and he knew he wouldn't be able to think straight until he had some coffee inside him. Standing there on the sidewalk, he glanced left and right, wondering where he might go. In the end, he decided to head left, past a row of tattered *America First* posters; it was downhill, at least.

Yawning, he walked down the shadowed street, gazing up at the bright blue sky between the tall buildings. Ahead of him, the sidewalks seemed busier, and it looked as though there would be more stores, more places to eat. He could hear the voices of hawkers raised above the rumble of traffic, saw a gleaming streetcar cut across the road, knew he was heading the right way.

Halfway between Kresge's and Macy's, he found a narrow-fronted diner that looked busy – always a good sign – and managed to squeeze himself in at the end of the counter. The waitress brought him coffee and he ordered a plate of eggs on toast, then lit a cigarette as he considered his next move. He had to find Faye, but all he had was an address for her brother Stanley and a vague description of her. It wasn't much to work with – he didn't even know for sure that she'd go to her brother – but he had to start somewhere. Briefly, he considered calling Adam – maybe his old friend could help out? – but then decided against it.

Not yet. He needed to see things clearer before he tried calling in any favors.

He stubbed out his cigarette as the waitress slid a full plate in front of him, and settled down to breakfast. Whatever the day held in store, he'd face it better on a full stomach.

The cab ride took ten minutes, cutting straight down Main Street, past the station and up the hill by the Liberty Memorial tower. Frank gazed out through the glass at the long, cream-colored streetcars, trundling along between the lanes of traffic in the middle of the road. They were bigger than the ones he'd rode in Bern – longer, with sleeker lines – but there was still something about them that took him back. So many things seemed to be reminding him of Switzerland lately.

'Coming up on 40th Street.' The cabbie was looking at him in the rear-view mirror. 'Any place special you want?'

Frank shook his head, fumbling in his pocket for some coins.

'Just drop me at the intersection,' he said. 'I can walk from there.'

He paid the cab, then stood on the sidewalk for a moment, looking around. This far out, it was all neighborhood places – drugstore, barber shop, church on the corner. He could probably ask around, see if anyone knew Stanley or his sister, but he wanted to find the address first. East 40th sloped away down the hill to his left, so he pulled the brim of his hat down and set off, walking like he belonged there. Soon he could see the apartment building, a broad red-brick block on the left. His eyes flicked along the line of cars dotted down the street, but there was no grey Chrysler; he felt both relief and a twinge of disappointment.

He went slowly down the hill, taking his time, getting a good look at the building and counting the windows: three stories, but not that big of a place. Probably no more than eighteen apartments, all told, which meant that apartment 16 would be on the top floor.

The entrance was in the middle of the frontage, with cement steps leading up to a half-glass door and a row of numbered mailboxes.

He continued on, following the sidewalk as it turned at the end of the block, pausing for a moment to glance up the side of the place, and again when he'd gone far enough to see round the back. It was an old building – no sign of any fire escapes here, but there seemed to be a back door opening onto the small yard where a group of trash cans stood, lost among the yellow weeds.

Not many ways in for him... but not many ways out for her, if she was here.

He stood for a moment, his eyes flickering between the third floor windows, searching for movement, then glanced at his watch. 10:20am – folk would be at work, kids would be at school – this was as good a time as any to take a look around. The place seemed quiet enough... and he might just get lucky.

Turning on his heel, he made his way back around to the front, right hand slipping casually inside his jacket for the reassuring touch of the gun. Walking up the steps, he saw an array of bell-pushes, arranged in three lines of six, names written beside each one. Reaching out a hand, he traced his finger down to number 16, and saw *Griffith* scrawled on a piece of yellowed paper, ink bleached by the sun.

This was the place, all right.

He tried the door, but it was locked. Leaning his weight against it, he felt the solid contact of the metal bolt and knew it wasn't going to budge easily. Through the half-glass panel, he could see a flight of old wooden stairs and a long, narrow hallway illuminated by a square of light at the far end.

The back door.

Turning away, he jogged lightly down the steps, then walked around the side of the building, eyes open, alert. Just because the Chrysler wasn't here, it didn't mean the thin man wasn't. He stayed close to the wall, ducking low as he passed beneath the windows, then rounded the corner onto the small yard at the back. Picking his way between the battered trash cans, he came to the door and peered in through the glass pane.

The hallway was empty. *Good.*

He tried the handle, just in case. Like the front, it was locked, but this door felt more flimsy – older, with a single latch bolt. As a cop, he'd seen just how easily these gave way. Glancing quickly over his shoulder, he took out his pocket knife and gouged it hard into the doorframe, working the wood in line with the lock and prying pieces out. After a moment, he grasped the handle with both hands, took a breath, then yanked backwards. The remaining wood around the lock split apart, and the door came open.

Brushing splinters from the sleeves of his jacket, Frank returned the knife to his pocket, then slipped inside.

The hallway was silent and smelled of floor soap. Keeping his right hand just inside his jacket, he made his way along to the bottom of the stairs and gazed upwards, listening. There was music coming from somewhere above him – something jazzy – but it was faint. He hesitated for a moment, then gripped the worn wooden banister and started to climb, the dry, old staircase creaking beneath his shoes. Pausing at the second floor, he looked along the corridor and listened again – the music was coming from one of the apartments on this level – then turned away and continued on up. He halted again at the top, reaching inside his jacket to draw out the .45.

A promise was a promise... and he owed Beth, no matter how things worked out.

Taking a breath, he started down the corridor, placing each footstep silently, eyes searching out the numbers on the doors.

...12... 14... 16.

This was it: a battered old panel door, held together by layers of peeling blue paint. A single lock with worn brass fittings. Leaning in against the frame, he held his breath, listening hard, but there was no sound except the echo of the music from downstairs and the heartbeat in his ears. Satisfied, he exhaled, then tucked the .45 back in its holster and bent down to study the lock. He couldn't risk forcing this one, but maybe he wouldn't need to.

Taking out his pocket knife again, he eased the blade in between the door and the frame until he found the latch bolt. There was a bit of play in the doorknob, and he twisted it back and forth while working the knife in against the bolt, horribly conscious of each scrape and rattle.

Come on... come on...

The blade jerked and the door suddenly moved freely under his hand. Frank held it shut while he stowed his knife and drew out his gun. Then, gulping down a breath, he pushed the door wide and took a cautious step forward.

Inside, the apartment was surprisingly neat. Frank paused, sniffing the air, trying to identify the smell. Shoe polish? There wasn't a lot of furniture, but everything looked clean and cared-for. He noted the large rug and the comfortable couch; neither looked as though they belonged to the building. Someone had clearly made the best of the place, but he could tell straight away that it was a man's apartment – there was no woman's touch in here.

He pushed the door closed behind him, treading softly on the old floorboards as he moved forward to glance through into the bedroom.

Nobody home.

Relaxing slightly, he holstered his .45 then turned and walked over to the large bureau, reaching out and pulling the front down. Letters – all addressed to Stanley Griffith – pay slips from St Luke's Hospital, pens and pencils, a neat stack of coins, and an envelope stuffed with old baseball cards.

He bent down, pulling out one of the drawers. This contained some folded linen and a square tin box with a picture of an eagle embossed on the top. He prized the lid off and carefully lifted out a tattered old medical ID, unfolding it and peering at the photograph inside.

This wasn't the thin man; a very different face stared up from the tiny black and white picture, stocky and determined-looking, with a solid jawline. According to the card, Stanley had been a frontline Army medic during the war, and that took a special kind of courage. Not the sort of person you could push around.

Beneath the ID, he found a very old and dented pocket watch, a set of dog tags with the name Lester Griffith, and a woman's engagement ring that showed many years of wear; family heirlooms, he guessed.

The bottom of the tin box was full of photographs, different shapes and sizes, some with clean corners where they'd been removed from an album. The first one showed Stanley in uniform, lined up with three other grinning medics... then a faded shot of a young couple marked *Mom and Dad*, smiling stiffly at the camera... and then – yes, there she was! – there, in a picture of the whole family.

Mom, Dad, Stanley and Faye – Lake Ozark, August 1947.

Frank leaned over, peering down at Faye. She was pretty all

right, just like everyone said, with wavy brown hair and an inno-cent smile... but smiles could be deceptive. Scowling, he shuffled through the rest of the photographs until he found one of Faye on her own. Stuffing the picture into his jacket pocket, he replaced the contents of the tin box and shut it away in the drawer.

The music from downstairs had stopped. Frank looked towards the door for a moment, listening for footsteps in the hall-way, but there was nothing. Eventually, he turned away and moved silently through to the bedroom.

The suitcase was the first thing he noticed, battered and scuffed, lying on the floor at the side of the bed. As his eye swept around the room, he spotted the lipstick and powder compact on the chest of drawers and, turning around, saw the dress hanging from the back of the door.

So she'd run to her brother... and he'd taken her in.

All her stuff was through here. He glanced back towards the couch, noted the neatly-folded quilt, resting on the arm; Stanley must have given up his bed and be sleeping out there.

Frowning, he made his way back through to the living room and looked around.

Should he wait for her to come back? Confront her?

No... the brother might get home first, or they could return together, and that would just complicate things. For now, it didn't look as though she was going anywhere in a hurry... and why would she? She had no idea that he was onto her.

Nodding grimly to himself, he walked across the rug, listened briefly at the door, then let himself out. Pulling the door shut behind him, he made his way quickly along the hallway and down the stairs.

He'd come back later, see if he could catch her on her own. And in the meantime, it wouldn't do any harm to ask around about her.

. . .

The drugstore on Main was quiet, and the greying little man behind the counter looked up, peering over the top of his spectacles as Frank approached.

'Help you find something, sir?' he asked.

'Some*one*,' Frank corrected him. 'I'm looking for an old acquaintance, name of Faye Griffith.' He took out the photograph, placed it on the counter, and slid it towards the man. 'Just wondered if you'd seen her around?'

Frowning slightly, the old man glanced at the picture, then adjusted his spectacles and leaned over to stare more closely.

'Fine looking girl,' he said. 'Very fine indeed.'

Frank drew the photo back and pushed it into his pocket.

'So?' he pressed. 'Have you seen her?'

The old man straightened up and shook his head.

'Can't say that I have,' he said, going back to the register. 'Pretty girl like that? Reckon I'd remember her.'

Frank sighed.

'Well, if you *do* happen to see her, just remember to get a message to me.' He tapped his chest. 'Edward Linden, and I'm staying at the Bradbury Hotel on 12th. You got that?'

'Yeah, sure. No problem.'

Frank turned to go, then paused.

'There's a reward,' he lied. 'If I find her.'

'Really?' The old man frowned, then reached into his apron pocket and brought out a pencil and paper. 'What did you say your name was again?'

There was a bright little diner, just along the block from the drug store. Frank slid onto a stool at the counter and nodded at the waitress who hustled over, coffee pot in hand.

'Can I get you something, mister?' she asked, pouring him a cup.

Frank glanced down at the paper menu.

'I could use a piece of pie,' he said, looking up.

'You got it,' she said, turning away.

'Excuse me, miss?' He took out the photograph, holding it up so she could see it. 'I'm trying to locate this woman, Faye Griffiths. Don't suppose she's been in here, has she?'

The waitress hesitated, gazing at Frank as though trying to read his intentions. He did his best to appear as unthreatening as possible.

'Someone she knew has recently passed away,' he explained. That much was actually true. 'So I thought I should try and get in touch with her.'

The waitress' expression became more sympathetic. She looked down at the picture for a moment, then shook her head sadly.

'Sorry, honey. I ain't seen her.' She straightened up. 'You still want that pie?'

Frank tucked the photograph back in his pocket.

'Yeah,' he said. 'And thanks for looking.'

The waitress flashed him a brief smile, then walked away. Frank noticed a payphone on the far wall, and frowned.

He knew where Faye was staying now, and he had a picture of her too; maybe it was worth calling Adam after all.

Getting to his feet, he wandered along the counter and picked up the phone. It was mid-morning – his friend ought to be at work. The number rang, then a voice answered.

'Kansas City Police Department?'

'Yeah, hi.' Frank leaned in against the wall. 'I'm trying to reach a Detective Adam O'Halloran?'

'One moment please.'

There was a click, then silence. Eventually, a familiar voice came on the line.

'Detective O'Halloran?'

'Hey Adam, it's Frank Rye.'

'Frank! Geez, I ain't heard from you in a while. How're you doin', buddy?'

Adam sounded genuinely pleased to hear from him. News of the suspension clearly hadn't made it this far up-state, thank goodness.

'I'm getting by,' Frank told him. 'How's life as a big city cop?'

Adam laughed.

'Well, it's busier than when we were in Joplin, that's for sure,' he said. 'How's the old place doing? Is Kirkland still busting your hump?'

'Oh yeah,' Frank said, shaking his head. 'He's my biggest admirer.'

'Well, his bite was always worse than his bark...' Adam paused, his tone softening. 'Say, I heard about poor old Pete Barnes. Must've been a real shock for everyone. Did they get whoever did it?'

Frank closed his eyes.

'Not yet,' he replied.

'Well, it sure makes you think, doesn't it?'

'Yeah.' Frank bowed his head and nodded slowly. 'It changes things, all right.'

'Well, anyway, I'm glad you finally decided to call.' Adam was trying to pick the mood up, just like he always used to. 'When are you gonna drag your ass up here to Kansas City? Celia's a great cook and we'd love to have you over for dinner.'

'That's the thing,' Frank said. 'I'm in town right now, wondered if you had some time for a drink?'

'*Right* now?' Adam hesitated. 'Damn, you shoulda told me you were coming... but I can probably duck out of here around five, if that's any good?'

'Five is good' Frank said. 'Where d'you want to meet?'

Adam thought for a moment.

'Well, there's a bar called Earl's on the corner of 12th and McGee, just a block over from City Hall.'

'Sure,' Frank told him. 'I'll find it.'

'Great. I'll see you there at five.'

'See you there.'

Frank hung up the phone and turned around. Walking back along the counter to his stool, he took a mouthful of coffee and waited for his pie to arrive.

17

It was a cop bar. The walls were lined with framed photographs of officers, old department pennants and sporting trophies, and it had a relaxed feel, full of laughter and lively conversation. Sure, a place like this might get a little tribal, with some minor resentments or rivalries in the ranks, but everyone was connected by the job, united against the world. Heaven help any outsiders who started trouble in here.

From across the small table, Adam caught him looking round and gave him a knowing grin.

'You look tired, pal. Kirkland working you too hard?'

Frank sighed and gave him a bleak smile.

'You have no idea.'

Adam sat back and loosened his tie. His dark brown hair was longer than it used to be, slicked back and carefully styled. He'd put on some weight in the last year too, his face a little rounder, his shirt a little tighter. Married life appeared to be suiting him.

'Well, I'm glad to see you finally took some time off,' he said. 'Figured you'd just drift up to Kansas City for a few days, is that it?'

Frank picked up his drink and nodded.

'Something like that.'

'You got any plans while you're here?'

Frank shrugged.

'Not really,' he replied. 'Just taking a break from being a cop.'

Adam spread his arms wide.

'And yet, here you are in a police bar.'

Frank looked around and smiled ruefully.

'Yeah,' he said. 'Some things you just can't get away from.'

Adam laughed and raised his glass.

'Well,' he said. 'If you're in town for a bit, you should come over one night. You haven't seen the house yet, have you?'

'Not yet,' Frank admitted. He looked at his old colleague. *Smile. Make an effort.* 'How's Celia?'

'She's good.'

Frank tried to recall what Adam's wife did. Couldn't.

'She enjoying being a cop's wife?' he asked.

Adam sat back and winked.

'Oh, I think she likes it just fine,' he said. 'We worked real hard to get the place fixed up just the way she wanted it, and she's got a lot more spare time now.'

Frank nodded politely, tried not to think about Beth, and how he'd helped her fill *her* spare time.

'So if you did want to come over, that'd be great,' Adam was saying. 'I'm sure Celia would enjoy talking to someone who knew me back in the Joplin days, and she'd fix you a first-class dinner.'

Frank lowered his eyes, not wanting to agree to anything, not wanting to offend.

'We'll see,' he replied. 'I wouldn't want to impose.'

'Hey, it's no problem,' Adam told him. 'Anything we can do for you, just ask. C'mon, you know that.'

Frank glanced up.

'Well...' he said 'I *was* gonna ask if you could do me a favor...'

'Damn,' murmured Adam, feigning disappointment. 'And here I thought this was a social call.'

'Oh, it is,' Frank lied. 'And I doubt there's anything you can do on this anyway. It just popped into my head and I thought I'd ask...'

He left the idea hanging, hoping his old colleague would take the bait.

'So what is it?' Adam asked. 'What do you need?'

Frank looked at him for a long moment.

'There's someone I'm trying to track down,' he said. 'A woman.'

Adam immediately raised an eyebrow and grinned, but Frank continued.

'Now I already know where she's staying, but I just wanted to check if you guys had a file on her up here.'

Adam shrugged.

'Sure,' he said. 'But why not just have Joplin PD put in a request?'

'Well...' Frank hesitated. 'This isn't really *work*, it's more of a... *personal* thing, y'know?'

'Personal, eh?' Eager now, he leaned closer. 'Who is she?'

Frank took out the photograph and placed it on the table.

'Her name is Faye Griffith,' he explained. 'I believe she's staying with her brother, here in Kansas City. You want the address?'

'Sure.' Adam set his glass down and fumbled in his jacket pocket, drawing out a small pad and pencil. 'Okay, go ahead.'

'210 East 40th Street. Apartment 16.'

Adam scribbled it down.

'And it's Faye...?'

'Faye Griffith.'

'Got it.' Admiring the photograph, Adam tucked the pad away, then smiled at Frank.

'So, who *is* she?' he asked again.

Frank stared at his glass, then took a sip.

'She's just someone I want to find,' he said.

'Yeah?' Adam had a mischievous glint in his eye. 'You and her...?'

'No.' Frank shook his head. 'Nothing like that.'

'Sure about that?' Adam persisted. 'She's a honey.'

Frank set his glass down on the table, firmly.

'Absolutely sure,' he said.

Adam's expression became thoughtful.

'Got someone else, waiting for you back in Joplin? Is that it?'

Frank thought of Beth standing there on the porch, watching him leave.

I want you to find whoever did this.

He sighed and lowered his eyes.

'Maybe...' he said. 'I... I don't know.'

Adam sat back and arched an eyebrow.

'Don't tell me *you're* settling down,' he said. 'I never took you for a one-woman guy.'

Frank gave him a withering look.

Adam chuckled.

'Is it that cute little blonde – what was her name? – the one from the library?'

Frank shook his head.

'Nah, that didn't last.'

Adam grinned.

'Ah well. They never last, not with you, eh?'

Frank stiffened and glared at him.

Adam caught the change in his manner and frowned.

'What is it?'

Frank shook his head and looked away. It wasn't just Beth, it was before her, before Adam's time... The dumb bastard didn't realize what he'd said.

'Nothing.' He picked up his glass and drained it. 'You want another?'

Adam watched him curiously.

'You okay, pal?'

'Yeah, it's nothing.' Frank summoned up a smile from some-where. 'C'mon, what'll you have?'

'Another nip of Wild Turkey, if you're buying.'

'Comin' right up.'

They stayed on far later than he'd intended. In the end, it was Adam who glanced down at his wristwatch, then looked up with a pained expression.

'Gee, I'm sorry, pal. I really should be getting home.'

Frank smiled at him. He hadn't been looking forward to seeing his old colleague, but the evening had panned out pretty well.

'No problem,' he said.

Adam tipped back the last of his drink and made a face, then got unsteadily to his feet.

'Damn,' he said, suddenly turning to Frank in dismay. 'I completely forgot to ask about Pete Barnes. What the hell happened?'

Frank sighed, then pushed his chair back and stood up.

'Beaten to death,' he said, quietly. 'Down in Newton County.'

'Newton County?' Adam looked puzzled. 'What was he doing down there?'

Frank picked up his drink and swallowed the last of the whiskey.

'Long story,' he said, setting the empty glass down. 'And it still has a way to go, from what I understand.'

'No arrests?'

'Not yet,' Frank told him. 'But someone's gonna pay for it, you can be sure of that.'

Adam nodded sadly, his eyes unfocused.

'Wasn't he married?' he asked.

Frank took a breath, keeping his face blank.

'Yeah. He was.'

'Damn.' Adam shook his head. 'His poor wife.'

The evening air seemed fresh and cold after the warmth of the bar. Frank followed Adam as he stumbled out onto the sidewalk. Clearly he wasn't quite so accustomed to drinking as he used to be.

'So you'll let me know?' Adam said, leaning heavily on a newspaper stand. 'About dinner?'

'Yeah, I'll give you a call,' Frank replied. 'And you'll ask around about Faye Griffith?'

Adam patted the notebook in his pocket.

'I'll let you know if I find anything.' He paused, then frowned. 'Where are you staying, anyway?'

'The Bradbury.'

'Oh, well that's quite close which is... convenient.' Adam wagged a finger towards the street. 'Listen, I'm gonna get a cab. Want me to drop you off?'

'No, it's okay,' Frank told him. 'I could use the walk.'

'Right. Well, sorry I can't stay later but... ah, you know how it is.'

'Yeah, I know. Go home, Adam. I'll speak to you tomorrow.'

Adam took a few steps, then turned around, smiling drunkenly.

'It really is good to see you, Frank.'

Frank managed a small smile.

'Go on,' he said. 'Get outta here.'

Adam grinned foolishly, then turned away to hail a passing cab.

Frank waved him off, then wandered slowly down to the street corner. He stopped to light a cigarette, then squinted at his watch. It was only a little after ten o'clock, way too early to be lying in bed, staring up at the ceiling. There was nobody waiting for him back at the hotel...

...but this time of night there might be someone at Stanley's apartment.

Standing beneath a street light, Frank blew out a long stream of pale smoke, then turned and hurried back up the sidewalk, looking for a cab.

18

Frank slumped in the corner of the back seat, staring out at the illuminated signs and storefronts as the cab cruised down Main Street. Yawning, he tried to shake off the fog of the evening's drinking. The city was still awake, but he figured that Faye ought to be back home by now, and at this time of night, she wouldn't be expecting visitors.

Cresting the bridge over the railroad tracks, he looked across towards the lights of Union Station, then settled back as the traffic slowed for the stoplight at the intersection. Ahead of them, on the hilltop above the station, the Liberty Memorial stood pale and tall, lit up against the night sky.

A siren was blaring behind them, and Frank turned to peer out as a fire truck roared past, red lights flashing as it cut across the road and went racing up the slope.

'Someone's sure in a hurry,' the cabbie observed as he put the taxi in gear and bumped across the intersection. He hunched forward over the wheel and jerked a thumb towards the hilltop. 'You ever been up there? The memorial?'

Frank leaned his head close to the window, peering up at the tower.

'No, I haven't.'

'Oh, you should,' the cabbie said. 'Hell of a view from the top, and there's a museum all about the war.'

Frank sank back into his seat again. The thought of a war museum didn't appeal to him at all.

'Was you in the last one?' the cabbie asked.

'The war?' Frank replied. 'Yeah, I was.'

The cabbie nodded his approval.

'My brother fought in Sicily with the 18th Infantry,' he explained. 'Me, I got a 4F on account of my asthma.'

Frank gazed out at the people on the sidewalk as they reached the top of the hill.

'Your brother get back home okay?' he asked.

'Yeah,' the cabbie said, with some satisfaction. 'But there's plenty that didn't, and there's plenty that's still over there.'

Frank sighed.

'True enough,' he murmured.

The cabbie slowed to allow a van to change lanes, then picked up speed again.

'Our boys are out in Siberia or wherever, freezing their asses off... and for what? I mean, we earned our piece of *Germany*, fair and square, but the rest of it?' He shook his head, jabbing a finger against the wheel to emphasize his point. 'America did what it had to do in '45, but we didn't *ask* for no war, so why should we be the ones to clean it up?'

Frank saw the frowning eyes in the rear-view mirror. He knew better than to get drawn into a conversation like this.

'Beats me,' he said.

'Yeah, well... sometimes I think that maybe those Brits ain't so stupid. Maybe they got the right idea.'

Frank glanced up.

'How's that?' he asked.

'Well, they got some trouble out in India, but that's *their territory* now.' He looked in the mirror, briefly making eye contact.

'Us? We done plenty of fighting, all over the map, so where's *our* empire, that's what I'd like to know? It's like that Lindbergh guy says: we got suckered into a bad situation.'

Ahead, a long line of tail lights were glaring red as the traffic slowed. Frank leaned forward, peering out through the windshield towards a yellow glow that lit the sky beyond the buildings further down the road.

'What's that?' he asked.

'I don't know, but we ain't going nowhere for a bit,' the cabbie murmured.

There were more sirens echoing in the distance now, and some people were starting to get out of their cars.

Frank checked the meter, then paid the fare and opened the door. Stepping out onto the sidewalk, he could hear the wail of the sirens more clearly and started walking quickly towards them.

Another fire truck forced its way through, driving up the wrong side of the road as he approached the intersection, and he saw it turn by the church, heading down East 40th Street. He began to run, weaving between the drifting people, and following it down the slope. The glow was much bigger now, flickering as bright flames danced above the roofs of the nearby buildings, touching the billowing smoke with an angry orange cast.

As the apartment block came into view, he slowed to a standstill, staring at the crackling blaze over the heads of the onlookers. The whole place was alight, a silhouette of blackened walls around a raging inferno, windows belching fire into the night. He started to move again, picking his way over the hoses that lay across the street like wet snakes, skirting the crowd as the police shouted and tried to keep everyone back.

Staring between the people, he saw a group of firefighters advancing, tiny dark figures against the glare of the flames, as jets of water played over the front of the building. He could feel the heat on his face, taste the mist of water and ash, smell the burning wood. Suddenly, a cry went up from the crowd, and he turned to see the silhouette of a firefighter, staggering down the steps from the burning entrance porch, dragging a limp figure away from the blaze as other fire crew rushed forward to help.

All around, anxious faces shone in the flickering light. Frank approached an elderly man in a bathrobe who stood staring at the scene.

'What happened?' he asked.

The old guy didn't seem to hear him at first, then turned with a haunted look in his eyes.

'I... I don't rightly know,' he stammered. 'The place just caught so fast. One minute it was just a little bit of smoke, then the whole damn building went up. Terrible thing.'

'You saw it start?'

The old man shrugged.

'I don't know about *start*, but when I first saw it there was just some flames in the entrance hall.'

'Did they get everyone out?' Frank demanded.

'They got some folks out, but maybe not everyone.' The old man shook his head. 'If the stairs were blocked early on, then I guess some folk on the upper floors might still be... oh dear Lord!'

He broke off as a sudden cracking sound came from the building, and everyone turned to see the end of the roof drop slightly, sagging downwards. Then, with a splintering groan, the whole roof caved in, blowing huge plumes of flame out of the top floor windows. There was a crash as the upper structure collapsed, sending clouds of sparks billowing up into the darkness, and screams as a wall of heat pushed the crowd backwards.

In the stumbling confusion, Frank could see a middle-aged woman in a housecoat being restrained by two police officers, shrieking that her husband was 'still in there, you bastards'. Sitting on the curb, a bald man in a soot-blackened vest hugged his knees, rocking backwards and forwards as people rushed around him, coughing, choking, sobbing.

Frank held up a hand, shielding his face from the intensity of the blaze. As the crowd broke around him, he saw the firefighters beaten back by the heat, and one of them collapsing to lay still on the asphalt. Others rallied to him, pulling the prone figure away from the building, and a desperate voice cried out, 'Is there a doctor here? Anyone with medical training?'

Frank stopped and looked around, expecting to see Stanley pushing his way to the front, but no one came. Frowning, he began to move grimly through the crowd, searching the illuminated faces. *They must be here, somewhere...*

But there was no sign of Faye or her brother.

An ambulance was nosing down the hill, bells ringing urgently, people parting to allow it through. Wearily, Frank stepped back to let it pass, then turned to stare into the ruin of the building, now totally engulfed in flames.

He didn't know whether Faye was alive or dead. His only lead – his only connection to the thin man – might just have gone up in smoke.

Summer, 1944
Bern, Switzerland

19

Rafe stood by the window, gazing down into the street. He stroked absently at the light brown mustache he'd been cultivating, then turned back to face the others and sighed.

'Honestly, I'm so bloody fed up of this wretched war,' he said.

Frank set his pen down and looked up at his friend.

'What do you mean?' he asked.

'Oh, I don't know.' Rafe shook his head slightly, then leaned in to rest his shoulder against the window frame. 'I rather thought we'd be making short work of the Germans by now, but since D-Day... well, the last month or so we seem to have got completely bogged down in France.'

Molly glanced up from her desk.

'The Russians are moving a *lot* quicker,' she noted.

'Well, that's something, I suppose.' Rafe seemed to brighten. 'Have your shady Eastern sources been whispering again, eh?'

'It's not exactly a secret,' said Molly, sitting back in her chair. 'The Germans are collapsing in the east, and Russia's hitting them hard. The way Stalin's going now, well...'

She hesitated, then frowned and looked away.

Watching her, Frank leaned forward.

'Well what?' he pressed her.

Molly stared at her desk for a moment, then said, 'When something gets that sort of... *momentum*... well, you just wonder how it's ever going to stop.'

Her tone was guarded now, but as she caught Frank's eye she managed a faint smile.

'Well, *I've* no sympathy for the Germans,' Rafe said. He raised his walking stick and rested it over his shoulder. 'I just thought we'd be giving a better account of ourselves, that's all.'

'Hey!' Frank protested, remembering his old infantry unit. 'I think we're doing pretty good.'

He could see from their faces that the others had caught something in his tone, and he shrugged self-consciously before adding, 'Anyway, it doesn't really matter which army gets rid of the Nazis, does it?'

Molly lowered her eyes.

'I suppose it depends what they do once they've liberated you,' she said.

'Ah, you've been spending too much time with your Red friends, comrade Molly,' Rafe grinned. 'You're starting to sound as miserable as they do.'

Molly gave him a withering look.

'Very funny,' she said.

'Sorry.' Rafe turned back to the window, smiling to himself as he peered outside. 'I'm just feeling a bit... restless. Can't be helped.'

Frank glanced over at him and nodded.

'I guess you *do* lose track of time in place like this,' he said.

'Ha!' Molly arched an eyebrow. '*You've* only been here a few months!'

'I know,' Frank replied, feigning modesty. 'And just look how well the war has gone in that time.'

'He's quite right.' Rafe glanced over at Molly. 'The Allied front line *has* done so much better without him.'

She smiled, a real smile this time, and the mood of the room lifted.

'Just watch that mouth.' Frank chuckled, shaking his fist at his friend. 'Loose lips may sink ships, but you're gonna have loose teeth.'

Rafe laughed, then turned to the window again, squinting down into the street.

'Hey!' he hissed, his voice suddenly serious. 'She's back!'

Turning, he limped quickly over to his desk.

Molly pushed her chair back and got to her feet. She gave Frank a meaningful look, then walked briskly across the room and disappeared through into the small kitchen area at the far end of the office.

Frank lowered his eyes and waited.

A moment later, the stairwell door swung open, and Jean came in.

'Afternoon, boys,' she said, making her way over to her desk and sitting down.

'Afternoon,' Frank replied.

He watched her as she unlocked her desk drawer and pulled it open.

'You've been gone a while,' Rafe said, peering over at her.

'Well, it was a beautiful day,' she said vaguely. Setting her purse in her lap, she withdrew something small, placed it in the drawer and slid it shut. 'Is Swift in his office?'

'He is,' Rafe replied, gravely. 'But he asked us to tell you something, immediately you came back.'

Jean looked up, alert.

'What?' she demanded.

Frank stood up and jabbed an accusing finger at her.

'Happy birthday!' He grinned.

Jean blinked at him in surprise, then her face broke into a broad smile.

'Oh... but how did you...?'

'You've no secrets from us, old girl,' Rafe laughed, getting awkwardly to his feet. 'Many happy returns!'

'Oh... thank you!' Jean beamed at them, then narrowed her eyes at Rafe. 'But not so much of the *old*, if you don't mind. I'm only twenty-six!'

Molly appeared from the kitchen. She was carrying a small round cake covered in chocolate, which she set down carefully on the desk.

'Oh my Lord!' Jean gasped, bringing her hands up to her face. 'It looks... it's amazing! Oh Molly, however did you manage this? I mean, with the rationing...'

'It's probably better that you don't ask,' Molly said, pulling a face, then smiling. 'Happy birthday, Jean. From all of us.'

They gathered round to sing *Happy Birthday*. There were no candles, but Frank leaned over and carefully inserted a long, lit matchstick into the centre of the cake. When they finished singing, Jean dutifully blew it out, then beamed up at them all.

'Thank you,' she said simply. 'Now, has anybody got a knife? This cake looks too good not to eat.'

Frank went through to the kitchen and came back with a knife. As he returned, Jean was talking to Molly.

'...but celebrating my birthday seemed such a trivial thing, you know, with the war and everything.'

Molly put a hand on her shoulder.

'Life's going on,' she said firmly. 'And that makes celebrating more important than ever.'

Frank walked over and offered Jean the knife.

'Come on, birthday girl.' He grinned. 'Let's cut that cake.'

They sat down and Jean passed around slices for each of them.

A few minutes later, the door at the end of the corridor opened.

'Is Jean back yet?' Swift called out, emerging from his room. He seemed to be in an impatient mood as he came stalking through to the office, though that was more and more often the case these days, Frank thought. As he drew nearer to them he slowed, seeing the cake.

'Special occasion?' he asked.

'It's Jean's birthday,' Rafe said.

Swift hesitated, then turned to Jean.

'Of course.' He smiled. 'Sorry, I should have remembered.'

'No, it's all right.' Jean shook her head, looking slightly embarrassed. 'Would you like a piece of cake?'

'Er... sure.' Swift nodded politely. 'It looks very impressive.'

'Oh, it is,' Rafe assured him. 'Molly made it.'

'Really?' Swift glanced over at Molly, who lowered her eyes. 'Well, good for you.'

Jean cut a slice of cake and offered it to him on a folded piece of paper.

'I'm afraid there aren't any proper plates,' she said.

'Thanks.' Swift accepted the cake graciously but made no attempt to eat it. 'Look, I'm sorry, but... there's a couple of things I need to go over with you.'

'Yes, of course.' Jean's face became serious. As Swift turned back towards his office, she bent down to lock her desk drawer, then got to her feet.

Catching Molly's eye, she hesitated, then leaned over to give her a brief hug.

'Thanks,' she said softly, before turning to look at the others. 'Thank you all.'

Then, with a quick smile, she hurried down the corridor after Swift.

Frank watched her go, then looked round to find Rafe shaking his head unhappily.

'Well, *that* was rotten timing,' he muttered, idly twisting his walking stick in his hand.

Molly got up and calmly smoothed her skirt down.

'It's a pity he didn't feel able to join us,' she said, turning away. 'But I don't think he trusts us *quite* as much as he trusts her.'

Frank frowned at this, but then he remembered Swift's comments, back when he'd first arrived: *Some of these people are Brits, not Americans... you can trust them, up to a point.*

Rafe nodded moodily.

'Well, trust or no trust, there's plainly *something* big going on. Heaps of radio traffic, Dulles chasing about all over Switzerland, and poor old Swift with a face like a wet weekend.' He shrugged his shoulders, then leaned over, helping himself to another piece of cake. 'I just wish it would hurry up and happen, whatever it is.'

They celebrated Jean's birthday that evening at a Bierkeller over in Länggasse. It was a rustic sort of place, set deep below the old cobbled streets and accessed via a steep wooden stair, but even with the shortages it still had a reputation for good food and excellent beer. There were long oak tables with rough wooden benches, and candlelight flickered merrily around the low arched ceilings, stained dark with years of smoke. As night fell over the city outside, the four friends leaned in close to hear each other over the sounds of clinking glass and laughter that echoed off the ancient stone walls.

'Which one?' Jean was asking. 'There are so many Sherlock Holmes pictures.'

'*The Hound Of The Baskervilles*?' Molly suggested.

'No, *The Voice Of Terror*,' Rafe said. 'It's a bit far-fetched but you'll enjoy it, I know you will.'

Frank took another swig of beer and set his glass down with a happy sigh.

'I like the guy who plays Doctor Watson.' Yawning, he began

to lean back, but caught himself just before he fell off the bench. 'Damn! I need to stop doing that!'

'Careful, old boy!' Rafe rested a hand on his back to steady him. 'Nigel Bruce; that's the actor you're thinking of. He's glorious, isn't he?'

'I prefer Basil Rathbone,' said Molly. She smiled to herself for a moment, then looked across the table with a twinkle in her eyes. 'I've always had a bit of a soft spot for Sherlock Holmes.'

Rafe shook his head.

'Never liked the look of him, myself,' he told her.

'Sherlock Holmes?'

'No, Basil Rathbone,' Rafe said gravely. 'I haven't trusted him since he was that *rotter* the Sheriff of Nottingham, in *Robin Hood.*'

Molly stared at him for a moment, then chuckled.

'You can hardly hold *that* against him!' she said, shaking her head.

'No, really.' Rafe leaned across the table and beckoned her closer. 'Who would you rather have a romantic assignation with: Basil Rathbone or Errol Flynn? Come on, you'd choose dashing Robin Hood over poor old Sherlock-of-Nottingham any day of the week.'

Molly shook her head again, then pushed her end of the bench back from the table.

'If I *were* to have a romantic assignation with anyone,' she said, standing up and gazing down with mock severity, '*you'd* be the last to know, Ranulph Cavanagh.'

Jean and Frank burst out laughing. Rafe clutched a hand to his chest and tried to look hurt, but couldn't stop himself grinning.

Molly winked at him, then whispered something to Jean and excused herself.

Frank glanced up as Jean yawned and got slowly to her feet.

'All right then, boys.' She stood up and stretched, her hands brushing the low ceiling. 'Thanks for a lovely evening. I really appreciate it.'

'I say...' Rafe gazed up at her in surprise. 'You're not running out on us are you?'

'I've been on the go all day,' she said, leaning on the table with both hands and giving him a weary smile. 'I'm practically asleep on my feet.'

'It *is* getting kind of late,' Frank said, nodding. 'You want me to walk you home?'

Jean looked at him and shook her head.

'Thanks,' she said, 'but Molly's taking me back. We'll be just fine.'

'Well, okay then.' Frank started to lean back again then stopped himself. 'Happy birthday, Jean.'

'Compliments of the season!' Rafe raised his glass.

Jean beamed and performed a small curtsey.

'Thanks, you two,' she said.

Molly appeared at her side.

'Night, boys. See you tomorrow, bright and early?'

'*Early*, perhaps,' Rafe muttered.

'Goodnight.' Frank smiled. He watched as Molly steered Jean across the room and saw the two women disappear up the stairs.

'Can't abide people leaving the party early,' Rafe said, with a sigh. He squinted at his watch for a moment, then gave up. 'What time *is* it, anyway?'

Frank glanced down at his wrist.

'It's late,' he said. 'I reckon we'll be walking home in the blackout.'

Rafe appeared to consider this for a moment.

'Oh well, if that's the case, we might as well have another drink.'

Frank got stiffly to his feet and walked over to the bar, noting that the place was finally starting to quieten down a bit. The clientele was mixed - some middle-aged men, and a few young couples - but everyone seemed to be having a good time. He returned to the table with two large beers and managed to set them down without spilling very much.

'Thanks awfully,' Rafe said. He immediately reached for his glass and took a long drink.

'No problem,' Frank replied, smiling.

The two men drank in sleepy silence for a moment, until Rafe drew himself up and pointed a finger across the table.

'You know, you're a bloody good chap,' he said, then added, 'for an *American*, I mean.'

Frank stared at him for a moment, then gave his friend a broad grin.

'Well now,' he replied, adopting an exaggerated drawl, 'that's mighty nice of you to make allowances for me.'

'No, really. I know there can be a bit of – what's the damned word? – *friction*, between the old nations, but you...' He trailed off and shook his head. 'You're a bloody good sort.'

Solemnly, he raised his glass then drained it.

Frank inclined his head slightly.

'You really think there's friction?' he asked, lifting his own glass and gently swirling the last of his beer around. 'Sure it isn't just chain-of-command crap? Little guys trying to make themselves feel important?'

'Swift's not a little guy,' Rafe replied quickly. 'And Dulles *certainly* isn't!'

Frank considered this for a moment, then shrugged.

'Everyone seems to get along,' he said.

Rafe shook his head unhappily.

'Easy for you to say,' he muttered. 'You're the right nationality; you're a *Yank*.'

Frank sat up, curious now.

'What's that got to do with anything?'

Rafe scowled at him.

'It means some of *us* have to listen very hard if we want to know what's going on, while *others...*' He looked pointedly at his friend. '...are simply told.'

'What?' Frank stared at him. None of this was making any sense.

'Oh, come on. You and Jean know what's going on at the moment. But was *I* told about it? Was *Molly*?' His voice was becoming shrill, but he broke off suddenly, looking away. 'Wrong bloody flag, apparently.'

Leaning forward, Frank whispered, 'What the hell are you talking about?'

Rafe gave him a withering glance, then frowned.

'You *know* who Dulles is talking to, what he's talking *about*.'

'Nope.' Frank shook his head.

Rafe stared at him with an expression of near-disbelief, before glancing around furtively to make sure nobody was listening.

'A German *coup d'état!*' he hissed. 'Why d'you think everybody's been so damned itchy, so impatient?'

Frank sat back, stunned. *A German coup?* But the army was still loyal to Hitler, wasn't it?

Rafe watched him carefully, then shook his head in wonder.

'Crikey! You really *didn't* know, did you?'

Disturbed from his thoughts, Frank blinked at him.

'No. I just...' He trailed off, then whispered, 'Are you sure about this?'

'Of course I'm bloody sure!' Rafe snapped. He pulled his bench towards the table and leaned in close. 'You remember when Dulles had those late-night meetings at Herrengasse?'

A movement caught Frank's eye. Over in the far corner of the cellar, a young couple had got to their feet and started towards them. Not knowing what else to do, he grabbed Rafe's wrist and began speaking over him in a loud voice.

'And *that's* why I won't drink schnapps any more. I don't think I ever felt quite so sick.'

'Eh?' Rafe blinked in confusion.

Frank shot him a warning look, then inclined his head towards the approaching couple. Rafe glanced up, then immediately fell silent as they squeezed past. The young man had his hand pressed firmly on the woman's behind and she was laughing at something. Frank watched them as they made their way over to the stairs. *Probably just an ordinary couple.*

When he turned back, Rafe was staring down at the table.

'Hey, sorry to interrupt,' he said. 'I wasn't sure if you'd seen them so I figured–'

'No, no. You're quite right.' Rafe looked up at Frank, a sheepish expression on his face. 'Thanks.'

They sat in uncomfortable silence for a moment. At the other end of the room, a group of men burst into raucous laughter at something.

Frank turned to his friend.

'You want one for the road?' he asked.

Rafe appeared to think about it for a moment, then shook his head.

'I think maybe I should call it a night,' he said.

Frank helped him up the stairs, and the two men emerged to find the city in darkness. The street seemed deathly quiet after the noise of the cellar, and there was a chill in the air.

Rafe stood for a moment, head tilted back, swaying as he gazed up at the stars.

Shivering, Frank buttoned up his jacket.

'Come on.' He yawned. 'It's a long walk back.'

Rafe turned and placed a hand on his shoulder. Staring deep into his eyes, he murmured, 'You really are a thoroughly decent chap.'

Frank managed an awkward grin.

'Oh, I wouldn't say that.' He chuckled.

'Well, I *would*,' Rafe insisted, then paused. A frown crept over his face. 'And that's what makes this all so damned irregular.'

'What's so irregular?'

Rafe stared at him, then shook his head.

'Why haven't they told *you?*'

20

Rafe looked rough when he arrived at the office. His blonde hair was sticking up untidily and there were several red nicks where he'd cut himself shaving. Limping across to his desk, he sat down heavily, then grimaced and closed his eyes.

'Are you okay?' Frank asked him.

'I've been better,' Rafe said. He managed a wry smile, then added, 'Thanks for getting me home last night.'

'No problem.' Frank grinned, stifling a yawn. It *had* been an effort to get up this morning, but the coffee was starting to kick in now. And he'd certainly come through the evening in better shape than his friend.

A few minutes later, he heard the door behind him open. Molly and Jean emerged from Swift's room and walked down the corridor into the main office. 'Oh dear!' Molly feigned dismay as she caught sight of Rafe. 'Look what the cat's dragged in.'

Rafe glanced up at her with a wretched expression, then hung his head.

'The comforting voice of the harridan,' he muttered.

Molly patted him on the shoulder and smiled brightly.

'Feeling good, are we?'

Rafe groaned.

'Oh, don't be so hard on him,' Jean said, walking round to her desk and sitting down. 'I had such a lovely time last night. It was perfect.'

Molly laughed, then turned to Frank.

'How about you?' she asked. 'Sore head this morning?'

Frank covered his mouth, yawning again.

'I feel okay,' he said with a shrug. 'It was cold walking home last night, though.'

Rafe lifted his head slightly.

'Well, that just proves you didn't drink as much as me. I barely felt a thing.'

Molly made her way around to her desk.

'I'm surprised you even remember.'

Rafe wagged a finger at her.

'I remember *everything*, thank you.' Turning to Jean, he muttered, 'It's terribly unfair, allowing her to badger me like this. I'm really not at my best just now.'

Jean glanced over and gave him a sympathetic smile.

'Well, grab yourself some coffee, mister,' she said, taking a firm tone. 'Swift says that Dulles is coming by this morning. Apparently he wants to talk to us all.'

Dulles breezed into the office on the stroke of ten, accompanied by Groth. Pausing to remove his hat and coat, he immediately made his way over to Jean.

'Happy birthday for yesterday, Miss Ellesworth,' he said, reaching into his pocket. 'I'm sorry to have missed it.'

He drew out a long, thin box wrapped in colored paper, placed it on her desk, then flashed her a quick smile.

'Oh, Mr Dulles.' Clearly surprised, Jean took the box and cradled it in her hands. 'Thank you very much.'

'That's quite all right,' Dulles replied pleasantly. 'Tell me, is

Mr Swift in his room?'

'He is.' Jean looked up from the box. 'Should I go and tell him you're here?'

'No need.' Dulles gestured for her to keep her seat. 'Herr Groth and I just wanted to consult with him on a matter, then perhaps we can gather the troops out here for a discussion?'

'Of course,' Jean said, nodding.

'Capital!' Dulles inclined his head to her, then turned to Groth. 'Let's go.'

Sitting at his desk, Frank watched them walk down the corridor. Dulles knocked once on Swift's door, then immediately opened it and went inside. Groth followed him in, pulling the door closed behind them.

'Oh my!' Jean gasped. 'Look!'

Frank turned to see her staring down at the open box. Inside, resting on a red velvet insert, was an elegant silver pen. Smiling proudly, she held it out for the others to see.

'That's a beauty,' Rafe whistled.

'It's lovely,' Molly agreed. But her eyes were on the door of Swift's room.

It was almost lunchtime when Dulles finally emerged from his conference. Groth came stalking along the corridor behind him, but Swift remained in his office. Slowing as he drew level with Frank's desk, Dulles cleared his throat and glanced around the room.

'Excuse me,' he said, pacing slowly over to stand by one of the filing cabinets. 'But if I might have your attention for just a few minutes?'

Everyone stopped what they were doing and looked up. Dulles rested an elbow on top of the cabinet, then took a moment to hold each of them in his piercing gaze.

'Tonight is a most important night,' he began. 'A rendezvous has been arranged to receive an unprecedented delivery of information that may, God willing, *significantly* hasten the end of the war.' He paused to let this sink in, taking out his pipe and tapping it thoughtfully in his palm. Groth walked slowly over to stand beside him.

'Now, I imagine that some of you may already be speculating about the exact nature of this information,' Dulles continued. 'Suffice to say, I consider it too sensitive to trust to the more usual channels of communication and, consequently, I and countless others are placing our trust in you.'

He looked round at the assembled faces again, as though challenging them to prove themselves, then nodded.

'Good! Now, this will be Herr Groth's operation, so I'll give way to him and let him apprise you of the details.'

Groth took a step forward, his face unreadable.

'Mr Cavanagh, Miss Pearson, and Mr Rye.' He glanced briefly at each of them. 'You will meet me at the bottom of Aargauerstalden at eight o'clock this evening.'

Jean raised her hand, a frown on her face.

'Am I not going?' she asked.

'No,' Groth told her. He turned back to the others. 'The rendezvous with our contact will be outside the city, so you will dress warmly. We may be out in the open for some time.'

'Can you tell us *where* we're going?' Rafe said.

'No. The man we are meeting will have travelled a great distance and taken many risks. It is vital that we do nothing to compromise him. That's all you need to know for now.'

Rafe sat back in his chair and glanced over at Frank with a shrug.

Dulles carefully lit his pipe and puffed on it for a moment, before looking up at them once more.

'I just want to impress upon you all the tremendous courage and commitment shown by our friends across the border. By their actions they place their lives in the gravest danger, for a cause they truly believe in.' He shook his head, his expression serious. 'We must show that same courage and commitment, and we must *not* let them down.'

Returning from his hurried lunch, Frank climbed the stairs to the office, absently munching on a piece of smoked sausage. As he opened the door and stepped inside, Jean looked up from her desk.

'He wants you,' she said, glancing along the corridor.

'What about Dulles and Groth?' Frank asked.

'They went back to Herrengasse. At least, I *assume* that's where they were going. Everyone seems so jittery at the moment, and nobody wants to tell anyone what they're doing.'

She spoke lightly, but Frank caught the troubled look that flickered across her face. *Left out of the operation... no reason given.*

'Don't worry,' he said. 'Nobody wants to tell *me* what they're doing either, so I'd say you're in fine company.'

Jean gave him a sidelong glance, then lowered her eyes and smiled.

'You're a smart man, Frank Rye,' she said. 'But you really don't need to tell me what I want to hear.'

Damn! He flashed her an awkward grin, wishing he'd been more subtle. She nodded towards the corridor.

'Go on, he's waiting for you.'

Frank leaned his head around the door.

'Jean said you wanted to see me?'

Sitting at his desk, Swift glanced up from a handful of papers, then beckoned him forward. Frank stepped into the room, pushing the door closed behind him.

'So...' Swift's expression became serious. He sat back in his chair and folded his arms. 'Is everyone all set for tonight?'

'I believe so, yes.'

'And you understand the importance of the operation?'

'In a general sense, yes,' Frank replied.

Swift studied him for a moment, then leaned down and carefully unlocked one of his desk drawers.

'I need you to keep your eyes open tonight,' he said, watching Frank intently as he slid the drawer open. 'Remember, it's not the Swiss police we're worrying about this time.'

'I understand that.'

'Good.' Swift reached into the drawer and took out a small cardboard box. It rattled slightly as he placed it in front of him. Printed across the top were the words *.45 Caliber ~ 50 Cartridges*. Next, he withdrew a cloth-wrapped bundle, something heavy that made a solid sound as he set it down. Wordlessly, he slid both across the desk.

Frank stared at them, then looked at Swift.

'Uh... thank you, sir.' He reached for the ammunition first, then hesitated. 'Do you need me to sign for this?'

Swift pushed his desk drawer shut and turned the key in the lock.

'Sign for what?' he asked.

They stared at each other for a long moment, until Frank nodded and picked up the bundle. It was a .45 automatic, dark-sheened metal with a brown wood grip. Slipping it free of the cloth, he inspected it briefly, made sure the safety was on, then slipped it into his jacket pocket.

Swift watched him, then picked up his papers again.

'That'll be all,' he said softly.

21

F rank stared out of the window as the car rattled along at speed. They'd been driving less than an hour, but he'd given up asking questions about the operation; Groth's oppressive silence only made the journey seem longer. Sitting beside him in the back, Rafe was yawning. Molly was riding up front with Groth, staring out at the road ahead.

The sleepy little villages that they passed through became smaller, and less frequent, and then the last of them was left behind them as night drew in around them. No more people, no more cars, just the weak illumination of the headlights and the dim glow of the sky on the mountains towering above them. They were climbing now, away from the rolling countryside and up into the steep hills. Peering through the windshield, Frank glimpsed an intricately-painted sign in the glare of the lights, but it was gone too quickly for him to read. Groth slowed a little, dropping a gear and turning off onto a dirt road, narrow and dark, with tall trees on either side.

It was pitch black here, with just a narrow wedge of night sky above and the twin beams searching out the way before them. The road continued to climb for a while, then leveled off abruptly as it opened out into a broad clearing ringed with pine forest. There were several buildings, set back among the trees, but they were all in darkness, angular silhouettes in the gloom. Groth swung the wheel left then right, turning around and slowing, so they stopped with the car facing back the way they'd come. A heavy silence fell as he killed the engine.

Twisting round to peer out of the rear window, Frank could just make out the steeply pitched roof of a large wooden structure, three stories tall, with shuttered windows.

'What is this place?' he asked.

Groth turned and looked at him.

'It's a ski-lodge, but they close it up in the summer months. Usually there would be a... hausmeister?'

'Caretaker,' Frank said.

'Ja, caretaker, but with the war on...' Groth shrugged, then reached for his door handle.

'Are we meeting him inside?' Molly asked, looking at the lodge.

'No. There's a path that leads up to a cabin beyond the first tree line. He's coming from the north so he'll meet us there.' Groth paused, squinting down at his watch. 'We should be going now.'

He opened the door. Frank and the others followed his cue and got out of the car. The night air was cold but fresh, and rich with the scent of the surrounding pine trees. There were two smaller buildings, set on either side of the main lodge: one low and long, the other squat and box-like. As his eyes adjusted to the darkness, Frank began to make out the curve of a huge spoked wheel protruding from the roof of the squat building, and the faint lines of cables disappearing up into the shadows of the mountain skyline.

Standing beside him, Molly was checking her gun. There was a sharp metallic snap as she pulled the slide back, eerily loud against the stillness of the clearing. Groth, who had been staring up at the lodge, turned to Frank.

'You and Mr Cavanagh will wait here. See that nobody comes up behind us, and make sure we still have a way out when we're done. If we're not back in one hour, you take the car and you drive to Herrengasse. Speak to Mr Dulles face-to face; *no* phone calls, understand?' His tone didn't invite any questions.

'Got it.' Frank nodded.

Rafe was glancing around at the dark woods.

'Do you need a torch or anything?' he asked.

'Only to make a signal,' Groth replied. 'Otherwise, it's better not to show everyone where you are.' He turned to Molly. 'Ready?'

Molly slipped her gun inside her coat pocket and lifted her chin.

'Lead the way,' she said.

Frank watched them as they walked across the clearing towards a path near the cable car wheelhouse, the crunch of their footsteps steadily diminishing. A moment later, they disappeared into the shadows beneath the trees, and were gone. Beside him, Rafe turned away and limped over to lean back against the car.

A sigh of wind swirled between them, sending a shiver of rustling movement through the dark trees, before passing away into the distance to leave a deathly quiet.

Frank glanced over at his friend.

'What do you think this is all about?' he whispered.

Rafe lifted his head, then shrugged.

'Dashed if I know. It's Groth's party, and he plays his cards pretty close to his chest.' He hesitated, then lowered his voice. 'But you can bet it's something to do with the German... *situation* that we discussed.'

Frank considered this, then frowned.

'Okay, but why did he take Molly with him? I mean, if it's dangerous...' He trailed off, looking back towards the trees.

'I think Molly's the only one who can identify tonight's visitor,' Rafe said, softly. 'Met him before somewhere.'

Frank nodded to himself then fell silent. Rafe and him were just backup.

Pushing his hands down into his coat pockets, he moved away from the car, his feet crunching slowly on the dirt. Above the trees, he could see the mountains more clearly now, the snow-capped heights still dimly lit by the last light of dusk. He stared up at them, so vast and majestic, trying to judge their true size, wondering about the view from those mighty peaks.

Everything down here so tiny and insignificant.

Rafe stirred and came over to stand beside him.

'Smoke?'

'Thanks,' Frank said. He turned and accepted the cigarette, lifting it to his mouth.

Rafe took one for himself, then struck a match, illuminating his face with a bright warm light.

Somewhere in the distance, there was the sharp crack of a gunshot. It rang out across the silent treetops, echoing back off the mountainside.

Rafe dropped the match and stood blinking in the sudden darkness. Frank whirled around to face the path, his hand going instinctively to his pocket, fingers wrapping themselves into place around the gun.

'That sounded close,' he whispered.

'Shhhh!' Rafe lifted up a hand for silence, and they both stood absolutely still. For a long moment, neither of them breathed as they strained to listen, but there was no noise except a faint rustle of the wind among the trees.

Frank put a hand on his friend's arm.

'What do we do?' he hissed. 'Do we check it out, or stay here?'

'I don't know!' Rafe whispered. 'It didn't sound like it was very far away, but...'

He glanced down at his walking stick then shook his head in frustration.

'Oh hell. You'll be quicker without me.'

Frank looked at him.

'Are you sure?'

'I'll be fine,' Rafe told him. 'Whatever it is, it's happening over there. Just be careful, will you?'

Frank gave a grim nod. Drawing his gun, he jogged stealthily across the clearing, moving on the balls of his feet to lessen the sound, eyes sweeping the darkness before him. Passing in under the shadow of the wheelhouse, he flattened himself in against the side of the wooden building for a moment, listening. Then, he darted quietly over to the beginning of the path and plunged into the gloom. Trees closed in around him as the path climbed, but the ground was soft underfoot here, and soon the only thing he could hear was the sound of his own breathing, nervous and urgent. He crouched low as he ran, trying to see into the blackness between the pines, but it was hard enough to make out the twists and turns of the path. And then, as he rounded a bend, ducking down to avoid a low-hanging branch, he came suddenly to a fork where the way split into two.

No!

Stumbling to a halt, he peered out into the forest shadows, trying to remember which direction the shot had come from, but it was impossible. He couldn't even be sure which way he was facing any more. Standing still, he listened hard for a time, but there was no sound.

What the hell was he supposed to do? Molly and Groth might be in trouble, but if he got it wrong now...

Frustrated, he turned this way and that, pointing his gun at the darkness, straining to see, straining to hear, but there was nothing.

Shit!

Taking a step backwards, he turned and started back along

the path, breaking into a run as he followed it down the slope. He had to get Rafe; maybe they could take one fork each.

Something on the ground caught the tip of his shoe and he went sprawling forward, almost falling but somehow managing to stay on his feet. Cursing under his breath, he slowed his pace a little, watching his footing now, breathing hard. The path led him on, twisting down through the forest, until he glimpsed the dipping black lines of the cables overhead, and the sharp silhouette of the wheelhouse. Bursting into the clearing, he turned towards the car, ready to call for Rafe, but the shout died in his throat as his eyes picked out two shapes in the gloom. Twenty yards in front of him, a dark figure was kneeling over something – no, *someone* – lying on the ground. They were struggling, movements frantic, the prone man's legs kicking at the ground in futile desperation. The kneeling figure hissed something, then grabbed his victim's head and slammed it down hard into the ground, blonde hair shining against the dirt.

Rafe!

Stifling a cry, Frank sprinted forward, leveling his gun at the shadowy attacker.

'Nein!' he screamed. 'Verschwinde! VERSCHWINDE!'

Immediately, the figure twisted round towards him, letting Rafe's head fall back. One hand went to his coat and there was a momentary gleam of light on the barrel of a pistol...

Frank squeezed the trigger hard. The muzzle flash burned bright against the darkness, and the recoil slowed him, as the deafening noise of the shot echoed up into the night sky.

A second flash erupted from his gun, a second booming report, as he closed the distance between them... then a third, and this time he saw the dark figure jerk backwards, slowly pitching over to slump onto the ground and lie still. Frank descended on him, kicking his pistol skittering away across the ground, but the man was finished, his pale face slackening into a vacant expression, unseeing eyes staring upwards as a dark stain bloomed out across the front of his shirt. A last bubbling rasp escaped his lips and he fell silent.

Wrenching his gaze away, Frank turned his attention to Rafe, crouching down to place a hand on his friend's shoulder.

'Hey buddy, you okay?'

Rafe's eyes were closed. There was a nasty-looking cut on his cheekbone, and blood glistened on his busted lip. He didn't respond.

'*Rafe?*'

Kneeling down, Frank eased a hand under the back of his neck, trying to cradle his head, then felt the sticky warmth in Rafe's hair as it spread over his fingers.

Oh please, no...

'Come on,' he pleaded. 'Say something, will you?'

Nothing.

A cold dread began to grip him. He tried to find a pulse – first at the wrist, then at the throat – but his own heart was pounding so hard that he couldn't feel anything else. In desperation, he leaned right down, putting his cheek close to Rafe's open mouth... then sighed with relief as he sensed the faint warmth on his face. His friend was breathing.

It seemed like hours before he heard the others returning. Over at the edge of the clearing, Groth emerged from the path, followed by Molly; both were grim faced, both had their guns drawn.

Seeing him on his knees, Groth hurried over, and stared down at Rafe.

'Scheiße!' he growled. 'Is he alive?'

'Yes,' Frank said. 'He's hurt but he's breathing.'

Molly halted a few feet away, an anguished expression on her face.

'What happened?' she demanded.

'We heard a gunshot,' Frank explained, motioning back towards the path. 'Rafe said to go and see if you two were okay.'

Groth glared at him, then turned away, his eyes sweeping warily round the clearing.

'You left him alone!' he hissed.

'I know, but...' Frank shook his head. 'Anyway, I went up the trail but when I came to the fork, I didn't know which way to go. I listened but I couldn't hear anything, so I came back here. That's when I saw *him*.'

He pointed over at the corpse. Molly walked around him to peer down at the body.

'He was on top of Rafe, smacking him into the ground.' Frank bowed his head. 'I... I think I yelled at him, but he pulled a gun on me, so I shot him.'

Scowling, Groth glanced over at Molly.

'Is he dead?' he asked her.

'Yes,' she replied.

'Any idea who he was?'

'A friend of the one *we* met, I should think,' she said, turning back to look anxiously at Rafe.

Groth shook his head slowly.

'What a damn mess.' He stood for a moment, deep in thought, then turned and pointed down at Rafe. 'Get him in the car. And check him over, make sure he isn't bleeding!'

Nodding numbly, Frank scrambled to his feet and, with Molly's help, managed to get his hands under Rafe's armpits. Half lifting, half dragging, they managed to haul their friend across to the car. Molly stretched out and opened the door.

'Gently,' she warned. 'Careful with him.'

Straining together, they lifted him and bundled him into the back seat.

Frank straightened up, breathing hard, but Molly immediately ushered him aside.

'Let me see him,' she insisted, quickly unbuttoning Rafe's shirt and sliding a hand inside to check for other injuries.

'Mr Rye,' Groth called softly. 'Give her some room. You can come and help me with this one.'

Frank looked round, then walked back across the clearing to where Groth was crouching down, going through the dead man's pockets.

'What are we going to do with him?' he asked.

Groth didn't answer. Standing up, he walked a few paces away, then stooped again to retrieve the attacker's gun. Studying it for a moment, he frowned, then slipped it into his coat pocket.

Frank was staring at the body. The dark patch had spread all across the dead man's shirt now, gleaming wetly in the faint light. The face, still staring upwards, looked so ordinary...

'Hey!' Groth was standing beside him, snapping his fingers impatiently. 'Get his legs.'

'Sorry.' Frank bent down, flinching as he touched the lifeless ankles, realizing he had to adopt a stronger hold. Grimacing, he forced himself to grip more tightly, his fingers pressing into the dead skin.

'You have him?' Groth asked, taking the dead man's wrists.

Wordlessly, Frank nodded.

'Okay then...' Groth grunted.

Together, they lifted the corpse, struggling as it sagged between them. It seemed unnaturally heavy, and Frank strained to keep it off the ground.

'Over there.' Groth indicated with his head. 'In the trees.'

They scuffed their way slowly across the dirt, hauling their burden up and over the grass at the edge of the clearing. Stumbling on beneath the shadow of the branches, pine needles soft underfoot, Groth finally dumped the body down behind a large tree, leaving it sitting propped up against a broad trunk.

'Good enough,' he muttered, straightening up and rubbing the base of his back.

The dead man's eyes were still open, staring out into the darkness. Frank shivered and looked away.

They started back towards the car. Groth paused at the edge of the trees, turning around and listening, then stepped into the clearing.

'You took his gun,' Frank whispered. He wasn't sure why he said it.

'Ja,' Groth said, walking ahead of him. 'We make use of it. Next time we have to shoot someone, if a German gun can be found beside the body... well, it gives the police something to think about.'

Molly stepped away from the car as they approached, her face troubled.

'Well?' Groth asked.

'Nothing other than the head wound,' she replied. 'But that looks *really* bad. I'm worried he may have fractured his skull.'

Groth's expression darkened and he clenched his fists. For a moment, it seemed as though he might be about to yell, but instead he lapsed into a brooding silence. Finally, glancing down at his watch, he appeared to reach a decision.

'Let's go,' he snapped, walking round and pulling open the driver's door. 'I was thinking maybe Basel, but it has to be the hospital in Bern. Come on; we work out how we deal with this on the way.'

Molly glanced at Rafe, lying slumped in the back of the car, then turned to Frank.

'You get in on this side of him, and I'll go on the other, so we can hold him steady, all right?'

'No problem,' Frank told her.

Groth started the car and the headlights blazed out, piercing the darkness and lighting up the gap at the bottom of the clearing. Lurching forward, they set off at speed, the car bouncing down the narrow dirt road.

Sitting in the back seat, holding their friend between them,

Molly met Frank's gaze for a moment, but quickly looked away. Turning her body towards Rafe, she smiled at him and murmured, 'Just sit back and enjoy the ride, you careless clod. You're going to be all right.'

But Frank had seen the fear in her eyes. He stared out at the winding road ahead of them, and willed Groth to drive faster.

22

The city was in darkness as they rounded a long downhill bend and raced past the first outlying houses.

'Not far now,' Groth called over his shoulder. 'How's he doing?'

'Just the same,' Frank said, his arm around Rafe's neck, keeping him upright.

'Okay,' Groth growled, accelerating slightly. 'You need to take his gun and any papers or identification out of his pockets. And clean him up a little, get some of the mud off.'

Frank turned to Molly and frowned. The gun and the papers made sense, but why did they have to clean him up?

'There'll be questions at the hospital,' she explained. 'We can't tell them where he really was or what he was doing so... oh, I don't know... we'll say it happened somewhere in the city... he got into a fight, or had a fall...'

'Say you were *told* he fell, but you didn't see it,' Groth called back. 'You *think* he had been drinking but you're not sure. The less specific you are, the better for everyone.'

Molly nodded thoughtfully, then looked hard at Frank.

'It happened down by the river somewhere... there's trees and grass down there and that'll help explain the mud.' She leaned over and began emptying Rafe's pockets, then glanced up again. 'Oh, and we flagged down a passing car to bring him up to the hospital, all right?'

'Okay,' Frank murmured. Bracing himself against the door, he held Rafe steady with one hand, and tentatively reached into his friend's pants pocket with the other.

They skirted around the northern side of the old town, rattling down a succession of empty cobbled streets, before sweeping round onto a bridge that crossed the railroad tracks. Groth flung the car through a couple more sharp corners before turning into a gated driveway, the headlights illuminating a large signboard that bore the words *Inselspital Bern* below the hospital crest. They pulled up in front of a modern concrete building, very long and several stories high. Blackout blinds gave the place a foreboding appearance, but there was a dim light visible at the entrance porch.

Groth left the engine running and twisted round to look at Rafe.

'Let me know how it goes,' he said.

'Aren't you coming in?' Frank asked, reaching for the door handle.

Groth shook his head.

'I have to go and tell Mr Dulles what's happened, that everything is screwed,' he said, frowning. 'I should probably have gone there first, but...'

Molly reached forward and placed a hand on Groth's arm.

'Thank you,' she said. '*Really.*'

Groth met her gaze, then looked away.

'Go on,' he muttered. 'And call the Herrengasse number when you have any news.'

Frank clambered out and, looping Rafe's arm around his neck, managed to maneuver him from the car. Molly slid across the back seat after him. Stepping out, she draped Rafe's other arm over her shoulder to prop him up, then pushed the car door closed with her foot.

'Can you manage?' she asked, as they struggled with their unconscious companion.

'Yeah,' Frank grunted, starting slowly towards the entrance. 'Just help make sure I don't drop him.'

It was well after midnight. Frank and Molly sat side by side on a row of four wooden chairs, wedged against the wall of a long, empty corridor. The whole place stank of disinfectant. Rafe had been lifted onto a stretcher and wheeled away almost as soon as they arrived, while they'd been left to fill out some paperwork with a yawning nurse. Now, they'd been sent here to wait.

'You okay?' Frank asked, breaking the silence. His voice echoed off the bare walls.

'Yes,' Molly said woodenly, her eyes staring straight ahead.

Somewhere nearby a door slammed, and they heard the sound of footsteps on the hard, polished floors, but the footsteps were receding, and soon they were left alone in the oppressive stillness once again.

Frank watched her for a while, then leaned forward to rest his forearms across his knees.

'I'm really sorry,' he said. 'I feel so bad about all this.'

Molly said nothing for a moment, then turned towards him.

'What do you mean?' she asked.

Frank bowed his head.

'It was a mistake. I should never have left him there on his own.' He paused, then sighed. 'I'm the reason he's in here now.'

'Don't be silly.' She bent down to meet his eye. 'You *saved* him, Frank. You're the reason he's still alive.'

Frank glanced up and gave her a grateful smile.

'I just *wish*...' He broke off, lowering his eyes. 'We heard that gunshot and I really didn't know what to do.'

'How *could* you know?' Molly said. She leaned back against the wall, and a bitter note crept into her voice. 'It was a setup, the whole *bloody* thing... and we walked right into it.'

Frank turned his head.

'What?'

Molly hesitated, then looked away.

'Tonight. Someone set us up. They were waiting for us.'

Frank was stunned.

'But what about the guy you were meeting?' he asked.

Molly shrugged to herself.

'Dead, probably. I don't know if they followed him to the rendezvous and killed him there, or if they picked him up earlier and...' She shook her head.

'There were two of them?' Frank asked. 'Bad guys, I mean.'

'That's right.'

'And the gunshot we heard?'

Molly looked at him, then got to her feet and smoothed down her skirt.

'The gunshot was mine.'

She turned on her heel and began pacing slowly back and forth along the corridor.

Frank watched her as she walked, her footsteps tapping out a steady rhythm, her fists clenching and unclenching as she moved. When she turned to come back, he looked away for a moment, then glanced up as she drew level with him.

'I'm sure he's gonna be okay,' he told her.

Molly stopped and looked at him, then silently nodded.

'I can tell you care about him,' Frank said gently.

She stared down the corridor, her eyes distant.

'Yes,' she whispered. 'Very much.'

Frank stared at her. He'd never seen this side of Molly before. Was there maybe something going on between her and Rafe?

'You two are...' He hesitated, unsure how to say it. '...close?'

Molly's brow wrinkled briefly into a puzzled frown, then she seemed to catch his meaning and gave him a curious glance.

'No,' she said, a faint smiling playing on her lips. 'I don't think I'm quite his type.'

'Sorry,' Frank said. 'I didn't mean to–'

'He's like a little brother,' Molly explained. She sat down again, a wistful expression on her face. 'An infuriating, stupid little brother but...'

'...but you care about him, right?' Frank finished for her.

'Yes,' she said, softly. 'I can trust him.'

They sat in silence for a moment, then Frank turned to look at her.

'You trust *me*, don't you?' he asked.

Molly turned her face to his, then reached over and squeezed his arm.

'I do now,' she said.

Brisk footsteps echoed along the corridor, and Molly jerked her head up from resting on Frank's shoulder. A nurse was approaching. They jumped to their feet, trying to read something in her expression as she made her way towards them, but then she smiled and they both sighed with relief.

'Ihrem Freund wird es bald besser gehen,' the nurse explained. *Your friend is going to be fine.*

'Thank God,' Frank said, grinning.

'May we see him?' Molly asked.

The nurse looked at her kindly.

'The doctor has given him something to make him sleep, but I'll show you where he is so you can see he is all right. You may visit him in the morning.'

They emerged from the hospital entrance and stood for a

moment, looking out at the dark buildings silhouetted against the night sky. Molly pulled her coat tight around her and shivered.

'I'm glad Groth told us to dress warmly.'

'It's gotten cold,' Frank agreed. He glanced down at his watch. 'C'mon, I'll walk you home.'

Molly tilted her head to one side.

'Are you sure?' she asked. 'I doubt it's any more dangerous than where we were earlier, and I *am* armed.'

'I just...' Frank hesitated, realizing how foolish he sounded. 'I was just trying to be gentlemanly.'

Molly's expression softened.

'That's very sweet of you.' She took his arm. 'If you really don't mind?'

'It'd be my pleasure,' he said. 'Besides, I don't really think I'm ready to turn in yet, after everything that's happened. My head's still spinning, you know?'

Molly looked up at him and nodded.

'I know,' she said quietly. 'Come on, it isn't far.'

They set off, passing out through the gates and into the sleeping city.

Molly's lodgings were in an imposing old villa on Waldheim-strasse, five stories tall with ornate stone detailing around the doors and windows, ringed with black iron railings.

'Nice place,' Frank said, staring up at the building as they stood together on the sidewalk.

'My room's at the back, on the third floor,' Molly explained. She gazed at him for a moment, then added, 'Did you want to come up for a drink? I think we both probably deserve one.'

Frank hesitated, glancing up at the shuttered windows. What would people think if they saw Molly taking a man upstairs so late at night?

'Are you sure it's okay?' he stammered. 'I wouldn't want to... you know... get you into any trouble.'

Molly gave him a bashful smile.

'There's a fire escape at the rear of the building,' she told him. 'It's very discreet.'

They made their way around to the back of the villa and slipped through a small gate in the railings. Molly led the way as they crept up the steep metal steps, then paused at a darkened window and placed the palms of her hands flat on the glass.

'There's no latch,' she whispered, then gave an upward shove. The window slid up a little, and she bent down, slipping her fingers into the gap to haul it fully open. Frank watched as she ducked inside, then reappeared at the window and beckoned him in.

Glancing back over his shoulder, Frank lifted his foot over the sill and climbed through into the shadowy room.

'Close the window and get the blind,' Molly told him, 'then I can put the light on.'

'Sure.' Frank slid the window shut, then found the blackout blind and pulled it into place. 'All done.'

'Thanks,' Molly said, and there was a click as warm light filled the room. She was standing beside a beautiful old writing desk with a tall electric lamp perched on it. 'Well? What do you think?'

Frank turned around. Molly's lodgings appeared to be a single high-ceilinged room, with a makeshift blue curtain dividing the narrow space into living and sleeping areas. At this end, there was a little round table with a white vase of drooping wildflowers and, by the door, a tall closet made of dark wood with elegantly carved double doors. To his right, he noted a small stove, with an enamel sink beside it. The exposed pipework looked recent.

'It's a lot nicer than my place over on Bantigerstrasse,' he told her.

'Thanks.' She smiled. 'But don't stand there, looming by the window. Have a seat and make yourself comfortable.'

There was a pile of folded clothes on the chair by the table, so he sat by the desk, turning his chair to face into the room.

'Sorry!' Molly gathered up the clothes and took them over to the closet. 'I don't have many guests here, I'm afraid.'

'It's okay.' Frank grinned. His gaze drifted past her, to the bed, just visible behind the blue curtain. There appeared to be a small rug on the polished wooden floor, and she'd hung a tiny picture on the wall above, but he couldn't make out what it was.

'Is gin all right?' Molly said, walking over and setting a bottle on the table. 'I'm afraid it's that or nothing.'

'Gin is fine,' Frank told her, reaching over and turning the bottle round so he could read the label. 'I got introduced to it while I was stationed over in England.'

'It reminds me of parties before the war,' Molly said softly, her back to him as she rinsed a couple of glasses in the sink. 'Whereabouts in England were you?'

'A town called Salisbury, but we weren't there long before they shipped us out again.'

'Oh, Wiltshire's lovely.' Molly brought the glasses over to the table, and poured them each a generous measure. 'Here's to home.'

Frank took his glass and clinked it against hers.

'Home,' he said, and knocked the gin back.

Molly sat down and sipped her drink, looking at him thoughtfully.

'How are you feeling now?' she asked. 'Head still spinning?'

Frank smiled and stared down at his glass.

'I'm okay, I guess,' he said, images of the clearing still flashing in his mind. 'It was... well, it was quite an evening, that's all.'

Molly nodded.

'Were you scared?' she asked softly.

Frank glanced up to meet her steady gaze, then looked away again.

'It's different than I expected,' he murmured. 'We saw plenty of action when our unit was in France, but this...'

He trailed off.

'I was scared too,' Molly told him. 'I think there'd be some-thing wrong with us if we weren't.'

She picked up the bottle and leaned across with it.

'Another?'

Frank raised his head, then pushed his glass towards her.

'I just don't know how I feel about it,' he said, wearily rubbing his eyes. 'I thought this was going to be some real death and glory stuff, you know, make a real difference to the war... and it kinda was, and we took out the Nazis, but...' He shook his head, remem-bering the dead weight of the corpse, the body whose life he'd snuffed out. 'It doesn't feel glorious, that's for sure.'

Molly poured another shot of gin. Her eyes shone as she slid his glass back across the table.

'You're a good man, Frank.'

He took the glass and raised it to her with a shy smile.

'To absent glory,' he said.

'Absent glory,' she repeated.

They sat quietly, sipping their drinks, until Frank glanced down at his watch.

'Well,' he said, swallowing the last of his gin. 'I should proba-bly...' He nodded towards the window.

Molly set her glass down on the table.

'Oh dear,' she said. 'I feel bad that I've brought you all the way over to the wrong side of the city.'

Frank's heart sank as it dawned on him how far he'd have to walk.

'It's no problem,' he assured her, getting to his feet.

Molly lowered her eyes.

'You could always sleep here,' she suggested. 'If you wanted to.'

Caught off guard, Frank stared at her for a moment, then glanced around the room.

'Er, I guess,' he said, looking doubtfully at the hard wooden floor. 'I could curl up in a corner somewhere.'

'If you like,' Molly said slowly. 'Or you could sleep in my bed if you'd rather?'

'In your bed?' he stammered.

Molly stood up and walked over to him.

'But I think you should probably kiss me first,' she said, her eyes twinkling as she took his hand. 'If we're going to sleep together.'

Her lips were soft and warm, and he closed his eyes, feeling her hands on his face as she pulled him close. For a moment, he was lost, overwhelmed by the sensation of her, then he felt himself growing hard and kissed her eagerly.

When he opened his eyes, her upturned face was close, and he could feel her breath on his skin. Arms around his neck, her eyes sparkled with a joyous mischief, and she suddenly drew him forward again, kissing him and playfully biting his lower lip.

'Take your clothes off,' she whispered.

He lost all sense of time. Later, when he finally gasped and collapsed on top of her, he felt her hands pressing down on his back, her legs wrapped around him, holding him tight for a moment more, before she relaxed and slumped back onto the sheets. Breathing hard, Frank propped himself up to gaze down at her.

Molly's eyes were closed, an expression of calm settling on her face as she sighed, stretching her arms up against the bed frame and slowly pointing her fingers towards the ceiling.

He stared at her for a long time, noticing the slight curve of her eyelashes, the shape of her mouth, the way her hair shone as it spilled out across the pillow. Then he leaned down to gently kiss her forehead. Molly's eyes fluttered open, and she gazed up at him with a smile.

'I just...' He hesitated, lost in her eyes. 'I don't know what to say.'

Molly's expression changed.

'Oh, Frank.' She put a hand to her mouth, covering her smile. 'That wasn't your first time, was it?'

'Of course not.' Blushing deeply, he bowed his head beside hers, thinking back to teenage fumbling at the county fair, and that long afternoon with Emily Walker in the hayloft on her father's farm.

'Frank?' Molly's finger traced a lazy spiral in the small of his back.

'No, really. It's just...' He faltered, suddenly aware of being still inside her.

'Just what?' she pressed.

Frank withdrew himself, then sat back on the bed, looking at her.

'You're so... calm,' he said. 'So matter-of-fact about it.'

Molly arched an eyebrow at him.

'Didn't you want to do it?' she asked.

Frank smiled helplessly.

'Yes of course, I just...'

'I wanted to do it too,' she soothed him. 'So what's the problem?'

'No problem, I just didn't expect it.'

Molly propped herself up into a sitting position, then scooted her naked body closer to his.

'You're very sweet,' she said, a hint of sadness in her eyes as she stretched out her hand to caress his cheek. 'And life is so *very* short. Don't you think we ought to enjoy the time we have?'

Frank met her gaze, then nodded.

'Yes,' he said, softly. 'I do.'

She smiled and reached down between his legs.

'Then kiss me again, Frank.'

23

Frank slowly surfaced into wakefulness. He was lying in a strange position, sheets bunched up against his back and his arm draped over something warm. He opened his eyes, blinking against the sliver of bright light that streamed in from a gap at the edge of the blackout blind... and remembered.

Molly. Her bare shoulder was just visible above the sheets, a mass of dark hair tangled on the pillow. He became aware of her breathing, the warmth of her naked body curled against his skin, and he sighed with contentment.

Had this really happened? It seemed impossible, and yet, here they were...

He went to lean back, but felt the chill of cold plaster on his shoulder, and remembered that Molly's bed was pushed up against the wall. Turning his head, he gazed up at the little picture, pinned above the bed: a blurry photograph of a small house – English, by the look of it – set on a grassy hill above a rocky sea shore. He squinted at it in the gloom, wondering about it, then felt Molly stir beneath his arm.

'Morning,' he whispered, gently hugging her.

She rolled over, a slight frown relaxing into a sleepy smile as she peered up at him.

'Good morning,' she said, hesitating for a moment, then lifting her head to kiss him lightly. 'What time is it?'

Frank turned to search for his watch, bumping into the wall again before remembering to check his wrist.

'Five after seven,' he yawned. 'Man, I feel like I've hardly slept at all.'

Molly groaned and slumped back onto the pillow, staring up at the shadows on the ceiling.

'We *did* hardly sleep at all,' she reminded him with a sheepish grin. 'But I suppose we'd better get up.'

Yawning, she threw the sheets aside and twisted away from him, rolling herself slowly into a sitting position on the edge of the small bed. Frank watched as she reached up and stretched, staring at the smooth lines of her silhouette.

'Oh damn, these are all crumpled.'

She stooped, retrieving her skirt and jacket from the floor, then stood up stiffly, trying to shake the creases out.

Frank sat up, rubbing one hand through his hair, the other keeping the sheets in place to cover his morning erection. Molly finished draping her clothes over the back of the chair, then turned towards him and smiled.

'It's a bit late for us to be shy with one another, don't you think?'

Frank gazed at her naked body, then lowered his eyes.

'I guess so.'

Sliding out from under the sheets, he twisted himself around and dropped his feet onto the small rug. If Molly noticed his arousal, she was too polite to mention it, busying herself around the room, taking a silk robe from the closet and slipping it on. Frank gathered up his things from the floor and quickly started to dress.

'Oh...' Molly was staring at him, a frown on her face.

Frank looked up from pulling on his pants.

'What is it?' he asked.

Molly bit her lip.

'I'm just wondering how we're going to sneak you along the hall to the bathroom without anyone seeing you.'

It was a bright, crisp morning as Frank stepped down from the fire escape and walked calmly round to the street. Standing on the sidewalk, he lit a cigarette and glanced along the road. There was a low wall around the front of the building opposite, so he crossed over and sat down to wait for Molly. She emerged from the front door a few minutes later, smartly dressed and professional-looking, falling in beside him and explaining the quickest route to the hospital. Suddenly she was the Molly he'd known *before*; just like that, the woman he'd woken up with was gone.

They walked down the quiet, tree-lined road and along the side of a sunken railroad yard, not really speaking now, just two colleagues going to visit a friend. As they followed the sidewalk up onto the bridge, a train passed beneath them, rattling along the tracks that curved away through the town. Not far ahead, the familiar shape of the hospital building was visible above the railroad sheds.

Molly slowed her pace a little.

'I was thinking,' she said. 'It might be better if we didn't arrive together.'

She looked at him for a moment, then added, 'More discreet?'

Frank frowned, then nodded as he understood.

'Sure,' he said. It made sense.

Molly gave him a bashful smile.

'I'd really rather that none of the others knew about...' She looked down. 'Well, about last night.'

'Of course,' Frank told her, but his heart sank a little. Was she beginning to have regrets about what they'd done?

'No hinting, no boys' gossip... not even to Rafe, all right?'

'Not a word from me,' he assured her, trying to smile. 'And no ladies' gossip to Jean.'

Molly's expression grew distant.

'I certainly wouldn't confide in Jean,' she said.

Passing on over the bridge, they followed the road round towards the hospital, then stopped at the curb opposite the main gates.

Turning to face him, Molly reached out to fix his collar and straighten his jacket. Then, she lifted her face and gazed deep into his eyes.

'We'll carry on at work like before?' she pressed him. 'As though nothing happened?'

'As though nothing happened,' Frank promised sadly. She'd made a mistake with him, understandable after everything that had happened yesterday...

But Molly's eyes were twinkling.

'Good,' she said. 'I'm busy tonight, but maybe tomorrow evening after work, or the weekend, maybe we could see each other then?' She lowered her eyes. 'If you like?'

'I... yeah,' Frank stammered, then grinned foolishly at her. 'Of course I'd like that.'

Molly's face broke into a bright smile. Standing quickly on tiptoes, she surprised him with a brief kiss, then stepped back from him.

'Wait a quarter of an hour, then come up to the ward, all right?'

'Fifteen minutes. Okay.'

Molly flashed a mischievous grin at him, then turned and hurried across the road towards the hospital gates.

Frank made his way along the echoing hospital corridor, retracing his steps from the night before. Turning a corner, he pushed through a set of swing doors and stopped beside a long desk where a nurse was busily noting something in a journal.

'Ja?' she said, glancing up at him.

'Ich bin hier, um Herrn Cavanagh zu sehen,' he told her. *I came to visit Mr Cavanagh.*

Nodding, the nurse closed the journal and got to her feet.

'Warten Sie bitte hier,' she told him. *Wait here please.*

Frank turned away as she bustled through another set of doors onto the ward. Walking over to the window, he stared out across the outbuildings and houses with their steeply-pitched roofs, his eyes resting on the snow-capped mountains, hazy and distant. Were those the same peaks he stared up at last night? Was there a dead man somewhere out there, sitting with his back to a tree?

Behind him, he heard footsteps and turned around to find Swift holding the door open for the nurse.

'Danke.' She smiled, returning to her desk.

Surprised, Frank walked over to him.

'Good morning,' he said.

'Morning,' Swift replied. 'How are you?'

'Er...' Frank's eyes flickered to the nurse, who was watching them. 'Okay, I guess.'

'Good.' Swift stepped forward, smoothly placing a hand on Frank's arm. 'Molly's in with him just now. Why don't we step out for a quick word before I go back to the office?'

He glanced meaningfully towards the exit.

'Uh, sure,' Frank replied.

Swift guided him back out into the empty corridor, letting the doors swing shut behind them.

'How's he doing?' Frank asked, worried. 'Is he okay?'

'Rafe's just fine.' Swift smiled. 'He's sitting up and cracking jokes. But how are *you*?'

Relieved, Frank turned away, then shrugged his shoulders.

'I'm okay,' he said, quietly. 'You heard what happened?'

'I did.' Swift's expression became serious. 'If it wasn't for you, we'd have lost a good man last night.'

Frank looked down.

'Thanks,' he said. 'I didn't feel like I had much of a choice.'

'Of course,' Swift told him. 'There was nothing else you could have done.'

'I guess...' Frank trailed off, remembering the glare of the muzzle flash, the figure pitching backwards, the dead eyes staring out into the night.

'Did he say anything?'

Frank glanced up.

'Who?'

'The guy you fragged,' Swift continued. 'He was German, right?'

Frank paused and frowned.

'I assume so,' he replied. 'He had a German gun.'

'But he didn't say anything?'

'It all happened really fast.' Frank looked at him, then lowered his eyes. 'I hardly had time to think, and then... well, it was done.'

Swift listened, nodding.

'Did you see the other one?' he asked. 'The one that Molly got?'

Frank shook his head.

'No, they went off to their meeting alone,' he explained. 'I didn't see anything.'

Swift considered this for a moment.

'Well, like I said, it's a good job you were there.' He clapped Frank on the back, then inclined his head towards the door. 'I'll let you go and see Rafe. Oh, and Dulles wanted a word with you, so maybe stop off at Herrengasse on your way back, okay?'

'Okay.' Frank turned back to the ward.

.   .   .

Molly stood with her arms folded, scowling down at Rafe, who was sitting propped up in bed. He had a large white bandage wrapped around his head, and his blond hair poked out from the top, giving him a comical appearance.

'Ah, there you are, thank goodness!' he beamed at Frank, then jerked a thumb towards Molly. 'Come and tell this frightful old battle-axe to stop grumbling at me.'

'*Grumbling?* I was simply telling him that he shouldn't have been so... so *reckless!*' Molly shook her head in exasperation, then sighed, composing herself. 'Good morning, Frank. How are you?'

Frank moved round to stand by the bed.

'Well, I'm a little tired, but I'm okay,' he told her, then turned to Rafe. 'And how about you?'

'Oh, you know, just a little delicate,' Rafe chuckled. 'A couple of aspirins and I'll be right as rain.'

'You're lucky you weren't *killed*,' Molly snapped at him.

Rafe's grin faded a little, and he shut his eyes for second, then reached over to take her hand in his.

'I'm sorry, old girl,' he whispered, gazing up at her. 'But I was worried about you, and Frank was always going to get there quicker.'

'But...' Molly stared down at him. 'None of us was meant to be alone.'

'I know,' he said, gently. 'But if the situation had been reversed, *you'd* have come running for *me*, alone or not.'

They looked at each other for a long moment, then Molly sighed.

'You're impossible,' she muttered, then turned to Frank. 'Maybe *you* can drum some sense into him, but I've got to get to the office. There's heaps of work to do, and Captain Bedrest won't be pulling his weight for a while.'

Her voice was angry, but Frank could sense her relief and, as she turned her back on the bed, she gave him a tiny secret smile.

'I'll see you back at Dufourstrasse,' she said, then glanced over her shoulder at Rafe. 'And I'll catch up with *you* later!'

They watched her as she walked briskly to the end of the ward and disappeared through the double doors.

'Think I'm going to be in the doghouse for a bit,' Rafe sighed.

'She's just worried about you.' Frank smiled. He moved closer and sat down on the edge of the bed. 'How are you *really* feeling?'

A weariness crept into Rafe's expression, and he reached up gingerly to touch his bandaged head.

'Well, I shall never complain about a hangover ever again,' he said, wincing. 'Tell me, what the hell did that wretched kraut hit me with?'

'He was banging your head on the ground when I got there.'

'Oh.' Rafe took a deep breath. 'That explains a lot. And I understand I have you to thank for saving me?'

'How'd you know about that?'

'Swift filled me in on the some of the salient points.'

Frank lowered his eyes.

'The whole thing was a mistake,' he muttered. 'I never should have gone off and left you on your own.'

'Now, don't *you* start with that nonsense,' Rafe interrupted him. 'Molly and Groth will have plenty to say on the matter, just as soon as I'm deemed well enough to receive their wrath. I want you on *my* side.'

Frank managed an unhappy smile.

'Sorry. Last night was just...' He trailed off and shook his head.

'I know.' All the joking silliness was gone from Rafe's voice now. 'And I expect it must have shaken you up a bit. Was it your first time?'

Frank raised his head, staring at Rafe, then realized what he was talking about.

'Killing someone?' He paused, then looked away. 'I don't

know... maybe. There was a time back in France when my unit was trying to clear a village...'

He remembered the crack of gunfire, the determined kick of the rifle against his shoulder... and the strangely conflicted feelings when that distant, grey-uniformed figure had finally stopped shooting back. Relief, elation, and a sickening sense of regret.

Rafe took a breath and sighed.

'Them or us, him or me... that's the trouble with this damn war.' He reached over and patted Frank's hand. 'Sometimes, the *right* thing to do is still a terrible thing to do.'

24

The streetcar doors swung open and Frank stepped down onto the sidewalk, stifling a yawn. Seeing Rafe had lifted his spirits but a deep weariness was beginning to take hold of him, and he wasn't looking forward to what he assumed would be a grilling from Dulles. Pale grey clouds rolled across the sky as he walked briskly past the Zytglogge clock tower and on towards Herrengasse.

A maid opened the door to him, but he was expected and she showed him through to the ground floor study where Dulles waved him in with an impatient gesture.

'Come in, Mr Rye,' he said, then turned to the maid. 'That'll be all, Anja.'

Frank nodded to the maid, who withdrew and pulled the door closed. When he turned around, he found Dulles staring at him critically.

'You look a mess, son.'

'Sir?' Frank blinked at him.

Dulles pointed a finger.

'The knees of your pants have mud on them, and your shoes need a shine.'

Frank looked down.

'Sorry, I–' He was about to say *haven't been home* but caught himself just in time. 'I stayed late at the hospital last night, and then this morning I was in a hurry to get over there and see Rafe...'

'I understand all that,' Dulles snapped, shaking his head irritably. 'But you have to assume that you're under surveillance, and there's no surer way to advertise that you were up to something clandestine last night. Why, you might as well wear a sandwich board and parade around the Bundesplatz.'

'I'll clean myself up,' Frank promised.

'Do it before you leave here; Anja will show you where the washroom is.' He turned and walked over to one of the chairs by the fireplace, gesturing towards the other. 'Now, come and sit down. I want to know what the hell happened last night.'

Frank moved across and sat down. Dulles immediately leaned forward, light gleaming off his spectacles.

'So. Four of you went to make a collection. You came back with nothing, and one of you actually ended up in hospital...' He narrowed his eyes. 'What went wrong?'

Taken aback by the abrupt question, Frank hesitated, then shrugged his shoulders.

'Er... they knew we were coming, I guess,' he said. 'They were waiting for us.'

'Is that your own theory?' Dulles demanded. 'Or are you repeating someone else's speculation?'

Frank met his eye, unimpressed by the suggestion that he couldn't think for himself.

'My own theory,' he replied, a little stiffly. 'But I expect everyone will be thinking the same thing.'

'Yes,' Dulles agreed, his voice becoming soft. 'I daresay they will.'

He leaned back and settled into his chair, pushing his glasses back up his nose, and studied Frank carefully.

'Exactly when was it decided that Mr Cavanagh and yourself should remain with the automobile?'

Frank considered this.

'When we arrived at the ski lodge,' he replied. 'We stopped in the clearing and got out. Groth told us to wait while he and Molly went to meet the contact at a cabin, somewhere nearby.'

'Did you object to this plan? Dulles enquired.

'No.'

'Did you think it was strange?'

'No...' Frank hesitated. 'Well, I did wonder why Groth was taking Molly with him, but Rafe said something about her being able to identify the courier.'

Dulles nodded to himself.

'So you had no issue with the plan,' he mused. 'And yet, a few moments later, you decided to set off through the woods. On your own.'

'We heard a gunshot,' Frank explained, as patiently as he could. 'And *I* didn't decide, Rafe *told* me to go.'

Dulles watched him with unblinking eyes.

'It was fortunate for him that you chose to come back when you did.'

There was an unspoken suspicion in his tone.

'I couldn't find the others, so I turned around and went back.' Frank scowled. 'When I got to the clearing, I saw a man attacking Rafe.'

Dulles paused for a moment, then drew a deep breath and sighed.

'Did you *have* to shoot him?' he asked.

Frank bristled.

'With respect, yes I did. He was trying to kill Rafe and he pulled a gun on me–'

'Did he shoot at you?' Dulles demanded, leaning forward suddenly.

'No, but–'

'Why not?' Dulles interrupted again.

'Because I shot him first,' Frank snapped.

They stared at each other for a moment, then Dulles allowed himself a faint smile.

'I see,' he murmured. Leaning back, he patted the arms of his chair thoughtfully. 'Well, that's *something*, I suppose.'

Sensing that the mood in the room had somehow changed, Frank also leaned back.

'I'm not sure I understand,' he said cautiously.

'You didn't hesitate,' Dulles explained. 'And you seem to know which side you're on, which is more than some people do.'

'Sir?'

Dulles raised a weary eyebrow to admonish him for saying "Sir", then got to his feet and walked over to the window. Pulling the tall drapes further apart, he gazed down at the river.

'Last night's operation was compromised, there's no getting away from that,' he said. 'And "compromised" really means "betrayed", though in this case we don't know whether they betrayal happened at their end or...'

Frank watched him. *At their end... or ours?*

Dulles straightened, and turned around to face him.

'Now then,' he continued. 'Thanks to you, Mr Cavanagh survived his encounter with the enemy. However, we must assume that our contact was less fortunate. And if *he's* blown, I have to ask myself what portion of his own contacts – his network – is also blown.'

Frank considered this.

'Can you find out?' he said.

Dulles looked at him thoughtfully.

'I'm afraid it's not quite as easy as that,' he sighed. 'You see, if there's ever any question about someone's integrity, or their status, or their loyalty... well, that's the end of it.'

Frank stared at him.

'You *don't* hesitate,' Dulles explained. 'You *can't* give them the opportunity to do more damage. Understand?'

Frank nodded uncertainly.

'So you just... shut down those parts of the network?' he said.

'That depends.' Dulles turned back to face the window again. 'If you think they have the trust of the other side, you might feed them false information so they mislead their masters. In other cases, it's too dangerous, and you have to cut them off entirely.'

Sitting back in his chair, Frank frowned. The word "entirely" sounded very final.

'Will it affect a lot of people?' he asked.

'What?' Roused from private thoughts, Dulles glanced around. 'Oh, I suppose so. These things happen from time to time – contacts and operatives don't last forever – but there are other... *costs* to consider.'

'Costs?' Frank looked up.

Silhouetted against the light of the window, Dulles bowed his head.

'It means I now have to question things I previously considered definite,' he said. 'And, most annoyingly, it means that I can no longer give active support to certain projects.'

Frank considered this. Rafe had believed that the operation was connected with the German coup, and Dulles had hinted that it was something significant enough to change the course of the war. But what were the implications for that, now that the network had been compromised?

'This is bad,' he murmured.

At the window, Dulles straightened and turned around.

'It's the game we play,' he said simply, as if that explained everything. Moving over to stand by the fireplace, he peered down at Frank through his spectacles. 'You've spoken very little today, but listened a lot,' he mused. 'You're learning.'

'Thank you,' Frank said, carefully keeping a neutral expression.

Dulles nodded to himself, then paced slowly over to his desk with a mildly distracted air.

'Now then, I'm going to be out of town for a few days,' he said, picking up a journal then snapping it shut. 'This whole business has become rather messy, and there are several things that need to be tidied up.'

'Is there anything I can do to help?' Frank asked.

'Maybe when I get back,' Dulles told him. 'In the meantime, just watch yourself, because others will *certainly* be watching you now.'

He held out a hand towards the door. Realizing he was being dismissed, Frank got to his feet and came over to him.

'You did well,' Dulles admitted, clapping him awkwardly on the shoulder.

Frank smiled despite himself.

'Thank you,' he said.

'Now go and clean yourself up,' Dulles said, shaking his head. 'And do something about those damn shoes!'

25

They left Bern behind, following the road west as it wound its way through lush green hills and cut across broad flat valleys. In the far distance, the hazy landscape seemed to rise up like a wall, dark with pine trees, and topped by a line of wispy white clouds. Here and there, pointed church spires marked small villages and wooden barns dotted the landscape.

'Isn't it wonderful?' Molly laughed. Wearing a pale yellow dress and sunglasses, she sat with one bare arm resting against the car window, staring out at the blue sky.

'It sure is,' Frank replied. He'd been looking forward to this since Molly suggested it and had arrived ten minutes early to pick her up from her lodgings on Waldheimstrasse. Seeing her emerge in a dress – so different to her usual work clothes – had brought an instant smile to his face and it underlined the fact that they would have the whole Saturday together.

Sweeping round a bend, the road ran alongside the railroad tracks for a time. Molly leaned an arm out of the window to wave as a train whined past, and they both laughed when the driver sounded his horn in response.

'So, this place we're going, have you been there before?' Frank asked.

'Neuchâtel?' Molly said, turning towards him. 'No, never. I always wanted to, though. Jean says it's lovely.'

'Well, it shouldn't be all that far now,' he said, glancing at his wristwatch, then frowning. 'Though I haven't quite got the hang of judging distances in kilometers.'

'I still prefer to think in miles,' Molly agreed. 'Oh, look... is that it?'

'Oh, wow, yeah.'

The road bent around a line of small houses and suddenly they saw the water – a startling blue-green that looked almost unnatural – stretching away into the distance. Not far ahead, the town spread along the shore, where forested mountain slopes ran down to the lake.

'It looks so pretty,' Molly said, leaning forward to peer through the windshield. 'We're going to have *such* a good day.'

The style of the buildings was different here – more ornate, like a French coastal town. All the road signs and street names were in French too, and Frank felt a momentary pang of anxiety as he recalled the bomb-blasted street signs he'd seen when his unit was advancing through Normandy.

They parked the car on the waterfront and strolled along the tree-lined esplanade, staring out across the lake and listening to the waves lapping against the shore. Molly startled him by slipping her hand into his as they walked.

'It's all right.' She smiled. 'Nobody knows us here. We can be whoever we want to be.'

'I guess.' He grinned, interlacing his fingers with hers. 'So, who *would* you like to be?'

Molly paused, giving him a coy look.

'I haven't decided yet,' she said. 'Tell me something about the man I'm with, first. In fact, *surprise* me; tell me something I don't know.'

'Something you don't know...' Frank tried to come up with an unusual story. 'Okay then, when I was a kid, maybe seven or eight years old, I saved a guy's life.'

'Really?' Molly said, looking impressed. 'What happened?'

'It's not quite as heroic as it sounds,' Frank explained. 'Where we used to live was near a railroad junction, and there was a place where the track bent around on itself, called Hobo's Curve.'

'Hobo's Curve?' Molly frowned.

'Yeah, it was a tight bend and the trains had to slow down as they took it. I guess it got its name because it was a place where they were slow enough for hobos to run alongside and jump up into the boxcars.'

'Oh!' Molly nodded in understanding. 'Hobos, as in tramps, homeless people.'

'That's right. Anyway, this one time I was down there and I found some homeless guy lying by the side of the tracks. He was still alive, but he was in a bad way – all covered in blood and with his leg busted – like he'd fallen from one of the cars or something.'

'The poor man.' Molly winced. 'What did you do?'

'Well, I knew he needed help, but he couldn't walk and I was too small to carry him. So I ran home and grabbed my grandma's crutches – she always slept in the afternoons, and left them propped up beside her chair – and I took them to this hobo.'

'Go on,' Molly urged him.

'Well, long story short, I got the hobo guy up onto the crutches and helped him into town. Got him to the church, and the pastor took him in.'

'Good for you.' Molly's eyes narrowed. 'But what did your grandmother do without her crutches?'

'Oh, I caught hell for that,' Frank said. 'But later, when the pastor stopped by to bring the crutches back, my family decided I must have been telling the truth after all. My mom even baked me an apple pie as a reward.'

'Bravo!' Molly laughed, clapping her hands together. 'So you were a hero in the end.'

Frank shrugged.

'My grandma maintained that it wasn't good for boys my age to be fooling around with train tracks and hobos,' he recalled, then turned and smiled. 'But my mom said *she* was proud that I'd helped the man.'

'Your mother sounds like a very sensible woman,' Molly told him. 'And she's from Germany, which is how you know the language so well?'

'Yeah. She spoke to me in German all the time when I was growing up, and we even went over there a couple of times.'

'But your father's American?'

'Yeah, he was an engineer. Spent some time working over in Hamburg, which is where he met my mom.' Frank paused, then shook his head. 'I used to think it was kinda fun, having extended families with such different backgrounds, you know, traveling and all, but having a German family isn't so great right now.'

Molly put her arm around him briefly.

'War spoils everything,' she said softly.

They walked on, past a short pier where several small boats were tied up, bobbing and creaking as the rippling waves pulled at them.

'What about you?' Frank said, as they continued along the waterfront. 'Whereabouts in England are you from?'

'I grew up in a tiny village called Littleworth, just outside Oxford,' Molly replied.

'Oxford as in the university?'

'That's right. Lots of lovely old stone buildings; rather like Bern, in a way.'

Frank caught the wistful tone of her voice, and the easy way she held his hand. He imagined her back in Oxford, before the war, beautiful and popular. *Someone like her couldn't have been unattached...*

'Got anyone waiting for you, back home?' he asked casually.

'Well, the family's decamped to London just now – father's got a job with the War Office – and my sister's a nurse at St Bartholomew's.' She glanced over at Frank, then hesitated. 'Oh, that wasn't what you meant, was it?'

'It's okay, really.' He gave her an awkward look. 'I just... wondered, you know?'

Molly slowed a little, hanging back from him and turning to stare out across the lake.

'I was... *nearly* married,' she said, a sad smile touching the corners of her mouth. 'His name was Harry. We met just before the war at a summer ball and... well, things just sort of happened, and we were engaged...'

They stood there for a long moment. The water slapped and sloshed over the stones below them.

'He was killed in France, two years ago,' she finished, simply. 'And that was that.'

Frank put a sympathetic hand on her shoulder.

'I'm sorry,' he told her.

'Thank you.' She turned to face him and he glimpsed the emptiness in her eyes, heard the hollow note in her voice. 'He was so much *fun*... and then... gone. Just like that.'

Frank reached down and took her hand, squeezing it gently. After a moment, she squeezed back and lifted her chin.

'Anyway,' she said, taking a deep breath and mustering a sudden, sunny smile. 'It's a beautiful day. Come on, I want to see if that museum is open.'

They walked across the road and climbed the steps of the imposing stone building. At the top, Molly pushed the heavy door open and Frank followed her into the cool stillness of a vast lobby.

The elderly man at the front desk spoke neither English nor

German. This defeated Frank, but Molly stepped in, smoothly exchanging pleasantries in French with the man, who seemed thoroughly charmed by her.

'What did you say to him?' Frank whispered, as they turned from the desk and started across the lobby towards the grand staircase.

'I told him you were an important American collector, touring the world in search of art treasures,' she said, innocently.

'Really?'

'Yes.' She grinned. 'Though I'm not sure he believed me.'

They started up the broad stone staircase, footsteps echoing around the huge space. Frank glanced up then slowed, pausing to stare at one of the mighty frescoes that towered above him, some sort of warrior angel, standing over the coiled wreckage of a slain dragon. He looked down to see Molly, a small figure at the turn in the stair, her face tilted up in wonder as she gazed at the enormous pictures. He moved up to stand by her side. After a moment, she noticed, and silently took his hand.

Upstairs, it became apparent that they had the museum to themselves. Moving from room to room, Molly studied the different paintings, while Frank nodded at her whispered commentary and enjoyed her obvious delight.

When they finally emerged, blinking into the sunlight, her mood seemed completely restored.

'Did you want to find somewhere we could get a drink?' Frank asked. 'Or maybe something to eat? We could take a walk through the town, see what there is.'

'Oh, yes.' Molly lifted her eyes towards the sun-bleached houses that looked out across the lake from the hillside above them. 'Let's go and explore.'

A few streets back from the shore, the ground rose sharply, climbing high above the grand buildings of the waterfront, with amazing views of the lake and the distant mountains. As the sun became hotter, they found welcome shade in some of the narrow, cobbled streets, where tall buildings crowded together, winding along the hillside.

Later, near the centre of town, the stopped at a tiny café with a window full of enticing hand-made chocolates. As Frank sat at their little corner table, sipping his café crème, he watched Molly tasting the last of their cocoa truffles, and smiled at her blissful expression.

'They're really good, aren't they?'

'Heavenly,' she sighed, putting a hand across her mouth. 'I do wish we could get chocolate like this back in England.'

'Things often taste better when you're away from home,' Frank said, taking out his cigarettes and offering the pack to her. 'You know, when everything's new and exciting.'

'I'm not so sure about that.' Her face darkened as she reached over and took a cigarette. 'I've been to a couple of places that were definitely new and exciting, but *nothing* tasted good.'

'Yeah?' Frank asked her. 'Where was that?'

Molly looked at him strangely.

'Let's not talk about work,' she said.

Sunlight sparkled on the blue water as they drove back along the main road.

'Oh, it looks idyllic,' Molly sighed, gazing out across the lake. 'I wish we didn't have to leave.'

Frank nodded, then glanced over at her.

'I'm not in any hurry,' he said. 'Do you have anything you need to get back for?'

Molly shook her head and smiled.

'Shall we see if we can find a way down there?' she said, looking back towards the water.

'Sure,' Frank told her. 'There's got to be a turning somewhere.'

In the end, they found a bumpy little dirt road that cut across the fields and dipped out of sight, but it took them roughly in the direction they wanted to go. When it eventually angled off to the left, they parked the car by a small patch of woodland, and continued down the hill on foot. After a few minutes, they emerged from the trees and stood shading their eyes in the afternoon sunlight. An expanse of lush, long grass swept down to the shore, where the glittering lake stretched out before them to the mountains.

'So, what do you think?' Frank grinned at Molly. 'Will this do?'

'Oh, it's simply perfect!' she laughed, staring down the slope. 'Come on, let's go and see.'

They found a tiny curve of stony beach between two outcrops of rock that jutted up from the rippling surface. Molly took her shoes off, then picked her way down to the edge and dipped a toe into the water.

'It's cold, but not *too* cold,' she called out. 'Shall we have a swim?'

Frank stepped down onto the beach and sat on a seam of rock. In the sunlight, it felt warm beneath his palm.

'I don't have a bathing suit with me,' he replied.

Molly turned around.

'Neither do I,' she said, unzipping her dress and pulling it up over her head.

Frank watched her as she removed her underwear, then draped her clothes over a large rock.

'What's the matter?' she asked him.

'Oh, nothing's the matter.' Frank smiled. He got to his feet and began undoing the buttons on his shirt. 'I just can't get used to seeing you naked, that's all.'

Molly gave an impish laugh, then turned her back on him and started out into the water.

Kansas City Herald

KANSAS CITY, MISSOURI - TUESDAY, July 18, 1944

ROOSEVELT HAILS MORE ALLIED GAINS IN EUROPE

GERMANY AND ITALY BEATEN BACK ACROSS THREE FRONTS

WASHINGTON, Jul 18 – In a special radio address, broadcast to US troops serving overseas, President Roosevelt spoke with optimism about the course of the war in Europe.

"The tide has turned at last," he explained. "There can be no doubt that our armed forces will soon wash away the ugly stain of fascist tyranny."

RUSSIANS POUND GERMAN EASTERN FRONT

His speech comes as American troops continue their push through Italy to Livorno, while Allied forces who liberated the French city of Caen are now driving the Germans out of Normandy. Meanwhile, the unstoppable advance of Russian units has liberated the cities of Minsk and Vilnius, steadily pushing back Germany's crumbling eastern front.

(continued on page 3, column 1)

26

The weather remained fair over the following week, and Frank was grateful when he had assignments that took him out of the office. Shielding his eyes against the sun, he took a last look back along the station platform at Brig, then climbed aboard the train, edging his way down the cramped corridor. Below him, through a window, he could see a uniformed railroad official with a bushy white mustache, wearily calling out the next station stops.

'Frutigen, Spiez, Thun, und Bern.'

Coming to an empty compartment, Frank slowed, then twisted around to smile over his shoulder.

'Here's one.'

Behind him, Jean smiled back. She was wearing a smart grey jacket and skirt, with a black pillbox hat.

Frank grasped the handle and slid open the door to the compartment, gesturing for her to go first.

'After you, darling.'

'Why, thank you, honey.' Her eyes twinkled with amusement as she eased past him and stepped inside. There were two wide bench seats facing each other and Jean hesitated as she looked at them.

'Which way are we going?' she asked. 'I prefer to face forward.'

Frank stepped into the compartment behind her and indicated the seats on the right.

'That side,' he told her.

As Jean sat down, he slid the door shut, sealing them in. Then he relaxed and let out a breath, moving over to slump down on the seat opposite her.

Jean looked at him for a moment, then raised an eyebrow.

'I think a *real* husband would likely sit *beside* his wife,' she reminded him.

Frank stared at her, then gave a reluctant nod.

'Yes, darling,' he sighed, getting to his feet and shifting across to her.

'Aw, was it really so bad, pretending to be married to me?' she laughed.

Frank rested his head back and rubbed his eyes.

'It's been exhausting,' he muttered, then caught sight of her expression. 'No, not being married to you, just... *concentrating*, you know? Concentrating on who I'm supposed to be, who you're supposed to be, what I have to do. Trying not to say the wrong thing or slip up; lying is tiring.'

Jean turned to look out at the last passengers hurrying along the platform.

'You get used to it,' she said. 'After a while it becomes second nature, and a whole lot easier.'

'I hope so,' Frank sighed.

Jean glanced back at him and her face softened a little.

'I think you did terribly well,' she said.

They heard the shrill blast of a whistle outside and felt the gentle jostling as the train started to move. Frank stared out of the window at the towering mountain peaks, grey and golden in the hazy sunlight, while the pretty buildings of Brig began to slide away. You could see the Italian influence on the architecture here – the arched window surrounds and the ornate verandas – but that was understandable, so close to the border. Brig was the last stop before the railroad plunged under the Alps to Italy; it was a critical transit route, and rumors were growing that the Germans might soon order the destruction of the tunnel if the Allied advance continued at its current pace. Preventing this was the reason that Swift had sent them down here.

'So, is that what you'll put in your report?' Frank asked, sitting up.

'What?' Jean frowned at him.

'That I did "terribly well".' Frank grinned. 'Is that what you'll say when you make your report to Swift?'

'Oh, I see.' Jean laughed. 'I think he'll be more interested in learning what we discussed with our partisan friends, don't you?'

'I guess so,' Frank said, smiling. He settled back into his seat, gazing out as the last buildings of the town disappeared. 'What did you think of them, by the way?'

Jean lowered her eyes for a moment, considering this.

'The one who called himself Luca seemed a bit... nervous, but that was understandable, I suppose. Did you see the way he kept turning that cigarette lighter over and over in his hand?'

'Yeah, I noticed that. You think he was on the level?'

'I think so,' Jean said, thoughtfully. 'I almost prefer when people are a bit anxious. Lord knows they have good reason to be, speaking to us. No, it's the quiet, confident ones that worry me.'

'Like his pal Carlo?'

Jean pursed her lips for a moment, then shook her head.

'No, I think they both seemed genuine enough,' she said. 'The real question is whether their group can actually stop the Germans if Hitler orders the tunnel to be blown.'

Frank nodded. They'd met Carlo and Luca in a restaurant just off the main square and spent a couple of hours in quiet discussion, though the tunnel itself was deliberately never mentioned. Posing as a married couple, he and Jean had asked questions about a "property their family was renovating" and Carlo had assured them that he had adequate staff to ensure the property remained open, as long as funds were available and his men were given "reasonable notice".

That was the part that worried Frank. Everything depended on them having sufficient warning; it all came down to information.

'How good is our intel?' he asked quietly.

Jean turned and looked at him.

'Good, I suppose.' She frowned. 'But why ask me? You know as much as I do.'

'You're closer to Swift,' Frank pointed out.

Jean's expression darkened.

'What are you saying?'

'I was just thinking about Carlo's "reasonable notice", and Swift seems to trust you...' Frank stopped. 'Sorry, I didn't mean...'

He trailed off, sensing that he'd said the wrong thing.

Jean regarded him stiffly.

'Is that what people think of me?' she demanded. 'That I'm Swift's private emissary? Or something worse?'

'No, that's not what I meant,' Frank assured her. 'Sorry.'

Jean glared at him, then turned her face back to the window.

'There's nothing going on between us, and there never has been,' she said, after an uncomfortable silence. 'Anyway, *Dulles* is the one who really knows what's going on. *His* sources seem to know everything, and the information isn't just coming from Washington.'

Frank opened his mouth to speak, then thought better of it. Sitting back slowly into his seat, he lowered his eyes and took a deep breath. How had he managed to get things so wrong with Jean? He hadn't been implying anything, but something he'd said had rubbed her the wrong way.

They sat in silence as the train trundled along beside the blue-grey water of the Rhône. After a few minutes, Jean turned back to look at him.

'I'm sorry,' she said, shaking her head slightly. 'I didn't mean to snap.'

'It's okay. I should have chosen my words better.'

Jean shifted in her seat.

'I hate the way this war gets into your head, you know?' She lowered her eyes. 'All the lying, the way it makes you angry, the way it makes you doubt people...'

Doubt people?

There was something there, something troubling her, but as Frank leaned over to ask, he saw her expression switch and suddenly she was gazing past him with a cheery smile on her face.

Behind him, he heard the compartment door open, and turned to see a young man in a conductor's uniform.

'Darf ich bitte Ihre Fahrkarten sehen?' the man asked, holding out a hand.

'I think you've got the tickets, darling.' Jean looked at him expectantly.

'Yes, of course.' Frank reached for his jacket pocket, drew out the tickets and handed them over. The conductor took a brief look, then returned them.

'Vielen Dank,' he said, withdrawing and sliding the door shut behind him.

Jean watched him leave, then calmly turned towards the window. Frank saw her smile fade in the reflection.

'Jean...' he began, but she silenced him with the tiniest shake of her head.

'Not now,' she murmured. 'There are some things I need to be sure of, things I need to decide.'

Frank eased himself slowly back in his seat, then stole a quick sideways glance at her. She'd been about to open up, confide in him... but what had she been about to say?

27

It rained heavily the next day. A wall of thick cloud rolled down off the mountains, turning the skies grey and washing the color from the city. People scurried between the shelter of the arcades and pressed into streetcars, leaving the cobbled plazas shining and empty.

In the Dufourstrasse office, Frank stood by the window, watching the droplets trickle down the glass.

'Anything you want me to do?' he asked, turning away from the light to look at Rafe. It was just the two of them in the office this afternoon and Jean hadn't left him her customary pile of dossiers to work through.

Rafe glanced up from his desk.

'You can help me sort these.' He indicated a stack of reports on the floor beside him, then smiled. '*A problem shared is a problem doubled.*'

Frank walked over, lifting half the remaining pile and taking it round to his desk.

'I think this is the quietest I've ever known it here,' he mused, sitting down and spreading the reports out in front of him.

'That's just because you're always the one out and about,

enjoying yourself,' Rafe said. 'Where was it yesterday? Lausanne?'

'Brig,' Frank corrected him. 'Playing *Mr and Mrs* with Jean.'

'She's far too good for you,' Rafe joked.

'I'll tell her you said that.' Frank laughed. He stared down at the reports, but his smile faded as he remembered the day before, and the long silent train journey home. Something had been troubling Jean, but a woman with a child had joined them in their compartment soon after they left Brig, and there'd been no opportunity to talk.

'I say.' Rafe looked up. 'If you were out all of yesterday, you won't have heard the good news about Cherbourg, will you?'

'Cherbourg?'

'Yes, the Germans there have been completely cut off.' Rafe beamed. 'It won't be long before the whole French coast is secured and our chaps are pushing on for a crack at Paris, just you wait and see.'

'It's the waiting that I can't stand,' Frank muttered. 'But you're right, it *is* good news.'

Rafe gazed over at him for a moment, then put down the report he'd been reading.

'What's the matter with you?' he asked. 'You've been like a bear with a sore head all day.'

Frank slumped back in his chair and sighed.

'Sorry,' he said. 'Maybe it's just... being here, so far from all the fighting, but it feels like nothing's happening, y'know? Or if it *is* happening, it's happening so slowly that it *feels* like nothing.'

He shook his head, not sure how to explain his frustration.

'But things *are* happening,' Rafe insisted. 'That's why everyone's chasing around all over the place at the moment. You and Jean in Brig yesterday, Molly up in Basel today, Swift off to the Bellevue for another briefing, and I don't have a clue where Jean is...' He tapped his desktop with a pointed finger for emphasis. 'Something's definitely going on. I don't know what it is yet, but it's big.'

Frank found himself smiling at his friend's enthusiasm.

'You're probably right.'

'It wouldn't be the first time.' Rafe grinned, then looked meaningfully at the pile of reports. 'Now then, I've got work to do. And by that, I mean that *we've* got work to do.'

Swift returned just before 3 o'clock. Stalking into the office, he leaned his wet umbrella by the doorway and pulled off his raincoat, shaking it irritably before hanging it up. Glancing around, he nodded a brief 'Hello' to Rafe and Frank, then paced quickly down the corridor and disappeared into his room. They heard the door slam behind him.

'Someone else is in a mood,' Rafe observed, turning back to his desk. 'Perhaps the Bellevue's cocktail bar was closed today.'

Frank chuckled.

'Maybe it's just this weather,' he said, looking over towards the window. 'It's still really wet out there.'

'I shouldn't grumble about the weather until you've had your first Bernese winter. The snow's not so bad, but there's a lot of slippery slopes to negotiate. Give me some good old rain, any day.'

'Spoken like a true Brit.' Frank grinned.

They worked on in silence, save for the steady patter of the rain against the window. The pile of reports on his desk was diminishing, but it was a slow, tedious job. Sitting back in his chair for a moment, Frank rubbed his tired eyes, then glanced down at his watch.

Ten after four. With luck, they'd be finished by six.

Behind him, he heard footsteps coming quickly along the corridor, and turned to see Swift approaching with a startled expression on his face.

'Um, listen....' Swift's voice was strange, almost trembling. 'At first I thought it was just a bit of wishful thinking, but the embassy says that radio traffic is going crazy...'

He took a breath, gathering himself.

'Somebody just blew up Hitler's headquarters at Rastenburg. They're saying he's dead!'

For a moment, they all stood frozen in silence, staring at one another.

'We actually *got* him?' Frank asked, his voice rising. His fists clenched of their own accord and he suddenly sprang from his seat and punched the air, snarling, 'Fucking-A!'

Rafe sagged back in his chair like a puppet whose strings had been cut.

'Oh, good God!' he whispered weakly, a bemused smile on his face. 'Are you certain?'

'There's no official confirmation yet, but the Germans have started turning trains back at the border, and there's reports of troops being rushed into Berlin.' He stood there, looking from one of them to the other. 'I think this is it!'

'Bloody hell,' Rafe sighed. He looked over at Frank, his eyes shining with tears, then burst out laughing. 'Bloody *hell*!'

Grinning, Frank turned back to Swift.

'Who got him?' he asked, eagerly. 'Was it the S.O.E? O.S.S? Who?'

'Nobody knows yet,' Swift replied, 'but I guess the whole of the Reich is in uproar at the moment. There's no saying what'll happen now.'

Rafe sat up suddenly, his eyes widening.

'A coup d'état,' he gasped, a smile spreading across his face. 'I say, maybe this is it! Maybe this is what everyone's been talking about!'

Swift stared at him for a moment, then nodded quickly.

'We'll need to wait and see what happens over the next day or two but... oh *hell*, it's exciting.' He punched his palm. 'I'm going to go and make a few calls but I'll let you know when I hear anything more.'

He turned on his heel and walked quickly back down the corridor.

Frank swung his arms and took a deep breath, trying to calm the tingling elation that was coursing through him. He forced himself to sit down, then looked over at Rafe.

'He's *dead*.' He grinned foolishly.

'And good *bloody* riddance, I say.' Rafe laughed, leaning back and putting his hands behind his head. 'Oh, please *God* let this be an end to the wretched war.'

'It will be, won't it?' Frank said. 'I mean, they must know they're finished. Between North Africa, Normandy, and the Russians... they *must* know it's only a matter of time.'

Rafe frowned.

'I suppose it depends who takes over. If Goebbels or Himmler grab the reins, well, we might have a year or two more before *they* chuck in the towel.'

'You really think so?' Frank asked.

'Oh yes, I imagine there's quite a few of them who'd follow their beloved Fuhrer into the abyss...' He paused, then slowly shook his head. 'No, we have to hope that someone from the army takes control: a soldier like Rommel, or someone like that. They're the ones who've been doing all the dying; they're probably the most eager to give peace a try.'

Molly walked in just after five o'clock, looking tired and bedraggled.

Frank glanced up, but Rafe was already calling over to her, his voice jubilant.

'I say, Molly, have you heard?'

She turned to look at him, shrugging off her wet coat, a weary expression on her face.

'Heard what?'

Rafe smiled at her.

'Hitler's dead,' he said simply.

Molly stared at him, and the coat slipped from her hands to fall in a crumpled heap on the floor.

'What?' she gasped.

'It happened this afternoon,' Frank explained, smiling broadly. 'Someone blew up his place in Rastenburg and...' He stuck a finger sideways into his mouth, then made a loud popping sound.

Molly's face broke into a radiant grin, and she started laughing.

'Oh, but that's wonderful news.' She beamed at them. 'Absolutely wonderful!'

'Swift says they've closed the borders,' Rafe told her. 'And Berlin's in complete chaos.'

'I'm not surprised.' Molly moved over to her desk and sat down. 'Any word on who's succeeded him?'

Rafe shrugged.

'Nothing yet.'

'I suppose we'll find out soon enough,' she said softly, then glanced up, her face brightening. 'For now, I'm just glad that Hitler's out of the picture.'

'Amen to that,' Frank said.

Swift came out of his room a few minutes later. Walking into the office, he paused as his eyes settled on Molly.

'I assume they've told you?' he asked.

'Yes,' she said, getting to her feet. 'Is there any more news?'

Swift looked at her, then glanced round at the others.

'Berlin's turning itself inside out, by all accounts,' he said. 'But I guess there was always going to be a huge power struggle when this happened. I'll know more when I speak to Dulles later.'

'Well, at any rate, I think this calls for a celebration,' Rafe said. He turned to Molly. 'Is there any of that Scotch left?'

She glanced towards the kitchen with a frown, then looked back and shook her head.

'All gone, I'm afraid.'

'We could go down to the bar on Thunstrasse,' Frank suggested, then turned to Swift for approval. 'If that's okay?'

Swift stared at him thoughtfully, then nodded.

'Yes,' he said. 'Yes, I think we *should* celebrate, all of us together.'

Rafe clapped his hands, then his smile faded slightly.

'It's a pity poor old Jean's not here for this,' he sighed. 'Where is she today, anyway?'

'Zurich,' Swift explained. 'But she's back now. She called me from the station a little while ago, and I told her to go straight home rather than get soaked in this weather.' He hesitated, then turned to look at Frank. 'Why don't you take the car, drive over there and pick her up?'

Jean had a tiny apartment in a large block on Sahlistrasse, not far from Waldheimstrasse – Molly had pointed the place out to him on their way back from Neuchâtel, and they avoided the street when walking together. In the car it should have been a ten-minute journey, but the rain was relentless, and Frank struggled to make out the road ahead as he peered through the windshield. One near-miss with a horse and cart sent him swerving across the wet asphalt, white knuckles wrenching at the wheel to avoid a stone wall. Excited as he was, he took it slower after that.

Now the building looked drab and grey as he ran across the road, coat pulled up over his head to fend off the rain. Flinging himself in under the meagre shelter of the porch, he peered at the array of bell-pushes, then pressed number 14. Waiting, he glanced back at the street, feeling the slow touch of cold water as it soaked through to chill his skin.

C'mon, Jean....

He jabbed the bell once more, but there was no sound, nothing to indicate whether it was working or not. Leaning into the doorway to avoid the rain, he felt the door give slightly against his shoulder, and realized it was open. He allowed Jean a moment more but, when there was no reply, he pushed the door and stepped inside.

The lobby was cramped and quiet, with polished old wood everywhere. Long strips of dark green carpet extended down the narrow corridor and zig-zagged up the staircase, too narrow to touch the walls or reach the sides of the steps.

Glad to be out of the downpour, Frank shrugged his coat down, shook himself vigorously to rid himself of any droplets. Then he sprang lightly up the stairs.

Jean's apartment was at the end of a corridor on the fourth floor. He knocked on the door smartly, hoping he wouldn't startle her, wondering how best to break the news. After her unsettled mood yesterday, this would be the perfect pick-me-up.

There was no answer.

'Jean?' he said softly, leaning in close to the door. 'Jean, it's Frank.'

The door moved slightly. He pushed it and it swung open a little.

'Anybody home?'

He put his head around the door, seeing the small living room, with a single armchair and a low table stacked high with magazines.

Out... but where might she have gone?

He stepped back into the corridor, pulling the apartment door closed, then hesitated as his nose caught a strange smell.

Frowning, he paused for a moment, then slowly turned the handle and opened the door again.

'Jean?'

Now that he was aware, he scented it more quickly, and it definitely seemed to be coming from inside. Nervously, he stepped into the apartment and pulled the door behind him.

There was no sound, and no sign of her. She must have been delayed coming back, or maybe she went out again afterwards. But as he stepped into the middle of the room he felt a curious unease.

He glanced down at the magazines, then looked through the doorway into the bedroom, his eyes flicking to something strange on the wall. He paused in mid-stride.

'Jean?'

His gaze was fixed beyond the bed, making out the dark spatter across the wallpaper, the strange organic pattern of marks that extended over the chest-of-drawers. He began to move, registering the stockinged feet lying still on the carpet, and stifled a cry, stumbling forwards to see if she was okay.

As he rounded the end of the bed, and the upper half of her body came into view, he saw what was left of her face and staggered back, choking.

Oh God, no...

One of her eyes was staring up at the ceiling, but her nose and the upper right side of her head were torn apart, flaps of ripped flesh and dark blood congealing in her hair. Her lips were slightly parted, as though she'd been about to speak.

Jean...

Putting a hand over his mouth, Frank stared up at the awful spatter on the wall behind her.

Shot. At close range. Whoever did it must have stood where he was standing right now.

He stared down into the wreckage of her face and felt the grip of nausea bubbling up as he turned away and ran from the room. He raced along the hallway and almost slipped on the stairs, taking them two at a time. Gasping, he burst from the front door into the stinging cold rain and sprinted for the car.

28

Dark clouds slid over Dufourstrasse as Frank slammed the car door and trudged along the sidewalk. Pausing at the gate, he put a hand on the glossy black railings and stared up at the office windows for a moment, squinting as the rain pattered down on his face. Numb, he made his way up the steps, pushed the door and went inside.

He hesitated again at the top of the stairs, wondering what he should do, how he might tell them. But there was no right way, not for something like this.

Feeling sick, he opened the office door.

'Ah, here he is,' Rafe crowed, lifting a hand in lazy greeting, then faltering as he saw Frank's face. 'I say, you look absolutely drenched. Where's Jean?'

Molly glanced up from her desk, her initial smile tightening into an expression of concern.

'Are you all right?' she asked, getting slowly to her feet.

Frank stood in the doorway, water dripping from him as he stared back at them.

'Frank?' Molly took an anxious step towards him. 'What's the matter?'

For a moment, he teetered on the edge of it, unable to speak, unable to breathe, then he gulped down a lungful of air and forced the words out.

'It's Jean,' he choked, his eyes brimming with sudden tears. 'She's dead.'

Everything slowed, and all he could do was stand there in the awful silence that followed, wanting it all to just... *stop*. Rafe had recoiled against the back of his chair as though struck by a physical blow, and Molly's face was caught in the moment between disbelief and anguish. A wave of nausea surged up from within him and he swayed, thrusting a wet palm against the wall to steady himself as he screwed his eyes shut.

'Swift!' Rafe was yelling. '*Swift*, come out here *now!*'

He felt a hand on his shoulder, and another at his side, steadying him. Molly's voice was in his ear, whispering something, telling him to breathe.

His eyes flickered open and he reached out to grip her forearm, taking a deep breath as he gazed into her face.

'What happened?' she said softly, staring up at him.

Through his tears, he could see Rafe getting up and, beyond him, Swift was hurrying along the corridor. Blinking, he looked down at Molly.

'I found her in her apartment,' he said, wretchedly. 'Someone shot her.'

Molly's lip quivered, but she leaned in closer, holding his gaze.

'You're certain she's dead?'

Frank blinked more tears away, nodding as he tried to drive the sickening image from his mind.

'She's dead,' he whispered.

He glanced over at Swift, standing stricken in the middle of the floor.

'I'm sorry, I didn't know what to do, so I came back here...'

He trailed off, looking round at them all.

'No!' Rafe swung an arm across his desk, sweeping everything aside and sending it all crashing to the floor. Then he slumped forward, head bowed, trembling. 'Why her?'

Swift's eyes were wide, but the outburst seemed to shake him out of his daze, and he stepped over, putting an arm around Rafe's shoulders.

'Easy, now...' he said, guiding Rafe back into his chair, then turning to look at Frank. 'Was there anyone else there? What happened when you found her?'

Frank stared at him, then slowly shook his head.

'She didn't answer the bell,' he said, sniffing. 'So I went upstairs to knock on her door, but it was open.'

'Did you see anyone?' Swift pressed him.

'No,' Frank replied. 'At first I thought she'd gone out or something... then I saw...'

He closed his eyes for a moment, felt Molly's hand squeezing his shoulder.

'What about on the way out?' Swift asked. 'Did you speak to anyone?'

'There was nobody around,' Frank said, drawing another breath. 'I just... I had to get out of there.'

Swift nodded slowly, then lowered his eyes.

'Poor Jean,' he said, quietly.

'What are we going to do?' Molly asked, twisting round to look at him.

Swift met her gaze, then frowned to himself.

'I'm going over there,' he said suddenly. 'I need to take a look, before the police get in there and mess things around.'

'I want to come with you,' Molly said.

Swift hesitated for a moment.

'I think it's better if you wait here,' he said, inclining his head towards Rafe and giving her a meaningful look. 'Frank can drive me.'

'Let me come too,' Molly insisted.

'No. Frank comes with me, you two stay here,' he said firmly. 'I mean it; I don't want *any* of us alone right now. We don't know what the hell we're dealing with.'

Molly glared at him, then turned back towards Frank. She gazed up into his eyes for a moment, her hand gently squeezing his arm, her face full of unspoken words. Then she stepped away from him and looked down at her feet.

'You better go,' she murmured. 'Before someone else finds her.'

Hunched forward in the car, Frank peered out through the smears of water on the windshield. Sitting next to him, Swift was drumming out a pensive rhythm on the side of his seat. Abruptly, the drumming stopped.

'I'm sorry,' Swift murmured. 'It must have been a hell of a shock for you.'

Frank gripped the wheel a little tighter.

'Yeah.'

He swallowed and stared out through the rain. They were approaching the turning for her road.

'I'll understand if you don't feel able to come in,' Swift said.

Grimly, Frank shook his head.

'Don't worry about me.'

He slowed and pulled hard on the wheel, rounding the corner onto Sahlistrasse, then applying the brakes as Jean's apartment building came into view.

'Drive past,' Swift muttered.

'What?' Frank looked across at him.

'Drive past!' Swift snapped, then continued more gently, 'Park round the corner and we'll walk back.'

Frank nodded wordlessly and straightened the wheel.

·   ·   ·

Trudging through the rain, they made their way slowly back up the hill. Swift went ahead, turning in at Jean's gate and walking up to the front door.

'Calm and confident,' he reminded Frank. 'Like we belong here.'

'Okay.' Frank took a deep breath, then pushed the door open and stepped inside. Glancing around the empty lobby, he stood and listened for a moment, but there seemed to be no one around. Satisfied, he started towards the stairs.

Behind him, Swift whispered, 'Wipe your feet.'

Frank halted and turned around.

'What?'

'Wipe your feet.' Swift pointed at the dark smudges of damp on the carpet. 'Or did you want to leave a trail of wet footprints leading up to her room? One of the neighbors might come up to complain.'

Frank stared at him, then moved back over and wiped his feet on the brush mat, shaking the water off his coat as he did so.

'Sorry,' he mumbled.

'If you want to catch a killer, you need to be able to think like one.' Swift motioned towards the stairs. 'C'mon, let's go.'

Upstairs, the door of apartment 14 was closed; Frank couldn't remember if he'd shut it on his way out. He supposed he must have. Swift glanced back along the hallway, his face a picture of calm, all except for his eyes.

'Ready?' he whispered, then reached for the handle without waiting for an answer. The door opened silently and they stepped quickly inside.

An oppressive stillness lay heavily on the room. Frank was more aware of the smell now, a dirty slaughterhouse stench that made him cover his nose and mouth with his hand. Swift looked at him and nodded slowly.

'Somebody's going to notice that soon,' he muttered. 'Come on.'

Treading softly, he made his way through to the bedroom. Unwilling to follow, Frank stood rooted for a moment, his eyes roving around the room. There was a stack of magazines on the table – movie magazines from the States. Beside them, he could see Jean's little gold cigarette lighter, her purse, the pillbox hat that she'd worn to Brig yesterday. He found himself thinking about the pen that Dulles had bought her, still sitting on her desk at work. Orphan items, now, a precious collection unravelling, meaningless without the person who had brought them all together. Gritting his teeth, he turned away and walked slowly through to the bedroom.

Swift was standing by Jean's feet, peering down at her where she lay behind the bed. Beside him, the spatter marks on the walls were now blackening to a grisly red-brown.

'Her eyes...' He paused, then corrected himself. 'Her eye is still reasonably clear. She hasn't been dead all that long.'

He leaned over the body for a moment more, hands clasped behind his back, then straightened up slowly.

'Poor Jean,' he said, with a sigh. 'She didn't deserve this.'

Frank nodded to himself.

Swift glanced over towards the doorway, then back down at the body.

'Someone got very close to her,' he mused. 'Three, maybe four feet away when they pulled the trigger.'

Frank didn't answer. From here, the wreckage of Jean's face was hidden by the bed, but he could still see it in his mind, no matter where he looked.

'Does anyone know you were here earlier?' Swift was saying. 'Did you speak to anyone? See anyone?'

Numbly, Frank looked at him, then shrugged his shoulders.

Swift came over and roughly grabbed his arm.

'You need to get yourself together!' he hissed. 'There'll be time for grief later, but right now I need you to snap out of it! Now, did anyone see you before?'

Blinking, Frank shook his head.

'I... I don't think so. There was nobody downstairs so I came up, found the door open... when I saw this, I just... ran.'

'Okay.' Swift patted him on the arm, then stepped past him, moving around to the side of the bed and retrieving a couple of document folders from the nightstand. He flicked through them briefly, then started working his way round the room, opening the closet doors and pulling out drawers.

'Look around,' he said. 'See if you can find her keys.'

Frank thought for a moment.

'Her purse is on the table out there,' he said, gesturing over his shoulder.

Swift glanced up at him.

'Show me,' he said.

They went through to the other room. Swift spent a moment rifling through Jean's purse, before triumphantly drawing out her keys.

'Got them,' he said, then moved over to grip Frank by both arms, leaning in close. 'Now listen to me; this is what we're gonna do. You and I will walk out of here, calmly and quietly. If we see anyone, you leave the talking to me, understand?'

Frank nodded vaguely.

'Good.' Swift straightened up and took a last look around. 'Let's go.'

Frank moved woodenly out of the room and into the empty hallway. Behind him, he saw Swift fumbling with the door and heard the sharp snick of a lock turning. Then he was being hurried along the corridor and quietly downstairs, outside into the rain once more.

'So who did it?' Rafe snarled. His eyes were puffy and red, and his hand shook as he leaned over his walking stick. 'Who the hell would want to hurt *her*?'

Molly stood in silence, watching Frank as he slowly pulled off his raincoat and hung it up to dry.

'I'm sorry,' Swift said, shaking his head. 'We just don't know. Not yet, anyway.'

He looked at Rafe for a moment, then lowered his eyes and moved over to the filing cabinets, pulling open a drawer and quietly stowing the folders he'd taken from Jean's apartment.

'We have to find out,' Rafe demanded. 'There must have been *something*, some indication...'

'She was shot at very close range,' Swift said softly, then looked round. 'If it's any consolation, she wouldn't have suffered; it would have been instant.'

Rafe's anger seemed to give way to grief, and he sagged, lowering himself heavily into his chair and letting his walking stick clatter to the floor.

'Poor old thing,' he whispered.

'So what are we going to do now?' Molly asked.

Swift looked at her, his face unreadable.

'Nothing for now,' he said. 'I need to talk to Dulles, figure out how we play this.'

'But what if someone finds her?' Molly pressed.

'We have time... well, a little time, anyway.' Swift patted his pants pocket, and they heard the jingling of keys. 'I locked the place when we left. It'll be okay for now.'

Rafe's head jerked up.

'You're not just *leaving* her there, are you?' he gasped, horrified.

The phone started ringing.

'I didn't say that,' Swift sighed. 'But we need to know what we're dealing with before we decide what to do.'

The phone continued to ring. Frowning, Molly walked over and answered it.

'She deserves better than this,' Rafe insisted. 'She deserves some dignity.'

'She deserves to be avenged,' Frank murmured, his voice bleak.

Across the room, Molly turned around, her hand over the mouthpiece of the phone.

'It's Groth,' she said urgently. 'He says to turn on the radio, right now.'

'Eh?' Rafe stared at her, confused.

Frank roused himself and walked over to the bureau, bending over and clicking the knob to switch the set on.

'What the bloody hell...' Rafe frowned, but Molly was turning away from them again.

'Thanks,' they heard her saying. 'Yes, you too.'

She put the phone down, then twisted round as the radio static hummed and a thin voice began to crackle faintly from the loudspeaker.

'Ich spreche zu Ihnen heute, damit Sie meine Stimme hören...'

Rafe leaned forward, cupping his hand to his ear, trying to make out the words.

Frank bowed his head, translating as well as he could.

'I'm speaking to you today... so that you will hear my voice... and know that I am unhurt and well... secondly, so that you will know of a crime... without equal in German history...'

The voice was louder now, and Frank lapsed into silence as it continued.

A small group of ambitious, dishonorable and criminally stupid officers have conspired to eliminate me and overturn the leadership of the German armed forces. A bomb that was planted by Colonel Graf Von Stauffenberg exploded two meters from my right side. It very seriously wounded a number of my faithful staff members. One of them has died. I myself am absolutely unhurt, except for very light scratches, bruises and burns. I interpret this as a confirmation of the order of

Providence that I continue to pursue the goal of my life, as I have done up to now...

Frank reached up and found the volume knob with his fingers, twisting it around and shutting the sound off. In the awful silence that followed, nobody spoke.

Hitler was alive.

Fall, 1953
Kansas City, Missouri

Kansas City Herald

KANSAS CITY, MISSOURI   -   Thursday, August 27, 1953

CITY APARTMENT BLAZE; AT LEAST TWELVE PERISH

FIRE DESTROYS 3-STOREY BUILDING; 12 DEAD AND SEVERAL STILL MISSING

KANSAS CITY, Aug 27 - Flames tore through a Westport apartment block last night, trapping many of the residents inside. Firefighters battled valiantly to control the blaze, but 12 people are known to have died, and fears are growing for at least 10 others who are missing since the three-storey building collapsed. Survivors of the tragedy, including two firefighters, are being cared for at nearby St. Luke's Hospital.

BUILDING 'WENT UP LIKE A TORCH'

There is still no explanation regarding the cause of the inferno, which raged on through the night. Neighbors who witnessed the tragedy described the fierce nature of the fire. According to Mr J. Eisenberg, "The whole place just went up like a torch. It happened so fast, there was no way for people on the upper floors to get out."

An official investigation is now underway to determine how the blaze stared.

(continued on page 2, column 3)

29

Frank opened his eyes, startled out of a troubled sleep, and sat up in bed. Grey light from the hotel window cast dirty shadows that moved across the sheets as he stretched his legs out beneath them.

He smelled smoke, and for a moment he was back in his dream of flames and burning... but then he remembered, and sank down wearily into the pillow.

It was on his clothes, from the apartment building fire last night.

Rubbing his eyes, he lay back and stared up at the ceiling for a while, then sighed and pushed himself out of bed.

Downstairs, the young man on reception nodded to him as he walked across the lobby. Frank paused, then turned and strolled back over to the desk, summoning the best smile he could manage as his eyes searched out the relevant pigeonhole and made sure the other guest's room key wasn't there.

'Morning,' he said. 'Any messages for me? The name's Edward Linden; room two-one-two.'

'Let me just check for you,' the young man said. He turned

away, reaching a hand into the pigeonhole, then glanced back over his shoulder. 'Nothing at the moment, Mr Linden.'

'Okay.' Frank inclined his head in thanks, then walked across the lobby and pushed through the glass doors.

No messages. No leads. He had nothing.

He ate a late breakfast in a neat little diner on Baltimore Avenue, then sat hunched over the table, drinking coffee and scanning the local papers. The noon edition had a piece about the fire on the front page under the headline *FATAL CITY APARTMENT BLAZE*. Frank leaned in closer, squinting at the smudged print. Twelve residents were confirmed dead, and at least ten more were listed as missing. Two fire-fighters were in hospital, one of them in grave condition.

Frank sat up and pushed the paper away. If Faye had burned, there was nothing more for him here. One way or another, he had to find out.

From his booth, he could see a payphone through the window. Gulping down the last of his coffee, he got up and made his way outside. Jamming a coin into the slot, he dialed the number and waited, staring gloomily at the endless stream of people moving along the sidewalk.

'This is Detective O'Halloran.'

'Hi Adam, it's Frank.' He spoke lightly, as though everything was fine. 'How are you feeling this morning?'

Adam's voice changed, as though he were whispering into the mouthpiece.

'Where are you?' he asked.

Frank hesitated, wondering what was wrong.

'I'm at a diner called...' He turned and checked the name on the sign. '...Martha's Café. It's on Baltimore Avenue.'

'I know it,' Adam replied. 'Stay there and I'll be right along.'

There was an abrupt click and the line went dead.

. . .

Adam entered the diner and stood in the doorway with a troubled expression on his face. Sighting Frank, he made his way over and slid himself in on the opposite side of the booth. Placing his palms flat on the table, he took a deep breath, then leaned forward.

'So, you wanna tell me what's going on?' he said in a low voice.

Frank edged back in his seat a little, unsure whether this was about him being suspended, or about the fire.

'What do you mean?' he asked, keeping his expression blank.

The muscles around Adam's jawline tightened visibly.

'That address you gave me...' He broke off for a moment, getting a grip on what he wanted to say. 'What's your interest in the place? Who's this woman you're looking for?'

It was the fire.

Frank lowered his eyes and spoke quietly.

'Like I told you last night; she's just someone I need to speak to, and I wanted to check whether you had a file on her before I–'

'Don't mess with me, buddy.' Adam raised a warning finger. 'You remember that address you gave me? Well, I go to start asking around for you this morning, and guess what: the whole place burned down last night. Sixteen people are dead.'

'Sixteen?' Frank sat back heavily in his seat, visions of the blaze playing out in his mind. 'I thought it was twelve.'

Adam stared across the table, eyes narrowing.

'So. You've been checking up on it, eh?' he mused, nodding grimly.

Frank bowed his head slightly, annoyed at himself. He'd forgotten how easy it was to underestimate Adam.

'I read about it in the paper,' he admitted.

'Oh yeah?' Adam said. 'Well, I got a newsflash for you. There's a huge investigation starting and you really *don't* want to be caught in the middle of it.'

Frank glanced up at him. A huge police investigation could only mean one thing.

'The fire was deliberate then?'

Adam shook his head unhappily.

'Seriously, you need to stay out of this, Frank. People *died.*'

There was something distasteful in his tone now, an air of self-importance that he'd never had back in the Joplin days.

Frank gripped the edge of the table.

'Think I don't *get* that?' he snapped. 'I was *there* last night; I *saw*...'

Adam gaped at him in surprise.

'You were *there*?' he hissed. 'What the hell...'

Frank quickly held up a hand to silence him.

'I took a cab down there, after you went home last night,' he explained. 'And before you ask, the place was already burning *long* before I got there.'

Adam looked at him in disbelief.

'But... why?' he demanded. 'Dammit, Frank. What the *hell* have you got yourself mixed up in?'

Frank met his gaze.

'When I figure it all out, I'll be sure to explain myself to you.'

They stared at each other for a long moment. Eventually, Adam turned away, shaking his head.

'Have it your own way, Frank,' he muttered. 'I wanted to keep you from getting dragged into this, but if you're gonna be a jerk–'

'Hey!' Frank leaned over the table. 'You *know* that fire was nothing to do with me. I was with you last night, remember?'

Adam glared at him.

'Yeah, so?'

'So you're my alibi,' Frank said. 'Now you can either play it by the book, and waste everyone's time by taking me in, or you can get out of my way and let me do my job.'

Adam said nothing for a moment, then frowned.

'Your job?' he asked. 'I thought you said this was personal.'

Damn. Frank rubbed his eyes wearily.

'It's both,' he sighed. 'Okay?'

Adam appeared unconvinced. He turned as though he was about to get up and leave. Frank reached out and put a hand on his arm.

'Listen to me,' he said. 'I just need to know whether Faye Griffith was in that building when it went up, okay? If she's dead, then there's nothing more I can do – I'll jump on a train and get out of town...'

Adam hesitated, suspicion still visible on his face.

'...but if she's alive?' Frank continued. 'Well, she may know something that can help me, and I need all the help I can get right now.'

Adam sighed, settling back into his seat and shaking his head.

'If you find anything – *anything at all* – about who started that fire...'

'I'll tell you,' Frank promised.

'You better,' Adam growled. He leaned back and folded his arms. 'So? What do you want?'

'I want to know if they ID any of the victims as her,' Frank said. 'That's all I need.'

Adam shook his head slowly.

'Good luck with *that*,' he muttered. 'You got any idea how *few* of those bodies we'll identify? You saw the fire; most of those folk were as good as cremated. There's nothing left of them but ash.'

Frank slumped back in his seat, frowning.

'How many people lived in that building?' he asked.

'Can't say for sure,' Adam replied with a shrug. 'Thirty, something like that?'

'You said there were sixteen dead?'

'Sixteen *so far*,' Adam clarified. 'But we still have some folks unaccounted for, and I reckon most of them'll turn out to be dead, sooner or later.'

Frank nodded, grimly.

'How many got out?' he asked.

Adam looked uncertain.

'Got out?'

'When I was down there I saw a couple of people who'd made it out of the building before it collapsed,' Frank said. 'You know how many there were?'

'No, I'd have to check.'

'Can you do that for me?'

Adam looked thoughtful.

'Maybe,' he said. 'But it'll take me some time.'

'How come?' Frank asked.

'I don't know where they all are,' Adam replied.

He glanced over at Frank, saw him frowning.

'It won't be just the one place,' he explained. 'I guess a few of them will be in hospital – St Luke's, probably – and I heard someone say that the others were taken to a local church for the night, but I don't know which church it was. I'd need to make some calls.'

'But you'll do it?' Frank pressed him.

Adam sighed.

'Sure, if it puts you on a train back to Joplin. Anything else?'

Frank paused, then nodded.

'A car,' he said. 'I'll need to borrow a car.'

Adam shook his head wearily. 'Dammit, Frank. I'd forgotten what a bastard you can be.'

Frank gave him a bleak little smile.

'And *you've* always had my back,' he said softly. 'Just imagine what a bastard I'm gonna be to the people who've *crossed* me.'

30

It felt strange, driving Adam's red Oldsmobile across the bridge and down towards the intersection. Pulling up at a stoplight, Frank glanced around the spotless interior, then leaned across and flipped the glovebox open, absently rifling through the contents.

A pair of white-framed women's sunglasses... a corkscrew with the cork still attached... a hairbrush with strands of long red hair...

He felt a sudden pang of jealousy for his former colleague – playing by the book and climbing the ladder, the willing little wife and the model home – but it wasn't for him. He'd figured *that* out long ago.

The stoplight changed. Frank slammed the glovebox shut and gunned the engine, heading south. St Luke's Hospital was down on West 43rd, and Adam had made a good point about the injured being taken there. It was certainly worth checking to see if Faye was among them. But if she *had* been taken there, chances were she wasn't going anywhere else for a while, and he had another stop to make first. Turning left onto East 40th, he pulled in and parked close to the curb. Switching off the engine, he gazed across the street at the small stone-clad chapel opposite.

Adam hadn't known which church the residents had gone to, but this one was just a few hundred yards from the burned-out apartment building. There was a good chance it was the place.

Getting out, Frank locked the car and strode across the asphalt. There was a small gate in the fence; beyond it, a gravel path led under the shadow of a large tree towards the main entrance of the church, and on around the side of the building. Glancing back over his shoulder, he crunched along the path and went up the steps to the arch of the stone entrance porch, where he hesitated.

Churches were supposed to provide sanctuary.

Awkwardly, he removed his hat, then frowned and forced himself to step inside. The porch was empty, and he moved silently to the inner door where his eyes scanned the interior of the church. Light streamed down from the tall, pointed windows, illuminating two rows of dark wooden pews. There were several figures sitting in the silence – including three women – but none of them looked anything like the photograph of Faye. Frank's gaze came to rest on the carved figure of Christ on the cross... then someone coughed, the sound echoing up around the high ceiling, and he quickly turned away.

Outside, he replaced his hat and continued on along the gravel path, following it around the side of the church. Ahead of him he could see another building – some sort of meeting hall – and beyond it, a small cemetery enclosed by hedges. A man was standing by the entrance to the hall; mid-forties, with soot-blackened clothes and uncombed hair, he stared at the ground, a cigarette hanging from his lip.

Yeah, this was the place all right.

Frank adopted an expression of kindly concern, then walked confidently up the path, nodding to the smoking man and going straight past him into the building.

The fewer people you spoke to, the fewer problems you'd have, as Rafe always told him.

Inside, there was a small lobby area, colorfully decorated in cornflower blue, with a large sign reading *Welcome to St Paul's Community Hall* surrounded by children's drawings. Below the sign, leaflets were arranged on a long trestle table, with bundles of old newspapers stacked neatly underneath. There was a small collection tin bearing the crest of the RAI – the charity for Russian-Americans still held in U.S. internment camps.

Frank walked over to a set of double glass doors and peered through into the main hall. It was a large space, almost as large as the church itself, with lines of small windows set high in the white walls and a raised stage at the far end of the polished wooden floor. A row of camp beds was set up along the left side of the room, dotted with bags and boxes and other possessions rescued from the fire. On the right, several sets of folding tables and chairs were arranged in groups. Here, a few disheveled people were sitting, some eating, some staring into the distance. A priest and two smartly-dressed women were moving between the tables, handing out bread and soup.

Leaning closer to the glass, Frank squinted, trying to make out the different faces, but he couldn't see everyone, not from here. Frowning, he straightened his jacket so that it concealed his .45, then pushed the glass doors open and went inside.

He kept his distance from the priest and avoided making eye contact, striding purposefully towards the far end of the hall as though he was going to speak to someone. As he walked, he noticed that the air had a stale taste to it, and he caught the same faint reek of smoke that he'd found on his own clothes that morning.

Not an easy smell to stomach, especially if you'd just lost everything in a fire.

Ahead of him, there was a solitary woman, sitting on the right with her back to the door and her head bowed. He went a little way past her, then slowed and turned around, just as she looked up.

It was Faye.

She looked a bit older than in the photo, but it was definitely her. Unlike some of the other people here, her clothes seemed clean – a patterned turquoise dress with a blue-grey jacket – but her brown hair was untidy and she had a forlorn expression, dazed and weary, as through she'd been through hell. He might have felt sorry for her, if she'd been anyone else.

Forcing a smile, he went over to her.

'Miss Griffith?'

She looked up at him, blinking sleepily.

'Yes?'

Frank sighed, feigning relief.

'Thank goodness I found you,' he said. 'Are you all right?'

Faye stared up at him; the makeup around her eyes was streaked, as though from tears.

'I... I guess so,' she replied.

Frank nodded sympathetically.

'I know you've been through a lot,' he said, talking quickly to keep her off balance. 'But if I could just speak with you for a few minutes, I'm sure it would help.'

'I'm sorry...' She looked uncertain now. 'What's this about?'

Frank lowered his eyes.

'You'll appreciate that it's a... *delicate* matter, so maybe we should speak outside?'

Without waiting for an answer, he started calmly towards the door, hoping that her curiosity would get the better of her and that she'd follow him. He made his way down the line of camp beds, nodding pleasantly to one of the women handing out soup. When he reached the far wall, he pulled the glass doors open, and glanced over his shoulder. Faye had got to her feet and was just a few yards behind him, a confused look on her face.

He smiled and held the door wide for her.

'After you.'

She gave him a doubtful look.

'I'm not sure what this is about.'

'Of course,' Frank said, kindly. 'I understand completely.'

He gestured for her go ahead of him.

Faye hesitated, then frowned sleepily and stepped through into the lobby.

He followed her towards the main door and ushered her outside into the sunlight. The smoking man had gone now, and there was nobody else around.

Good.

Faye turned towards him, a curious expression on her face.

'So what's this about Mr...?'

Frank drew the .45 out from beneath his jacket. Her eyes widened as she glimpsed the gun, but he grabbed her sleeve and hissed, 'Keep quiet and do as I say, or I'll finish you right here. Understand?'

She stared up at him, paralyzed with fear, as he jammed the gun into her side.

'Understand?' he repeated.

Swallowing hard, she managed a trembling nod.

'What... what do you want?' she stammered.

Frank glanced around, wondering which way to go. *Not back towards the street – too many people.*

'Come with me,' he growled.

Linking arms with her, he dragged her along the path towards the corner of the building. A small cemetery occupied the space behind the hall, with lines of well-kept headstones jutting up from the newly mown grass, all surrounded by a thick hedge that offered some privacy and shielded them from the road.

'I don't understand,' Faye whimpered. 'Is this about the fire? Why are you doing this?'

'That fire was no accident,' Frank growled.

'What?!' Faye gasped, her body stiffening. 'What do you mean? Let go of my arm.'

He ignored her, increasing his pace so that she stumbled on the gravel, trying to keep up.

Ahead and to the left, he could see a large mound of dirt, partly covered by an old grey tarp, and turned towards it, dragging Faye across the grass.

He felt her pull back when she saw the open grave, heard her little gasp of fear as they took the final few steps and stopped right at the edge.

'No!' she whispered, shrinking away from it. 'Please, no!'

Frank gripped her arm tightly with his, moving the gun around so the barrel was angled up into her chest. Her eyes were staring wildly at him as he turned his gaze on her and paused.

'Do you know who I am?' he asked.

Faye shook her head, tears beginning to stream down her face.

'No, I don't!' she sobbed. 'And I don't understand what's–'

'That's all right,' Frank interrupted, calmly talking over her. 'I guess you could say I'm a friend of a friend. Remember that police officer you met, down in Neosho?'

He saw the recognition in her eyes, the dread as he spoke the name.

Yeah, she remembered all right.

'C'mon.' He smiled down at her, as though he wasn't about to blow her heart out through her back. 'You wouldn't forget *him*, would you? All beaten to death in your room?'

'Oh Lord, please...' She tried to recoil from his gaze, but he was holding her tightly. 'You don't understand... I didn't know, I *swear* I didn't know...'

'Hush now,' he soothed her. 'Shhhhhh... look at me.'

She was trembling, her breathing erratic, eyes hunting around wildly.

'*Look* at me!'

She flinched and stared up at him as he leaned in close.

'You're going to tell me everything I want to know, understand?'

Blinking fearfully, she managed a stiff nod.

'Good.' Frank regarded her thoughtfully for a moment. 'Now then, we're gonna start with an easy question: did you kill him?'

Faye's body jerked back against his hold.

'No!' Her eyes widened in horror and she shook her head violently. '*No!* It wasn't me who killed him. Please, you have to believe me.'

She seemed genuinely terrified by the suggestion... but he hadn't expected her to admit it.

'Why should I believe anything *you* say?'

'Because it's the truth!' she pleaded. 'I didn't kill anyone.'

Frank scowled, allowing a cold edge to creep into his voice.

'So you got your friend to do the killing, is that it?'

'No!' Faye sobbed, staring up at him in fear. 'Oh God, no!'

'I'd be careful about taking the Lord's name in vain,' Frank warned her. 'You may be about to meet him.'

Faye took a ragged breath.

'I didn't know. I *swear* I didn't know.' She blinked, trying to see through the tears. 'He said nobody would get hurt, that it was just a way of keeping someone in line, that's what he told me...'

'That's what *who* told you?'

But Faye's head had dropped, and her shoulders were shaking.

Frank pulled her close, sliding the barrel of the gun up to her throat.

'Who?' he demanded.

Faye lifted her face to him, tears streaming down her cheeks.

'Ellis,' she whispered.

'Ellis who?'

Faye tried to turn away again.

'I don't know...'

'TELL ME WHO HE IS!'

'I don't *know*...'

She sagged, as though she was about to collapse, but with his arm linked through hers he jerked her upright.

'Listen to me,' he hissed. 'Is Ellis a short guy, grey hair, a bit overweight?'

For a moment, Faye didn't respond. Then she slowly shook her head.

'No,' she sniffed. 'He's about six foot... dark hair and skinny...'

The thin man.

He bowed his head close to hers, speaking softly.

'Who is he, Faye?'

Faye looked up at him, wretchedly.

'I swear I don't know,' she said. 'But he's the one who killed that cop, not me.'

Frank relaxed his grip on her just a little, and she slumped away from him, sobbing quietly.

It looked as if he'd been right about the thin man being the killer, but he felt less sure about Faye. What was her part in all of this?

A noise somewhere behind them made him twist around. A small man in overalls was crunching along the gravel path towards the grave.

Frank grabbed Faye's arm.

'Come on,' he said, dragging her towards a small gate that opened out onto the street. 'We're gonna go someplace we can be alone.'

31

Frank lifted his foot off the gas and turned, bumping the Oldsmobile down the narrow alley that ran along the side of the hotel. He pulled up in the empty lot at the back of the building, switched the engine off, then glanced across at Faye.

'We're here,' he told her.

She sat there, unresponsive, head bowed so that her hair spilled forward to hide her face.

'I *said*, we're here.'

Her head snapped up and she jerked herself away from him, suddenly a desperate blur of movement. Clawing at the handle, she fought to wriggle free as the door swung open, but he managed to catch her arm, hauling her back down onto the seat.

'Don't!' he snarled, showing her the .45 gripped tightly in his left hand, aimed across his body. 'You wouldn't get ten feet away.'

She stared at the gun, then at him, and the last of the fight drained out of her. As he gently relaxed his grip on her arm, she seemed to shrink, shoulders drooping, face slackening into a numb expression.

Frank twisted round in his seat to look at her. What the hell had happened in that room in Neosho? What was her part in all this? And who was Ellis?

'Let me lay it out for you,' he said. 'You're gonna give me everything I want. Everything. Your one chance to make it through this is to do exactly what I say. Is that *fucking* clear?'

She flinched as he swore, but managed to nod her head slightly.

Frank held her gaze for a moment, seeing the fear in her eyes, then turned his head away.

He'd seen that look before, years ago, and still hated himself for the memory of it.

'Okay,' he said, speaking more gently. 'Now, we're gonna get out, and we're gonna go into the hotel, arm in arm.'

Without taking his eyes off her, he reached back and opened his door, pushing it wide, then slid his leg over and lowered a foot to the ground.

'Out you get,' he said, gesturing with the gun. 'Nice and easy.'

Faye slowly raised her head and blinked at him, makeup streaked below her eyes, then slid her legs across the seat and got out on the far side.

Frank put on his hat and glanced around. The lot was enclosed on all sides by buildings: high walls and locked back doors. As long as he kept himself between her and the alley there was nowhere for her to run. Satisfied, he walked slowly around the car, nudging her door closed and linking his arm through hers. She offered no resistance.

'Just remember, you can't go to the cops, and nobody's gonna help you.' He searched her face, waiting for a response. 'Got that?'

Faye stared straight ahead, then nodded slowly.

'Good.' Frank took a final glance round at the overlooking windows. 'Let's go.'

They followed the alley back to the street, then went along the front of the hotel to the main entrance, Faye drifting at his side like a sleepwalker. Guiding her up the broad steps, Frank slipped the gun inside his jacket, but made sure she understood it was still there, still aimed at her.

Pushing the glass doors open, he led her into the lobby. Ahead of them, the young man on the desk glanced up, taking an uncomfortably long look at Faye and her smudged makeup. Frank caught his eye, then winked. The young man quickly lowered his gaze, a knowing smile spreading across his face.

That's right... just another lonely out-of-towner, taking some poor working-girl up to his room. Nothing memorable, nothing to be concerned about...

Holding her arm, Frank guided Faye across the lobby and up the stairs.

She seemed to become more alert as he led her along the dimly-lit corridor, half turning her head to peer behind them, pulling back a little as they came to the room.

'Don't.' He gave her a warning look, then slowly slipped his arm free of hers, so he could reach for the key without holstering his gun. Opening the door, he gestured for her to go first. She hesitated for a moment, as though trying to think of an alternative, then her shoulders dropped and she wearily went inside. Frank hung back for a second, glancing back along the empty corridor, then followed her into the room and pushed the door shut.

She was standing at the foot of the bed, a forlorn figure, half-silhouetted against the light of the window. The sight troubled him. Frowning, he turned away to lock the door, then took off his jacket and hat, and hung them up.

'Might as well make yourself comfortable,' he said, over his shoulder. 'We're gonna be here for a while.'

He slid the clip out of his .45, checked it, then slotted it back into the grip. She flinched at the sound, turning towards him with a startled expression, then she seemed to wilt again, sitting down on the edge of the bed and staring at the floor.

Frank watched her.

Was she really as resigned as she looked, or might she still try and run? His handcuffs were clipped to the belt of his uniform pants back in Joplin, but he wouldn't have had the heart to restrain her anyway. She was frightened enough without that.

He walked slowly over to the nightstand, set his gun down and picked up the half-empty bottle of bourbon.

'You want a drink?' he asked her, pulling the cork out.

She glanced round at him, then shook her head.

'No.'

'Sure? You look like you could use it.'

She didn't answer. Frank shrugged, then lifted the bottle to his mouth and tipped it up, knocking back a good measure, feeling the heat of it going down. Wiping his mouth with the back of his hand, he walked slowly to the corner of the bed and stared down at her. It was time for her to talk.

'Well?' he asked, expectantly.

Her gaze flickered up to his, then she gave an unhappy sigh and lifted a hand to her throat.

'Just don't rip my clothes, okay?' She lowered her eyes and began to unbutton the front of her dress. 'I won't fight.'

Surprised, Frank recoiled from her.

'Hey... *hey!*' He waited until she glanced up at him, then gave her a stern shake of his head. 'I don't know what you think this is, but *that's* not why I brought you here.'

Faye's expression became confused.

'I thought...' She trailed off and fell silent.

Frank shook his head again, wondering what sort of company she must have been keeping for her to think like that. He took another slug of bourbon, then pushed his hand through his hair.

'I brought you here to *talk*,' he explained.

'To talk?' Faye frowned, twisting her body round and gazing up at him, as though trying to read something in his eyes.

'To talk,' he said, firmly.

Faye stared at him.

'Who *are* you?' she asked.

He moved over to lean his back against the wall.

'My name's Frank Rye.'

Faye's eyes grew wide.

'*You're* Frank Rye? But...' She sank back onto the bed in bewilderment.

Frank gave her a chilly little smile.

'Remember the guy you took to your place, down in Neosho?' he said. 'The cop?'

'I... I thought...'

'You thought he was me?'

Faye's expression became fearful again, and she shrank back from him a little, then nodded.

Frank sighed.

'We had... one or two things in common... but no. That guy you met? That was a guy called Pete Barnes.'

Faye turned away from him slightly, frowning as she tried to take it all in. Frank watched her for a moment, then pushed himself away from the wall to stand upright.

'So what happened?' he asked. 'You say you didn't kill him, but he still wound up dead in your room.'

Faye raised her head.

'I *didn't* kill him!' she insisted. 'And I swear I didn't know Ellis was going to.'

She was starting to sound desperate, with a rising note of panic in her voice. Maybe he'd ridden her a little too hard. He had to back off a bit, keep her focused.

'Start at the beginning,' he told her. 'Where exactly did you meet Pete?'

Faye regarded him with suspicion for a moment, then appeared to relax slightly.

'I met him outside the Skordeno factory,' she explained.

'Outside?' he asked.

'That's right.'

'Okay,' Frank shrugged. 'But did you ever work there? Or know anyone there?'

'No. I was just supposed to wait at the front gate for a cop called Frank Rye, then ask him back to my place to collect some letters.'

Frank remembered the message: "Several letters, of a sensitive nature, relating to that poor mill owner... when would Officer Rye be free to come down and collect them?"

Someone had asked for him by name.

'You still have those letters?' he asked.

'There weren't any letters,' she explained. 'It was just a story, an excuse to get him back to my place.'

Frank scowled.

'Where Ellis would be waiting, right?'

Faye gave him an unhappy look.

'I didn't know what he was going to do!' she protested.

'No?' Frank goaded her. 'What did you *think* was gonna happen?'

Faye lowered her eyes.

'I was supposed to invite the cop upstairs and... you know... be friendly with him.'

Frank paused.

'How friendly?' he asked.

Faye blushed and stared at the floor.

Frank sighed.

'Okay, but why?'

'Ellis had it all figured out,' Faye explained. 'He was going to bust in on us and threaten to make trouble for the cop if he didn't do what Ellis wanted. Nobody was supposed to get hurt.'

Frank looked at her doubtfully.

'So you're saying it was some kind of *blackmail* plan?'

This didn't sound right. It should have been him in that room, not Pete. Unlike Pete, he wasn't married and Faye was old enough to be legal... *but of course, blackmail wasn't really what the thin man had in mind.*

Sitting on the edge of the bed, Faye nodded, miserably.

'I swear I didn't think anyone was gonna get killed,' she said.

'But...' Frank looked at her. 'Why would you agree to... do *that* with some cop you'd never met?'

Faye lifted her face and he saw her eyes were glistening with tears once more.

'I got in trouble with some... bad people,' she said quietly. 'This... this was supposed to make it right.'

Frank studied her for a moment, then took another shot of bourbon. Ever since that moment in the churchyard – with her desperate denial, and her insistence that it was just a way of keeping someone in line – he'd had an uneasy feeling about her, that maybe she wasn't involved the way he'd thought she was. Now it looked as if she was just another mark – not exactly innocent, but a long way from being guilty – caught up in something she didn't even understand.

But she was still his only link to the thin man.

He rubbed his eyes.

'So you met Pete and he drove you back to your place. Then what?'

'We went upstairs.'

'He didn't ask you for the letters?'

Faye looked at the floor and said nothing.

Frank sighed.

Pete must have stopped thinking with his head by that stage.

'Go on,' he told her.

Faye swallowed hard, as if she was gathering her courage.

'When Ellis did bust in on us, that's when I knew something was wrong,' she explained. 'He was carrying a bat, and he had this look on his face, like nothing I ever saw before. He didn't say anything, just smiled this awful smile...'

She broke off and shivered.

'What did Pete do?' Frank asked.

'The cop?' Faye's eyes were glassy as she relived the moment. 'He tried to protect me, put himself between me and Ellis... but he didn't have his gun on him by then. So when Ellis started swinging the bat... well, he just yelled for me to get out.'

Frank shook his head.

Poor old Pete, valiantly trying to protect the woman who'd lured him to his death.

'What did you do?' he asked.

'I just ran.'

'Ran where?'

Faye glanced up at him.

'I hid. There's a bathroom at the end of corridor and I went in there and locked the door.'

'But why hide?' he said. 'Why not get the hell out of there?'

Faye blushed, looking down again.

'I... I wasn't dressed,' she admitted.

Frank nodded thoughtfully.

That's why she'd gone back to the room afterwards. She needed her clothes.

'How long were you hiding there?' he asked.

Faye considered this.

'I don't know... five minutes, maybe ten? I heard Ellis leaving, and then I heard Mr Furnier, the old man who lives in the apartment underneath – he called out and came up to see what was going on. I guess he took a look in my room, then went to get help. I know I heard him going down the stairs pretty fast. Well, pretty fast for *him*.'

It all fitted together... she might just be telling the truth.

'All right,' he said. 'Then what?'

'Well, when it was quiet, I opened the door and went back along the corridor to my room...'

She trailed off, a faraway look in her eyes.

'Go on,' Frank urged her.

'He was dead, lying there on the floor... it was...' Faye shook her head. 'It was just awful.'

Frank turned away. He could still see the interior of the room, Pete's body, broken and bloodied, the whole sickening aftermath.

'Tell me what happened then,' he said softly.

Faye bowed her head and took a breath, composing herself.

'I got dressed,' she said, shrugging slightly. 'Then I grabbed what I could, and got out. There was nobody downstairs, so when I made it out onto the sidewalk I just... started walking.'

Frank frowned.

'But you didn't go to the cops.'

Faye's head jerked up.

'Of *course* not!' she snapped. 'The *dead* guy was a cop! And those people I owe, Ellis' people, they don't like it when someone calls the cops.'

Frank weighed the bourbon bottle in his hand, then turned and set it down on the dresser.

'Tell me about Ellis,' he said, pacing slowly towards the window. 'What happened to him?'

'I don't know,' Faye replied. 'I didn't want anything more to do with him. That look in his eyes when he started swinging the bat...'

Frank looked round at her.

'How do you know him?' he asked.

'I didn't know him,' Faye explained. 'I just got a call from a friend in Kansas City. We... we worked for the same guy, and she said he wanted to talk to me about something. When I called him, he only told me I had to telephone Joplin Police Department, and what I had to say to them... you know, about the letters. It didn't sound so bad.'

She paused and her face darkened.

'I didn't meet Ellis till the next day. He showed up early and told me... you know... what else I had to do.' She lowered her eyes. 'I didn't want to but... well, I figured it was just one time, and it wouldn't be so bad if it meant I was free of them.'

Frank turned back to the window in disgust.

'Yeah, not so bad,' he growled, staring down at the street below. 'Except you and your friend Ellis killed the wrong guy.'

Behind him, Faye stirred.

'You think I *wanted* any of this?' she said angrily.

Frank rested his forehead against the glass and closed his eyes.

'I think Pete's dead,' he muttered. 'And you sure played your part.'

Just as he had played his.

'So that's why you're here?' she demanded. 'To get revenge?'

Frank sighed, picturing the smug way Ellis had nodded to him at Pete's funeral.

'A score like this has to be settled,' he said softly. He opened his eyes, blinking up at the bright sky above the buildings, then wearily stepped back from the window and turned around.

Faye was standing by the nightstand, pointing the gun at him.

'Is that why you did it?' she demanded. 'Is that why you killed my brother?'

Frank stared at her.

'*What*?!' he gasped.

Faye moved cautiously round to the end of the bed, staring at him down the barrel of the gun.

'To settle your score?' she snarled. 'You wanted to get rid of me so you thought you'd burn the building down. But you killed Stanley instead.'

Frank slowly held a hand up.

'Now wait just a minute,' he said carefully. 'I didn't start that fire.'

'No?' She bared her teeth in rage. 'You told me it wasn't an accident; how did you know that?'

Frank shook his head.

'I... look, you've got this whole thing wrong,' he said. 'I didn't start that fire, but I think maybe Ellis did.'

Faye hesitated.

'Ellis?'

'Think about it,' he urged her. 'You're a loose end; maybe he figured it was time to cut you off.'

Faye swallowed, looking less certain for a moment, then raised the gun again.

'He's not the one who kidnapped me, who threatened to *shoot* me!' she hissed.

Frank bowed his head. He *had* been rough on her, *too* rough, as it turned out.

'I'm sorry,' he sighed. 'I just needed to know the truth but... well, I guess I was wrong about you.'

'You *guess*?' She managed a bitter little laugh.

Frank shrugged.

'I'm right about Ellis, though,' he said. 'And sooner or later he's gonna catch up with you.'

There was a hunted look in her eyes now, and he saw her glancing towards the door.

'What's the use of that?' he challenged her. 'Where could you go? Back to the church hall? It didn't take *me* long to find you there, so it won't be difficult for him.'

Faye raised her chin.

'I'll go to the police,' she said, defiantly.

'I *am* the police,' he told her. '*Officer* Frank Rye, remember?'

Her face twisted in dismay.

'Shut up!' she cried, jabbing the gun at him. 'Just shut up!'

Very slowly, Frank stepped forward, reaching out and picking up the bourbon bottle from the dresser.

'Stop!' Faye warned him, despair rising in her voice. 'Don't come any closer!'

'It's okay,' he told her gently. 'I don't blame you for being mad at me. But you know I'm right.'

'Stay back!' she insisted, the gun shaking in her hands.

Frank looked into her eyes, then took another step forward.

'Faye, please...'

'I mean it!' Stumbling backwards, she pointed the gun at the ceiling and pulled the trigger.

There was a sharp *click*.

Panicked, she stared at the gun, then aimed and pulled the trigger again.

Click. Click. Click.

Frank took a long swig of bourbon, then set the bottle down and held out his hand for the gun.

'You've got heart,' he told her. 'But you haven't got any bullets.'

She gaped at him.

'Clip's empty,' he explained, reaching out and gently taking the gun from her. 'I didn't come here to kill *you*.'

Trembling, Faye put out a hand, leaning against the wall to steady herself.

'I... I don't understand this...' she whispered.

'I'm here for Ellis,' he said, checking the gun and sliding it back into his holster. 'The bastard killed Pete, and your brother Stanley, so I'm gonna blow his brains out.'

He met her startled gaze, then turned and walked back over to the window.

'And until I do, the safest place for you is with me.' He glanced back at her. 'Unless you have someone else you can go to?'

Faye walked over to the bed and sat down heavily, bowing her head into her hands.

'Stanley was the only friend I had left,' she sniffed.

Frank stared down at the street.

'No,' he said softly. '*I'm* the only friend you have left.'

32

The early evening traffic rumbled by as they turned the corner and walked slowly down the long line of restaurants on Central Street. Frank stared in through a few different windows, then stopped outside a grill joint called The Cook Out. Turning to Faye, he raised an eyebrow.

'Well?' he said. 'What do you think?'

She gave him a cold stare, then shrugged her shoulders.

Frank sighed, then turned and pushed the door open.

'After you,' he told her.

The place was small and dimly lit, but a delicious smoky aroma of cooking hung in the air. They took a booth in the corner near the back and sat on opposite sides of the table. A waitress with long black hair came over and offered each of them a menu.

'Our specials today are the smoked chicken and the blackened salmon.' Straightening up, she flashed a brief smile. 'I'll be right back with some water.'

Pivoting on her heels, she clicked away across the wooden floor. Frank followed her with his eyes, then turned to find Faye watching him. Frowning, he picked up his menu and studied it for a moment. He hadn't eaten since breakfast and the smell of barbecue always stirred his appetite.

Glancing up, he noticed that Faye was sitting with her hands folded on the red and white table cloth, one thumb stroking the other in a soothing motion. Her menu lay untouched on the table.

'Not hungry?' he asked.

She stared past him for a moment, as though not wanting to acknowledge him, then lowered her eyes.

'I don't have enough money,' she said.

Frank looked at her awkwardly. Of course she didn't. The poor kid had been on the run for days, and everything she owned would have been lost in the fire.

He frowned and fumbled in his pants pocket, drawing out his wallet and thumbing through the worryingly thin fold of bills that remained.

'Eat,' he said gruffly. 'It's on me, okay?'

Her gaze met his for a second, then she reached for the menu and lifted it, so he couldn't see her face.

The waitress brought their food out and set the plates down carefully on the table.

'One chicken platter...' She turned to Frank. '...and a rack of ribs. Enjoy.'

She moved away.

Across the table from him, Faye had already seized her knife and fork and was attacking her food hungrily.

Frank watched her for a moment, then picked up his own cutlery.

'Is it all right?' he asked her.

She looked up at him, her face unreadable, then gave a slight nod.

Frank stared down at his plate.

'Good,' he said.

They ate in silence for a time. After a while, Frank paused and glanced across at her.

'So,' he said. 'Have you lived in Kansas City long?'

Faye lifted her head, then slowly put her knife and fork down.

'Moved here when I was fifteen,' she said quietly. 'We were in Jefferson City before that.'

'You got any family here?'

He spoke casually, with an encouraging tone, but he knew he had to figure out how he was going to keep her safe. Whatever she'd done, she wasn't a willing accomplice to the thin man... and she was still his best chance of finding the bastard. Either way, he didn't want anything to happen to her.

Faye's expression darkened and she stared down at her plate.

'Mom and dad passed away, year before last. Stanley...' She faltered, then cleared her throat and continued. 'He was the only family I had.'

Shit. Feeling stupid, Frank looked away.

'I'm sorry,' he said.

Faye took a breath, then picked up her fork and continued eating.

For a time, neither one of them spoke. Eventually, Frank sat back in his seat and tried again.

'So what took you down to Neosho?'

Faye hesitated, then looked up.

'I just... felt like a change.' She paused for a long moment, then added, 'I heard there was a job going down there.'

Frank noted the unease in her voice.

'Didn't you have a job *here*?' he asked.

Faye lowered her eyes and nodded. Setting her cutlery down, she picked up a napkin and dabbed at her mouth.

Frank frowned. Had she been running away from something? Or someone?

'Who did you work for when you were here?' he asked.

Faye slowly folded the napkin, then raised her eyes to meet his.

'Can we talk about something else?' Her voice seemed calm, but there was something in her expression, something that warned him not to press her.

'Sure, I guess.' He gave a shrug, as though it was nothing to him. 'What would *you* like to talk about?'

She sat back, studying him for a moment.

'You said you're a cop...'

It was more of a challenge than a question.

'That's right,' Frank replied. 'Joplin PD. Joined up after the war.'

'You don't *act* like a cop,' she said.

He managed a brief, rueful smile.

'Maybe I'm not a very good one.'

Faye crumpled the napkin in her hand and placed it at the side of her plate. He could see the suspicion in her eyes.

'What's a Joplin cop doing all the way up here?' she asked. 'Are you here about a case? About that other cop...?'

Frank sighed, then nodded.

'About Pete Barnes, yeah.'

Faye appeared to consider this.

'Was he a friend of yours?'

Frank shifted in his seat, then rubbed his eyes, wearily.

No. He really *hadn't* been much of a friend to Pete Barnes.

'Can we talk about something else?' he sighed.

He caught a tiny glimmer of interest in her eye before the waitress appeared, clearing away their plates and sparing him further questions.

It was dark when they stepped out onto the sidewalk. Frank put on his hat and took out his cigarettes, then held out the pack to

Faye. She hesitated, then took one, and waited while he lit it for her.

'Thanks,' she said.

'Forget it,' he told her. 'Come on, let's walk.'

They made their way back up Central Street, moving slowly, both of them wrapped in their own thoughts.

'Did Ellis ever talk about me?' Frank asked suddenly. 'Did he mention anything, other than what he wanted you to do?'

Faye slowed, shaking her head.

'No, nothing,' she replied. 'That day was the only time I ever saw him.'

Frank scowled.

'Then I don't get it,' he muttered.

'Don't get what?'

Frank stopped and turned to face her.

'I don't get why he was after me,' he sighed. 'I mean, I'm sure I don't know the guy.'

Faye's brow crinkled into a frown.

'Maybe you didn't,' she said, simply.

Frank shot her a questioning look.

'Think about it,' Faye told him. 'Ellis didn't know you either, did he?'

Frank stared at her, then began to nod.

'Or he wouldn't have killed the wrong man,' he said. 'Yeah, you're right.'

He took a drag on his cigarette, turning this over in his mind. Ellis didn't know who he was, so it wasn't anything personal... but *someone* had sent the bastard down to find him.

He glanced at Faye. Didn't she say that her first contact with Ellis had come via her old boss? That she'd been in trouble with some "bad people"?

Faye caught his look, and her expression became wary.

'What is it?' she asked.

He took a step towards her.

'Faye, I need to know who used to work for.'

For just a second, fear flickered in her eyes, but she took a long draw on the cigarette and said nothing. He stared at her, reaching out to take her arm, but let go when she flinched from his touch.

'I'm sorry, I just...' He held his hands up, taking a step away from her to give her space. 'I just want to understand who Ellis is, who he works for.'

Faye turned away, taking another drag on the cigarette before looking back over her shoulder at him.

'Bad people?' Frank prompted her. 'We're talking about the Mob, right?'

Faye stared at him for a moment, then lowered her eyes and managed a slight nod.

The Mob.

Frank took a breath as the implications started to sink in.

'And that's who you worked for too, right?' he continued. 'That's who you owed...'

Faye hesitated, then nodded again.

Frank took a final hit on his cigarette, then dropped the butt and ground it out under his shoe.

The Mob.

It certainly explained why she'd gone along with Ellis' instructions, but the rest of the pieces still didn't fit. Why him? He was just a small-time cop, screwing up his life in a small-time way.

Why the hell would the Kansas City Mob be interested in him?

Shaking his head, he glanced across at Faye.

'Come on,' he said, starting along the sidewalk.

Faye took a nervous step forward.

'So... we're going back to the hotel now?' she asked.

'Yeah.'

He frowned, head down as he walked, trying to think.

Did the Mob have interests as far south as Joplin? Had he busted someone "connected" without even knowing it?

Behind him, Faye had slowed her pace. He turned to look back at her, saw the doubt in her eyes.

'What's the matter?' he demanded.

She hung back and gave a slight shake of her head.

'Faye?'

He turned, trying to read her, then suddenly remembered the way she'd looked before, as she reluctantly unbuttoned her dress. Bowing his head, he rubbed his eyes again.

'Listen, you can come with me or not, it's up to you, but I really think you'll be safest if you stay with me.' He straightened up and gave her a long, steady look. 'And you can have the bed, if that's what you're worried about.'

Faye met his gaze.

'What about you?' she asked. 'What will you do?'

Frank shrugged his shoulders.

'Well, I guess I get to sleep in the chair,' he replied.

A strange light came into Faye's eyes and she bit her lip.

Frank sighed and held his hands out wide.

'What is it?' he said wearily.

Faye gave him a thoughtful look.

'You really *don't* act like a cop,' she said.

33

They were still a block away when he spotted the police cars skewed across the road, the shadowy figures beginning to form a crowd. The steady rhythm of his footsteps faltered and he slowed.

'What's wrong?' Faye caught something in his expression and turned to see what he was looking at. 'Is that the hotel?'

Frank hesitated, then nodded.

There were three black-and-whites that he could see, and an ambulance. Spotting it, he relaxed a little. Whatever the police were here for, it had already happened.

He lifted his chin, straightening up.

'It's all right,' he told her. 'I'm a cop too, remember? We'll be okay.'

Putting a hand gently on the back of her shoulder, he gave her a reassuring smile and they started walking again.

It was strange, feeling uneasy at the sight of the police cars. When had that happened to him? Was this how ordinary people felt?

He glanced at Faye, sensing the tension in her shoulder,

seeing the tightness in her jaw, wondering what she meant when she said he didn't act like a cop.

What kind of cops had she known?

He could see a couple of uniforms now, patiently turning people back, trying to maintain a perimeter. Absently, he patted his pocket, then made his way towards one of them, leading Faye between the onlookers.

'Evening,' he said before he was challenged.

The officer, a stocky man in his early thirties, raised a hand to stop them.

'Sorry folks, I can't let you through here just now.' He gestured back up the street, the way they'd come. 'You'll have to go around.'

'Oh.' Frank feigned concern, looking at Faye, then pointing towards the hotel entrance. 'But we're staying right there. At the Bradbury.'

The cop planted his feet a little wider apart.

'I'm still gonna have to ask you to wait, sir.'

Frank fixed his politest smile, then reached into his pocket.

'Hey, I understand. And don't worry...' He pulled out his badge, and let the officer see it. 'We're on the same side – I'm Joplin PD myself.'

Suspended... Maybe for good...

The officer peered down at the badge, then seemed to relax slightly.

'Now I appreciate you gotta keep undesirables from crowding the place,' Frank continued. 'I was just wondering if you had any idea when we'd be allowed to go back to our room? It's been a long day.'

He put a protective arm around Faye's shoulder, the way a husband might.

The officer hesitated, then gave him an awkward smile.

'Well, I guess there's no harm if you go inside,' he said. 'You might not be able to get to your room... I think they have one of the floors shut off just now. But at least you can wait in the lobby.'

Frank inclined his head.

'Much obliged,' he said, putting his badge away, then looking up at the hotel. 'Say, do you happen to know what's going on in there?'

The cop glanced around, then leaned over, his voice low.

'Nothing official yet, but I hear it was a shooting. Real nasty.'

'You don't say.' Frank shook his head. 'We don't get many shootings down in our part of the world.'

The officer's face became grim.

'Sadly, it ain't so unusual up here.' He stood aside and beckoned them past. 'You folks have a good night now.'

'Thanks, you too.'

Frank took Faye's hand and led her past the police cars towards the hotel entrance.

There were several more uniforms in the lobby. Over by reception, one of them looked up, then turned around to the elderly man behind the desk. Frank saw him mouthing the words *Is he a guest?* and the old man peering across and nodding slightly.

The cop straightened up and started walking towards them. He was older than the officer who'd waved them through, with a calm expression and patient blue eyes.

'Excuse me, sir?' He moved to position himself in front of them, blocking their way to the staircase. 'Can you tell me which floor you're going to?'

Frank hesitated, then reached into his pocket and drew out the key.

'Fourth floor, room four-one-three.' He gave the cop a questioning look. 'Why? What's the matter?'

The cop glanced at Faye, who shrank back a little, then turned to Frank.

'There's nothing to be concerned about,' he said. 'You can go up to your room, but I'll need you to stay away from the second floor. It's closed off while we conduct an investigation.'

Frank nodded, then assumed a grave expression and lowered his voice.

'One of the people outside said there was a shooting?'

But the cop remained impassive, too clever to be drawn.

'Everything's in hand,' he said. 'Just please, keep to your own floor.'

'Of course.' Frank turned to Faye. 'Let's go up.'

They started across the lobby once again, Faye's heels clicking quickly on the hard floor. They'd almost reached the staircase when a voice called out sharply behind them.

'Hey!'

Frank turned around.

It was Adam, marching over to them with a grim expression, his fists clenching and unclenching.

'Wondered when you'd show up,' he snapped.

Frank took a half-step back from him.

'What's the matter?' he asked.

Adam moved closer.

'I thought maybe you could tell me,' he said. His eyes were glittering, the way they used to when he was about to take down some lowlife. It was unnerving to be on the wrong end of that gaze.

'What's that supposed to mean?' Frank demanded.

Adam took a breath, as though trying to restrain himself.

'I got a guy, here, shot dead in his room,' he said. 'Now tell me, where have you been this evening?'

'We were at a grill on Central Street. The Cook Out.' Frank stared at his old colleague. 'You can check if you want.'

Adam smiled, but there was nothing pleasant about it.

'Oh, you *bet* I will.'

'Why? What's this got to do with me?'

'I'll tell you why,' Adam hissed, leaning forward and grabbing the sleeve of Frank's jacket. 'You mention an address to me, and the same day the place gets burned down. You tell me you're staying at a hotel, and a guy gets shot there. I don't know what you're mixed up in but I want to know what the *hell* you're doing here.'

Frank snatched his jacket free and glared at his old colleague.

'Quit screwing around, Adam,' he growled. 'You *know* where I was for the fire. And we really *were* at The Cook Out tonight.'

Adam scowled at him for a moment, then seemed to notice Faye for the first time.

'What about you?' he asked her. 'You were with him tonight?'

Faye blinked up at him, then nodded.

'And they'll remember you when I ask at the restaurant?'

Faye nodded again.

Adam stared down at her, then narrowed his eyes.

'Faye Griffith, right?'

The sound of her name appeared to startle her.

'Y-yes?' she stammered.

Adam's expression became thoughtful.

'What's the story here?' he asked. 'You know that Frank's been looking for you?'

Standing at her side, Frank stiffened.

What would she say? If she cracked now, it was all over.

Faye glanced up at him, then looked back to Adam.

'Yes,' she said. 'He found me.'

Frank exhaled.

Adam nodded slowly, suspicion still evident on his face.

'Uh-huh... Anything you might want to tell me? Anything I should know?'

He was fishing now, sensing there was something below the surface, even if he wasn't quite sure what it was. But he sounded so damned convincing... she was going to think he already knew, she was going to talk.

Blinking again, Faye hesitated, then slowly shook her head.

Adam studied her for a moment longer, then sighed and turned back to Frank.

'So you really don't know anything about this?' he demanded. 'Some guy gets machine-gunned in his hotel room, right after you tell me you're staying here, and it's just... *coincidence?*'

Frank met his gaze and held it.

No coincidences... only warnings.

He straightened, allowing a note of irritability into his voice now.

'Like I told you, we weren't here, so no; I really *don't* know anything about it.' He paused, frowning. 'Who the hell uses a *machine* gun anyway? You think it was... I don't know... rival gangsters or something?'

Adam hesitated, then something in his eyes changed, and for a moment it was almost like they were fellow cops again, discussing a case.

'Doesn't seem very likely,' he said. 'Victim was seventy years old; some retired college professor, name of Edward Linden.'

Edward Linden.

The name hit him like a bucket of ice water. Frank stared straight ahead, fighting to keep the shock off his face, trying to remember all the places he'd used that name while searching for Faye.

...well, if you do remember anything, contact me at the Bradbury Hotel. The name's Edward Linden...

He looked at Adam, but his old colleague had lifted a hand and was waving to someone on the far side of the lobby.

He hadn't noticed.

'Anyway, I'm still gonna want to speak to you,' Adam said. 'Don't leave town, either of you.'

Frank took a breath, then made a point of straightening his jacket.

'You know where to find me,' he said.

Adam sighed wearily.

'Yeah, I do.'

He turned and walked away. Without a word, Frank touched Faye's arm and nodded towards the stairs. They climbed in silence, their footsteps in sync, as they made their way upwards. As the staircase angled back on itself and they approached the second floor, Frank saw another uniformed officer standing at the end of the corridor that led to the rooms. The cop watched them carefully as they continued past, climbing on towards the fourth.

Entering the room, Frank threw his hat onto the chair, then walked over to stand by the window. Peering down into the street, he watched the people milling around beyond the police cars, eager strangers all trying to get closer.

It was like being in a siege.

Behind him, Faye pushed the door closed.

'So?' she asked quietly.

Frank turned to look at her.

'So what?'

She took a couple of steps towards him, then halted, arching an eyebrow.

'Who's this Edward Linden?'

Damn. Frank tried his best to look puzzled.

'How should I know?' he replied, speaking carefully now. 'You were there with me, you heard what Adam said.'

'Yeah, and I was watching you when he mentioned the name. You know something.'

Frank gave her a long look then shook his head wearily.

'It's nothing,' he told her. 'Forget about it.'

Faye was silent for a moment, then she glanced towards the door.

'Listen,' she said. 'Either you level with me, or I go downstairs and take my chances with that detective. He... he seemed like a straight-up guy.'

Frank bowed his head, then sighed. Adam *was* a straight-up guy. *He wouldn't have got himself into a mess like this, wouldn't have got some old college professor killed.*

'I didn't think this would happen...' he said softly, then trailed off.

'What do you mean?' Faye pressed him.

Frank took a deep breath.

'When I was asking around, about you and Ellis... well, I didn't want to leave my *own* name, so I gave out a different one.' He shut his eyes. 'One I lifted from the hotel register.'

'But...' There was a long pause, as Faye put it together. 'But why would you *do* that? Why not just use a false name?'

'So they could get in touch if they had any information.' Frank opened his eyes slowly, staring down at the floor. 'So they could find me.'

Faye sat down heavily on the bed.

'Ellis,' she said softly.

Frank paused, then nodded.

'The bastard must have heard that someone was asking questions... decided to come over here and deal with it.'

He extended an index finger, them mimed pulling a trigger.

Faye sat motionless, staring at nothing.

'He's not gonna stop, is he?'

Frank looked at her, then turned away and moved back to the window.

'Do you know *anything* else about him?' he asked. 'Where he lives? Where he works? Anything at all?'

'Sorry, no.' She sounded distant now, drained.

Frank clenched his fist as he stared out at the illuminated windows in the building opposite.

'There must be *something*,' he muttered.

Behind him, Faye sighed.

'I told you before; they got in touch with my friend and she asked me to call them. I don't even know who *they* are, only that they're the kind of people you don't say "no" to. Ellis... well, he just showed up the next day. I'd never seen him before, and I haven't seen him since.'

Frank turned around.

'You still have that number?' he asked.

'What?'

'The number you were asked to call. Do you still have it?'

Faye stared at him blankly, then picked up her purse and snapped it open. She rummaged through the contents for a moment, then stopped, drawing out a folded paper napkin with a number scrawled on it.

Frank stepped over to her and took the napkin, turning it over in his hand. She gazed up at him.

'What are you going to do?'

Frank hesitated.

'I'm not sure,' he admitted. 'Call the number, I guess.'

Faye gave him a doubtful look.

'What good will *that* do?' she asked.

Irritated, Frank turned away, staring down at the scrawl on the napkin.

'I don't know,' he said, after a moment. He couldn't call in any more favors from Adam, not right now. 'Maybe we can figure out where he is. And if we can do that, maybe I can get to him before he gets to us.'

He glanced over, but Faye was staring at the floor, her expression bleak.

'I've got to do *something*,' he told her. 'And anything's better than just waiting for him to hunt us down.'

Turning his back on her, he walked over to the telephone and picked it up, wondering what the hell he was going to say.

Figure out if Ellis was there... try and arrange a meeting, perhaps?

Frowning, he stood for a moment, then carefully dialed the number. It rang three times, then there was a click and a man with a gruff voice answered.

'Sugarhouse Haulage Company.'

Frank tightened his grip on the receiver and leaned close to the mouthpiece.

'Let me speak to Ellis,' he demanded.

'He ain't here,' the gruff voice replied. 'Who's this?'

Frank hesitated. Ellis wasn't there, but they knew him all right. This might be just the opening he needed.

'Listen to me,' he snapped. 'You tell Ellis I've got information about his friend Rye and the girl. He'll understand. Tell him I'll call again tomorrow afternoon. You got that?'

There was a pause, then the voice returned, sounding less sure now.

'I don't know what the hell you're talking about.'

'Ellis will,' Frank growled. 'You tell him I'll call tomorrow afternoon.'

'But–'

Frank quickly replaced the receiver, then stood staring at the phone for a moment. His heart was racing.

This was it. At long last, he had a chance to be one step ahead of Ellis, to call the shots rather than play a blind defense. Excited, he turned to look at Faye, but she just gazed up at him unhappily.

'Come on,' he told her. 'This is *good*. How about a little optimism?'

Faye leaned back, studying him.

'Why?' she said. 'How do you think you're gonna fix this?'

Frank gave her a grim smile.

'By killing Ellis, that's how.'

But Faye just shook her head.

'And *then* what?' she asked.

Frank hesitated.

'What do you mean?'

Faye got slowly to her feet and walked over to the window.

'Whoever sent Ellis,' she said, turning back to look at him. 'Won't they just send someone else?'

34

It was a small warehouse on Campbell Street, tucked away in a quiet corner of the North End neighborhood. Frank had got the address from the phone book. Now they were sitting in the Oldsmobile, parked at the far end of the block, watching the front of the building.

Faye shifted in her seat.

'You think he's in there?' she asked.

'Hard to say,' Frank mused. 'His car isn't here. Assuming the one I saw before *was* his car.'

They'd driven right around the block, and there was no sign of the grey Chrysler. A tan Ford and a blue Studebaker were parked outside the warehouse. Beyond them was a large truck with the Sugarhouse Haulage name painted down the side.

'Have you figured out what you're gonna say?' Faye asked.

'I don't know exactly,' Frank replied. 'I want him riled up though. Maybe he'll get mad and say something useful.'

'Not much of a plan.'

'Right now we don't have much of anything.' Frank drummed his fingers on the steering wheel. 'We need to know why he sent you after me, whether he's working for someone. Until then, we're just groping around in the dark.'

Faye ran her fingers along the chrome door lining.

'He *has* to be working for someone else. Don't you think so?'

'Most likely,' he agreed. 'But I'll be a lot happier once I know for sure. And I want to know *who*.'

They lapsed into silence for a while. Further down the street, a group of children ran laughing out of an apartment block, then disappeared round the corner.

Frank yawned and checked his watch.

Faye leaned across to see the dashboard clock.

'Shouldn't he be here by now?' she frowned.

Frank's eyes flickered to the rear-view mirror then back to the street.

'He's leaving it late,' he admitted.

'You think he'll come?' There was an anxious note in her voice.

'He'll come,' Frank said, doing his best to sound confident. Ellis *had* to come. If he didn't, they were screwed.

'What if he doesn't tell you anything?' she asked. 'Anything useful, I mean.'

'Well, then...' Frank broke off, trying to figure out what the hell they *could* do. 'I guess we follow him, find out where he goes, where he lives.'

Faye considered this.

'You're not going to grab him right here?'

Frank shook his head.

'Not here, no.' He pointed a finger towards the warehouse then gripped the wheel again. 'This place smells like a Mob operation, so he'll probably have friends inside. I want him on his own.'

Preferably someplace quiet, private. It could take a while to sweat the truth out of Ellis, and he might not want to rush things...

A green Plymouth sedan appeared at the far corner of the block and turned onto the street. Frank leaned forward as it crept towards them, but it continued on past. He watched it disappearing in the rear-view mirror, then relaxed back into his seat.

'Mind if I ask you something?' Faye said.

Frank sighed. *More questions.*

'Sure,' he replied without enthusiasm.

Faye twisted around in her seat to face him.

'You're a cop...' she began.

'Yeah?'

'So, why are you doing this by yourself?'

Frank stared straight ahead.

'This isn't just some... everyday crime; this is personal.' He thought of Beth, the way she'd greeted him when he came to the house that last time, that slender hand reaching up to touch her hair...

The last time he'd seen her smile.

'I made a promise.'

Faye paused, tilting her head slightly.

'To who?' she asked.

Frank sat motionless and said nothing.

Faye watched him for a moment, then shrugged and settled back into the corner of her seat.

'Okay, but what about the police? You don't trust them?' she asked. 'Your detective friend from the hotel?'

Frank glanced at her, then looked away.

His time in Switzerland had taught him not to trust anyone.

'Friends let you down,' he said, quietly.

The grey Chrysler turned onto the street a little after two-thirty. Resting his head against the window, Frank blinked and sat up. He watched as the car slowed, then swept over to park across the street from the warehouse. Faye leaned forward, squinting through the windshield, as a thin figure in a suit got out.

'That's Ellis!' she said.

Frank nodded grimly.

'I know.'

They watched as he strode quickly across the road to the warehouse and disappeared inside.

Faye continued to stare at the building for a moment, then turned to look at Frank.

'Are you going to call?'

'Not yet.' Frank checked his watch, then folded his arms. 'He's kept us waiting. Let *him* twist in the wind for a while.'

It was almost three o'clock when Frank finally stirred, reaching into his jacket pocket to make sure he still had the paper napkin.

'Okay,' he said.

Faye sat up.

'Now?'

'I'll be back in a few minutes,' he said. 'While I'm gone, you watch the place. If Ellis or anyone else comes out of there, I need to know which direction they go. If they drive, I'll want to know the color of the car, and the license tag if you can see it.'

Faye's eyes were nervous, but she nodded quickly.

'Got it.'

Frank pushed his door open, then glanced back at her.

'And stay low in your seat,' he warned. 'Don't let them see you.'

'Okay.'

Frank got out and put his hat on, pulling the brim down.

'Wish me luck,' he muttered, then slammed the door shut and began walking back up the street. At the corner he turned left, following the sidewalk past a neighborhood deli and a pizza parlor, his eyes on the shiny new phone booth ahead of him.

Pushing inside, he unfolded the napkin and took a brief moment to collect himself. Then he lifted the handset, dropped a nickel in the slot, and dialed the number.

Click.

'Sugarhouse Haulage Company.'

The same gruff voice he'd spoken to yesterday. *Good.*

'Let me talk to Ellis,' he said.

There was recognition on the other end of the line, and the voice became hesitant.

'Who wants him?'

Frank leaned into the mouthpiece.

'Ellis is expecting my call,' he snarled. 'So quit stalling and go get him!'

There was a crackle and a series of muffled sounds, then a new voice came on the line.

'This is Ellis. Who are you?'

Frank straightened up, staring out through the glass.

'I'm the guy who can help you solve your missing persons problem.'

'Oh yeah?' Ellis sounded amused. 'Who says I need any help?'

'I do,' Frank replied. 'So far you've taken out a small-town cop, burned down an apartment building, and machine-gunned an old man in a hotel room. You've killed a lot of people, but none of them were the ones you're after.'

There was moment of stunned silence, then Ellis' voice returned, troubled.

'Now listen, I don't know anything–'

'No, you really *don't*,' Frank said. 'And that's why you need my help, before you make things any worse for yourself.'

Another pause, then Ellis snapped back, angrily, 'Who the *fuck* do you think you are, talking to me like that?'

Frank smiled, leaning back against the inside of the booth.

'I'm the one who's gonna help you finish this,' he said. There was a note of uncertainty in the other man's voice; it was time to test their theory that he was working for someone else. 'Now, I guess you're getting paid for all this, right?'

'Oh, and you're gonna make me a better offer, is that it?' Ellis sneered.

Staring out at the street, Frank shook his head.

'No, I want to be paid, just like you.' He paused for a second. 'But there's no reason why we can't *both* do well out of it.'

Ellis hesitated.

'What do you mean by that?'

He was trying to sound tough, but Frank could feel the anxiety in him.

'Your boss didn't tell you *why* he wanted Rye gone, did he?' He spoke in a mocking tone.

'No,' Ellis snarled down the phone. 'And I ain't dumb enough to ask.'

Frank silently punched the air. Ellis *was* working for someone!

'Listen,' he said firmly. 'I can deliver what your boss wants... what he *really* wants. He'll have to pay for it, but I think that's better than letting you kill half the city.'

'What he *really* wants?'

Frank grinned and adopted a smug tone.

'He didn't tell you, did he?'

'He told me enough,' Ellis retorted.

'Well, now I'm telling you: I can deliver the girl, *and* Rye, both alive...' Frank paused, then added, 'I might even fix things with the Kansas City PD, so they find someone else to pin that fire on.'

There was a long silence at the other end of the phone.

Had he pushed it too far? Would Ellis get mad and hang up on him?

He waited, straining to hear anything... then Ellis spoke again, his voice quieter, closer to the mouthpiece.

'And what would *you* want?'

Frank closed his eyes. He had the bastard now.

'Two grand, cash.'

'Two *grand?*'

'And I'll cut you in for two hundred of that,' Frank continued. '*If* you can make it happen by tomorrow.'

There was a pause, as though Ellis was thinking about this.

'Who the hell are you?' he asked.

Frank turned around in the booth, staring back along the sidewalk.

'I'm your only way out of this mess,' he said. 'Now go speak to your boss, and see if he wants to pay for a nice neat solution, or if he'd rather have you shooting into the crowd on Main Street and hoping for the best.'

'Now listen, whoever you are,' Ellis hissed. 'You don't just–'

'I'll call again tomorrow,' Frank said, and hung up the phone.

He stood for a moment, breathing hard. His hands were sweating and his muscles were tense, but it felt good to be calling the shots at last.

Ellis *was* just muscle – a hired-gun working for someone else – and the phone call had really shaken him up.

But which way would the bastard jump?

He stepped out of the phone booth, lit a cigarette, then turned and made his way back towards Campbell Street.

The next move was down to Ellis. If he agreed to a deal, they'd need to find somewhere to meet. But how could they possibly meet without Ellis bringing a squad of his thug friends? No, they'd have to arrange a meet, then try to hit Ellis earlier in the day, before he was ready. And that would mean tailing the bastard, figuring out where he lived...

Frank turned the corner, walking slowly. Reaching the Oldsmobile, he tossed his cigarette butt and opened the door.

'Get in!' Faye hissed at him. 'Quickly!'

'What is it?' He'd been reaching to remove his hat, but now his hand went for his gun.

Faye pointed towards the warehouse.

'It's him!'

He turned, just in time to see the thin man walking briskly across the street, his head down.

Ellis was on the move.

Sliding into the driver's seat, Frank started the engine just as the grey Chrysler pulled out into a broad U-turn and set off down the street. Eyes fixed on it, Frank nosed the Oldsmobile out from the curb and began to follow, keeping a good distance between them.

'Well?' Faye demanded. 'Did you speak to him? What happened?'

They bumped over an intersection.

'I think I got his attention,' Frank mused. 'And you were right about him working for someone else. I'm not sure who it is, but I got the feeling they don't trust Ellis very much.'

'Smart move,' she said, squinting at the Chrysler up ahead of them. 'You think that's where he's headed now?'

Frank gripped the steering wheel.

'I guess we're gonna find out.'

They drove for a while. Before long, it became clear that they were heading out of the city. As the houses and vacant lots gave way to trees and open fields, Frank pulled the sun visor down to shield his eyes.

'Where are you going?' he muttered under his breath.

Faye stared out at the road, shading her eyes with her hand.

'You think he's running?' she asked. 'Just getting the hell out?'

Frank glanced over at her. He hadn't considered that, but it was a possibility.

'I don't know,' he said. 'Maybe.'

'But we still follow him, right?'

'Yeah,' Frank told her. 'The way I see it, we don't have any other choice.'

·   ·   ·

They'd been on the move for almost an hour when the Chrysler turned off onto a side road that led away into an expanse of rolling woodland. There was a little gas station by the turn-off, with a distinctive yellow ribbon tied around the sign pole.

Suddenly, Faye stiffened, then slumped back into her seat. Frank turned to look at her and saw that she'd clapped her hand across her mouth.

'What is it?' he asked, seeing the dread in her eyes. 'What's wrong?'

Faye shook her head slowly, then turned towards him.

'I think I know where he's taking us.'

Winter, 1944/45
Bern, Switzerland

Kansas City Herald

KANSAS CITY, MISSOURI - MONDAY, January 29, 1945

NATION MOURNS ROOSEVELT; TRUMAN BECOMES PRESIDENT

F.D.R. DIES OF CEREBRAL HEMORRHAGE; TRUMAN PLEDGES TO PRESS FOR VICTORY

WASHINGTON, Jan 29 – Franklin Delano Roosevelt, President of the United States, died suddenly in the Oval Office at 6:55pm yesterday evening. Stricken by a cerebral hemorrhage, he lost consciousness and, despite efforts to revive him, died soon after. He was 62.

The White House announced his death at 8:15pm. Less than two hours after the official announcement, Harry S Truman of Missouri, the Vice President, was sworn in as the thirty-second President. The oath was administered by U.S. Chief Justice Harlan F Stone in a short ceremony at the White House.

TRUMAN WILL GO TO YALTA SUMMIT

President Truman stated his intention to attend next month's summit meeting with British Prime Minister Churchill and Russian Marshal Stalin at Yalta, saying it was "vital that the Allies press on to victory".

(continued on page 2, column 1)

35

Frank turned the corner and trudged along Waldheimstrasse, his shoes crunching through the thin crust of snow. Above him, the sky was darkening, the last golden glow on the horizon fading into a deep and distant blue. Walking across the intersection, he took a quick look behind him, but the street was deserted. Rubbing his hands together, he slipped around to the back of the building and started up the familiar steps of the fire escape. He moved quickly but quietly, remembering to be careful of the ice that formed below the roof gutters – impossible to see in the dark.

When he got to the window, he leaned down and rapped gently on the glass, then stood up, shivering. His breath bloomed out in pale clouds, billowing up into the evening sky.

There was movement, and a sliver of warm light flashed out across the fire escape, making the frost on the guard rails glitter. Molly's face appeared at the window, her expression already breaking into a smile. She helped him to raise the window, then leaned out and whispered, 'You're late.'

'Rafe wanted to talk,' Frank said with a sigh. 'Let me in; it's cold out here!'

Molly stepped back, holding the blackout blind for him. Frank bent low to clamber inside, then turned around to slide the window shut.

'Skies are clear,' he said, gazing out across the silhouettes of the city, dark shapes topped with white rooftops. 'I think it's gonna snow again tonight.'

He stepped back, letting the blind drop into place, then turned to face Molly. She flung her arms around him, then stiffened.

'Ugh!' she gasped. 'You're freezing!'

Frank kissed her forehead then released her.

'What did I tell you? It's cold out there.'

'Come over to the fire,' she urged him. 'Warm yourself up.'

'Well, okay,' Frank said. 'But I was kinda hoping you might do that for me.'

Molly arched an eyebrow at him, but there was a faint smile playing on her lips.

'We'll see,' she said, removing the blackened metal fire guard. 'Come on.'

He moved over to stand by the fireplace, holding out his hands to the small glowing grate, and feeling the prickle of heat as his face began to thaw.

'Oh yeah,' he sighed. 'That's good.'

Molly smiled at him.

'Shall I make us some gluhwein?' she asked. 'It won't take long.'

Frank nodded.

'That'd be perfect.'

Molly opened the closet and lifted out a dark green bottle, followed by the little patterned tin where she kept her precious stash of spices and sugar. Moving across to the stove, she began pouring wine into a small pan.

'So,' she said, glancing over at him, 'what did Rafe want to talk about?'

'Oh, some conversation he thinks he overheard between Dulles and Swift.' Frank yawned, feeling the heat returning to his hands. 'But you know what Rafe's like for getting excited over things.'

'Yes, I do.' Molly gave a sigh as she switched on the stove. 'What was it this time?'

'Something about Dulles being lined up as station chief for an OSS office in Berlin.'

'*Berlin?*'

'I know, it's kind of crazy.' Frank shook his head wearily. 'I mean, I get that the war's going well, but the Germans haven't surrendered yet.'

'And they won't, as long as Hitler's still in charge,' Molly said, then frowned. 'Assuming he *is* still in charge, of course.'

Frank looked over at her and nodded. It had started out as whispers among the embassy staff but speculation was certainly growing.

'No speeches in the last six weeks... and nobody's even seen the little rat-bastard in public, not since the bombing in July.' He turned back to stare into the flames. 'I think Rafe's right about one thing: I think the Führer's injuries were a lot worse than they let on.'

Molly added some spices as she slowly stirred the pan.

'It would explain the change in their strategy,' she said thoughtfully. 'Militarily, I mean.'

'The withdrawal from France...'

'And in the east, too.' Molly said. 'They're conserving their forces so much more than before, trying to slow the Russians down rather than fighting battles they can't win.'

'I wonder who's pulling the strings now,' Frank mused. 'Göring, I suppose.'

Molly stopped stirring and gazed down at the stove.

'When I was last in London, I was speaking to...' She hesitated, then continued. 'I spoke to someone about Hitler. He told me they'd had several opportunities to get him, but that an assassination was actually the *last* thing they wanted. The reasoning was that Hitler didn't listen to his generals, and almost *anyone* who succeeded him would do a better job, so I suppose it's not just *who's* pulling the strings, it's who *they're* listening to.'

'Knowing our luck, that's probably Rommel,' Frank said, with a sigh. He glanced across at her. 'Hey, the wine's starting to smell good.'

Molly peered down into the saucepan.

'I think it's about as mulled as it's likely to get,' she said. 'Hang your coat on the fireguard then get me a couple of cups, will you?'

Frank nodded slowly.

'Yes, ma'am,' he said, straightening up and pulling off his coat.

Molly glanced up from the stove with a slight smile.

'I've told you about calling me that,' she said. 'I'm not royalty.'

Frank carefully draped the coat over the fire guard, then moved over to stand behind her, circling his arms about her waist and nuzzling her hair.

'Well, maybe you are to me,' he whispered.

They pulled the chairs over to face the fire and sat down with the hot wine. Frank lit two cigarettes and passed one to Molly.

'Thanks.' She took a slow drag and blew out a long stream of smoke. 'Have you thought about what you'll do? After the war, I mean?'

'After?' Frank sat back in his chair. When the attack had come on Pearl Harbor, with conflict raging across Europe, the future had looked so uncertain; there hadn't seemed much point in planning too far ahead. 'I haven't really considered it.'

'I thought you'd be eager to get back to America,' Molly said.

Frank shrugged.

'I guess so,' he admitted. 'But there's nothing special waiting for me back there. And it's not as though I had my life all mapped out.'

Molly smiled.

'Most people know what they want,' she said. 'Or *think* they do, anyway.'

'Not me.' Frank leaned over to flick his cigarette ash into the grate. 'Maybe that's why I enlisted.'

Molly studied him, firelight dancing in her eyes.

'Well, I think you're very wise not to plan too far ahead,' she said. 'If you don't expect too much, you probably won't be disappointed.'

Frank grinned and took a sip of his drink.

'How about you?' he asked. 'Any grand plans?'

Molly appeared to consider this.

'Not really,' she replied. 'But I can see myself staying on the continent. Here, in Switzerland maybe... or even in Germany. There's sure to be a lot of important work to do when the fighting stops but... oh, I don't know.'

Frank looked at her for a moment, then nodded slowly.

'Hey, I could see myself living in Germany.'

Molly gave him a brief smile, then lowered her eyes. Lifting her cup, she took a sip then pulled a face.

'This would have been better if I'd had some orange juice,' she apologized. 'But you just can't get it any more...'

'Hey, it tastes good, and it's hot,' Frank told her, warming his hands on the cup. 'It's fine.'

Molly glanced up at him.

'You're easily pleased,' she said.

'Well, I'm just glad to have you back.' He tossed his cigarette butt into the fire, then reached over and placed a hand on her arm. 'You've spent so much time away lately.'

Molly looked down and sighed.

'I know. I wish I didn't have to but...' She shook her head slightly. 'It can't be helped, I'm afraid.'

With France liberated, Switzerland was no longer surrounded by enemy territory and that made travel a lot simpler. But with Molly's eastern connections, Frank didn't think she'd been spending much of her time in France.

'Where were you this time?' he asked. Rafe had said it was probably Czechoslovakia, but he hadn't sounded too sure.

Molly gave him an unhappy look.

'Please, Frank. You know I can't.'

He held her gaze for a moment, then lowered his eyes.

'Yeah, yeah... I get it,' he sighed. 'I just worry about you, okay?'

Molly's expression warmed a little.

'Nothing's going to happen to me,' she assured him.

'You don't know that. When Jean...' He broke off, bowing his head, then mumbled, 'Sorry.'

After a moment, he felt her hand on his shoulder.

'Is that what's troubling you?' Her voice was quieter now.

'Maybe,' he replied. 'Doesn't it trouble *you*?'

Molly withdrew her hand and leaned forward to stare into the fire.

'Is this the first friend you've lost?' she asked.

His thoughts went immediately to those early days in France... the sudden flash and the deafening roar of the explosion... being lifted from his feet and thrown across the road... the bewildering rain of dirt and rubble... then the eerie silence that followed, the stillness of the figures laying in the road ahead... Billy Jackson on his back, staring up at the sky, and Ron Cunningham, a few yards to his left. At first, he couldn't figure out why they didn't just get up...

'There was a mortar attack on our unit, not long after we got to France...' He glanced up at her. 'I've lost people.'

Molly nodded slowly.

'Were you close to them?'

'We were in the same unit.' Frank shrugged. 'I don't know about *close*.'

Molly's eyes were distant.

'When you lose the person you expected to spend the rest of your life with, you feel as though you've lost your whole future... all that remains is the now.' She took a breath, drawing herself up, then turning to look at him. 'But in a strange way, it means you can cope, because you know that the worst has already happened. After that, you can face anything, *do* anything...'

Frank stared at her, then shook his head.

'The way you say that, it's as if you–'

He broke off suddenly and they both sat up, listening.

From outside, the mournful howl of an air raid siren rose, echoing in the distance. A few seconds later, it was joined by another, then another.

Molly got to her feet, and moved quickly over to the window, her hand on the blackout blind.

'Switch the light out,' she said.

Frank reached over and turned the lamp off, then went across to join her at the window.

Outside, the city was in darkness, dim shapes outlined by snow, but here and there he glimpsed the tell-tale flicker of blinds being drawn back, as people came to peer out. Air raids weren't common in neutral Switzerland, and especially not here in Bern.

Molly leaned close to the glass, staring up into the night sky as the wailing sound continued.

'Anything?' Frank whispered.

Molly crouched down a little, eyes uplifted, then slowly straightened up.

'No,' she said. 'Nothing.'

'Want to open the window?' he asked. 'Maybe we can hear something when the sirens stop.'

Molly appeared to think about this.

'It's too cold, and we'd let all the heat out.'

'Yeah, you're right,' Frank sighed. 'And it's probably one of ours anyway.'

Molly reached back and held his hand.

'I expect so.'

They stood for a while, staring out at the darkened city. Eventually, Molly turned and paced slowly across the room, lit by the red glow of the fire.

'It's getting late,' she said. 'We should go to bed.'

Frank pulled the blackout blind down, then moved over to the chair, sitting down and easing off his shoes.

'Where are my things?' he asked, glancing around the room. He usually kept a few items of clothing folded beside the nightstand, but they weren't there now.

'Oh, I put them in the suitcase,' Molly said, pointing. 'Just there, under the bed.'

Frank looked up at her, puzzled.

'While I was away,' she explained. 'I didn't want the landlady coming in and seeing them. How would I explain?'

'Yeah, that might be tricky.' Frank grinned. He stood up and arranged his damp socks on the fire guard, then padded over to the bed and dragged the suitcase out. 'Okay if I unpack this stuff now?'

Bending over the stove, Molly hesitated.

'I'm... only back for a couple of days,' she admitted.

'But you've only just...' He put the case down heavily, then scowled. 'How long will you be away *this* time?'

Molly avoided his eye, running a cloth around the inside of the saucepan, then setting it down carefully.

'A few weeks,' she murmured. 'Maybe longer.'

Frank hung his head and sighed.

'Wanna tell me where you're going?'

She looked over at him briefly, then carried on tidying up.

Frank watched her for a moment, then shook his head.

'Have it your way,' he muttered, turning his back and squatting down to open the suitcase.

. . .

The fire burned low in the grate, reducing the room to a wavering red glow.

They undressed in silence. Molly pulled on a cardigan over her nightgown, then stood aside while she waited for him to climb into the cold bed. He lay down awkwardly, shivering at the chill touch of the sheets against his skin. She sat down wearily, slipping under the covers and laying with her back to him for a while. Then, just before he went to sleep, her felt her reach back for his hand and pull his arm over her, drawing him close.

Neither of them spoke. For tonight, the warmth of each other was all that mattered.

36

The Bellevue Palace was a very large, and very grand hotel. Set high above the bare trees that lined the icy river, it occupied a prominent position in the old town skyline, between Casinoplatz and the snow-capped domes of the Bundeshaus parliament building.

Glancing up at it as he walked across the exposed heights of the Kirchenfeld bridge, Frank paused to check his watch, then pulled his coat around him and hurried on. Hunching his shoulders against the wind, he made his way around to the canopied main entrance, hurrying up the steps and into the warm.

The lobby was bright and open. Light streamed down from the beautiful stained glass ceiling and cream-colored columns lined the polished marble floor. Frank checked his coat at the desk, then made his way over to Swift, who was sitting in an easy chair, reading a newspaper.

'Ah, there you are.' Swift folded his paper and left it on the low table in front of him. 'Very punctual. That's good.'

'Well, you told me not to be late,' Frank said.

'So I did.' Swift got to his feet. 'First time you've had lunch at the Bellevue?'

'Yes.' Frank glanced around, taking in the ornate detailing round the edge of the ceiling. 'I've never had cause to come in here before.'

'It's an experience,' Swift said. 'Let's go through.'

They made their way across the lobby and on towards the restaurant.

'I appreciate you inviting me.' Frank smiled. Walking through the cold had fired his appetite, and he found that he was looking forward to his lunch.

'Don't thank me yet,' Swift said, under his breath. 'This is business, not pleasure.'

The restaurant was a long room of wood-paneled walls lined with tall, arched windows that looked out over the Aare to the snowy city beyond. Huge chandeliers hung like glittering teardrops from the smooth, vaulted ceiling, while smartly-dressed diners spoke in hushed tones across gleaming white table linen.

The maître d' was an eager man in his fifties, with greying hair and a neat mustache. He wore a diner jacket and came gliding over, smiling as he approached.

'Ah, Herr Swift,' he said, inclining his head respectfully. 'Always a pleasure to have you here at La Terrasse.'

'Hello, Bruno,' Swift said. 'We're not expecting anyone else, so it's just the two of us today.'

'Very good.' The maître d' ushered them in. 'This way please, gentlemen.'

He escorted them down the length of the room. Following him past the other diners, Frank became acutely aware that they were being watched.

The maître d' led them to a small table in the corner. Swift went to occupy the chair against the wall, then appeared to change his mind, and offered the place to Frank.

'Sit here.' He smiled. 'The view's better.'

Frank glanced at him, then did as he asked.

'Thanks,' he said, pulling his chair in.

The maître d' waited until they were seated, then stepped closer.

'May I offer you something to drink?' he asked.

Swift glanced up at him.

'Maybe you could just give us a couple of minutes, Bruno,' he said, pleasantly.

'Of course.' The maître d' bowed his head slightly and moved away.

Swift watched him go, then turned to Frank.

'Welcome to the lunchtime farce,' he said in a low voice. 'And it really *is* a farce, just about the most ludicrous situation you could imagine.'

Frank leaned forward, listening intently.

'La Terrasse is one of the finest places to eat in the whole city,' Swift murmured. 'Naturally, the great and the good don't like their dining to be inconvenienced by a mere world war; everyone still wants to eat here. So, the restaurant has become a bit – how shall I put it? – *territorial*.'

Puzzled, Frank looked at him.

'Territorial?'

Swift smiled.

'This end of the room is reserved for the Allied diners,' he explained. 'The other end is for the Axis guys. We sit here and we eat, and we politely ignore the enemy sitting a few tables away. All very civilized... and completely crazy.'

Frank leaned back in his chair.

'You're kidding me,' he whispered.

Swift shook his head.

'Straight up,' he said. 'It's been like this for years, now.'

Frank glanced surreptitiously towards the far end of the room.

'You know, I *felt* like everyone was looking at me as we came in.'

Swift nodded.

'They probably were,' he said. 'People like to know who's speaking with who. But that's why I told you to get here early.'

Frank looked at him and frowned.

'Sorry, what do you mean?'

Swift reached into his jacket pocket, took out his cigarette lighter, and set it down on the tablecloth in front of him.

'There's somebody I want you to see,' he said, quietly. 'But I figured it was better for us to be safely tucked away at a table *before* he showed up.'

'Who is it?' Frank asked.

'Just keep your eyes open,' Swift told him. 'I'll explain in a minute.'

He turned around and raised a hand to summon the maître d' over.

Frank sat silently, his gaze flickering constantly towards the door, as Swift ordered for both of them. But nobody came in.

'Very good, Herr Swift.'

'Thank you, Bruno.'

The maître d' inclined his head, then turned on his heel and walked away. Frank waited until he was out of earshot, then leaned over.

'Okay,' he said. 'What's this all about?'

Swift gave him a long look, then lowered his eyes.

'In a way, it's about Jean,' he said, sighing.

Frank stiffened.

'Alongside her other duties, Jean was also...' Swift paused, as though considering how to explain. '...*keeping track* of someone for us. We deliberately kept it very quiet; only a couple of people knew what she was doing.'

He reached over and picked up the cigarette lighter.

'The person in question isn't permanently based here. He hasn't been seen in Bern for a couple of months, but he's back now.'

Frank stared past him towards the far end of the room, his eyes sweeping across the people sitting at the Axis tables.

'Who is it?' he whispered.

Swift shook his head very slightly. He casually glanced over to his left, then turned back to make eye contact with Frank.

'Over there by the window,' he murmured. 'The grey-haired guy who's just sat down with his two gorillas.'

Frank looked over, doing his best not to be obvious about it. Three tables away, the man appeared to be in his fifties, balding, with a grey beard and small round eyeglasses. He wore a sombre three-piece suit and was frowning at something written on a scrap of paper. Flanking him, two solid-looking younger men sat like statues; both had their hair cut short in a military style.

Frank lowered his eyes.

'Is that him?' he asked.

'No,' Swift replied. 'But keep watching that table, and we'll see who joins them.'

It dawned on Frank that the men were sitting at this end of the room... *in the Allied section.*

'But they're...' He frowned. 'Who are those guys?'

Swift shrugged, his voice barely audible.

'They're the Russians.' He met Frank's eye, nodding calmly at his surprised expression. 'Yeah, *that's* why we had to keep it quiet.'

'But...' Frank stared at him. 'Why were we watching them? They're on *our* side.'

Swift toyed with his cigarette lighter.

'Just because we all hate the Nazis, it doesn't mean we're all on the same side.'

'But, surely–'

'Oh, *wake up*, Frank.' Swift leaned forward, his voice low and urgent. 'The only thing we really have in common is a common enemy, and that enemy isn't gonna last forever.'

Frank sat back in his chair, his mind racing ahead as Swift's earlier words sunk in.

In a way, it's about Jean... but he'd always assumed that the Nazis had murdered Jean.

'You think the Russians killed her?' he asked, suddenly.

Swift took a deep breath and studied Frank for a moment.

'I didn't say that,' he replied, carefully. 'The relationship with Moscow has never been easy and there are always concerns. Jean thought she was onto something, some connection to our own operation, but she died before she could figure it out.'

'So?' Frank pressed him.

'So that's not the same thing as *knowing*,' Swift hissed. 'There's no proof. We don't know if her death was sanctioned from the top, or if it was somebody operating on their own. We don't know if the Russians had anything to do with it at all.'

Frank slumped back in his chair, glaring down at the table. There had to be *some* way of finding out.

'What about Molly?' he asked, looking up. 'She's got connections with the Russians... wouldn't she know?'

Swift slowly shook his head.

'I asked, but she says she knows nothing about it.' He paused, lowering his eyes. 'Of course, she works for the British, not for us, but...'

He shrugged again. The gesture annoyed Frank.

'You think she's *lying*?' he snapped.

Swift shook his head slowly again, a pained expression on his face.

'She may hear things... things that she isn't allowed to share with us.' He turned the cigarette lighter over in his hand. 'You have to consider the bigger picture; the war isn't won yet, and it's a fragile alliance.'

Frank scowled at him.

'How can you *say* things like that?' he hissed. 'We all want the same thing; we all want the Nazis gone.'

Swift gave him a withering look.

'Is that what you think?' he asked.

'Well... yeah. Of course.'

'And afterwards, *after the Nazis are gone*, what then?'

Frank stared at him.

'I don't know...' he said, frowning. 'Peace?'

Swift took a breath and sighed.

'Everyone wants different things,' he muttered. 'The British have been dragging their feet in this war. Think about it; Churchill spent *years* chasing around North Africa and the Mediterranean rather than going back into France. And why? Trying to preserve his precious British Empire.'

He leaned forward, his face serious.

'But it isn't Churchill that worries me, it's Stalin. Because *that* guy has imperial ambitions of his own. You just watch; the Russians are going to annex Poland and then they're gonna look west and keep on coming. And I don't know who's gonna stop them, because so far the only way America has managed to keep Stalin in line is by giving Stalin whatever the hell he wants.' He paused. 'Trouble is, Stalin wants the whole of Eastern Europe.'

Frank sat in silence for a moment, trying to take it all in.

'So what do *we* want?' he asked, quietly.

Swift gazed over at him thoughtfully.

'I don't know,' he said. 'Peace, I guess. But a peace that *lasts*. I want to stop the fighting in such a way that it doesn't start right up again as soon as we go home.'

'Okay, but...' Frank broke off. Over by the doorway, the maître d' was welcoming a bearded man, and escorting him towards the Russian table.

Staring over Swift's shoulder, Frank watched them approach.

'Short man in his forties, thinning on top, black beard,' he murmured. 'Does that sound like him?'

Swift accidentally dropped his cigarette lighter to the floor and calmly bent over to retrieve it. He didn't appear to glance back or turn his head, but when he sat up again, he was nodding slightly.

'Yeah. That's him.'

Frank watched as the man sat down at the Russian table, noting the familiar way that the men all greeted each other.

'So who is he?' he asked.

'He calls himself Yakov Nikolayevich Levkin,' Swift replied, tucking his cigarette lighter back into his pocket. 'He's an assistant to the Russian military attaché.'

'And you think he might have... might be responsible for Jean.'

Swift narrowed his eyes.

'If I thought *that*, he'd already be dead.' He frowned. 'I think Jean found out something while she was watching him, something that someone doesn't want us to know.'

Frank quickly averted his eyes as the Russian glanced over in their direction.

'All right,' he said, stiffly. 'What do you want me to do?'

'I want you to pick up where Jean left off,' Swift explained. 'I want you to keep an eye on this guy for a while. Get a feel for where he goes, who he meets.'

Frank nodded.

'Understood.'

Swift absently reached out to straighten his cutlery.

'You report only to me on this, and you *don't* speak to anyone else about it.' His eyes flickered up to hold Frank's gaze. 'Not to *anyone* else.'

Sitting there, Frank was gripped by an uncomfortable feeling. He wondered if Swift had somehow found out about Molly and him.

'Don't worry,' he said. 'I can be discreet.'

Swift looked at him for a moment, then gave him a faint smile.

'Yes,' he said. 'I know.'

37

F rank picked up the two steaming cups of coffee and walked slowly through to the office, being careful not to spill them.

'Here you go,' he said, setting one of the cups down on Rafe's desk. 'Just the way you hate it.'

'Can't be any worse than your tea.' Rafe smiled. 'But thanks.'

'You're welcome.' Frank sat down, looking again at the illegibly scrawled notes he was attempting to transcribe, and sighed.

Rafe got stiffly to his feet and moved over to one of the filing cabinets. Propping his walking stick against the wall, he pulled open the middle drawer and started flicking through the files. Frank heard him muttering to himself.

'What's the matter?' he asked.

Rafe looked round at him, frowning.

'I do wish people would learn to put things back in their proper place,' he grumbled. 'I say, could you just pop along and see if there's any files on Swift's desk? He's forever borrowing things and forgetting to put them back.'

'Sure.' Frank scraped his chair back, glad of any excuse to leave the transcribing. He got to his feet and walked down the corridor to Swift's room. Opening the door, he went inside and took a quick look around, but there were no files visible. On a whim, he went around and tried the drawers in Swift's desk, but they were locked.

'Nothing there,' he said, walking back into the office. 'And it wasn't me, before you ask. I *know* how much you enjoy things being out of place.'

'Damn,' Rafe said, regarding the filing cabinet with trepidation. 'It's so tiresome when people just stick things back in the wrong drawer.'

The telephone started ringing.

Frank glanced at his watch and jumped to his feet.

'It's okay,' he told Rafe. 'I'll get it.'

Moving quickly across the room, he stooped over the phone and picked up the receiver.

'Bern 261,' he said.

There was a crackle, then a voice spoke in heavily-accented English.

'This is Stephan calling for Herr Rye.'

Frank turned his back on Rafe and lowered himself down to perch on the edge of the desk. Swift had pointed Stephan out to him when they went for lunch at the Bellevue. One of the concierge staff, he was a nervous young man, with tidy blonde hair; Frank wasn't sure what hold Swift had over him, but he was an invaluable source of information on the hotel's guests.

'This is Rye,' he said, quietly. 'Go ahead, Stephan.'

'Your gentleman has just returned.' There was an anxious pause, and Frank could just make out the muffled sound of another conversation in the background. Then, Stephan was back again, his voice close in the earpiece. 'No lunch reservation today, but he's booked a table for dinner at seven thirty.'

'Understood.' Frank nodded. 'Any visitors? Messages?'

'Nothing new.'

'Okay. Thanks.'

There was a click and the line went dead. Frank gently placed the receiver back in its cradle.

It had only been a couple of weeks, but he was already getting a feel for Levkin's routine. He'd learned that the Russian invariably spent the morning at the ambassador's residence, over in the Muri neighborhood, but usually returned to the Bellevue for lunch. Stephan's information helped him to keep track of Levkin's movements at other times.

He walked back over to his desk, picked up his cup, and gulped down the coffee. Rafe was leaning against the filing cabinet, gazing out of the window.

'The place seems awfully quiet when it's just the two of us,' he muttered.

Frank gathered up the transcription notes and dumped them into his desk drawer.

'It's about to get even quieter,' he said, walking over to get his coat.

Rafe turned to look at him.

'What? Oh, not *again*...' He shook his head in disappointment. 'Where are you off to today?'

Frank jerked a thumb towards the phone.

'I just go where I'm told,' he said, smoothly. 'Don't wait up.'

In the afternoons, Levkin usually went for a walk. At first, these excursions from the warmth of the hotel had intrigued Frank, and he'd tailed the Russian excitedly, certain that his subject was making for an illicit rendezvous, particularly as he always went alone. Someone from the east might feel at home in this bitter winter climate, but surely Levkin's afternoon strolls around the old town had more significance than exercise or sightseeing.

So far, Frank had followed him six times, and nothing out of the ordinary had happened. Levkin's route varied slightly, sometimes cutting across the Bundesplatz towards the station, sometimes setting out via Casinoplatz, though he usually ended up treading the ancient streets down by the Cathedral. In all these walks, Levkin had spoken to no one, except a brief exchange with the vendor at a station newsstand when he'd bought a newspaper. But something about the man was wrong.

Today, he was walking east along the covered sidewalk of Marktgasse, pausing every now and then to gaze in a shop window. On the opposite side of the street, Frank watched him from the shadow of a stone pillar, then casually glanced over his shoulder, alert for sudden movements or familiar faces.

You couldn't be too careful.

Satisfied, he set off again, matching his pace to Levkin's as the Russian drifted along. There was a moment when a streetcar passed between them, briefly obscuring Frank's view but when it passed there was Levkin again, passing between the vaulted arches.

At the end of Marktgasse, they emerged from the shelter of the arcades into bright winter sun. Frank glanced up, captivated by the way the light gleamed and glinted on the golden hands of the enormous Zytglogge. He looked across to see which way Levkin would go, but the Russian had already turned his back on the impressive clock tower and was strolling down the broad expanse of Kornhausplatz, stepping lightly over the shining tram lines as he crossed the street.

Frank held back a little, allowing the distance between them to grow as they made their way down the narrow, cobbled slopes of the old town. Levkin had emerged to walk on the road itself now, but Frank still kept to the cover of the arcades wherever possible, knowing that it was better to lose sight of the Russian than be sighted himself. Levkin showed no concern, rarely lifting his head, as though the idea of being followed simply hadn't occurred to him.

They came to the Rathaus, the ancient town hall building with its ornate frontage of carved stone balustrades. Opposite, the mighty statue of a medieval knight holding a banner stood above a large, frozen fountain. Levkin walked past without slowing, turning right to cut along a side street, his pace unchanged. Frank paused by the fountain, waiting until his target was fifty yards ahead before he continued. If the Russian had intended to disappear, or double-back, he would surely have done so by now.

The side street emerged by the cathedral. Frank made his way around the rear of the towering stone building and approached the tall iron gates of the Münsterplattform, a large square of tree-lined gardens built out from the higher ground of the old town with a hundred-foot drop to the streets below. Open on three sides, it provided stunning views along the edge of the medieval town and across the river, where the winter sunlight touched the mists in the valley with a golden glow.

There was Levkin, sitting on one of the benches, as he often seemed to do when he came here. Frank stayed well back, leaning up against a stone pillar just inside the gate, trying to figure out what was troubling him.

Was he wasting his time, trailing round the town like this? Levkin wasn't doing anything out of the ordinary coming down here. Taking in the Zytglogge, the Rathaus, the Münsterplattform... these were just the places that someone *would* go for a walk, with so much impressive architecture and stunning views across the Aare valley.

But as he stood there, watching the Russian, with sunlight glittering on the frosted tree branches, he finally realized what was bothering him: Levkin wasn't interested.

He was going to the most beautiful places, but he wasn't looking at them.

Shivering a little, Frank rubbed his hands together, then took out a cigarette and lit it. Across the gardens, Levkin sat on his bench, doing nothing.

What the hell was he up to? If he wasn't taken by the old town buildings or the stunning Alpine views, what *was* the man looking at?

Pulling his coat tight around himself, he frowned.

Levkin certainly didn't *behave* as though he was planning to meet someone. He'd drifted calmly through the streets, no furtive glances, seemingly unaware and unconcerned about who might walk past him.

But if he wasn't meeting anyone, what *was* he doing?

Levkin stayed for ten minutes, which wasn't unusual for him. Then he bent forward, hands gripping the front edge of the bench, and slowly got to his feet. Watching him, Frank got ready to follow, then hesitated.

Something about the way the Russian had leaned forward, something *odd*. He often seemed to have difficulty rising from that bench...

...but if the bench was so uncomfortable, why sit there?

As the Russian turned and made his way towards the exit at the far end of the gardens, Frank stared at where he'd been sitting.

He knew he had to be careful. If he was obvious, if he just marched over there and felt under the bench like an amateur, he might be spotted; the Russians would know they were being watched and change their routine. No, he had to be smarter than that.

He waited for a few minutes, calmly surveying the gardens, noting the faces of the people. Then, when he felt sure that nobody was paying him any attention, he set off at a slow pace, his eyes turned towards the river, enjoying the view like anyone else would. He followed the path around, taking his time, his breath rising like pale smoke in the cold sunlight. A couple of yards before the bench, he frowned, then stooped and pretended to tie his shoelace. Kneeling over, head low, he glanced up to look along the underside of the bench... but there was nothing there.

Damn.

He got slowly to his feet and continued on along the path, carefully hiding his disappointment. He'd felt so sure that there would be something stuck under there – an envelope, a scrap of paper, *something* – but he'd come up empty. Levkin hadn't left any secret messages and now, thanks to this delay, he was gone.

Frank trudged over to the edge of the garden and leaned on the low stone wall, feeling the cold frost on his palms as he looked over the edge. Far below, there was still a little snow on some of the shadowed rooftops, and he caught the smell of wood smoke as thin grey wisps curled up from the chimneys.

Unless...

He paused and looked over his shoulder.

Unless Levkin wasn't here to *leave* a message, but to *receive* one.

38

Frank left his lodgings early the following day, stepping down onto the sidewalk and pulling his coat tight around him. The air was cold, despite the pale sunlight, shocking him into wakefulness, and he looped his scarf about his neck before setting off at a brisk pace. His usual route to the office took him down through the trees overlooking the bend in the river, but today he cut back on himself, following a narrow path down the steep grassy slope towards the bear pit. A large brown bear with a matted, shaggy coat had clambered to the top of the man-made rock-pile within, and he paused to watch it for a moment, steam rising from its muzzle as it yawned. Frank smiled. Then, remembering why he was here, he turned away and hurried onto the old Nydegg bridge, a lonely stone causeway stretching out through the morning mist.

He'd spent the evening thinking about Levkin, going over the man's routine, searching for patterns. If the Russian always went for his walks after lunch, then it seemed likely that any messages would be left for him earlier in the day. Of course, it was just a theory, but Frank was keen to test his idea, and he owed it to Jean to learn the truth about the man she'd been watching.

The cobbled streets of the old town were grey and still as he made his way up the hill towards the cathedral, shadowed spaces filled with a damp chill that the sun couldn't reach. High above, the bells tolled eight o'clock as he approached the gate and passed through to walk down the broad stone steps. The Münsterplattform gardens were quiet. Looking across the space, he could see a couple of figures strolling among the bare trees, silhouetted shapes against the white mist that hung over the river valley beyond. The bench where Levkin had sat was empty.

Frank glanced over his shoulder, then started along the gravel path. So far, all of his surveillance had turned up nothing; he didn't have anything definite that he could take to Swift, but if he could find something here, intercept a secret Russian communication, all that would change.

The bench was a few yards ahead when he slowed, bending down and pretending to tie his shoelace. Lifting his head slightly, he peered along the underside of the bench, scanning the wooden slats, but there was nothing there.

Frank bowed his head, swearing under his breath. Scowling, he got slowly to his feet and walked on, his shoes crunching on the gravel.

Maybe this was just the wrong day. Just because Levkin came here regularly, there was no reason to suppose that there were messages waiting every day.

Or maybe he was too early...

Frank looked down at his watch. He would come back later, at lunchtime, perhaps... *before* Levkin took his walk. It was certainly worth another try.

Frowning, he jammed his hands down into his coat pockets and strode away.

Rafe glanced up at him as he walked into the office.

'Not like you to be late,' he said. 'Sleep in, did we?'

'I had an errand to run,' Frank murmured, pulling off his scarf and undoing his coat. 'Is Swift in today, or is it just us?'

'He'll be in later,' Rafe replied, studying a paper on his desk. 'But you just missed Molly.'

Frank looked over at him.

'She's back?' he asked, being careful to hide his excitement.

'She just stopped in to get a few things,' Rafe said, leaning over to note something on the paper. 'Off to Geneva or somewhere this afternoon – no rest for the wicked. Said she'd be in the office tomorrow.'

Frank nodded. It would be good to have her back again. Smiling to himself, he went through to the kitchen area to make a coffee.

Swift arrived at eleven. He appeared to be in an unusually good mood, taking the time to perch on one of the empty desks and chat, rather than shutting himself away in his room.

'Have either of you seen the newsreels?' he asked. 'There's a new one showing, with some pictures of the Yalta conference.'

'And how were our great leaders looking?' Rafe said, grinning. 'Rather smug, I should think, what with the Germans retreating everywhere.'

'The newsreel said that the allies were making "great strides towards victory and the security of Europe",' Swift replied. 'But they didn't look too pleased about it.'

'Really?' Rafe asked. 'I thought they'd be all smiles. Well, maybe not Stalin... he's usually rather grim.'

'Truman and Churchill were the ones who looked grim,' Swift explained. 'And that ties in with some of the chatter going round the embassy these last few days. I don't think they're very happy with Comrade Stalin.'

Frank looked up, remembering his talk with Swift at the Bellevue.

'Well, Churchill's never been fond of him,' Rafe observed. 'The only thing he loathed more than Stalin's Communism was Hitler's Nazism.'

'Maybe Hitler's time is coming to an end,' Swift said, quietly. 'Assuming he's even still alive.'

Rafe turned to Frank with a triumphant look.

'I *told* you so, didn't I?' he said, excitedly. 'And if Hitler *is* dead, or dying, then old Göring's got a tiger by the tail. If he lets on that his precious Fuhrer's dead, he risks losing his authority, but the longer he hides it, the worse it'll be for him when it does come out.'

'Hey, let's not get ahead of ourselves,' Swift said, holding up a hand. 'This is all just speculation at the moment. Hitler could simply be lying low after the assassination attempts, which we *know* he survived. He *may* still be running things, just as Göring says.'

Frank nodded thoughtfully.

'But you don't believe that, do you?' he asked.

Swift gave him a long look, then eased himself forward off the edge of the desk and got to his feet.

'It doesn't matter what we believe,' he said, quietly.

At midday, Frank pushed open the tall front door and stepped out into the cold, squinting in the thin winter sunlight. Dufourstrasse was deserted, and he made his way briskly along to the end of the road where he knew he could get a streetcar that would take him into the city.

As usual, Rafe had wanted to know where he was going, but today the questions had felt a little more awkward, especially being asked in front of Swift. Frank had carefully avoided specifics, explaining that he felt like wandering around the shops in town, then slipping out into the stairwell before the conversation could go any further. He didn't like lying to his friend, but he was under strict orders not to tell anyone what he was doing. And there was nothing to tell, anyway – just a Russian sitting on a bench, and an uneasy feeling. No secret messages, no proof.

He got off the streetcar at Casinoplatz. An icy wind was blowing up from the river, and he paused to wrap his scarf around his mouth and throat before striding away down the sloping cobbled street that led to the cathedral.

Away from the sunlight, the cold air hung heavy, and his doubts began to grow. Maybe he was imagining things. Maybe he'd not found anything because there was nothing to find. If someone wanted to pass information to Levkin, would he really do it like this? Wouldn't it be easier to leave a message for the Russian at his hotel, or simply telephone the embassy...?

Emerging from the shadows of the narrow street, Frank stepped out into the broad plaza in front of the Cathedral. Frowning, he looked over at the gap between the buildings that led through to the Münsterplattform gardens, then turned and made his way around to the quieter gate at the far end of the church.

Head down, he went over the questions in his mind. Dulles had warned him that the Swiss police routinely monitored telephone calls in the city, especially calls to and from people with links to foreign governments. And he knew first-hand how hotel staff could intercept messages left for their guests. No, the more he thought about it, the more possible it seemed; Levkin *could* be receiving messages this way.

Frank came to the eastern gates and peered through the railings. He was tempted to go straight in, to walk over and check under the bench, but he forced himself to wait. It wasn't even twelve thirty yet, and Levkin rarely left the hotel before two. He had time.

A bearded old man in a fur hat shuffled past him, being pulled along by an excited young Labrador with a glossy black coat. The dog's tail wagged eagerly as they made their way down the stone steps and into the gardens. Frank watched them for a moment, until his eye was drawn to a man standing beneath the trees, stepping forward to meet a woman who'd entered from the other gate. They embraced for a time, then set off slowly, walking towards the far wall, hand in hand. A sudden clamor of barking made him look back to the gravel path, where the Labrador was now straining at its leash, while a large woman in a fur coat called out in alarm, jerking her own smaller dog back out of its reach.

Frank smiled at the commotion, until some inner warning drew his gaze back to the bench. Leaning up against the railings, he felt a momentary thrill as he glimpsed a silhouetted figure sitting down on the bench, then frowned as he realized it was a woman.

Damn it!

He turned away, scowling, wondering how long she was going to stay. Even if there *was* something hidden beneath the bench, he could hardly walk over and stoop down to check, not now she was sitting on it; he should have gone over there when he first arrived. Worse still, Levkin's contact might not have come yet; he wouldn't be likely to stop and hide a message if he found the bench was occupied when he got here.

Angrily, Frank turned and glared between the railings, wondering what the hell he could do. Staring at the distant figure, he willed her to move, then bowed his head in frustration.

Of all the dumb luck...

High above him, he heard the tower bells toll their mournful chime; twelve thirty. He glanced up, then felt a flicker of excitement as the woman shifted her position.

Was she moving? Yes, she was leaning forward, doing something with her purse and getting to her feet...

He watched as she stood up, saw her pausing to take in the

view over the river, and then she turned, stepping out from beneath the shadow of the trees.

Frank stiffened, gripping the railings tightly, staring in disbelief as she moved calmly away along the path towards the other gate.

It was Molly.

39

It couldn't be a coincidence. He walked in a daze, shoes scuffing across the cobbles, trying to make sense of it, trying to think of some circumstance... *anything* that would explain it away. Because he knew it *couldn't* just be a coincidence.

In front of him, an elderly laborer was maneuvering a laden handcart out from between a pile of wooden crates, and Frank slowed, waiting for the man to pass. Without thinking, he took out a cigarette and struck a match.

He pictured Molly sitting on the bench, saw her leaning forward, one hand closing her purse, the other discretely reaching downwards... What was she doing there? She wasn't even meant to be in Bern today.

The match was scorching his fingers. Cursing angrily, he dropped it and shook his hand, trying to escape the burning pain. Beside him, the laborer had stopped, and was peering at him curiously. Frank lowered his eyes and pushed through the gap beside the cart, anxious questions pressing in on him.

What if he was making a mistake? Was it possible that Levkin was somehow working for her?

No, Swift had been very clear about the situation. Levkin

wasn't a friend; he was someone they'd been watching for some time, someone who Jean had suspected of having some sinister link to their *own* operation.

The more he thought about it, the worse it became.

Numb, he looked up, wondering what he should do, where he could go. His first instinct had been to race back to the Dufourstrasse office and find Swift... but what if *she* was there?

He turned to his left, staring down the side street that cut between the tall buildings. Herrengasse was just two blocks over, less than a minute away; he could walk there right now and knock on the door... but who would answer it? Groth? Swift had been very specific; report *only* to him.

Sighing, Frank gazed up at the vast clock tower that loomed in front of him, staring at the two faces and the wheels within wheels. It was twelve fifty-five. Absently, he calculated that Levkin would have left the embassy and returned to the Bellevue by now.

The Bellevue.

Clenching his fists, he turned right, making his way around the base of the clock tower and out into the cold wind.

Molly. Why did it have to be Molly?

The doorman tipped his hat respectfully but Frank ignored him, taking the broad steps two at a time. Entering the hotel lobby, he made straight for the desk where, he noted with grim satisfaction, Stephan was on duty. The blond concierge looked up with a pleasant expression, but his smile faded and he glanced around nervously as Frank bore down on him.

'Good afternoon, sir,' he said in a low voice. 'I did call but they said you were out. The Russian gentleman returned shortly after midday; he's in the restaurant just now.'

'I don't care,' Frank snapped. 'Just give me the damn phone, will you?'

Stephan looked at him unhappily, then nodded and lifted a telephone onto the counter. He stepped back as Frank picked up the receiver and called the office number.

Rafe answered.

'Hello,' he said curiously when he realized who was on the line. 'What's all this then? Wherever are you calling from?'

Frank ignored the questions.

'Is Swift there?' he asked, trying to keep his voice calm.

'Yes, he's in his office.'

'Tell him to get over to the Bellevue. Right now,' Frank said.

Rafe started to say something, but Frank was already placing the receiver back in its cradle.

He looked up at Stephan, who was watching him anxiously.

'Thanks,' he said, taking his hand off the telephone and indicating that he was finished with it. 'Could you get me a drink, Stephan? A whiskey or something?'

Stephan lifted the telephone and returned it to its place under the counter.

'Of course, sir,' he said.

'Appreciate it,' Frank said. Turning away, he trudged across the lobby and slumped into one of the lounge chairs.

Swift came in through the revolving door and paused to remove his hat. Looking round the lobby, he spotted Frank sitting in the corner and calmly made his way over.

'Good afternoon,' he said, unbuttoning his coat. Glancing down at the low table, he noted the empty glass and turned to beckon one of the hotel attendants, a fresh-faced youth with short dark hair.

'I'll have a whiskey and soda,' he said, then turned to look inquiringly at Frank.

Frank shook his head.

'That'll be all, thank you.' Swift handed his hat and coat to the attendant, who gave a curt nod and walked briskly away.

'So,' he said, lowering himself into a chair, his eyes on Frank. 'I got your message. I assume this is about our Russian acquaintance?'

Frank looked over at him.

'That's right,' he said.

'Well?' Swift prompted him.

Frank rubbed his eyes, wondering where to begin.

'I've been watching him, like you asked,' he said. 'Stephan's kept me informed of his movements, who visits him, who calls, that sort of thing. And I've shadowed him when he goes out on his own.'

Swift nodded encouragingly.

'Well, in the afternoons, he often goes for a walk through the old town. At first, I thought he might be meeting somebody, but he doesn't speak to anyone, not so far as I can see. The time varies, and the route he takes, except...' Frank broke off, shaking his head. 'This whole thing is so messed up. I wondered if it might be some sort of coincidence but...'

Watching him, Swift shifted in his chair.

'In my experience, *there's no such thing as coincidences*,' he said, quietly. *'Only warnings.'*

Frank met his eye, then looked away again.

'Levkin always seems to end up at the Münsterplattform gardens,' he explained. 'There's a bench down there, and he sits on it for a while, then comes back here to the hotel. I started to think it was... *significant.*'

Swift frowned.

'Always the *same* bench?'

'I thought maybe he was leaving messages – you know, pieces of paper tucked under the seat, that sort of thing – but he wasn't.'

'No?' Swift asked.

Frank shook his head.

'So then I figured someone *else* might be leaving messages, and Levkin might be the one collecting them. So I started watching the bench, checking it earlier in the day...'

Swift leaned forward in his chair.

'*And?*' he said.

Frank swallowed, staring down at the floor.

'Molly,' he whispered. 'She was there this afternoon.'

Swift gaped at him in disbelief.

'You mean *our* Molly?' he stammered. 'Molly Pearson?'

Frank nodded wretchedly.

Swift sagged, sinking back into his chair.

'But... no, there must be some other explanation.' He stared at down at the table, his expression an agony of doubt. 'Even if she was there, it doesn't mean...'

Frank reached into his coat pocket and drew out a crumpled piece of paper.

Wordlessly, he leaned across and handed it over.

Swift took the paper and carefully unfolded it. His eyes took in the rows of two-digit numbers, arranged in twelve-by-twelve squares, then flickered up.

'What the hell is this?' he demanded.

'I found it pinned to the underside of the bench, right after she left,' Frank explained. 'It wasn't there this morning.'

Swift stared down at the paper, then looked up again, appalled.

'And you *removed* it?'

Frank shook his head, wearily.

'I put the original back under the bench, *after* I copied it.'

The two men sat in silence for a time. Swift seemed almost to have shrunk, hunched over in his chair, staring at the grids of numbers. He slowly drew a hand across his face, then looked up at Frank.

'Shit,' he whispered.

A waiter approached, his shoes clicking smartly on the

marble floor. Carrying a small silver tray, he inclined his head politely, then bent down to place Swift's drink on the table.

'Thank you,' Swift said, his voice immediately calm and measured again. Frank marveled at the man's self-control, watching him as he tipped the waiter and settled back into his seat as though nothing had happened.

The waiter bowed and made his way back through to the bar.

Swift picked up his glass, turning it in his hand to see the play of light on the crystal, then took a small sip.

'Well,' he said, sadly. 'Now we know.'

He set the glass down carefully, then gave Frank a long, thoughtful look.

'Is there... anything else?' he asked.

The question seemed so strange that, for a moment, Frank wondered if he'd misheard.

'Anything *else*?' he said, allowing an edge of bitterness to creep into his voice. 'What, you don't think this is bad enough?'

Undaunted by his tone, Swift continued to watch him.

'I just wondered if there was anything more that you wanted to tell me.' He paused, then added, 'About Molly, for example.'

Too late, Frank realized what Swift was driving at. He scowled and looked away, not wanting the pain to show in his eyes.

'You and her?' Swift asked, pressing him.

Cornered, Frank stared down at the floor.

'What do you mean?'

Swift took a breath, as though growing weary of his own questions.

'I *mean*, are you sleeping with her?' he demanded.

Frank closed his eyes.

It was no use; this was *far* beyond any personal promises he'd made to Molly. At the very *least* she'd put him in an impossible position, and he couldn't lie for her, not now.

He hung his head, then nodded.

For a time, Swift was silent. When he did finally speak, his voice seemed gentler.

'If it makes you feel any better, I already suspected,' he said. 'About the two of you, I mean.'

Frank lifted his head.

'I try to keep an eye on my people,' Swift told him. He paused, then reached over and lifted his glass once more. 'It's been going on for a while, hasn't it?'

Frank took a deep breath, thinking back to that first night, when he walked Molly home from the hospital.

'Since the summer,' he murmured. Just a few months, but it seemed like a long time ago now.

Swift sat back in his chair and sighed.

'And I guess that *she* was the one who initiated the relationship,' he said.

Frank looked up sharply.

'What are you saying?' he hissed.

But deep down, he already knew.

40

Standing in the shadows, Frank glanced quickly over his shoulder towards the lights of the street, then started up the fire escape. He moved warily, silently, one hand jammed deep in his bulging coat pocket.

Somewhere in the distance, a clock chimed seven. He'd wanted to come here earlier, but Swift had been adamant that he should go and follow Levkin as usual, make sure he was right about the message pick-up, then meet again at a café near the station. The delay had vexed him at the time but, in a way, this had worked out well; he couldn't have come up the fire escape until it got dark, not if he wanted to avoid being seen.

He reached the third floor and slowed, pressing his body flat against the wall and sliding his hand carefully out of his pocket. The gun gleamed black in the darkness, the grip warm in his palm where he'd been holding it for so long.

He checked to make sure the safety was off, then lifted his head and looked along towards the window. Taking a cautious step forward, he brought his ear close to the edge of the frame, holding his breath and listening.

Nothing.

Another step, and he leaned in close, shading the dim reflection with his free hand, peering inside... but the room was in darkness. He allowed himself to exhale, slipping the gun back into his coat pocket before placing his palms on the cold glass. Exerting gentle pressure, he felt the window start to move, sliding up with a dull scraping sound. Immediately, he dropped to a crouch, his right hand easing back into his pocket, fingers finding their place on the gun. Leaning in close to the gap, he whispered, 'Molly?'

No answer.

He listened for a moment more, then adjusted his grip and drew out the gun. Bending forward, he eased his body over the sill, bracing himself as he tentatively lowered a foot to find the floor.

Once inside, he straightened up and turned quickly, training the gun left and right, eyes registering the dim shapes in the shadowed room. Satisfied, he slid the window shut with his free hand, then ghosted silently to the door, leaning up against it and listening hard.

Nothing.

He allowed himself a couple of deep breaths, then drifted about the room, placing a hand on the seats of each chair, on the bed, on the little kettle resting by the stove.

Everything was stone cold; she hadn't been back here this afternoon.

He relaxed just a little, his right arm wavering then dipping, lowering the gun. Swift had assured him that Molly wouldn't be back from Geneva until eight at the earliest, but Frank didn't trust her to stick to a schedule, not now.

He didn't trust her at all.

For a time, he just stood there in the middle of the floor as the initial storm of adrenalin drained slowly out of him. Then, shivering slightly, he began to pace, stopping here and there to gaze down on some small object, or brush his fingertips along the familiar lines of the furniture. He opened the closet and peered inside, making out the little spice tin on the upper shelf, running his hand across the rack of clothes that hung below it, watching the way that the fabric came briefly to life then settled into stillness again.

The pale yellow dress she'd worn that day in Neuchâtel...

He sighed and lowered his eyes, starting to shut the closet door, but something caught his attention. Bending down, he reached in below the hem of the dress and lifted a carelessly crumpled blouse.

Beneath it, he saw a small stack of folders, the kind they used at the office for the more sensitive dossiers. Squatting, he pulled them out and flicked through a few pages, his jaw tightening as he recognized them.

How long had it been going on? How much information had she passed to the Russians?

Standing up, he recalled Rafe complaining about documents being mislaid. He'd suggested that it was simply a matter of Swift being untidy, forgetting to bring files back, but now here they were in the bottom of Molly's closet where they should never have been.

Gripping the folders, Frank caught himself wondering about Rafe, whether he and Molly might be in it together, him trying to cover for her by blaming Swift...

No! Not Rafe.

Clenching his fist, he banged the closet door hard, slamming it shut as his anger grew. What she'd done was bad enough, without making him doubt his friends, the people he cared about.

Yet the person he'd cared about most was her.

Turning, he gazed at the blue curtain that hung across the far end of the room, framing her small bed. He walked over, stepping through the gap and staring down at the neatly smoothed quilt, the white pillows shining pale in the gloom.

Weary, he turned and sat down, feeling the mattress creak beneath him as he placed the gun on top of the folders and rubbed his eyes.

He'd cared about her so much...

Lifting his head, he looked up to see the last light of dusk in the sky at the window, picturing her silhouette moving about the room, wishing that it hadn't been her, wishing that it wasn't true, wishing that none of it had happened.

But Jean was dead. And Rafe had almost died. This was a war, just as surely as the battles that still raged beyond the Swiss border.

And what had she planned for *him* once he'd outlived his usefulness?

He stiffened, recalling how she'd asked about what he was going to do after the war, how she'd praised him for not having any plans. Telling him it was better that way, that he was less likely to be disappointed...

Snarling, he snatched up the gun, thumbed back the hammer, and stared over at the door.

It was late when he heard the muffled sounds of movement in the hallway outside. There had been several false alarms, but each time the footsteps had passed by. This time they halted right by the door.

Leaning forward, Frank lifted the gun, settling it in his palm as he eased the muzzle out beyond the edge of the curtain. There was a pause, then more movement, and he heard the sharp scratching of a key sliding into the lock.

He took a slow, calming breath, aiming down the barrel as the door opened. A shaft of light spilled across the wooden floor, and Molly stepped in, half in silhouette. She was wearing a long woolen coat, yawning as she slipped her keys back into her purse and turned to push the door. He heard it close, heard the catch snap shut, saw her shadowy form walk across the room to the small table lamp. As the switch clicked on, illuminating her with a warm glow, Frank spoke.

'Don't make a sound,' he hissed.

Startled, she jumped and whirled around, her eyes wide.

'Oh!' she gasped, recognizing him. 'Bloody hell, Frank; you scared me...'

Her voice trailed off and her expression tightened as she saw the gun.

'Not a damn sound,' he warned her.

She took a half-step backwards, fear and confusion on her face. Frank's finger tightened over the trigger.

'Stand *absolutely* still,' he said, the anger clear in his tone.

Blinking at him, Molly opened her mouth to speak.

'Frank, what are you–'

'Shut up!' he snapped. Swift had warned him to be careful; not to be distracted, not to take any risks. 'Are you armed?'

Molly was at a loss, staring blankly.

'No, I–'

'Kneel down,' he demanded. 'Kneel down and slide your purse over to me.'

'But I–'

'NOW!' he snarled.

She looked as though she was about to cry. Woodenly, she dropped to her knees, then slowly took her purse and placed it on the floor with a trembling hand.

'Slide it over to me,' he told her.

Staring up at him with wide eyes, she hesitated, then shoved the purse towards him. It slid across the bare boards and he stopped it with his foot.

'Please Frank,' she began. 'I–'

'Shut *up!*' he growled, jerking the gun to point at her head. 'Just shut the hell up, will you!'

Eyes locked on hers, he squatted down, one hand keeping the

gun level, the other reaching down and feeling for the purse. His fingers closed on it and he slipped his hand inside, rummaging through the contents until he felt the unmistakable touch of something solid and metallic. Nodding grimly to himself, he drew out the small pistol.

'Not armed, eh?' He shook his head in disgust, tossing the weapon onto the bed behind him. Swift had told him she'd be carrying a gun, and warned him just how dangerous she could be, even without it.

'Lie down on your front, hands behind your head,' he said, motioning towards the floor.

On her knees, she stared up at him, eyes bright with fear.

'Frank, I just—'

'On your front!' he snapped. 'DO IT!'

With a helpless look, she got onto all fours, then lowered herself to lay flat on the floor.

'Hands behind your head.'

Trembling, she slid her arms around and placed her hands behind her head.

Frank stared down at her, determined to feel no sympathy, stoking up his rage so it burned hot.

'I *know* about you,' he snarled. 'Don't you get it? I know all about you.'

'Wh-what are you talking about?' Molly's voice was muted, stammering into the floor. 'Please, Frank, I don't—'

'The Russians... the documents...' He snatched up the folders from the bed and threw them down onto the floor beside her. 'I know every damn thing.'

He broke off, his fist clenching.

Molly twisted her head around, eyes white as she stared at the folders, then strained to look up at him.

'And *Jean* knew too, didn't she?' he hissed. 'Is that why she was killed? Because she knew too much about *you*?'

'Oh God, Frank, *please* don't...'

Moving restlessly on the balls of his feet, he gave her a bitter half-smile.

'Who was it, Molly? Who killed Jean?'

Molly lowered her head and began to weep.

She'd been out that afternoon, so she'd had the opportunity to do it... but he wanted to hear it from her own mouth.

'WHO WAS IT?'

'I don't know what you're talking about,' she sobbed. 'I don't *know*!'

He stepped closer, leaning down to press the muzzle of the gun against the side of her face

'Don't... *fucking*... lie to me,' he hissed.

He could feel her trembling through the barrel of the gun.

'I don't know!' she wept. '*I don't know!*'

Frank tensed, his finger tightening round the trigger.

'Did you kill her?'

'*What?!*' Molly choked. 'No! *No!*'

'You're lying!'

She was shaking her head, trying to look up at him, and he saw the pale impression on her cheek where the muzzle had pressed into her skin.

'I swear, I'm not lying.'

He clenched his fist.

All those nights together, gaining his trust, pretending she cared about him...

'You've been lying to me from the very beginning,' he growled, pressing the gun in against her temple, forcing her to lean her head over to one side as she sobbed into the floor.

And he'd cared so much about her...

'Oh God.' She gulped down a breath. 'I swear–'

His trigger finger squeezed a little harder.

'Last chance, Molly.'

But she was weeping uncontrollably now, her body shaking, her breathing ragged.

He'd cared so much...

The sound was becoming unbearable, like the desperate crying of an injured child, and he found that he was grinding his teeth together, trying to shut it out.

Too much...

He stood up straight, aiming the gun at the back of her head, but then he recoiled. There was a dark puddle spreading out across the floorboards from beneath her hips. He stared down in shock, realizing what he'd done, how much he'd terrified her. Sickened, he took a step back, lifting his free hand to cover his mouth and lowering the gun slightly.

Too much...

He glanced hurriedly round the room, then moved over and stooped to retrieve the bundle of folders, his eyes fixed on her, face down and sobbing.

Swift had been very clear: detain her, or eliminate her. There was no third option.

But how the hell was he supposed to get her out of here? And where was he going to find a phone to call for transport? There was really only one choice.

Standing up, he raised the gun again, aiming, taking a breath and holding it.

Do it quickly, cleanly.

His heartbeat counted out the seconds in double time... then his finger eased off the trigger and he exhaled quietly.

If she'd just admitted it, if he didn't still care about her.

Keeping the gun trained on her, he took a few steps forward, then nudged her elbow with his shoe. She didn't seem to notice, still trembling and crying.

'Molly?' He tapped her arm with his foot again. She flinched, then turned her head slowly, her face a mess, wide eyes blinking up through the tears. He stared down the barrel at her, sickened by her betrayal and what it had done to them. Then he let the gun fall to his side.

'You're dead, okay?' he said quietly, holding up the stolen document folders so she could see them. 'Get out of Bern. Fuck it, get out of Switzerland. And do it tonight.'

With that, he turned his back on her, opened the door, and walked away down the long, empty hallway.

41

He hadn't slept. His body felt light and eager, still coursing with all the emotion and urgency of the night before, but now it was a restless energy, directionless and distracting. Standing by a closed door in the bare corridor at Herrengasse, Frank turned to squint at the morning sunlight, streaming in from the window at the back, and wished he could go outside. The weight of the building seemed to press down on him, a heavy silence broken only by the thin ticking of a clock that tested his patience. Bowing his head, he glanced down at his leather satchel and peered at the bundle of folders inside.

She'd made a fool of him... made fools of them all.

Sighing, he closed the satchel then leaned back against the wall, wondering about this meeting he'd been called to and how long they would keep him waiting.

Eventually, the door opened and Groth appeared, wordlessly summoning him with a hurried gesture. Frank followed him through into the study, blinking at the thick haze of pipe smoke that hung in the air. Dulles was over at the fireplace, carefully polishing his glasses with a handkerchief, while Swift stood by the tall window, staring down at the river far below. Groth ushered Frank inside, then closed the door behind them.

'Come and join us, Mr Rye,' Dulles said, looking up. 'We were just discussing the delicate matter of Miss Pearson.'

Indicating one of the chairs by the fire, he hooked his glasses back into place then peered at Frank speculatively.

'Mr Swift is of the opinion that we may have misjudged her. He feels that she may be in league with our Russian friends. It's quite a theory.'

Over by the window, Swift stirred but didn't turn around.

'I can't take *all* the credit,' he said quietly. 'Frank was the one who figured it out.'

Dulles raised an eyebrow, then stared at Frank.

'Is that so?'

Frank hesitated, then sat down uneasily.

'That's correct, sir.'

There was an air of tension in the room, and he had the uncomfortable sense that he'd walked into the middle of something, an extra opinion brought in to help settle an argument.

'And this is based on her visiting a dead-letter drop?' Dulles asked. 'Down in the Münsterplattform gardens?'

Frank nodded. He glanced across the room for guidance, but Swift still had his back to them, staring out the window, so he pressed on.

'I've been following this Levkin guy – he's part of the Russian consular team – and I noticed that his afternoon walks always took him to a particular bench down there. I guessed that maybe it was a way of passing messages, so I started to watch the place. Then, one day...' He shrugged and looked up at Dulles unhappily. '...there she was.'

Dulles said nothing for a moment, turning to the mantelpiece and retrieving his pipe. Tapping the stem against his palm, he glanced back at Frank, his expression guarded.

'You're certain that Molly wasn't *receiving* information?' he asked. 'Running this Levkin fellow as one of her stooges?'

Frank shook his head.

'*She* left a message for *him*,' he explained.

Swift finally abandoned the window, turning and pacing slowly across the room towards Dulles.

'That was the paper I showed you earlier,' he explained. 'With the grids of numbers.'

Dulles looked at him thoughtfully.

'And you believe this ties in with Miss Ellesworth's suspicions, about a foreign agent in the Dufourstrasse office?'

Swift stared back at him, then inclined his head slightly.

'Doesn't it suggest that to you?'

Dulles looked away, his brows wrinkling into a frown.

'Suggestions aren't enough,' he muttered. 'If there was something else, something more tangible...'

Frank's head snapped up.

'There is,' he said. Reaching for his satchel, he lifted out the bundle of folders and handed them to Dulles. 'These were in Molly's apartment.'

Dulles took the folders and began flicking through them, his expression darkening.

'I found them when I went there last night, looking for her,' Frank added. After all, what other reason would he have for being in Molly's apartment?

Glancing up, he wondered if Swift had told Dulles that he was sleeping with her.

'*You* found these?' Dulles asked, peering down at him.

Frank nodded.

For a moment, Dulles looked as though he was going to challenge him further, but then his shoulders dropped and he turned away, tossing the folders onto the other chair as he faced the fireplace.

'Where is she now?' he said, with a heavy sigh.

'We don't know,' Swift replied. 'She was in Geneva late yesterday afternoon.'

Dulled glanced over at Frank.

'She didn't come home last night?' he asked.

Frank willed his face to remain blank.

'There was no sign of her when I got there,' he replied. Technically, that was true.

He took a silent breath, then looked over to find Swift watching him, his expression unreadable.

Dulles nodded slowly, staring down into the fireplace.

'And you took the folders,' he mused. 'Yes, of course; she must have come home late, found the folders were missing, and realized we were onto her.'

Frank sat in the chair, feeling increasingly uncomfortable.

What would they think of him if they knew he'd had Molly at his mercy, but been unable to eliminate her?

Dulles turned around. Seeing Frank's face, his expression softened and he forced a brief smile.

'Don't be too hard on yourself, son; it's an easy mistake to make.' He glanced over at Swift. 'And it seems we may all have been mistaken about Miss Pearson.'

Swift acknowledged him with a look.

Dulles jammed his pipe between his teeth then patted his pockets.

'Such a capable young woman,' he said, quietly. 'What a shame.'

He found a box of matches on the mantelpiece and took a moment to light his pipe, then turned to look at them again.

'But was she working entirely without the knowledge of London?' he asked. 'Or did they have some inclination about what their young lady was up to?'

Frank stared at him.

'You think the British were involved in this?' he gasped.

Dulles tossed the spent match into the grate and drew thoughtfully on his pipe.

'I don't know,' he admitted. 'But I believe it's prudent to consider every possibility. And that brings us to the matter of Mr Cavanagh, another child of Empire.'

Frank lowered his eyes, remembering his own doubts about Rafe.

'I sent Rafe down to Brig, first thing this morning,' Swift told them. 'I thought it was better to keep him occupied elsewhere, until we decide what to do with him.'

Dulles nodded his approval.

'Very practical of you,' he said softly, then looked around at the others. 'So, what do we think? Where do Mr Cavanagh's loyalties lie?'

Swift's eyes went to Frank, who shifted uncomfortably in his chair.

'Well... *I* trust him.' He made a face. 'I know, I trusted Molly too, but I haven't seen anything – not ever – to suggest that Rafe's crooked.'

Groth stepped forward, clearing his throat.

'And he was very nearly killed, back in the summer.'

'That was by the Nazis,' Dulles reminded them. 'They'd have no reason to spare him, even if they suspected he was working for Moscow.'

There was an awkward silence. Frank looked around at the grim faces.

'You don't *really* think Rafe could be selling us out, do you?' he asked.

Dulles moved across to the chair. He reached down and picked up the folders, slowly shaking his head.

'No. I don't,' he said, weighing the folders in his hand. 'However, like you, I also believed that Miss Pearson was on the level... and it appears I was wrong about her.'

'So?' Swift asked. 'What are we going to do with him?'

Dulles narrowed his eyes, then looked towards the window for a moment.

Frank had a momentary vision of Groth following Rafe down a darkened alley, carrying that convenient German pistol they'd obtained at the ski lodge. He shuddered, and looked at Dulles anxiously.

'Well, Rafe's always been useful, and he's not done anything wrong that we know of,' Dulles mused. 'He's also a British asset, which means there are certain diplomatic issues to consider. For now, I think we have to give him the benefit of the doubt. But there *are* doubts... serious doubts.'

'So we watch him,' Swift said calmly. He nodded to himself, as though planning how he would do this, as though they were discussing someone who was a stranger, rather than one of their own. 'Keep him at arm's length on operations, that sort of thing.'

'Yes, handle with care,' Dulles replied, then added, 'until we're sure about him, one way or the other.'

Frank looked at them. Dulles had an uncharacteristically bleak expression, and Frank realized just how close Rafe was to being branded an enemy.

Their group had been held together by such a fragile trust, and after Molly's betrayal, that trust was finally beginning to fracture.

42

Frank walked slowly up the hill, listening to the rush of the river and the wind sighing through the bare branches of the trees. Hunching his shoulders forward, he dug his hands deeper into the pockets of his coat, shivering as he tried to hold on to the last of his warmth. Away to the right, the lights of the old town twinkled merrily but it was getting dark now and the long chill of evening was settling across the city. Ahead, the road swept up and round into the darkness.

Things had looked black for Rafe after the revelation of Molly's betrayal, and he wasn't out of the woods yet. Sure, everyone liked him, but those sorts of feelings didn't count for much when the person might be selling you out to some foreign power. Once more, Frank wondered what they would have done if Dulles hadn't decided to give Rafe a chance... then he shook his head and shivered again.

Not something he wanted to think about.

At the top of the bend, bright against the gloom, a lonely street lamp illuminated the turn-off to a small side road. Frank followed the sidewalk round to the right, trudging up a gentle slope, where the trees finally gave way to a series of large villas that loomed up above thick hedges, slivers of golden light gleaming between their closed shutters.

Yes, everyone liked Rafe, but *trusting* was more important than liking now, and trust had to go both ways. Frank sighed, thinking about the news he was going to have to break to his friend. It wasn't going to be easy, explaining about Molly, but he understood why he'd been chosen to do it; they'd been close from the start, and he'd saved Rafe's life. If there was bad news to deliver, it was better that it came from him.

Cresting the rise, he started slowly down the far side, wishing that things could have worked out differently.

Rafe had a ground floor apartment in a crumbling old building, just a few blocks away from the Dufourstrasse office. Standing in the porch, Frank leaned in close, squinting to find the number six bell-push by the dim light of the streetlamp opposite. Pressing it, he waited, then checked his watch. It was almost nine – Rafe ought to be back from Brig by now. Drawing his coat tighter around him, he stamped his feet, moving this way and that to try and drive away the cold. He turned to glance back along the street, half expecting to see his friend limping along the sidewalk, but there was nobody around.

The lack of sleep was beginning to tug at his senses, and he stifled a yawn. His own lodgings weren't that far, but he'd promised he'd come and speak to Rafe tonight.

He rang the bell again, then decided to let himself in and try knocking – anything was better that waiting outside in the wind.

Walking along the ground floor hallway, he followed the corridor towards the rear of the building and turned the corner at the end. Standing in front of number six, he rubbed his cold hands to get some feeling back into them, then rapped smartly on the door.

'Rafe?' He yawned again, leaning up against the wall. 'Rafe, if you're in there, open up. It's me.'

There was no answer. Frank bowed his head and sighed, trying to think where his friend might have stopped for a meal or a drink. *The place on Thunstrasse, maybe? Or somewhere in town?*

Pushing himself away from the wall, he turned around, then stiffened as Molly stepped into view, just a few yards away from him at the corner. She stared for a moment, her eyes cold, then slowly drew a gun from her purse and held it loosely at her side. He recognized it as the pistol he'd left on her bed, now fitted with a silencer, and cursed himself for not taking it with him.

'Rafe's not home,' he said, trying to keep a lid on the sudden surge of anger he felt at seeing her. He'd given her a chance to get out, to get far away from here, far away from *him*, but now here she was again.

'I know,' she replied, her voice measured. 'I've been waiting for him.'

'Yeah?'

For a moment he hesitated, doubts about Rafe flickering in his mind again... then he dismissed the idea. No, if these two were working together, she wouldn't be lurking out here in the hallway.

'Feeling lonely, were you?' he said, goading her. 'Looking for someone else to charm?'

'Oh, don't be so bloody stupid, Frank.' She spoke as though his words were just foolish, but he could see her jaw tighten, the muscles in her neck stiffening – he'd touched a nerve.

'Now that I'm wise to you, it's Rafe's *turn*, is that it?' He lifted his head in defiance and took a step forwards, spitting out the words. 'You're really *something*, Molly.'

'Stay where you are, Frank.' She was doing her best to sound dangerous but he wasn't fooled.

'Or what?' he growled.

Molly raised the pistol, her knuckles shining small and pale as she tried to keep the barrel steady.

'I mean it,' she whispered.

Frank looked at her with disgust.

'What the hell do you want, Molly?' he demanded. 'Haven't you done enough already? Why are you still here?'

Molly glared back at him for a moment.

'I have to speak to Dulles,' she said. 'He... he trusts me.'

'Yeah?' Frank sneered. 'Like *I* trusted you? Did you sleep with *him* too?'

Molly's face went pale.

'He trusts me because I *refused* to sleep with him,' she snapped.

Frank shook his head and sighed bitterly. Swift had warned him she could talk her way out of anything, but he wasn't going to be fooled again.

'Oh, give it a rest, will you? Damnit all...' Weary of the exchange, he rubbed his eyes, then started towards her. 'I should have just brought you in when I had–'

Molly angled the gun slightly and there was a brief flash.

For a second, he didn't understand what had caused him to stumble, but then the agony exploded up through his leg like a splash of scalding water, and everything tilted and he was pitching over to fall against the wall.

'Nnnggghhhfuck!' The cry burst from him as though he'd been holding his breath, and he gaped in shaking disbelief at the dark stain spreading down his pants leg. 'You... fucking *shot* me!'

'Oh God!' Molly gasped. She moved to stand over him, her face ashen, the gun still pointing at him. 'Keep your bloody voice down, and press hard on that wound.'

'Shit!' Frank gasped. He could feel the warm wetness against his calf, sensed the panic rising in his chest as he stared up through a mist of tears. 'Shit!'

'Press down hard on the wound,' Molly snarled. 'DO IT!'

Slumped against the wall, Frank lifted a trembling hand and clamped it over the sticky dent in his lower leg. A flash of burning pain seared through him and he twisted his face away, shrieking out a muffled howl into the shoulder of his overcoat.

He wasn't sure how long he'd been lying there. The pain made it seem like a long time, but the pool of blood on the floor didn't look all that big...

He closed his eyes. Molly was speaking, but it was difficult to follow what she was saying; her voice was rapid, agitated.

'...with Hitler out of the picture they've been looking for a way to surrender – Dulles knows that better than anyone – and when they do? Well, that's when it could all change, that's when it could all *really* go to hell...'

Frank lifted his head, vaguely aware that he was sweating profusely despite the sudden chill in the hallway. He gazed up at her, mouthing the word "traitor" but she didn't hear him, just carried on talking.

'...and after the problems at Yalta, between Stalin and Truman, things are so much worse. We're going to have a whole new war unless I can–'

Suddenly, she broke off, listening intently.

Straightening up, she took a step back, keeping the gun trained on him as she turned her head towards the bend in the corridor.

Dimly, Frank thought about grabbing for her, but it was all he could do to keep his palm pressed against his leg; he knew he wouldn't be able to get up, let alone snatch the gun from her.

He could hear it now: approaching footsteps, and something else...

The tapping of a walking stick.

'Rafe!' he croaked, the effort of sitting up sending waves of agony through him. 'Get back!'

Molly's expression became anguished.

'Just wait there, Rafe,' she called. 'Don't come round here.'

But it was too late.

Rafe limped into view round the corner, bundled up in a hat and coat, and carrying a small briefcase.

'I say, what are you...?' He stopped, eyes flickering from Molly gripping her pistol, to Frank lying in a pool of blood. 'Oh dear God.'

His face went slack and the walking stick slipped from his hand to fall, clattering on the floor.

'Rafe,' Molly implored him. 'Rafe, it isn't what you think.'

'Don't listen to her,' Frank gasped, struggling to sit up. 'She's a fucking traitor.'

'Shut up!' Molly snarled, whirling around and brandishing the pistol at him. 'Just shut up and let me *speak*, will you?'

Behind her, Rafe had reached inside his coat and was slowly pulling out a gun.

'Oh God,' he gasped. 'Molly, what the hell have you *done*?'

Molly held up her free hand to silence him.

'Just... just wait a minute, *please* Rafe... I promise you it's not...'

Breathing hard, Frank raised his voice over hers.

'She *shot* me.'

'BE QUIET, FRANK!' There was panic in her eyes as she glared down at him.

Standing behind her, Rafe had raised his gun. He swallowed, a sick expression on his face.

'Molly,' he stammered. 'Put the gun down.'

'You don't understand!' She rolled her eyes, stifling a cry of frustration. 'I'm not the one who–'

'Don't listen to her,' Frank rasped.

'SHUT UP!'

Rafe was trembling.

'Put the gun down,' he told her. '*Please!*'

'She betrayed us,' Frank grunted.

'Put it down!' Rafe insisted.

'She sold us out.'

'MOLLY, *PLEASE!*'

'NO!' Molly shrieked. She spun around to face Rafe, her pistol hand swinging round wildly. 'Both of you just SHUT UP and–'

The sound was deafening, a shattering crack that seemed to shake the walls and echo away down the corridor. Frank flinched, slipping sideways onto one elbow, unable to protect his ears.

Standing over him, Molly staggered. In the awful silence, her arms dropped to her sides and the pistol slipped from her fingers. For a moment, she was still. Then her knees buckled and she crumpled, falling backwards. There was a dull crack as her head struck the floor.

At the corner of the corridor, Rafe still hadn't moved, standing there like a horrified statue, the gun still clenched tightly in his hand.

'Oh God...' His voice trembled and he started to cry. 'Oh dear God, *no...*'

Frank blinked through his shock, gulping down a desperate lungful of air.

'Rafe,' he whispered, then slumped against the wall, trying to keep his hand pressed against his leg. Through the ringing in his ears, he thought he could hear a voice, calling out from somewhere else in the building.

Rafe stumbled over to him, backing up against the wall as he stepped around Molly, then looking down at Frank with fear in his eyes.

'Are you badly hurt?' he gasped. 'Can you stand?'

Frank shut his eyes.

'Can't get up,' he said, weakly.

'You need a doctor,' Rafe said, glancing around anxiously. He seemed to come to a decision, and bent down quickly, grasping Frank by the lapels of his coat. 'Come on, old chum, I've got you.'

Frank drew a ragged breath as Rafe hoisted him up, pulling him round so that his arm was hooked over the other man's shoulder.

'That's it, lean on me.'

Dimly, he wondered why he couldn't feel his leg so much now, just an occasional flash of pain in the throbbing numbness as he scuffed his shoe, leaving a trail of smeared blood.

'Stay with me, Frank.'

From somewhere further along the corridor, a voice shouted something.

Rafe was weeping openly now, tears running down his face as he struggled along without his stick, every step an effort.

As they came to the corner of the corridor, Frank struggled to lift his head and look back.

She lay in a heap, legs splayed awkwardly, an ugly stain of darkening scarlet in the middle of her chest. Her expression was strange and empty, dead eyes staring blankly at the wall...

Negotiating the turn, Rafe jarred against his wounded leg, then glanced up wretchedly.

'Damn,' he puffed. 'Sorry.'

Frank's eyelids drooped, and he slowly shook his head.

He felt nothing.

𝕶𝖆𝖓𝖘𝖆𝖘 𝕮𝖎𝖙𝖞 𝕳𝖊𝖗𝖆𝖑𝖉

KANSAS CITY, MISSOURI - WEDNESDAY, June 20, 1945

GERMAN PRISONERS TO FIGHT AGAINST REDS, CHURCHILL SAYS

WESTERN ALLIES CREATE NEW GERMAN DEFENSE FORCE TO HALT RUSSIAN ADVANCE

LONDON, Jun 23 – British Prime Minister Churchill tonight gave a special statement regarding plans to enlist captured German soldiers into the continuing battle with Russian forces occupying Poland.

"It is an opportunity for Germany to begin the repayment of her great debt to the world, and to regain some small measure of honour," he told Parliament. "As one dictatorship is vanquished, so another, long-foreseen, seeks to subjugate weary nations to its will. Tyranny may come with different faces, but it is a threat to all people and all people must stand against it. In this great endeavour, Germany must play her part."

General Eisenhower, Supreme Commander of the Western Allies in Europe, voiced his support for the plan. "Allied troops have shouldered a great burden in the battle for European liberty. Now, with that battle on their home territory, the Germans cannot stand idly by while others fight for them."

(continued on page 2, column 2)

43

Frank shifted awkwardly in his narrow bed, unable to move, unable to get comfortable. Shafts of late afternoon sun touched the far wall with patches of pale gold, making the nurses squint as they paced back and forth on their rounds. He sighed and let his head sink back against the heaped pillows, trying to ignore the wheezing snore of Herr Baumann, an elderly patient who'd arrived last week and seemed to sleep all the time.

How he wished he could do that, just close his eyes and slip away into nothing...

But his leg was still imprisoned in a casket of plaster and steel clamps, elevated at an angle that made a full night's sleep impossible.

He twisted his neck around, craning to see out of the window behind him, enjoying the distraction of drifting clouds against the sky. The pain wasn't so bad today – just a steady dull ache that worried at the edges of his awareness – but it was a constant, unwelcome reminder.

'Herr Rye?'

He looked round. It was the pretty nurse with the black hair and deep brown eyes.

'Sie haben einen Besucher,' she said with an encouraging smile. *You have a visitor.*

Frank sat up in surprise, flinching as the weight pulled on his leg; he wasn't expecting Rafe until Saturday.

The nurse turned towards the door, beckoning, but it was Dulles who stepped into view. He was wearing a light grey over-coat and carrying a small briefcase of brown leather. Approaching the foot of the bed, he inclined his head politely at the nurse.

'Danke, Fräulein.'

She grinned at him and moved away to attend another patient.

Dulles watched her go, then turned to peer at Frank through his spectacles.

'Good afternoon, Mr Rye,' he said, leaning over to study the plaster cast and its supports. 'Dear me, I thought they might have let you out of this contraption by now.'

'Shattered femur,' Frank said, with a shrug. 'Some things take a long time to mend.'

Dulles looked at him for a moment, then nodded.

'True enough,' he agreed. Moving awkwardly around to the side of the bed, he pulled up a small chair and sat down, keeping his coat on despite the warmth. Frank watched him, thinking how he looked ready to leave despite having only just arrived.

'Very capable-looking nurse there,' Dulles remarked, glancing back towards the door. 'And the room seems pleasant enough. How's the food?'

'Not quite up to the standard of the Bellevue Hotel,' Frank confided in a low voice.

Dulles chuckled.

'No, I imagine the menu here is rather different.'

'But it's not too bad,' Frank continued. 'And I get breakfast in bed every day.'

'Well, that's one silver lining, I suppose.'

A particularly loud snore made Dulles glance across the room, and he shook his head with a smile.

'So how are things at the office?' Frank asked. 'Rafe comes to see me each week but he doesn't say all that much, and I don't like to push him.'

'There's quite a lot happening at the moment.' Shifting in his seat, Dulles reached into his pocket and drew out his pipe. 'You'll have seen the newspapers?'

'I try and find time in my busy schedule.' Frank looked pointedly at his plastered leg, then back to Dulles. 'So, I guess our coup finally happened. But for Germany to side with us against the Russians...' He whistled softly.

Dulles shrugged.

'Germany was a spent force. Once Hitler was out of the picture, there was no reason for them to prolong the war any longer and they needed to negotiate a surrender with us before the Russians wiped them off the map. And there was no reason for *us* to prolong things, either...' He shook his head disapprovingly. '...wasting *more* American lives just to humiliate a nation that's already on its knees.'

Frank considered this, then frowned.

'But... the conflict with Russia: *haven't* we prolonged the war?'

Dulles fixed him with a steely gaze.

'If something is inevitable, you may as well meet it on your own terms,' he said quietly. 'And I don't think the advancing Russians were likely to stop at their own border, do you?'

'No, I guess not,' Frank conceded. 'Still, it's strange to think of the German army being on *our* side.'

What was it Molly said? "We're going to have a whole new war..."

Behind his spectacles, Dulles' sharp blue eyes twinkled.

'Come now, you know better than that,' he said. 'There *are* no sides, just common interests.'

Frank leaned back against his pillows, wincing.

'Now you sound like Swift,' he said.

'Maybe *he* sounds like *me*,' Dulles replied, flashing a faint smile.

He opened his tobacco pouch and started filling his pipe.

'I guess it does suit *our* interests,' Frank mused. 'But what about the British? Rafe says it's a complete betrayal of everything we've been fighting for.'

Dulles snorted.

'The British *people* might not like it, but Churchill is secretly delighted.' He paused and looked up. 'It was his idea, you know.'

'Really?' Frank said, surprised.

'Oh yes, Roosevelt wouldn't back the plan because he always wanted to keep Stalin sweet, but Truman is a very different man, and a very different president. After Yalta, when it became clear what the Russians were intending... well, Churchill's a clever man, and he chose his moment perfectly.'

Dulles appeared to have warmed up now. He spoke at length on a subject he was clearly comfortable with, and Frank listened eagerly.

It was easier to discuss a war that was far away, than to talk about what had happened right here in Bern.

'Anyway, there you have it,' Dulles concluded. He lifted his pipe to his mouth, then seemed to remember where he was and grudgingly lowered it again. 'As you can imagine, it's going to mean some big changes – a major restructuring, in fact – so I thought I should pay you a last visit before things get any busier.'

Frank looked at him sharply.

'*Last* visit?'

Dulles gave him a wry smile.

'You're very attentive,' he said. 'Yes, I'll be leaving Bern for a new post in the next few days.'

It was clear that he didn't intend to discuss the matter in any detail, but Frank's mind flickered back to his conversations with Rafe.

'Berlin, right?' he said.

Dulles peered at him thoughtfully.

'What makes you think that?' he asked.

Frank shook his head.

'Just some talk around the office,' he said, keeping his answer deliberately vague.

Dulles frowned.

'I see. Not much of a secret now then, I suppose.'

Frank smiled to himself.

'The office will be quiet...' He trailed off.

Quiet without Dulles, without Jean... and without Molly.

Perched on his chair, Dulles zipped his tobacco pouch shut and took a moment to push it firmly down into his pocket.

'There isn't going to *be* a Bern office,' he said quietly. 'That's what I came to tell you.'

Frank stared at him.

'You're taking me to Berlin?' he asked, sitting up. The idea excited him – a fresh start, away from everything he'd ever known, a chance to lose himself in something that really *mattered*.

But Dulles was shaking his head.

'Things are changing,' he said. 'What with the German surrender, and the Russian situation...'

Frank hesitated, then frowned.

'I'm not sure I understand,' he said.

Dulles sighed.

'I think we've asked enough of you for now,' he said, eyeing Frank's injured leg. 'Quite enough.'

'But...' Frank looked at him helplessly. 'What will I do?'

'You're done,' Dulles told him gently. 'I've made some calls and it's all taken care of; as soon as you're well enough, the embassy will arrange for your passage back to the States.'

Frank slumped back heavily onto his elbows.

'You're washing me out?'

Dulles shook his head firmly.

'No, I'm just being pragmatic.' He took a deep breath, then continued. 'The war will soon be over, but you'll need time to heal. You can't go back to your old infantry unit, and there's nothing for you here. Go back to Missouri, son. Go home.'

Frank stared at him, then nodded thoughtfully.

Home. There was nothing for him there either.

'Is that an order?' he asked, then added, 'Sir?'

Dulles got slowly to his feet and stood by the bedside, gazing down at Frank.

'Call it sound medical advice.'

He extended his hand and waited. After a moment, Frank reached out and shook it.

'I'll be seeing you, Mr Rye,' Dulles said.

Frank looked up at him, then gave a reluctant nod.

'Good luck, sir.'

Dulles smiled, then turned and walked briskly away.

Kansas City Herald

KANSAS CITY, MISSOURI - TUESDAY, August 7, 1945

FIRST 'ATOMIC' BOMB DROPPED ON MOSCOW

NEW DEVICE EQUAL TO 20,000 TONS OF TNT; TRUMAN WARNS REDS OF 'RAIN OF RUIN'

WASHINGTON, Aug 6 – The most powerful force ever harnessed by man - atomic energy - has been unleashed on the Russians, destroying their capital city. President Truman today announced that the first atomic bomb had been dropped on Moscow some 16 hours before. He noted that Marshal Stalin had rejected a final ultimatum to withdraw from Poland and Czechoslovakia, where American and European troops have been battling Red Army forces since the German surrender.

A-BOMB 'WILL SHORTEN THE WAR'

President Truman stated his belief that the new weapon, which has a blast force greater than 20,000 tons of TNT, will "prove a tremendous aid" in shortening the war and that Russia "may expect a rain of ruin from the air the like of which has never been seen on this earth".

(continued on page 2, column 1)

Fall, 1953
Jackson County, Missouri

44

The road climbed steadily, a smooth ribbon of blacktop sweeping up the hill in a series of long, lazy curves. Trees pressed in on either side of them now, unending walls of red-golden leaves that offered brief glimpses of the grey Chrysler up ahead before the next bend hid it from view.

Frank drove with one hand on the wheel, keeping as much distance between them as he could. They hadn't passed any other vehicles since they turned off the main road, and he couldn't afford for Ellis to notice them.

Better to lose him than be seen, especially as the girl seemed to know where they were going.

He glanced over at Faye, her head resting against the window glass, blank eyes staring out at nothing. She hadn't said a word in almost ten minutes.

'So...' he began. 'You gonna tell me about this place?'

For a while, she didn't speak. Then, she shifted in her seat, raising her chin slightly.

'It's a big lake surrounded by trees, way out in the middle of nowhere,' she said, her voice distant. 'One of the Kansas City bosses had a house, right down on the shore. I went there, just one time... and we passed that gas station, the one with the yellow ribbon tied round the pole? I remember looking up at it and wondering who they'd put it there for. Someone from the war, probably. Whoever it was, I guess they never came home...'

She trailed off. Frank's eyes flickered briefly to her then back to the road.

'Who lives at the house?' he prompted her.

'I don't think anyone lives there,' she replied. 'Not full-time, anyway. It's just a place they have, for fishing and... you know... entertaining important people.'

Frank allowed himself a wry smile.

A country retreat for the Mob.

'How come you were out there?' he asked.

Faye fell silent again. She turned her head away and stared out of the window.

Entertaining important people.

Frank sighed as it dawned on him what she'd meant.

'Hey,' he said. 'I'm sorry.'

Faye managed a small shrug but her cheeks were flushed red.

The road crested the top of a rise and swept around to the right, then dipped down into a hollow, snaking back and forth through tight, tree-lined curves.

Frank snatched another quick look at Faye.

'Well, at least we have an idea where Ellis is headed,' he said, trying to shift the conversation onto safer ground. 'And the bastard wouldn't come all this way without a reason. My guess is, he needs to meet up with whoever it is he's working for.'

He tightened his grip on the steering wheel and frowned.

That was someone he wanted to meet too.

They were descending now, the line of the road dropping away before them. The trees here were taller, older, and the sky became a narrow strip of light as branches and foliage reached over to enclose them in shadow. Rounding a bend, they could see that the road ahead angled away sharply to the right, while a dirt trail continued straight on, sloping down to disappear among the trees.

'Slow down a minute.' Faye sat up in her seat, pointing towards the start of the trail. 'There... I think that's it.'

Frank stepped on the brakes, bringing the car to a gentle halt. He leaned forward over the steering wheel, peering out through the trees, but there was no sign of the Chrysler now, nothing to indicate if this was the right place.

'Are you sure?' he asked.

Faye hesitated.

'No, but... oh, I don't know.'

Letting the engine idle, Frank studied her expression, then nodded grimly.

Something had jarred her memory. And just because she couldn't say what that was, it didn't mean she was wrong.

'Okay,' he said, indicating the turn-off. 'Is the house far from the road?'

Faye shook her head.

'I don't think so,' she replied. 'Why?'

Frank paused, frowning to himself.

'Well, we don't want to blunder into Ellis, or whoever he's working for, and that trail doesn't look wide enough for me to turn around easily.' He glanced across at her. 'Maybe it's best if we find someplace to ditch the car, then walk down to the house.'

Faye's expression was nervous, but she nodded quickly.

'Okay.'

Frank lifted his foot and allowed the car to creep forward again. They rolled past the turn-off and pulled slowly around the bend.

'What can you tell me about the place itself?' he asked. 'Is it walled in? Are there fences, anything like that?'

'I don't know,' she said, frowning. 'But I remember a little grassy slope that led down to a jetty, and a long shore that curved away into the distance.'

Frank considered this.

'Okay then,' he said to himself. 'So I guess I just need to find a way down to the water, then follow the shoreline back to the house.'

He drove on slowly, peering out between the trees, then pointed.

'There! Is that the lake?'

'I think so. Yes, it is.'

Frank slowed the car to a crawl, then carefully bumped the wheels down onto the patchy grass at the side of the road. Switching off the engine, he took a deep breath, then twisted round in his seat to look at Faye.

'This is liable to get ugly,' he warned her. 'I really think you'd be better off staying here.'

Faye held his gaze without blinking, an expression of cold determination on her face.

'No,' she told him. 'I'm coming with you.'

Her eyes challenged him to refuse, and he looked away.

'Your choice,' he sighed.

'That's right.'

Frank got out and stood for a moment, listening to the forest. The air beneath the trees was cool and still, rich with the scent of decaying leaves. He took his gun out and checked it one more time, wincing at the sharp metallic snap as he pulled the slide back.

He glanced over at Faye, standing on the other side of the Oldsmobile, her eyes on the trees, large and watchful.

'Ready?' he said softly.

For a moment, he thought she hadn't heard him, then she gave a slight nod.

'Ready.'

They left the road and started to pick their way down the uneven, forested slope. Some distance below them, Frank could just make out the early evening light reflecting off the water, but their progress was slow, particularly where the ground fell away more steeply. Faye matched his pace, but the carpet of fallen leaves made it difficult to find any sure footing and, despite their efforts, it was impossible to move silently.

Halfway down the slope Frank paused, lifting a hand and motioning her to stop so he could listen, but there was nothing, just the faint sigh of a breeze in the branches above them. His eyes swept left and right, searching between the trees...

...like that night at the ski lodge near the Swiss border, when he'd almost lost Rafe.

He turned back to Faye, standing absolutely still a few feet behind him, her face alert and anxious. She looked so small among the towering trees.

'Stay close to me,' he told her.

They continued their descent. Eventually the ground leveled off, and they emerged from the shadow of the trees to step out beneath a vast open sky. The light was just beginning to fail, and the first dark clouds of evening were drawing in from the eastern horizon.

Cautiously, Frank walked out onto the rough grass, glancing left and right, before beckoning Faye to follow him. Together, they made their way down to the stony shore and gazed out over the broad expanse of the lake. The surface was calm, maybe half a mile across to the far side, where rolling hills rose from a dark line of trees. Gentle waves lapped and gurgled against a large shelf of rock that extended out into the water.

'Quite a view,' Frank said softly.

'Yeah,' Faye nodded, but her eyes were staring along the shore to their left.

Towards the house.

Frank came over to stand beside her.

'Let's go take a look at the place,' he said.

They made their way back up to the strip of ground that separated the forest and the lake, and followed its course along the meandering shoreline. Here and there, the trees came right down to the water's edge, but they were always able to pick their way through, and the grass allowed them to move more quickly and quietly.

Before long, they rounded a bend where a ridge pushed further into the lake and, looking ahead, Frank made out a long straight line that stretched from the shore.

That must be the jetty.

His eyes flickered to the trees behind it and there, on a gentle grassy slope, he finally saw the house. It was a modern, timber-frame construction, two stories tall with a sloping roof. A broad balcony looked out over the lake, supported on wooden stilts above the incline.

He turned to alert Faye, but she'd already halted mid-step, bad memories visible in her eyes as she stared towards the house.

'Let's get back under cover,' he told her. 'We don't want to be seen out here.'

She remained still for a moment longer, then wordlessly turned and followed him into the trees.

The shoreline curved round towards the jetty but Frank took them deeper into the forest, picking his way back up the wooded slope so that they could approach the house from the side, where there were fewer windows.

It was beginning to get darker now, especially here under the canopy of branches, and it took them some time to reach it, but eventually they crested a shallow rise that overlooked the front corner of the building, and the open clearing beside it.

Frank motioned Faye to get down, and they both dropped to their knees, peering out from behind the barrel trunk of a gnarled old tree.

'There.' Frank pointed at the broad gravel area where the dirt trail emerged from the trees. There were three cars parked there: a sleek blue Cadillac convertible, a brown Chevy, and the familiar grey Chrysler.

'So his car's down there.' Faye shrugged. 'So what? We already knew this was the place.'

Frank looked across at her then gently shook his head.

'There's *three* cars down there.'

'So?' she said, frowning.

'So we need to know how many people we're dealing with here.' Frank turned back to study the cars. 'The grey one is Ellis, and I'm guessing the Cadillac belongs to whoever he's working for. But the third one? That could mean three or four extra guys.'

He reached inside his jacket and carefully withdrew the .45, weighing it in his hand for a moment.

'This isn't going to be easy,' he muttered.

45

A breath of wind created a faint rustling in the leaves of distant trees, like the stirring of some ancient spirit. They could hear it approaching from down by the lake, growing nearer until it seemed to pass right over them. Faye gazed up nervously into the branches above them, then turned to Frank.

'So?' she asked. 'What are we going to do?'

'I'm working on it.' He had squatted down low, still staring at the three cars outside the house.

Had he really come this far only to find himself outgunned?

'We need to do *something*,' Faye pressed him. 'It'll be getting dark soon.'

Frank nodded unhappily.

'I really want to go in there and find Ellis' boss, but it's too risky without knowing who else is with him.' He paused, then stared along the trail that led back to the road. 'I guess we could wait until Ellis leaves, but even then...'

Faye looked appalled.

'You aren't going to let Ellis *go*, are you?' she gasped.

'I don't want to.' Frank scowled. 'But there's only two of us against who knows how many. We can't just walk in there and hope they all surrender.'

Beside him, Faye frowned.

'Couldn't you just get Ellis as he comes out?'

Frank looked down at the .45 in his hand and wished he'd brought his suppressor. Without it, the noise would be too much.

'This thing isn't quiet,' he told her. 'If I pull the trigger out here, everyone in the house will know about it.'

Faye frowned, then slumped against the tree in frustration.

'I can't believe we're just going to let him drive out of here,' she muttered. 'There must be *some* way to stop him. What if you let the air out of his tires or something?'

'But that would just keep them all together.' He paused, staring down the car, thinking. *Something that Groth had told him, a late-night story in the Bierkeller.* 'Unless...'

'Unless what?' Faye asked.

Frank turned to her, the ghost of a smile playing on his lips.

'I have an idea,' he whispered. 'Stay here and keep out of sight.'

He crept down the slope, moving from one tree to another, pausing now and then to listen. His own footsteps seemed terribly loud, crunching through the fallen leaves, but as he drew closer he thought he could make out music coming from the house.

Good.

Reaching the last tree before the grass gave way to gravel, he paused to compose himself, then took off at a crouching run, quickly covering the ground and ducking down at the side of the grey Chrysler.

Taking a breath, he listened again, but there were no voices, no sounds of alarm, just the music. Was that Sinatra? Cautiously, he lifted his head and peered through the car interior towards the house. From this angle he was relatively well shielded; none of the windows looked this way.

His luck seemed to be holding... so far.

Steeling himself, he edged around to the back of the Chrysler, feeling for the trunk release button with his fingers and pressing it until it clicked. Easing the trunk open just a little, he peered inside.

Yeah, there it was.

Reaching in, he located the long metal lug wrench and drew it out, then carefully eased the trunk lid down again until it clicked shut. With another anxious glance towards the house, he moved back around to crouch by the rear wheel. Using the flat end of the wrench, he managed to pry off the chrome hub cap, remembering just in time to catch it so it wouldn't clatter on the gravel. Then, flipping the wrench around, he set to work undoing the lug nuts.

It was hard work, and it seemed to take forever, but eventually he was able to press the hub cap back into place. Gripping the wrench, he made a dash across the gravel and disappeared into the shadows of the forest.

'Frank?'

Faye's voice startled him, and he whirled around to see her standing with her back to a large tree.

'Damn it!' he hissed, lowering the wrench as the shock slowly ebbed from him. He'd been wound up so tight, waiting for a noise, and then just as he started to relax... 'I thought I told you to stay put.'

'I couldn't see what you were doing,' she whispered. 'What *were* you doing?'

Frank beckoned her to follow him. Together they made their way back up the slope and dropped down on the sheltered far side, out of sight of the house.

'Well?' Faye asked.

Frank caught his breath, then reached into his jacket pocket and pulled out the lug nuts to show her.

'I loosened one of the wheels,' he explained, with grim satisfaction. 'It'll come off when he tries to take that winding trail back to the road, hopefully a good distance from the house.'

Faye nodded in understanding.

'So you can get him on his own,' she said.

Frank managed a grim smile.

'Ellis isn't going anywhere far.'

'Okay.' Faye considered this. 'But what do we do for now? And what if he doesn't leave until late, or stays till the morning?'

Frank gave her a weary look, then sighed.

'We didn't want him to drive away, and now he *won't* drive away,' he said, with as much patience as he could muster. 'For the moment, we're going to wait.'

'Wait for what?' Faye asked.

Frank settled down and leaned back against the base of a tree, dropping the wrench on the ground beside him.

They needed an edge, something that would let them get close to the house and keep their advantage.

'Darkness,' he told her.

Dusk was closing in and it was getting colder. Frank had offered Faye his jacket once already, but she'd refused, assuring him she didn't need it. Now she was pacing back and forth a little way down the sheltered side of the rise, trying to keep warm.

A voice, indistinct and distant, made him sit up suddenly. He raised a hand to warn Faye, then rolled onto his knees and snatched up the wrench. Keeping his head low, he crawled to the top of the slope, and peered down at the house. A shaft of light spilled out, cutting a bright path across the gravel while a lean figure stood talking in the doorway. It was impossible to make out what was said, but there was no mistaking who it was.

Ellis.

The thin man turned and walked across the gravel. Behind him, someone shut a door and the light was suddenly gone. Backing away, Frank crawled down below the crest of the rise, then got stiffly to his feet.

'It's Ellis,' he whispered to Faye as she came up to stand beside him. From the other side of the ridge, they heard something that might have been a car door slamming, then the waking roar of an engine. 'Come on, he's leaving.'

Turning he started to move along the slope, keeping far enough down to be out of sight from the trail. The exact direction of each sound was confused among the trees, but they could hear that the car was moving quickly and a moment later they saw the glow of its headlights illuminating the forest ahead of them.

Frank ran, almost stumbling over fallen branches and tangled undergrowth but desperate not to let Ellis get too far ahead. He saw the reflection of the lights raking around to the left as the car began to turn... then there was a sudden awful scraping noise, like stony ground being gouged under metal, and a final grinding crunch.

Frank hurried on, angling directly towards the sound as he rounded the shoulder of the rise and saw the car ahead of him. The engine was still running, revving fast like it had got itself stuck, and the headlights glared out, illuminating the trees at the side of the trail where the car had finally come to rest. It lay at a slight angle, stooped down on one corner as though it was lame.

As Frank closed the distance between them, the engine abruptly switched off. Tensing, he skidded to an immediate halt, his crashing footsteps suddenly way too loud against the silence. He twisted around, gesturing to Faye, motioning her to be careful, then turned back towards the lights.

A door squeaked open, metal scraping against metal, and

they heard Ellis' voice, cursing and swearing as he forced his way out of the car.

'Dannazione, you useless piece of crap...'

He stomped around to the near side of the car, bending down to stare at the empty wheel arch, muttering angrily to himself.

Frank stepped quietly out from the trees, his gun leveled at the thin man's back, the wrench gripped tightly in his other hand.

'Don't *fucking* move,' he said, in a tone that froze Ellis where he stood. 'Hands above your head, where I can see them.'

Slowly, Ellis raised his hands.

'What the hell is this?' he demanded gruffly, but there was a note of fear in his voice. 'I just lost a wheel and damn near killed myself, so ain't in the mood for no...'

He trailed off as Frank walked around into his line of sight, illuminated by the glow of the headlights.

'Surprised to see me?' Frank asked.

A flicker of shocked recognition passed briefly over Ellis' face, but he managed to regain his composure.

'I... I don't know what you mean,' he said, stiffly.

'But you've been *looking* for me,' Frank reminded him. 'Looking quite hard.'

'What are you talking about?'

Frank paused and smiled down the gun barrel.

'You just didn't know *why* you were looking for me,' he continued. 'Isn't that right, *Ellis*?'

The thin man frowned, then his eyes widened.

'That was *you* on the phone!' he gasped.

'That's right,' Frank replied. 'Now, get down on your knees.'

He glanced over as Faye stepped out from the shadow of the trees. Ellis caught his look, twisting around to see Faye, then turned back with an expression of bewilderment on his face.

'On your knees!' Frank growled.

Hands still raised, Ellis sank to his knees, staring up in mounting panic.

'Hey look,' he stammered. 'You wanted money, right? Well, I *got* your money. I got it right here...'

He began to lower one hand, reaching towards his jacket, but Frank jerked the gun at him.

'STOP!'

Ellis' face fell and he raised his hands again.

'It's in my jacket pocket,' he insisted. 'I swear!'

Frank took a step closer, aiming directly at his head now.

'First, I want to see the gun,' he said. 'Take it out carefully, thumb and forefinger only.'

Watching him, Ellis nodded and pulled open his jacket to reveal a shoulder holster. Very slowly, he used his finger and thumb to take out a Beretta, then tossed it over. It landed in the dirt with a dull thud.

'Good,' Frank said, without enthusiasm. 'Now, the money.'

Ellis reached to his inside jacket pocket and drew out a thick manila envelope.

'Come *on*,' Frank barked.

Flinching, Ellis threw the envelope over and raised his hands again.

'There, see?' He licked his lips, nervously. 'I did what you asked.'

Ignoring the money, Frank scowled down at him.

'I'm not done asking yet,' he hissed.

'But...' Ellis stole a fearful glance at Faye, then turned back again. 'What else do you want?'

Frank stared down at him.

'I want to know who sent you,' he demanded. 'Who wants me dead?'

Ellis' eyes flickered briefly towards the house.

'Some out-of-towner, calls himself Spree.' He looked up fearfully. 'I never heard a first name.'

Frank began to pace around him, watching him, keeping the gun trained on his head.

'Who is he?'

'I don't know, but he ain't one of us.' Ellis gave a shudder. 'Some big-shot from back east, I guess.'

'You weren't curious about him?' Frank said, moving round to his side.

Ellis shook his head emphatically.

'When *my* boss tells me to go help someone out, I don't ask questions.'

Frank considered this as he walked around behind the kneeling figure.

'How many people are in the house?' he demanded.

'There's three,' Ellis replied, without any hesitation. 'Spree, some little whore we got for him, and the cook.'

Frank lifted his head and glanced over at Faye.

Whoever this big-shot was, he was unguarded.

'And how did you leave things with Spree?' he asked.

Ellis hesitated.

'The truth,' Frank snapped. 'Or I'll shoot you in the spine.'

'Okay, *okay!*' Ellis jerked his hands even higher, then drew a breath. 'He said to give you the money...'

'*And?*'

'And then...' His head dropped slightly. 'Then I was supposed to kill you.'

Directly behind him, Frank stopped pacing.

'Hey, come on,' Ellis cried, panicking now. 'You said you wanted the truth, and that's what he told me, I swear.'

Frank tightened his grip on the gun, then looked across at Faye. Her face was like stone.

'Don't shoot me!' Ellis begged. 'C'mon, I did what you asked!'

Staring down the barrel at the back of his head, Frank swallowed, one finger tight against the trigger.

Don't shoot...

In his mind, he saw them again.

The lifeless body, propped up against the tree in that dark

alpine clearing... the German soldier in France who'd suddenly stopped firing back...

His shoulders were taut, and he was rhythmically beating the wrench against the side of his leg as he slowly lowered the gun.

'I won't shoot you,' he murmured.

Ellis' upstretched arms sagged a little in relief.

And then he remembered the firefighter collapsing on the sidewalk, the woman screaming for her husband... Pete's broken body sprawled across the floor... the bitter promise he'd made to Beth...

Everything tightened as he raised his arm high, guilt and pain and *anger* bursting through his muscles as he brought the wrench down hard on Ellis' head. He heard the sickly wet cracking of bone, saw the skull deforming horribly under the blow, but he couldn't get a hold of the rage inside him, lifting the length of steel once more, bringing it down again and again as the useless limbs twitched in the dirt beneath him...

When he came to himself, stooping over the ruined corpse, he jerked his head away, fearing he would vomit.

Oh God, no!

He turned anxiously towards Faye, expecting her to be hysterical, but she was staring down at the body, her expression eerily calm. Dimly aware that he was still gripping the wrench, he tried to drop it, but for some reason his hand wouldn't let go. Glancing down, he saw the bloody mass of hair and brain matter on it, and felt his stomach lurch. Staggering to the nearest tree, he bent over, his hand pressed against the cold bark, retching until he had nothing left to bring up.

'Are you all right?' Faye had come over and was standing by his side.

'No,' Frank gasped. He spat, trying to get rid of the acid taste, then slowly looked round at her.

Faye stepped forward and held out her hand, offering him the manila envelope. Frank took it, feeling the weight of the cash as he jammed it down into his jacket pocket, nodding in acknowledgement.

She stared at him thoughtfully, then glanced over her shoulder, back towards the road.

'You wanna get out of here?' she said quietly. 'Go back to the car?'

Frank sighed.

Yes. That was what he wanted, what he'd always wanted: to get far away, to leave it all behind.

He looked down the trail towards the house, then slowly shook his head. Standing up, he wiped his mouth on his sleeve.

'We're not finished here yet.'

46

They made their way back towards the house, staying in the shadow of the trees for as long as possible. As they approached the corner of the building, Frank turned to Faye and beckoned her close.

'Step on the dirt, not the gravel,' he whispered. 'Less noise.'

Her large eyes glittered in the dim light.

'Okay.'

He gave her an encouraging nod, then turned and gazed up at the house. Most of the place seemed to be in darkness, but there was a warm glow from a small window at the far corner.

Someone was in there. *Spree maybe? Or perhaps the cook...*

Gripping the .45 tightly, he moved across to the front wall and waited for Faye to follow him. Then he sidled forward, hugging the wall and ducking low under each window. His shoes sank into the soft ground, but he made it over to the entrance porch without any noise to give them away, and paused for a moment, listening.

Music again, but muffled, distant.

Glancing back at Faye, he held up a hand for her to wait, then turned and crept round to the front step. Normally he wouldn't have entertained an entry via the front door, but this place was built to look out across the lake, and he figured that whoever was inside would be enjoying the view at the back.

Time to see if he was right.

He reached out and gripped the handle, twisting slowly; it turned and he felt the door come free in his hand. Grabbing a breath, he took a half-step back and raised his gun. Then, using the tip of his shoe, he eased the door open. As it swung slowly ajar, a wood-paneled entrance hall came into view, thankfully deserted. Directly in front of him, a broad flight of stairs ascended into the darkness of the upper level. On the left there was a passage that looked as though it led through towards the rear of the building, and a short corridor ran off to the right, where the lit window was.

The music was louder now, a Dean Martin song, upbeat and cheerful.

Frank leaned forward, twisting his body left and right to look down the gun barrel, but there was no sign of anyone.

He stepped back and waved for Faye to come join him. Turning, he kept watch on the hallway until she was by his side, then cautiously stepped over the threshold. To his left, there was a small table with an antique chair beside it. All around him, the walls were hung with a selection of paintings that alternated between racehorses and naked women.

'Maybe we should find the cook first,' he whispered, peering down the corridor. 'You know where the kitchen is?'

Faye didn't answer. Frank glanced round to see her standing pale and tense, her eyes staring up the dark stairs.

'Are you okay?' he asked her softly.

She blinked at him, then raised her chin.

'I'm okay,' she said.

'The kitchen?' he prompted her.

'I'm not sure,' she said gazing past the stairs. 'Down there, I think.'

She indicated towards the right.

'Stay behind me,' he whispered.

They edged down the corridor, placing each foot carefully to avoid any sound on the polished wooden floor. Behind them, the music had changed to a different song, with swooping strings and a light, airy feel.

Frank approached the door at the end of the corridor, then turned to Faye.

'Wait here,' he mouthed to her. 'Warn me if you hear anyone coming.'

Faye turned around to look back towards the entrance hall.

Frank raised his gun, then carefully twisted the door handle and pushed his way inside.

It was a long kitchen, with a single window overlooking the gravel parking area, and a plain wooden door set in the far wall. The air that hit him was warm, heavy with cooking smells. A glass-topped table sat in the middle of the room with four modern chairs around it, and an impressive array of electrical appliances lined the wall on the right. Standing over by the sink, a fat man in his fifties was sluicing water around in a large steel pan, humming to himself. He looked up with mild interest, then took a stumbling step backwards as he saw the gun.

'Shhh.' Frank raised a finger to his lips, easing the door quietly closed behind him. 'Not a sound, okay?'

The man had a red face and gentle eyes, but he looked frightened. Perspiration shone on his balding head, and what hair remained was grey and wavy. Setting the pan down, he wiped his hands on a striped apron that was covered in stains and scorches.

'You're the cook, right?' Frank asked.

The man nodded anxiously.

'And what's your name?'

'Carlo.'

'Okay then, Carlo.' Frank held up one hand in what he hoped

was a calming gesture. 'I need you to tell me who's in the house. Spree and the girl, right?'

'Right,' the cook replied, staring at the gun.

'Nobody else? You're not expecting anyone?'

'No. Nobody.'

'Okay, good.' Frank gave him a serious look. 'Now, if you do as I say, you won't get hurt, understand?'

Carlo nodded eagerly.

'All right then.' Keeping the gun trained on him, Frank glanced around, his eye settling on the door in the far wall. 'What's through there?'

Carlo turned to see where he was looking, then shook his head.

'Nothing,' he said. 'It's just a pantry.'

Frank considered for a moment, then motioned him towards it.

'Show me.'

Carlo hesitated, then moved across to the far wall and pulled the door open. Beyond it was a small, dark storage area, with shelves of canned goods, jars and bottles. There was no window.

'In you go,' Frank said, pointing. 'Get in there and keep quiet, okay?'

With some reluctance, the fat cook stepped inside, then turned around to face him.

Frank moved over and put his free hand on the door.

'Don't come out, no matter what you hear, okay?'

Panic showed on Carlo's face.

'But... what do I...?' he stammered. 'How long...?'

Frank paused.

'You got a watch?' he asked.

The cook glanced down towards his pocket then nodded.

'Wait until midnight,' Frank told him. 'After that, it won't matter.'

Staring at him in confusion, Carlo began to say something

else, but Frank pushed the door shut, then turned around, looking for some way to lock it. Eventually, he had to settle for dragging the glass table over the floor and resting it across the doorway. As an afterthought, he took the large metal pan from beside the sink, and balanced it precariously on the edge of the table. If Carlo *did* try to get out, at least they'd hear him coming.

Out in the corridor, Faye jumped and gripped her purse, startled as Frank stepped up quietly behind her.

'Hey, it's okay,' he hissed. 'It's only me.'

Faye shut her eyes and took a deep breath to settle herself.

'What about the cook?' she whispered.

'Locked in the pantry,' Frank told her. 'Heard anything from the rest of the house?'

'Only the music.'

It was another Dean Martin song, and it sounded as though it was coming from the rear of the building.

'Okay.' Frank eased past her and stood, gun in hand, gazing towards the entrance hall. 'We'll check downstairs first. Stay a few steps behind me and tell me if you hear anything.'

Faye was slipping off her shoes, and Frank nodded in approval.

'Ready?' he asked.

'Ready.'

They moved down the corridor, Frank walking on the balls of his feet, Faye ghosting along behind him. Passing through the entrance hall, he paused, gazing up the stairs into the darkness for a moment, then turned and pointed towards the other passageway.

'It's definitely coming from down there,' he whispered.

They could make out the music more clearly now, the crooning voice, and the romantic strings.

Gripping the gun, Frank eased around the corner and crept

on towards the back of the house. Ahead of him, he could see a set of double doors: dark wood, with carved detailing and a pair of ornate gold handles. He was just a few feet away from them when the song finished.

Holding his breath, Frank gestured for Faye to stop. He stood there, frozen, waiting for the next song to begin, but there was nothing. Only silence.

No, not silence...

Straining to hear, he thought he could make out a rhythmic bumping noise. At first, he guessed it might be the crackle of the needle as it hit the groove at the end of the record, but it was different somehow, less regular. He frowned, unable to place the sound, wondering whether it was better to open the door or wait longer.

Go! Go now!

Tensing himself, he reached for the handle, grasping it tightly and easing it down. He felt the door give way and eased it back slowly, aiming the gun through the widening gap. It was a broad room, with a polished wooden floor that stretched out before him; directly ahead, full-length windows looked out onto a balcony and the darkening lake beyond.

The bumping sound was clearer now – coming from somewhere off to the right – but he couldn't see that far around the corner. Without looking back, he held up a hand for Faye to wait, then stepped silently into the room.

It stretched back further than he'd imagined. There was a huge rug, with several easy chairs arranged round a low table, a collection of empty glasses and open bottles. He could see a portable record player lying there, the turntable still spinning, needle crackling softly in the groove, but that wasn't what was making the bumping noise.

He took another step forward, staring right down the gun as they finally came into view.

Facing away towards the windows, a waif-like young woman,

bent naked over the arm of the couch, her long red hair hanging down across her face. Behind her, a broad naked man was hunched over, holding her hips firmly as he humped his weight against her, making her small body jolt.

Discarded clothes were strewn about their feet; they still hadn't seen him. He swallowed a breath as he noticed Faye at the edge of his vision, her face ashen, a hand across her mouth.

Entertaining important people.

Frank tensed his muscles and thumbed the hammer back with an ominous click.

'Don't move!' he barked, aiming the .45 at the middle of the man's back. The red-haired girl gave a startled cry and tried vainly to cover herself, but the man froze, pinning her in place.

'You must be Spree,' Frank snarled. 'Turn around *very* fucking slowly.'

The girl buried her face in the seat cushions as the broad man raised his hands. He paused for a moment, then very slowly – very deliberately – looked back over his shoulder.

Frank gasped as their eyes met; the face was older but there was no mistaking who it was.

'*Swift?*' he croaked, taking a step back.

Beside him, Faye's head jerked around, her expression wary.

'You *know* him?' she demanded.

Frank pulled his free hand across his jaw, trying to take it in, trying to shake off the sense that he was somehow transported back to Switzerland...

'From the war,' he told her, staring along the barrel at his old commanding officer. 'His name's Swift. Major James Swift.'

'Hello, Frank.' Hands still raised, Swift withdrew himself awkwardly from the redhead and turned around, his erection swaying in front of him. 'Ellis did promise me that he could deliver you both, but... well, this isn't quite what I expected.'

'You don't need to worry about Ellis any more,' Frank growled.

Swift started to raise a questioning eyebrow, then his expression became more serious as he grasped what this meant.

'Oh,' he said, swallowing. 'I see.' His dick was shriveling noticeably now.

Frank grimaced and motioned irritably towards the discarded clothes.

'Put something on,' he muttered.

Cautiously, Swift leaned over and picked up a robe from the floor, his eyes never leaving Frank as he slid his arms into the sleeves and pulled it on. Behind him, the red-headed girl huddled down against the side of the couch, peering up at them fearfully through her tangled hair.

Faye stepped forward.

'Get away from that poor girl!' she demanded. '*Right* away from her!'

Swift moved awkwardly aside as she snatched up a crumpled silk robe and went to drape it around the young woman's shoulders.

'I'd do as she says,' Frank warned him, gesturing with the gun.

Faye had her arm around the girl, helping her up.

'It's okay,' she whispered. 'It's all right.'

Swift watched them, then shook his head.

'She's *fine*,' he protested. 'I wasn't going to hurt–'

'You *animal!*' Faye hissed, something in her voice making him take a step back. She placed herself between Swift and the girl, her teeth bared. 'Just stay the hell away from her, you filthy son of a bitch! You think you can just use people however you like?'

'Hey!' Frank brandished the gun, trying to keep control of the situation. 'HEY!'

He waited until they both turned towards him.

'Okay.' He looked at Faye. 'Take care of her, will you? Make sure she's all right.'

Faye glared at him for a moment, then nodded.

'And you...' Frank turned to address Swift. 'Let's you and me step outside, give them some privacy.'

He gestured with the gun, then followed Swift towards the balcony.

The air was cooler now, but the faint evening breeze had gone and a deep calm had descended over the lake. Frank stepped out onto the raised wooden balcony and reached behind him to slide the glass door closed. Silhouetted against the dusk, Swift was standing by a flight of broad steps that led down to the grass, staring out at the view. For a moment, he said nothing. Then his shoulders dropped and he turned around.

'You're looking well,' he said.

Such a reasonable tone. As if he wasn't responsible for a string of deaths, as if there wasn't a gun pointing at his chest.

'No thanks to you,' Frank growled.

Swift sighed and gave a small nod of regret.

'Yeah, I'm sorry about all that,' he said. 'This whole business...'

He trailed off, as though that somehow explained everything.

'Oh, you're *sorry*?' Frank retorted.

Swift met his gaze for a moment, then looked away.

'Yes,' he said quietly. 'I am.'

Thrown by this, Frank stared at him. There seemed to be no animosity in the man, and yet he wasn't denying what he'd done.

'I don't get it,' he said. 'Why did you send Ellis after me?'

Swift sighed and rested a hand on the wooden railing.

'Some decisions are forced on us, Frank; you know that.' He paused, lifting his head to stare out across the lake. 'But this is part of something that goes far beyond any individual considerations... and I'm just one man in a much bigger operation.'

Frank stiffened.

'Yeah, I forgot,' he said coldly. 'You work for the *Mob* now.'

Swift twisted round and gave him a contemptuous look.

'Don't be stupid,' he snapped. 'The Mob works for *me*. I work for the government.'

The government?

Frank gaped at him.

'But... I thought...'

'You thought I was a *criminal*?' Swift shook his head bitterly. 'Thanks a lot!'

Frank blinked, trying to grasp what this meant.

'So... you're saying the *government* wants me dead?'

Swift sighed again, but his expression became more sympathetic.

'Not really,' he said. 'And I didn't want you dead either. You must understand, this isn't personal. It's just... well, your time in Bern. You were there during a very sensitive period, and we couldn't be sure how much you knew.'

'Knew about what?' Frank demanded.

Swift's eyes flickered briefly to the windows behind him, where Faye and the red-head were moving around.

'Let's... take a walk,' he said, then paused, glancing at the gun. 'If it's all right with you, of course.'

Frank hesitated, then frowned and motioned him towards the stairs.

'Go ahead, but no sudden moves.'

They made their way down the wooden steps, descending below the light from the windows and stepping out onto the shadowy lawn that sloped away to the water. Swift walked slowly, barefoot on the grass, his voice calm and quiet.

'There were always two wars going on. The one people saw in the newsreels, with troops and tanks and colors on the map... and then there was the other war, the one you were part of in Switzerland, with people and information and negotiation. Some of the biggest battles were won there, won without ever being fought, but whenever warring nations try to talk to each other there are... compromises.' He glanced over, his eyes flashing in the gloom.

'Sometimes, the only way to secure what our countries want is to do things they would never countenance.'

Walking beside him, Frank shrugged.

'So you're saying that sometimes the ends justify the means. So what?'

'No, I'm saying that sometimes the truth behind a nation's success is *utterly* incompatible with what that nation stands for, what it *believes* in.' Swift looked out across the water. 'Great things are often built on terrible secrets.'

Unimpressed, Frank shook his head.

'Okay, but...?'

Swift slowed, then turned to face him.

'You know that the Bern office helped negotiate the German surrender?' he asked.

Frank kept the gun trained on him.

'I knew Dulles was speaking to a lot of people from Berlin.'

'He was working to support the German resistance for months, long before the attempt on Hitler's life.' A faraway look came into Swift's eyes. 'You remember that night at the ski lodge when Rafe was almost killed? That was a rendezvous with one his German couriers, communicating with... well, with someone who would probably have been hanged for war crimes if Dulles hadn't succeeded.'

'But the Nazis intercepted that courier,' Frank reminded him.

Swift nodded calmly.

'They did, but the point is, we had to do all kinds of unpalatable things to secure that surrender. Deal with some terrible people, cover up some unbelievable atrocities, sacrifice so much. But it was worth it.' He looked up, and managed a grim smile. 'As long as people didn't *know*, of course; they'd be appalled if they learned the truth... but that surrender shortened the war and saved countless lives.'

Frank rolled his eyes.

'I'm not interested in old war stories,' he snapped. 'I was *there*, remember?'

'Well, what *are* you interested in?' Swift replied, a note of irritability creeping into his voice.

Frank glared back at him.

'I want to know what all this has to do with *me*,' he demanded. 'What the hell d'you think?'

Swift paused and looked at him.

'Maybe you didn't know as much as we thought,' he murmured.

Frank waved the gun at him.

'Let me worry about that,' he said. 'Just keep talking.'

Swift scowled at him, but reluctantly continued.

'Try and understand. German surrender was important, but it wasn't the *main* goal.'

Frank frowned.

'What do you mean?' he asked.

'Well, there were some who wanted to inflict an absolute defeat, wipe the Germans off the map.' Swift turned towards the lake again. 'Others were focused on getting them to surrender. But *our* aim was to achieve a lasting peace, quickly, and with as few casualties as possible.'

'Of course.'

'No, *not* of course.' Swift shook his head. 'They're three very different things. And what *we* wanted involved looking further than just Germany, Italy and Japan.'

Frank considered this.

'You're talking about Russia,' he said. 'About Truman dropping the bomb on Moscow.'

Swift glanced at him, then turned back to continue gazing out over the water.

Frank moved to stand by his side.

'But the Bern station didn't have any involvement in that...' He trailed off, suddenly less sure of what he was saying. 'Anyway, it all happened years ago; why does it suddenly matter now?'

A smile ghosted across Swift's face.

'Because Truman's gone,' he said. 'And there's real resentment among the new Eisenhower administration. There's a growing feeling that we shouldn't have bombed Moscow, or sided with the Germans, and some very significant people are asking questions about why we did.'

Frank snorted.

'So let them ask,' he said defiantly. 'We had no choice about Russia. We *had* to arm the Germans against them, we *had* to drop the bomb on Moscow. Stalin was gonna sweep right across Eastern Europe, he wasn't gonna stop.'

Swift looked at him for a long moment, his eyes glittering.

'Sure of that, are you?'

Frank hesitated. He'd heard the talk, read the briefings; Poland, Czechoslovakia, Yugoslavia. Stalin would have seized them all.

Wouldn't he?

'But I saw the intelligence reports,' he protested. 'All the evidence suggested– '

'Oh come *on*, Frank. You were *there!*' Swift interrupted. '*We* wrote those reports. *We* were the eyes and ears of our government, you know that!'

The meaning of his words began to dawn on Frank, and he looked at Swift in shock.

'What did you do?' he asked.

Swift shot him a cold grin.

'You mean, what did *we* do?'

Frank took a step back, his mind reeling.

All that time in Switzerland, all those documents he'd translated...

'They were false?' he gasped. 'It was all a *lie?*'

'No, we just made sure the message going back to Washington was unambiguous,' Swift explained. 'We clarified the picture that the intelligence reports painted. We made it easier for people to come to the right conclusions.'

Frank stared at him.

'But... why would you *do* that?'

'Because it needed to be done!' Swift snapped. 'You think just because we didn't have enough evidence of Stalin's intentions that he wouldn't have acted? Or maybe you'd rather we waited until half of Europe was under Soviet control and the Russians had built their own bomb... because that would have happened.'

'You can't be sure of that.'

'Can't I?' Swift gazed up at the dark sky, clenching his fists in frustration. 'Think about it, Frank. Imagine if we *hadn't* acted, if Stalin had been allowed to continue, unchecked. Imagine the whole world divided up between two superpowers – east and west – each with enough atomic weapons to...'

He broke off, shaking his head. When he spoke again, his voice was quieter, and tinged with regret.

'The road not taken,' he sighed, turning away again. 'Innocent lives were going to be lost *whatever* happened. We simply tried to minimize those losses. Even if it meant sacrificing some of our own.'

Frank watched as he bowed his head, a weary figure now, standing alone on the grassy slope. Was this Swift's way of justifying the attempt on his life? He frowned as another possibility occurred to him. Maybe Swift was talking about someone else...

'Jean?' he said softly.

Swift's shoulders dropped.

'I wish it hadn't come to that,' he murmured, glancing back over his shoulder, his face full of remorse. 'I tried so hard to keep her out of it, but she was clever, and she started noticing things. And her loyalties weren't exclusively to me...'

Frank stared at him in disbelief.

'So that was *you?*' he gasped. 'You *killed* her?'

Swift's head snapped up, glaring at him.

'You and Rafe killed Molly.'

The words hit like a physical blow and Frank recoiled, taking a shaky step backwards as the memories of that night rose in his mind.

He brandished the .45 at Swift, trying to ward off the accusation, feeling the pistol grip become sweaty against his palm despite the cool evening air.

'What the hell do you mean by that?' he cried. 'Molly shot *me*. She was a traitor, working for the damn Russians.'

Swift gave him a bitter smile.

'Sure of that, are you?' he said, then turned back towards the stillness of the lake. 'You found what you *expected* to find. What I *sent* you to find.'

Numb, Frank stood there in the darkness, listening to the gentle lapping of the water below them. The sound recalled that day in Neuchâtel, standing by the lake shore with Molly smiling up at him...

'What she was *actually* doing... well, she could have compromised everything, and I couldn't allow that.' Swift took a deep breath. 'People think wars are won by bravery, but they're not. Wars are won by sacrifice.'

Frank swallowed. The gun seemed cold and heavy in his hand, and he slowly let his arm fall to his side.

He saw Molly's arm fall to her side, the gun slipping from her fingers to clatter on the floor outside Rafe's apartment...

'No!' With his free hand, he rubbed his eyes, trying to drive away the visions. 'This is all... wrong.'

Swift shivered and pulled the robe tighter about himself.

'You think we're to blame because we intervened, because we *did* something... but there were *no* innocent options. Because doing nothing is also a choice, and in this case, it would have been the coward's choice.' He bowed his head and sighed. 'Sometimes there are no solutions, only actions and consequences.'

They stood in silence for a time.

Eventually, Frank looked up.

'So that's all this was,' he murmured. 'A cover-up. To keep people from knowing about what happened in Bern, about how we came to bomb Russia.'

Swift stared out across the lake and nodded.

Frank shook his head.

'Pete Barnes, Edward Linden, the people who burned in that apartment building... they're all dead because you wanted to silence me.'

'I'm sorry, Frank.' Swift glanced over his shoulder with a sad smile. 'It really *should* have been you.'

His expression suddenly changed and he looked past Frank, his eyes widening.

The gunshot cracked the stillness of the evening, echoing out across the lake, and Swift stumbled back with a cry, frantically clutching at his leg.

Frank whirled around to see Faye walking out of the gloom behind him. Her face was twisted with anger and she had Ellis' gun.

'Faye!' he gasped. 'What are you doing?'

She turned and leveled the gun at him now, her eyes gleaming in the darkness. Startled, Frank raised his hands.

'Back away,' she hissed. 'This time I *have* got bullets.'

Frank gaped as she aimed past him, flinching as she pulled the trigger again and a sudden flash lit her face. Out of the deafening gunshot, he heard an awful scream and turned to see Swift falling, blood spilling from his leg and a second wound in his pelvis. Robe flapping open, the broad man tumbled to a bloody heap in the grass, braying like a dying animal.

'Oh, dear God,' Frank stared in revulsion. 'Faye, stop!'

Her eyes, glaring with rage, flickered over to him.

'My brother,' she snarled. 'My brother *burned* because of him!'

Frank held up a hand, imploring her.

'I know but...'

She looked away, raising the gun again.

He saw Rafe raising the gun to point at Molly... saw his own hand raising the wrench above Ellis' head...

'No!' He stepped in front of her. 'You don't want to do this!'

'Yes I do!' she hissed.

'No, you don't!' He looked at her and saw the hatred burning in her eyes, saw what he himself had become. 'You never killed anyone.'

'Get out of my way,' Faye shrieked.

'Please don't do this.' He could still taste the bile in his mouth.

The gun was shaking in her hand, tears streaming down her face.

'You can't stop me, Frank,' she whispered.

He stared into her eyes. Behind him, Swift was screaming and swearing, an incoherent babble of English and German.

'You're right,' he told her.

There were no solutions, only actions and consequences.

Twisting round, he leveled his .45 at Swift's forehead, and squeezed the trigger.

The screaming stopped and echoes from the gunshot rolled out across the surface of the lake.

When he looked back to her, Faye was trembling. She dropped Ellis' gun on the grass and stood there, a small figure in the darkness.

'I'm so sorry,' Frank sighed.

Faye stared down at the body for a long time, then looked up at him.

'Why did you do it?' she asked.

Frank bowed his head.

'Because doing nothing would have been the coward's choice.'

47

They made their way slowly back up the slope towards the light of the house, the grass soft and springy beneath their feet.

'You said you knew him from the war...' Faye said, leaving the question open.

'That's right.' Frank hesitated. 'At least, I *thought* I knew him.'

Faye glanced over at him.

'So he was a German?' she asked.

Frank shook his head.

'No.' He paused then glanced back over his shoulder, down towards the darkness of the lake. 'Actually, I don't know. Maybe.'

A faint wind began to stir among the trees as they climbed the wooden steps to the balcony. Reaching the top, Frank peered in through the glass, then frowned.

'Where's the girl?' he asked.

Faye walked over to the door and pulled it open.

'I gave her that bastard's wallet and the keys to his car.' She looked over at Frank, as though daring him to complain. 'She was just a *kid*, for pity's sake. You saw what he was doing to her, what men like that *always* do...'

She broke off, biting her lip, composing herself.

Frank walked over to stand beside her.

'You okay?' he asked, quietly.

Faye shut her eyes for a moment, then nodded.

'I just figured she deserved a second chance,' she explained.

Frank looked at her thoughtfully, then sighed.

'Yeah.'

He followed her inside and pulled the door closed behind them. When he looked round, Faye was standing in the middle of the floor, staring across the room towards the couch. She gave a little shiver, then turned to him.

'What about you?' she asked suddenly. 'What will you do now?'

He stared at her for a moment, realizing that he hadn't ever thought this far ahead. When he'd set out, everything had been about revenge; now, it was about responsibility.

'I honestly don't know,' he said, shrugging. 'I did what I set out to do... what I *had* to do.'

Faye tilted her head to one side.

'You said you made a promise,' she said, looking at him intently. 'Who to?'

Frank turned away from her and paced slowly across the room, halting by the double doors.

'Beth,' he said wearily. 'Pete Barnes' wife.'

'Oh.' Faye was silent for a moment, then she walked slowly over to him. Frank opened the doors for her.

'You can go back and tell her you got the man that killed her husband,' she said, softly. 'She'll want to hear that.'

Frank followed her out of the room.

'Not from me she won't.'

Faye paused, frowning.

'Why?' she asked. 'It isn't *your* fault that Ellis killed the wrong cop.'

Frank lowered his eyes and nodded.

'Yeah. It is.'

He pulled the doors shut behind them, then started slowly down the corridor.

'I sent Pete down there, to Neosho. Instead of going myself.'

Faye stared up at him.

'Does she know that?'

Frank nodded grimly.

'She does, yeah.'

They came to the entrance hall at the end of the corridor. Faye slowed, her expression sympathetic.

'You think she blames you for what happened?'

Frank halted, then turned and met her gaze.

'She was in bed with me when it happened,' he said miserably. 'So yeah, I think she blames me. And I think she's right.'

Pete Barnes, Edward Linden, Faye's brother... even Molly, according to Swift... How many people were dead because of him?

He felt a tentative touch on his arm as she patted him awkwardly with her hand.

'You can't take it all on yourself,' she told him. 'No one's completely guilty because no one's completely innocent.' She blushed. 'Your friend *certainly* wasn't... and neither was his wife, if she let you take her to bed.'

Frank looked round at her and gave her a sad smile.

'But it should have been me,' he said simply.

'Ellis would have killed you if you'd gone to Neosho.'

Frank shrugged, then nodded.

The road not taken...

'He'd have killed us *both*, wouldn't he?' she continued, moving around so that she could stare up into his eyes.

'I guess,' he muttered.

'But we're *alive*,' she told him. 'And I won't feel guilty about surviving.'

.   .   .

They stepped out onto the gravel parking area. Faye gazed up at the evening sky, deep blue above the silhouettes of the trees, her eyes wide as she turned around to stare at the stars.

'Where will you go now?' he asked her.

She turned and looked at him.

'Kansas City.' She shrugged, then her expression clouded. 'Back to that church hall, I guess.'

Frank gazed over at her, then reached inside his jacket and drew out the envelope of money they'd taken from Ellis.

'You wanted to travel, right?' he said, holding up the envelope, then tossing it to her.

Startled, she caught it, then looked up at him with a strange expression.

'Yes.' Her eyes narrowed. 'But... how did you know that?'

He thought back to that tiny room in Neosho, with the pictures of exotic places cut out from magazines and pinned up around her bed.

A bed surrounded by dreams.

'So travel,' he said.

Fall, 1953
Joplin, Missouri

48

Frank dropped down from the fence and straightened up, brushing his hands off. Lifting his head, he stood for a moment gazing towards the back of the house. The place looked better since he'd been gone. Someone had watered the grass and mown it. The tattered old lawn chairs were gone, and even the birdhouse pole had been straightened.

Kaitlyn, he supposed, *or Beth's aunt, keeping everyone busy.*

Lowering his eyes, he made his way slowly across the yard and climbed the steps that led up onto the porch. From habit, he reached out for the door handle, then stopped himself. After a moment's hesitation, he knocked on the door instead, then turned away to stare out across the yard. Beyond the railroad tracks, the leaves were falling from the dogwood trees, burning red in the afternoon sunlight.

He heard the approach of soft footsteps behind him and turned around, removing his hat. Beth opened the screen door partway and stood there peering out at him. She was wearing a simple floral print dress and her hair was tied back in a ponytail. He couldn't read her expression but she seemed tired somehow, with a resignation deep in her eyes that never used to be there.

'Hello, Beth,' he said.

'Frank.'

She opened the door a little wider, stepping out onto the porch, then pushed it closed behind her and leaned her back against it like she didn't want it to open.

Frank's eyes flickered up to the house.

'Someone else here?' he asked quietly.

Arms folded, Beth stared at him for a moment, then gave the slightest shake of her head.

'No.'

Frank nodded slowly, turning the brim of his hat between his fingers.

'Your sister... she went back to St Louis?'

'Kaitlyn stayed long enough,' Beth replied with a shrug. 'Now, it's just me.'

Frank looked at her, the way she held her chin up, the way her eyes followed him. For the first time in a long time, he had no idea what she was thinking.

'Are you managing okay?' he asked.

Beth shifted slightly, letting her arms drop to her sides, turning her head away.

'Everyone's been real kind,' she said. 'The department gave me some money, and Pete's brother says he's gonna get me a job at the newspaper.'

Frank considered this.

'The paper, huh?'

'That's right.' There was a note of defiance in her voice, as though she expected some smart-mouth response.

Too much history between them, and not enough of it good... that was the problem.

He sighed to himself.

'Well, if there's anything you need...'

She stared at him for a time, appearing to relax a little, but saying nothing. He stood there, feeling increasingly awkward.

'I've been away,' he told her. 'Kansas City.'

'Oh?'

'Yeah,' he said, pausing. 'I found the guy.'

Beth stiffened and looked at him.

'Did you arrest him?' she asked, her voice tight.

Frank turned away and looked along the porch.

'No,' he said quietly.

'What did you do to him?'

For a moment, he could taste the bile again, see the bloody wrench in his hand, the twitching limbs on the forest floor...

'You don't wanna know,' he told her, shaking his head.

'Well, I guess it doesn't matter,' she said. 'So long as he's dead.'

'He's dead all right.'

They stood in silence for a time. When he finally turned to look at her, Beth was toying with a loose strand of hair.

'So... you're back now?' she asked.

Frank leaned on the porch rail.

'For now, yeah.'

Beth studied him for a moment, then tilted her head to one side.

'You don't sound too sure,' she said.

Frank shrugged. He was a lot less sure of things than he used to be.

Beth lowered her eyes.

'You wanna come in?' she asked.

Frank looked at her. She was as beautiful as ever, leaning back against the door frame, her dress pulled tight across her breasts.

'Yeah,' he said.

She met his gaze, opening her mouth as though to speak, when he interrupted her.

'But I'm not going to.'

She frowned at him, unsure what he meant.

'Why not?'

Frank took a deep breath, then moved to stand close to her.

'You've said it often enough,' he sighed. 'I'm a bastard.'

He leaned in and kissed her softly on the forehead.

'I reckon you deserve better than that.'

Beth stared at him as he lightly touched her cheek, then turned and walked slowly down the steps.

'Frank?'

He looked around to see her standing there, an unfamiliar sparkle in her eyes.

'Thank you,' she said.

Frank nodded, then turned and walked away.

EPILOGUE

F rank stood by the corner of the long Reflecting Pool and stared up at the white columned façade of the Lincoln Memorial, pale against the slate grey sky. Shivering, he pulled his coat tighter around himself, trying to keep out the wind that squalled up from the river. The cabbie had assured him that the weather was unseasonably mild for Washington, but he'd been waiting here for fifteen minutes and the cold was really starting to bite.

He turned and looked down the edge of the pool, studying the different figures that dotted the path, searching for a familiar face. Men in overcoats and hats, women bundled up in scarves, everyone walking briskly to keep themselves warm. Frowning, he slid his hand from the shelter of his jacket pocket, tugging back the sleeve to check the time once more.

He should have been here by now.

Stamping his feet to get some feeling into them, Frank turned back towards the Memorial building. A man was walking down the steps towards him, wearing a long black coat and a grey homburg hat. Frank saw the light reflect off his glasses and, as he drew closer, he raised a gloved hand in greeting.

'Mr Rye!' Dulles looked grayer than he had during the war, his hair now a uniform silver, but he appeared otherwise unchanged.

'Good afternoon, sir.' Frank walked over to meet him and they briefly shook hands.

Dulles smiled then stood back as though appraising him.

'Truth be told, I wasn't sure you'd come,' he said, lifting his head to squint through his glasses.

'Well, I wasn't sure I should,' Frank replied. 'Certain people seemed to think it might be better if I was dead.'

'And you thought I might be one of them?' Dulles asked with interest.

Frank hesitated, but there was no polite way of answering.

'The thought had crossed my mind,' he admitted.

Dulles grinned and clapped him on the back.

'You think I'd be standing out here in the cold if I wanted you killed?' he chuckled.

Frank looked at him uncomfortably, then managed a wary smile.

Dulles shook his head.

'I certainly wouldn't be mean-spirited enough to drag a man halfway across the country for *that*.' He beamed, then turned and gestured towards the path that led around the edge of the water. 'Let's walk, shall we? This town's colder than Bern. Stand still too long and you'll catch your death.'

They walked slowly, talking quietly, falling silent every now and then when a passer-by came close, but the weather meant they had few such interruptions. For the most part, Dulles let him talk, and Frank told him everything; there seemed no reason not to. After all that he'd been through, it was somehow a relief to be able to say it out loud.

It soon became clear that Dulles knew much of what had

happened already, but he probed Frank on several points, and was particularly interested in Swift's admission that he'd killed Jean.

'Poor Miss Ellesworth,' he sighed, turning away to look out over the silver-grey water for a moment. 'Did he mention why he stopped her from attending that rendezvous at the ski lodge?'

'He just said that he was doing his best to keep her out of things,' Frank replied.

'And did he tell you who the courier was carrying messages *for?*'

'No. He said it was someone who might have been hung for war crimes, but he never told me who it was.'

Dulles nodded to himself.

'There are so many unpalatable truths on the road to peace,' he muttered.

They walked on. Frank stole a sidelong glance at the older man, who appeared to be lost in thought.

'Sir?' he asked. 'Do you think Swift was acting on his own?'

Dulles raised his head and frowned.

'That's really *not* the sort of question you want to be heard asking,' he replied.

Frank caught the warning note in his voice.

'Oh, I didn't mean...' He shook his head. 'I was talking about during the war.'

Dulles very deliberately gazed out across the water.

Frank lowered his voice and continued.

'Only, when he died, he started screaming out in German...'

Dulles glanced across at him.

'Did he really?' he mused. 'Well, well... I've often thought that a man's true self emerges at the most difficult times. I suppose that, if defeat were inevitable, a patriotic German agent *might* feel his country stood a better chance siding with the Western Allies, making a common enemy of Russia.' He held Frank's gaze for a moment, his eyes twinkling. 'But you must draw your own conclusions, naturally.'

A gust of wind blew up from behind them, scarring the surface of the Reflecting Pool with dark ripples. Frank turned up his collar and hunched his shoulders, looking into the distance where the Washington Monument stood proud and white against the dirty sky.

'Swift implied that Molly...' He took a breath, then stared down at his feet. 'He said she wasn't the traitor we thought she was.'

'Ah,' murmured Dulles. 'So, we come to it at last.'

Frank clenched his fists in his pockets.

'I mean... if *Swift* was the traitor, then I guess it sort of puts her in the clear, doesn't it?'

'One person's guilt doesn't necessarily prove another's innocence,' Dulles began, then trailed off as he looked at Frank. 'You were sleeping with her?'

Frank slowed to a stop and turned to face the water.

Beside him, Dulles sighed.

'I see,' he said softly. 'We did have our suspicions, of course, but Swift always assured me that...' He shook his head. 'I'm sorry. It's hard to lose someone you care about, especially when you can't acknowledge them. I know...'

Something in his voice made Frank glance up. He recalled Swift saying that Jean's loyalties were not exclusively his, but... *her and Dulles?*

'Jean Ellesworth?' he asked.

The light in Dulles' eyes faded just a little.

'Miss Ellesworth and I were... close,' he said carefully. 'We spoke quite often, and she *did* come to believe that we had a traitor in our midst, though she never implicated Miss Pearson. Nor did she suggest that the agent was Russian.'

'So Molly...' Frank swallowed. 'Molly was innocent?'

Dulles paused, gazing up at the grey clouds, then sighed.

'When I finally returned to Washington, after my time in Berlin, her name came up in conversation, quite by chance. It seems that she may have been acting as go-between for... well, for certain British and Soviet officials who didn't want a war between their two nations.' He gave a small shrug of his shoulders. 'If that's true then she was an extremely brave – and *loyal* – British agent.'

Frank bowed his head.

'And I hung her out to dry,' he muttered.

'No,' Dulles said firmly. 'Swift manipulated you into a position where you would be compelled to doubt her. And, whether or not you had the opportunity to deal with her yourself, it was Mr *Cavanagh* who actually pulled the trigger.'

Frank looked at him unhappily.

'Poor Rafe,' he said.

Dulles shrugged.

'We must hope that he never finds out.'

'You aren't going to tell him?' Frank asked.

Dulles stared at him in horror.

'Why on Earth would I want to do that?' he gasped.

Frank shrugged uncertainly.

'You don't think he has a right to know?'

'I think he has a right *not* to know,' Dulles insisted. 'The truth would bring him nothing but pain, and he's suffered quite enough, wouldn't you say?'

Frank nodded. Rafe had come to visit him a few times while he was in hospital, but it was obvious that Molly's death had hit him harder than anyone.

'I guess you're right,' he sighed.

Dulles turned and began walking again. Frank fell in beside him, brooding on all the things *he* knew and wished he didn't.

'I'm sorry, sir, I shouldn't ask... but what Swift said, about manipulating intelligence reports to justify using the bomb on Russia...'

'Mr Rye...' There was a warning in Dulles' voice.

'I know, it's just...' Frank looked at him anxiously. 'Do you think it's true? Would the Russians really have taken over half of Europe? Would they really have been able to develop their own atom bomb?'

'Really, Mr Rye!' Dulles glared at him. 'I made it quite clear that I wished no harm upon you. Don't make me regret that position.'

Frank looked away, shaking his head.

'I... I just need to know if what he said was true.'

Dulles sighed, as if worn down by continual questions.

'Oh, very well,' he muttered. 'If you must know then yes, I believe that the world *would* have been in great peril *if* the Russians had been allowed to continue. Does that satisfy you?'

Frank felt a strange sense of relief.

'I was just worried,' he explained. 'You know, worried that we'd been doing something wrong – that *I'd* been doing something wrong – without even realizing it.'

Dulles frowned as he walked.

'You cannot allow yourself to think that way, son.'

Frank looked at him.

'But, knowing what we know now–'

'No,' Dulles said firmly. 'Fools judge history with the benefit of hindsight, and think themselves wise. But the people who matter, who change the world, have to make the best decisions they can with the information they have *in that moment*.' He turned to look at Frank. 'When Rafe saw Molly with her gun drawn on you, he did what he believed was right. When you shot that German at the ski lodge, when you told me about Molly and the Russian, you did what you believed was right. That's the only truth there is.'

Frank considered this and nodded.

'I wish more people saw it that way,' he said.

Beside him, Dulles gave a grim little laugh.

'Don't fear the condemnation of fools,' he said. 'Just because there are so many of them, just because they're loud, it doesn't make them right.'

They reached the far end of the Reflection Pool, and Dulles continued on, following the path up and around the fountains. Just ahead of them, parked by the side of the road, was a sleek black sedan. A tall man in a suit was pacing back and forth beside it.

'My next appointment,' Dulles muttered. 'You know Charles Lindbergh?"

'Of course. The airman. America First, right?'

'He might not agree, but I like to think we've *all* put America first, in our own way...' Dulles smiled, then turned to face him. 'So, this is where I say goodbye.'

'It was good to see you again.' Frank shook him by the hand.

'You'll be going back to Joplin, I suppose?' Dulles asked. 'I understand you managed to patch things up with Chief Kirkland?'

Frank looked at him, wondering how he knew about that, then gave a wry grin as he remembered who he was talking to.

'Yeah, I'm still a cop,' he said. 'Until something else comes up.'

Dulles nodded.

'One never knows what surprises the future may hold,' he said. 'Well, good luck to you, Frank.'

He turned away and started walking towards the car, then paused and glanced back over his shoulder.

'What about the young lady?' he asked. 'Miss Griffith, wasn't it?'

Frank looked at him and sighed.

'Gone,' he said. 'I gave her the money we got from Ellis and told her to take off.' He shook his head sadly. 'I've no idea where she is now.'

Dulles appeared to consider this, then smiled.

'Well, I have,' he said, touching the brim of his hat. 'If you should ever want to find her, give me a call.'

Raising his hand in farewell, he turned and walked back to his car.

THE END

Author's Note

This book is entirely fictitious. However, towards the end of World War II, it's said that Winston Churchill really did order plans to be drawn up involving large numbers of captured German troops who would be re-armed and sent to fight the Russians. Known as 'Operation Unthinkable', these plans were never acted upon, not least because President Roosevelt didn't share Churchill's mistrust of Stalin and, without determined American military support, the Russians would have proved too strong to subdue. Things might have been different if Harry Truman had been president at the time of the Yalta summit.

Allen Dulles really was a director of the O.S.S. and spent much of the war in Bern, running a series of vital American intelligence networks. He lived at Herrengasse 23, where he conducted many clandestine meetings despite the attentions of the Swiss police and had a team of people working from a house on Dufourstrasse. He went on to become director of the CIA.

It is rumored that during the war the U.S. government struck a deal with imprisoned mobster Charles 'Lucky' Luciano. As well as aiding the war effort by blocking dockworker strikes and preventing sabotage in Mafia-controlled ports, the arrangement is said to have involved covert support for the U.S. intelligence community. Shortly after the war, Governor Thomas Dewey (who had secured Luciano's conviction and 30-year prison term) reluctantly commuted the sentence and allowed him to be deported to Sicily.

ALSO BY FERGUS MCNEILL

The Detective Harland series

EYE CONTACT

KNIFE EDGE

CUT OUT

BROKEN FALL (short novella)

ABOUT THE AUTHOR

As well as writing crime novels, Fergus McNeill has been creating computer games since the early eighties, writing his first interactive fiction titles while still at school. Over the years he has designed, directed and illustrated games for all sorts of systems, from consoles to mobile phones.

A keen photographer and digital artist, Fergus lives in Hampshire with his wife and their very large cat. He is the author of EYE CONTACT, KNIFE EDGE and CUT OUT, plus the short novella BROKEN FALL.

Fergus is represented by the Eve White Literary Agency.

Read his blog at www.fergusmcneill.co.uk

ACKNOWLEDGMENTS

This book began its life on my laptop in a Missouri hotel room and, rather like Frank's story, it became a journey that spanned several years and two continents. I'm deeply grateful to everyone who offered help and encouragement along the way.

My thanks to Kate Ranger, John Popkess and Liz Barnsley for their feedback on early drafts, to Susi Holliday and Steph Broad-ribb from Crime Fiction Coach for their structural edits, and to John Rickards for his copy-editing. German translations were provided by Dr. Kat Hall and Alyce von Rothkirch via Peabody Ink. You all made the story so much better.

A special clandestine nod to my fellow crime writers (you know who you are) for your daily encouragement, support, and that wonderful sense of belonging.

Thanks to my family for... well, everything.

And finally, thanks to you, for reading.

Printed in Great Britain
by Amazon

42863492R00253